MASQUERADE

To Denise,
I hope you enjoy reading
this as much as I did
writing it.

Anne

By the Author

Femme Tales

Masquerade

Visit us at www.boldstrokesbooks.com

MASQUERADE

by
Anne Shade

2021

MASQUERADE

ISBN 13: 978-1-63555-831-9

This Trade Paperback Original Is Published By
Bold Strokes Books, Inc.
P.O. Box 249
Valley Falls, NY 12185

First Edition: February 2021

CREDITS
EDITOR: CINDY CRESAP
PRODUCTION DESIGN: STACIA SEAMAN
COVER PHOTO BY ANNE SHADE
COVER DESIGN BY TAMMY SEIDICK

Acknowledgments

Special thanks to my sister, Tammi Purnell, for allowing me to use you to grace the cover so beautifully. Thank you to everyone on the Bold Strokes Books team for taking a chance on me. You all sure know how to make an author feel loved. Thank you to my Bold Strokes Books editor, Cindy Cresap, for not denting my ego too much. I've learned so much with your guidance. Working with you all has been an amazing journey that I hope never ends.

This story is dedicated to the brave LGBTQ People of Color
in our history who lived without shame or apology in their own truth.
Langston Hughes, Countee Cullen, Ethel Waters, Florence Mills,
and so many others famous and not so famous.
I am honored to carry on their legacy.

PROLOGUE

New Orleans, 1923

Celine had been Mrs. Montré for ten years, and in that ten years of marriage to her husband, Paul, she thought she was content with her life just the way it was, but Paul seemed to believe otherwise. He had just returned home from an evening out with his friends and was annoyed to hear that Celine had spent her evening not with her friends but mending his clothes and reading.

"Celine, why do you torture yourself this way?" Paul asked.

"I'm not torturing myself. I'm simply doing what any normal wife does for her husband, and I'm reading a book you gave me," she said as if it should have made perfect sense to him.

Paul sat beside Celine on the sofa. He took her hands in his and placed an affectionate kiss on her fingertips. "You know how much I adore you, but we are not any normal husband and wife. The whole purpose of this arrangement was to be able to live our lives the way we choose and not the way our parents think we should."

Celine nodded. "I know, and I am content with the way things have been."

Paul gave her a look of skepticism. "You cannot tell me that you dreamed of puttering around the house doing chores, going to bourgeoise card and tea parties with women you have nothing in common with except your Gens de Couleur upbringing, discussing tedious subjects such as who wore what to what event and what new thing their child learned today. Celine, you are a vibrant, beautiful, and intelligent woman who should not be locked away like a virgin in a nunnery."

Celine looked guiltily down at their clasped hands. "Paul, I don't have your courage."

Paul placed a finger under Celine's chin and raised her eyes to meet his. "I have courage because you allow me to be me. Let me do the same for you."

Celine thought back to when she and Paul were children and found it hard to believe that she could give him courage. Their parents were lifetime friends, so she and Paul practically shared a crib. He had always been the brave, outgoing one of the two of them whenever they played as children and socialized as young adults. The only times Celine had ever had to be the stronger one were the moments he would feel as if their parents loved their standing in the community more than they did their own children's happiness. At those times, Paul's usual jovial mood would turn dark and depressed. He would worry her with talk of how his family would be happier if he just disappeared or worse, died, to avoid the embarrassment his true nature would cause them. She would refuse to leave him alone, no matter how much he railed at her to do so, until she was able to draw him out of the dark place he had retreated to.

Celine shook her head. "If my parents were to find out..."

"We will continue to be as discreet as we have been these past ten years. Besides, if anyone from their circles is going to the same parties and events that we would be attending, I'm sure they wouldn't want to be found out any more than we do."

Celine thought, just for a moment, what it would be like to finally allow herself to let go the way Paul had after their first five years of marriage, but fear continued to hold her back.

She patted Paul's hand and stood. "I'm entertained enough with all your wonderful stories when you come home and the books you bring me. I don't need any more than that. I love seeing how happy you are."

Paul followed her into her bedroom and lounged on her bed as she stood behind her dressing screen to change into her nightclothes.

"My poor Celine, forever sacrificing herself for everyone's happiness but her own. I don't deserve such a precious gift. You should have married a man who would have at least been willing to give you children to keep you company."

Celine joined him on her bed, cuddled into his side, and placed an affectionate kiss on his cheek. "I get to spend the rest of my life with my best friend in a beautiful home he gifted to me. What more could I ask for?"

"You could ask for passion."

"My passion is my sketching and making my custom hats for Father to sell at the shop."

"If you won't accompany me out on my little *liaisons dangereuses*, allow me to bring a companion home for you," Paul said.

Celine gazed up at him in shock. "You are not suggesting..." She blushed at the very thought of what Paul might be suggesting.

"That's exactly what I'm suggesting. You can indulge in your heart's, or body's, desire in the privacy of our home."

Celine wrinkled her brow in thought. Paul placed a kiss on the folds of her skin.

"Don't think too hard about it. Just allow me to do this one thing for you, and if you don't like it, then we will never speak of it again," Paul said.

Celine swallowed nervously and nodded, too afraid to say her answer out loud.

Paul clapped happily. "Excellent!" He placed another kiss on her forehead, stood, and assisted with tucking Celine under her covers. "It's late and Father wants me in the store early to help restock. We will discuss this further tomorrow. *Je t'aime, mon cher.*"

Celine blew him a kiss. They had not slept in the same bed in five years. There was no longer a need to continue putting up appearances at home as long as they behaved as the loving, affectionate couple in public. That wasn't too difficult to do, as they truly did love each other, they just felt no passion for one another and were completely fine with the fact that they never would. That wasn't the reason they married. Marrying each other was the most logical thing to do after spending their entire lives together already. They were able to appease their parents, avoid being placed in arranged marriages to strangers, and not have to hide who they truly were from each other.

❖

Three weeks later, Celine sat in front of her vanity happily humming a tune as she smoothed the front of her dress down. She was getting ready for a surprise outing Paul had planned for her birthday.

"Ah, you're ready!" Paul walked into her bedroom.

"I believe so. I wish you would tell me where we're going."

"Then it wouldn't be a surprise, now would it?"

Celine loved seeing Paul happy and excited the way he was now. This was the Paul she had loved to be around growing up. The little boy who saw excitement and adventure in everything he did.

Paul offered his arm to her. "Shall we?"

Celine took his arm and Paul escorted her through their upstairs foyer to the other side of their second story toward one of their larger guest rooms.

Celine looked at the closed door with confusion. "Paul, what is this?"

"On the other side of that door is your birthday gift. As much as I hope you will, I will not force you to accept it. Whether you participate or watch, the choice is yours and yours alone."

Celine looked toward the door, surprised at the sensuous sound of women's laughter. Her body reacted in ways she had never felt before. A heat spread throughout her body and gathered at the juncture of her thighs. Hearing the women's enjoyment had curiosity overriding her fear.

"All right."

Paul handed her a peacock feathered face mask. "I promised we would be discreet. We'll all be wearing masks, and I blindfolded the women when I brought them here, so they wouldn't know where we lived." He put a domino mask on himself.

Celine couldn't believe he had done all of that for her. "Thank you, Paul." She gave him a hug.

Paul held her for a moment longer, then took her hands and led her through the door. The bedroom was lit with candles instead of electric lighting which gave the room a more clandestine feel.

"How did you manage to do all of this without me knowing?" she asked.

She could tell Paul quirked a brow beneath his mask. "While you napped and bathed."

Celine shook her head in disbelief, then turned her gaze toward the bed. She gasped at the sight of two women lying cuddled together looking in her direction. One was a blonde with pale, smooth skin wearing a black feather mask. The other was a brunette of light tan complexion wearing a white feather mask. They smiled seductively at her as the blonde leisurely ran her hand along the curves of the brunette's body. Curves so full and luscious that they had Celine aching to be the one touching her.

"Come." Paul distracted her from the tempting sight and led her to a pair of chairs in a dimly lit corner near the bed. "Ladies," was all he said to signal them into action.

Celine watched in utter fascination as the erotic books Paul had given her came explicitly to life on the bed before her. A throbbing heat at the juncture of her thighs blocked all reasonable thought as the women stroked, touched, and licked each other. Celine felt herself drawn to the darker of the two women with her full breasts and hips, and long, thick black hair that hung in loose curls down to her waist. Her eyes shone through the mask like dark, hypnotic pools of water pulling Celine into what the woman's lover's lips and fingers were making her feel. Her full lips spread into a sexy smile as she reached toward Celine, beckoning her to join them on the bed. Celine gripped the sides of the chair as if trying to keep herself from giving in to a need that was overwhelming her body.

Celine stared into the beckoning woman's eyes, picturing herself between the two women on the bed, and the receiving end of their acts of desire. She shook her head in response and received a pout from the woman in return. The pout disappeared as her eyes closed and her hand dropped to tangle in the hair of the blonde, who had lowered herself between the brunette's open thighs. Moans of pleasure filled the room as the dark-haired woman received the most intimate of kisses. She writhed on the bed in agonizing pleasure, and Celine found herself writhing in her chair as well.

As the woman's moans became more frantic, Celine's breathing turned to pants as she reached down and cupped her sex through her dress, stroking it in rhythm with the dark-haired woman's hips. The woman turned her head to face Celine, and when their eyes locked, it was as if their bodies had become one. She felt a pressure she had never felt before when she touched herself on those rare occasions her physical needs outweighed her prim sensibilities. When the dark-haired woman's hips rose off the bed and she cried out in pleasure, so did Celine as her orgasm rocked her body and left her undergarments soaked through. She collapsed back in her chair feeling utterly spent.

"You are so beautiful in your passion," Paul said beside her.

"Yes, she is," Celine heard a feminine voice say.

Celine opened her eyes and looked first at Paul, who gazed at her in awe, then at the women on the bed. The blonde had the same look as Paul, but the dark-haired beauty looked as if she would ravish her on the spot, and it made Celine's sex throb. Having all eyes on her made Celine shift in her seat nervously.

Paul took her hand and leaned over to whisper in her ear. "If I were not a lover of men, I would never leave the house knowing you awaited me in bed."

Celine blushed and playfully swatted Paul's arm.

"Would you like to continue to watch?" he asked.

"Yes," she said.

Paul smiled indulgently and nodded at the women to continue. When they did, the dark-haired woman became the dominant one. She shifted their position on the bed so that they lay crossways. As she made love to her partner, she kept her eyes locked with Celine's. It took all of Celine's willpower, and a few prayers, to keep herself from stripping off her clothes, which had now grown too restrictive, and joining the women on the bed.

By the time the women were sated an hour later, Celine's body was aching with unreleased desire. The dark-haired beauty had tried coaxing her to join them again, but Celine had remained strong with the help of her death grip on Paul's hand. Paul escorted the ladies back to wherever he had collected them from, and Celine retreated to bed hoping sleep would stave off the hunger she was feeling. She had tossed and turned for a half hour when a soft knock sounded on her door.

"Come in," she called out.

Paul opened the door and peeked his head into her room. "Can't sleep?"

"No." Celine frowned.

Paul walked into the room. "I've come bearing a gift."

His broad smile was lit by candles on two chocolate cupcakes he carried on a plate. "Happy birthday, *mon cher*." Paul sat beside her on the bed.

Celine turned on her bedside lamp and sat cross-legged across from Paul. Just like when they were children, he placed the plate between them and gave her a fork.

"Make a wish," he said.

Celine closed her eyes and took a moment to think of something, but all she could see when she did was a pair of intense dark eyes beckoning her. She blinked her eyes open and tried to hide her discomfort, but Paul knew her too well.

"You're still thinking about them, aren't you." He dug his fork into one of the cupcakes.

"I feel as if something has been unleashed that I cannot tuck back into its cage." She moaned in delight as she slowly chewed the cake.

"I've been where you are, Celine, and whenever I tried to lock that part of me away it put me in an awfully bad place. I don't want to see you go through that. We're in this together, remember? How fair is it to you when you allow me to be free but keep yourself from doing the same?"

"I'm afraid," Celine said.

Paul took her hand. "There is no rush. Take your time to think about what you truly desire, and I will be here to guide you, holding your hand along the way until you feel free enough to fly on your own."

Celine smiled gratefully and nodded. "What would I do without you, Paul?"

Paul leaned over and placed an affectionate kiss on Celine's forehead. "Since we will be together forever, we will never need to find that out."

❖

Celine stared at her father in confusion. "There must be some mistake."

Her father grasped her hands. "I'm afraid not, Celine. When they didn't find you at home, one of the sheriff's men came by the shop to tell us what happened. Paul was killed in an apartment in the District early this morning."

Celine's heart felt as if it skipped a beat. The District was the section of the city where the cabarets, gambling halls, and speakeasies were. It was also where men seeking other pleasures escaped when they couldn't, or preferred not to, find it at home with their wives. Celine looked from her father to her mother and could see in their eyes that the latter was more than likely what got her husband killed, but she still needed to hear the words.

"What happened?" she asked her father.

He hesitated in answering.

"Papa, please, I need to know the truth."

"Paul and Robert Cole Jr. were shot by Robert's father after he found them together. It seems Judge Cole had become aware of his son having an affair with Paul and warned him to put a stop to it. When the judge became suspicious that the affair hadn't ended, he decided to take matters into his own hands. He had Robert followed to an apartment in the District where he found them together and shot them both, killing Paul and wounding his son, then he turned himself in."

"Celine, did you know of Paul's relationship with Robert Cole?" her mother asked.

Celine lowered her head hoping her parents wouldn't see the truth in her eyes. "I knew that he and Robert were acquainted."

Her mother sat beside her and placed an arm around her shoulder. "You poor thing. If your father and I had known of Paul's…tastes… we wouldn't have approved of the marriage," she said sympathetically.

"As cold as this may sound, it's too late for regrets, Lanie," her father said. "What we have to focus on now is how to get past this with minimal amount of damage to our reputation. We're going to have to distance ourselves from Paul's parents."

Celine's mother's eyes widened in surprise. "But, Francois, they've been our closest friends since before Celine and Paul were born. Our friendship is what brought our children together. We can't abandon them when they'll need us most."

"We have no choice. I've worked too hard with what little my father left to build the reputation I have. Broussard's Tailors was almost driven to the ground because of his gambling and drinking, and I built it up to one of the finest Negro-owned establishments in the city. I will not lose it because Paul had no self-control."

Celine could imagine that the decision for her father to abandon his friendship with a man he considered a brother since they were children was not easy for him, but when it came to the pride of their community, the Creoles of Color had very little tolerance. Although they were only related by marriage, the Broussards' reputation could be at stake because of Paul Montrés's indiscretion, so it was imperative to cut ties immediately.

"He's right," Celine said. "You know that if we continue to associate with Paul's family it would seem as if we thought what he did was acceptable. His actions could possibly be forgiven if Robert were one of us, but he isn't. He's White and the son of a local influential judge who's also rumored to be associated with the Ku Klux Klan."

"I suppose you're right. But what about you?" Celine's mother asked. "It will be easier for us to disconnect from the scandal than for you as Paul's widow. Maybe we should send you to Atlanta to stay with Aunt Liz."

Celine shook her head. "I'm not going to run and hide. With any luck, everyone will look on me with the same pity you and Father are doing now."

Celine knew she had to become the clueless widow who knew nothing of her husband's "tastes," as her mother had so delicately put it. Fortunately, very few knew the truth of her and Paul's marital arrangement. It was an arrangement that had worked well for them until several months ago when he'd met Robert Cole Jr. When they married, Celine had asked Paul to make two promises to her—don't fall in love and be discreet—both of which were vital for them to keep up the appearance of their marriage. After Robert entered their lives, Paul would stay away for days at a time. When he did return home, he would be moody, snapping at her when she showed the least bit of concern for him. There were no more colorful stories as he withdrew from her more each day. Her loving, witty, happy companion since childhood had become someone she no longer recognized.

She finally found out the reason for his distance the week before his murder when he confessed that he was in love with Robert. Celine insisted that Paul immediately break it off with him before someone got hurt. They argued, for the first time in their lifetime of friendship, as she tried to make him see how dangerous it was to be involved with Robert. Eventually, she was able to reason with Paul. Although she could see it hurt him deeply, he promised he would end the relationship as soon as he returned from a trip to Baton Rouge with his father. He had phoned her from his family's store after their return to tell her he was on his way to see Robert and that everything would be back to normal by morning.

Now Celine sat in her parents' living room wondering if she had not insisted so strongly that Paul break off his relationship with Robert, would he be with her right now? Could his death have been avoided? She would never know. What was worse, she had been so afraid of losing the safe little life they had that she had not considered what he was going through, loving someone he knew he could never truly be with. She had been selfish, sending him away with threats and fear as his motivation for ending the relationship. Now he was gone, and it was too late for apologies.

Tears pooled in Celine's eyes and slowly slid down her face as she grieved for the man who had been her one true companion for as long as she could remember.

"Ooh, *mon enfant*, it's going to be all right." Her mother pulled

Celine into her arms. "It's going to be difficult, but we'll get through this if we just stay strong."

Unfortunately, despite their best efforts, Celine's family could not escape the aftershock from the scandal Paul's death caused. Following Robert Cole Jr.'s damaging testimony on his father's behalf and Judge Cole's acquittal for Paul's death, everyone associated with Paul was ostracized by their community. Robert had accused Paul, who was almost ten years his senior, of seducing him. He claimed that when he tried to break it off several times, Paul had threatened him and his family. When asked why he didn't tell his father about these threats, Robert said he was too humiliated by what he had done. He also claimed that the night his father found them together he was going to put an end to their relationship once and for all, but Paul had a gun and forced him to do things he would always be ashamed of. The jury considered the shooting a father's only hope of saving his son and found Judge Cole innocent.

Celine was appalled and had to be physically restrained by her parents as they sat in the courtroom listening to the lies being said about her husband. To defend him would put her and her family in the same shameful light that Paul was in. She could only watch as his parents and younger brother were treated like the worst kind of criminals while their son's reputation went from respectable businessman, loving son, brother, and husband, to a lecherous, sexually depraved seducer of young men. It was soon too much for the Montrés. Celine wasn't the least bit surprised when they packed up and slipped away in the middle of the night just weeks after the trial, more afraid of what Judge Cole's associates would do to them than of being treated like lepers by the community they had spent their lives in.

What did surprise her were the rumors that began circulating about her involvement in Paul's liaisons. That she had probably been a part of his seductions by luring the young men in. Those who traveled in Celine and Paul's small circle of friends knew it wasn't true, but they could not come to her defense for fear of their own secrets coming out. White and Colored customers began pulling their business from Broussard Tailors. Invitations to Lanie Broussard's tea socials and card parties, which had been two of the most sought-after events within their community, were either declined or returned unopened. Celine watched her parents suffer silently through it all as they prayed it would blow over. They finally realized their life in New Orleans was over when Celine began receiving threatening letters from anonymous sources and became the object of snickers and malicious whispers by those from within their own community. Like the Montrés, the Broussards decided it would be best for their own safety, and sanity, to leave town.

❖

Celine tried to comfort her mother, who sat in tears as they rode in a taxi to the train station to board a train for New York. At Celine's request, they made one stop. She wound her way through the above ground crypts of Lafayette Cemetery until she found the one she was looking for.

She gazed down at her husband's final resting place with tears in her eyes. "How did we get here, Paul?" she asked, even though she already knew the answer.

"We were so happy and now look at us. You're lying here in a tomb, brought down in the prime of your life because you dared to love someone in spite of the danger it could bring, and I'm being run out of the only home I've ever known because of the scandal it caused."

Celine laid white roses before the stark crypt. "I never told you enough, but I do love you. I miss your company so much, and I hope you can forgive my selfishness when you needed me most. Goodbye, Paul, my friend, rest in peace."

She blew a final kiss toward his grave, wiped away her tears, and went back to the car. As they drove through town toward the train station, Celine sat silently watching the city she knew like the back of her hand sweep past the window, wondering if she would ever see it again.

"Do we truly have to go?" her mother tearfully asked her father.

Celine's father grasped her mother's hand. "You know we do. The scandal has practically ruined our business. It's better to leave now while we still have something other than our dignity to leave with."

"But New York, Francois? Why not Baton Rouge or even Atlanta?" her mother asked.

"It'll be all right, Lanie, you'll see. Your sister has already acquired a storefront for the tailor shop and a nice townhouse in a good neighborhood. She will have everything we shipped unpacked and set up by the time we get there," he said. "All you'll have to do is settle in and become the queen of your domain once again." He gave her an indulgent smile.

"You always take care of everything, don't you?" Lanie turned back to gaze out her window.

Celine met her father's gaze for a brief moment, but it was long enough for her to see that, in spite of his assurances, he was just as worried about this new life they were embarking on as she and her mother were. She turned back toward the window, said goodbye to her beloved New Orleans, and pulled her aunt's letters from her purse. She hoped reading them once more would help her feel all the excitement of life in Harlem that her aunt had described.

CHAPTER ONE

Harlem, 1925

Celine strolled down St. Nicholas Avenue barely aware of the appreciative glances from the men she passed along the way. Although she sent them friendly smiles and nods in greeting, she kept her clipped pace to let them know she didn't have time to extend her response beyond that. Celine cared more about the sights and sounds of the city as she left the quiet of the neighborhood known as Striver's Row and headed toward downtown. This was the part of Harlem she had come to love since they arrived almost a year ago. During the day, it was the gritty heart and traffic of the working class heading off to their jobs dressed in maid uniforms or laborer dungarees. After dark, the working population gave way to crowds coming uptown, dressed to the nines and ready for a wild and exotic night in Harlem, where class and color lines were blurred when it came to people looking for a good time. From overcrowded rent parties to the decadence of the Cotton Club, there was something for everyone.

What drew Celine's love for this part of the city most was the people. Like New Orleans, Harlem's Negro population consisted of every hue of color, from mulatto to ebony, and every aspect of class, from the street corner hustler to the wealthiest doctor, but unlike New Orleans, at some point and time these same people met on the streets of Harlem and realized that they were not as different from each other as they might think. Separation of color and class was the one thing she didn't miss about her Southern home. That separation was what chased her family from New Orleans. There, she was a Creole of Color whose light skin and social class afforded her a cultivated and comfortable life many people of color were denied. It also afforded her few friends and associates outside of their tight community, leaving her outcast and alone when the scandal of her husband's death rocked their safe little world.

In Harlem, she was just a young widow working as a hat designer in her aunt's shop. It didn't matter what she did before coming to New York because it seemed everyone in Harlem had a story, possibly no worse or better than hers. Aunt Olivia, who had been living in Harlem for five years before Celine and her parents arrived, told her that if anything, her story would make great material for one of the many Negro playwrights making Harlem their home. Celine had been thrilled over the opportunity to start over in a life that gave her the comfortable sense of anonymity she craved since Paul's death.

As she rounded the corner from St. Nicolas Avenue onto 125th Street, Celine was greeted by two familiar faces she saw every morning as they waited for the bus that would take them to their jobs downtown.

"Ooh, Miss Celine is working it today with that hat," one of the women said to the other.

"Now, Miss Viola, I told you to stop by my aunt's shop anytime and I'll fix you right up with one," Celine said.

Miss Viola laughed. "Child, that hat would probably cost me a month's pay at that fancy shop of yours."

"Only way to find out is to stop by." Celine gave her a conspiratorial wink.

"I just might take you up on that. I do need a new one for Easter," Miss Viola said.

"I have just the hat for you, so I'm going to hold you to that. You two have a good day," Celine said in parting.

A few moments later, she arrived at Rousseau's Fashions, not surprised to see two customers already there that early in the morning. She greeted them then went to the backroom where her aunt was.

"*Bonjour, mon bijou,* Celine," Aunt Olivia greeted her.

"*Bonjour, Tante.* I see we have some early birds."

"Yes, they're here to pick up the Sherman order."

The Sherman order had been an interesting one to say the least. It was a white satin and sequin tuxedo with matching top hat and feathered face mask. It had also been the first of at least a dozen more similar orders. What made the orders interesting for Celine was that they were being made for women. Rousseau's specialized in women's apparel, and tuxedos were not a common item in a woman's wardrobe.

Celine had refrained from asking Aunt Olivia about the orders because she assumed her aunt would tell her in her own time, but after a few men came in looking for women's dresses to be made for them, she was determined to find out what was going on.

After she assisted with wrapping and boxing the order and gave it to the young women waiting in the shop's sitting area, she joined Olivia behind the display counter.

"*Tante*, I've been meaning to ask you about all of these unusual orders. Are they for something special?"

Olivia grinned. "I wondered how long it would take for you to ask me about that. They're for a special masquerade ball."

"I love masquerades. Paul and I would go to one every year during Mardi Gras."

"I don't think you've been to a masquerade quite like this one. It's a bit more risqué."

As Celine took a moment to put the pieces of information together, women dressing as men, men dressing as women, it all sounded too familiar not to be what she was thinking. She began rearranging her hat display in an attempt at nonchalance while her stomach fluttered nervously.

"What kind of masquerade is it?" she asked.

"It's being organized by a social club I'm a part of," Olivia said.

Celine looked up at her in surprise. "You're helping to organize it?"

Celine remembered stories Paul told her about the masquerade drag balls he attended. She couldn't imagine her sophisticated aunt attending one of those. Her imagination was probably working overtime because she had been so bored lately socializing with all her mother's friends and their daughters.

"Maybe I can help? If I have to go to another one of Mother's teas or society luncheons, I'll go mad," Celine said.

Olivia chuckled. "Your mother has always been one for the society functions, which is why I don't think she or your father would want you involved with this particular event."

Celine frowned and felt as if something inside her clicked, releasing frustration she had managed to hold back since her father told them they were leaving New Orleans.

"I am so tired of being told what I can and cannot do because it wouldn't be proper. I've been the proper little Creole child my whole life, now here I am, thirty years old, widowed, and still not allowed to enjoy my life the way I choose." She shoved the hat she had been fidgeting with aside.

"It's not fair! Paul spent our entire marriage trying to get me to enjoy life more, and I refused because it wasn't what a proper Creole woman did."

"Look where his enjoyment of life got him, an early grave," her aunt pointed out.

"Carelessness put Paul in an early grave, not his joy for life," Celine said. "That joy was what drew me to him when we were children. I lived vicariously through his antics. There were so many times I wished I had been born a boy so that I could get away with some of the things he did."

"Celine, what if you could, for one night, be that boy. Would you do it?" Olivia asked.

Celine laughed off her question. "That's ridiculous because it could never happen."

"Think about it. For one night you could live the life of a man. Openly enjoy the same pleasures a man does, drinking, cigars, entertaining beautiful women," Olivia said.

"To entertain such an idea would be foolish." There wasn't much conviction behind Celine's statement.

"Not if I let you help with the masquerade." Olivia grinned mischievously.

In that one sentence, Aunt Olivia confirmed what she had thought the true nature of the party was.

"Paul used to tell me about the type of masquerade you're talking about, the extravagant costumes, the champagne flowing, the beauty and freedom of the guests. He hoped telling me about them would convince me to go, but as much as I wanted to, I could never bring myself to do it."

"Well, here's your chance."

Celine thought about what her aunt was offering, and she realized that Olivia understood what Celine was going through, that they shared a bond that went beyond blood relatives. They shared a common desire that could not be openly expressed without going against everything they were raised to believe was wrong.

One night, Celine thought. One night to be free of all societal restraints and do things she only fantasized about. The offer was too tempting for her to turn down.

❖

"Miss Hampton, I'd like to see you in my office," Nurse Porter called.

Dinah sighed heavily. She had been so close to making her escape. Only a few feet stood between her and the exit. She could act as if she had not heard her supervisor, Hilda Porter, but then that would just get her into more trouble than she was obviously in, so she turned back the way she came and was met with her disapproving glare. Dinah walked past Nurse Porter into her office, wondering what she could have possibly done wrong this time.

Nurse Porter sat at her desk in the only chair the office had. She shuffled through a stack of papers, making Dinah wait several minutes before acknowledging her. When she finally did, it was with a frown as she folded her hands on her desk in front of her.

"Miss Hampton, do you enjoy being a nurse at this facility?"

"Yes, ma'am, I do," Dinah lied smoothly.

"Then why were you two minutes late for your shift?"

"Ma'am, I explained when I came in that the train was delayed." Dinah tried not to sound annoyed.

Nurse Porter's mouth curved into a condescending smile. "We have rules here, Miss Hampton. One of them is that all nurses are to be here at least five minutes prior to their shift and ready to begin that shift on time. Our patients depend on us to support them in every way we can, and that cannot happen if we are shorthanded because you're late. Now, if that rule is too difficult for you to follow then maybe you need to reconsider your career choice."

Nurse Porter's glare dared Dinah to do or say something that would probably get her in more trouble or fired, but Dinah refused to take the bait. It was widely known among the nurses at the small privately owned facility where Dinah worked as a nurse that Hilda Porter despised working with the Negro nurses. There were only four under her charge, and she made sure they knew how much she disliked them. All four were put on the night shift and given the most menial tasks possible, such as dumping bedpans, collecting dirty linen, and delivering patient meals. None were allowed to do anything that would give them direct contact with the elderly patients in the facility other than those jobs. Being reprimanded for the trains being late was the last straw.

Attitudes like Porter's were the reason Dinah left Alabama. She had worked too hard for her nursing diploma to be treated as if she were not worth the paper it was printed on. For months, she had been considering putting in an application at Harlem Hospital, which had begun accepting Negro nurses a few years ago, but she held off because, in spite of the treatment she was receiving at this facility, the pay was better than what they were offering in Harlem. Now she knew she had no choice but to apply if she wanted to do more than empty bedpans for the next five years. Dinah decided she would stop by Harlem Hospital later that afternoon and hoped they either had positions available or Nurse Porter got run over by a bus. She preferred the latter, but since that was unlikely, she would have to bide her time.

She pasted a smile on her face to hide her disdain for Nurse Porter. "I apologize, Nurse Porter. I will make sure I'm not late again."

The disappointment obvious on Porter's face almost made Dinah laugh.

"Yes, well, I hope it doesn't become a habit. You may go."

Dinah turned and didn't look back. As she rode the train uptown, she could feel the weariness of working the night shift dragging her down. It was only four days a week, but having to deal with Porter and the tasks she and the other Negro nurses were assigned made it tiresome. Between that and her second job dancing at Flynn's Nightclub two nights a week, she was beginning to wonder if she would ever be able to enjoy a leisurely day of simply walking or reading in the park the way she used to before Porter became head nurse.

She took the subway to 125th Street in Harlem and wearily climbed the steps to the street. She got off work at a time most people were heading into their jobs, so she greeted friends and neighbors as they rushed for buses and trains as she dragged herself the two blocks home to Hampton Place, a boardinghouse owned by her aunt, Josephine Hampton.

"Hey, baby girl, you look beat," Aunt Jo said in greeting.

"Hey, Aunt Jo." She gave her a kiss and hug. "A few of hours of sleep and I'll be fine."

"Well, Fran's warming up some breakfast for you. Go eat and I'll get a hot bath ready for you."

"You spoil me, Aunt Jo. Mama would have a fit if she knew you were cooking and drawing baths for me."

"What my sister don't know won't hurt her." She gave Dinah a conspiratorial wink. "Now, get yourself some breakfast. You got a big night and need your rest."

"Speaking of tonight, did Curtis bring my costume over last night?" Dinah asked.

Aunt Jo frowned. "Mm-hmm. I don't know why you insist on working for that two-bit hustler."

"I know you don't like him, but dancing for Flynn's Follies gets me the extra money I need to send home to Mama and Coretta."

"Fran and I told you we'd be happy to give you the money for them."

"Mama won't take it if it's coming from you. She would consider it a handout and you know how prideful she can be."

"Mm-hmm, like I said, what she doesn't know won't hurt her," Jo said.

"Jo, stop nagging the girl. She can handle herself with Curtis Flynn."

"Thank you, Fran," Dinah said to Fran Walker, her aunt's partner.

"I'm just looking out for Dinah. I trust that man about as far as I can throw him," Aunt Jo said.

"I'm sure Dinah feels the same way. Don't you?" Fran asked.

Dinah smiled. "Yes, I do."

Fran turned back to Jo and slid her arm around her waist. "See, nothing to worry about."

"You're just saying that to shut my nagging up," Aunt Jo said.

"Maybe. Or I'm more accepting of the fact that Dinah is a grown woman who's got the same stubborn fearlessness as a certain young woman I knew who came from Bam to the big city all by herself twenty years ago," Fran said.

"I guess you're right," Jo said.

"You know I am. Now, let the girl go eat and get some rest." Fran gave Jo's waist a quick squeeze before leaving the room.

As Jo watched Fran leave, Dinah couldn't help but see the adoration in her gaze for Fran.

"Do as Fran said, go eat. I'll get your bath ready."

Dinah gave her a hug. "Thanks, Aunt Jo."

Dinah truly admired her aunt and Fran's relationship, which began twenty years ago when Jo first moved to New York. They were both maids at an upscale Manhattan hotel and became friends. After a year, they rented an apartment together, which they shared for ten years before they decided to admit that their feelings for each other had grown into something more. Five years ago, they purchased two vacant brownstones from a German business owner who abandoned them due to the fear of the rising Negro population in Harlem, and they turned them into a boardinghouse. A business they could call their own and a home where they could live freely together without the prying eyes of fellow coworkers and neighbors.

It was a loving relationship that Dinah always hoped she would find but knew, despite changing times and ideals, that it was not openly accepted. It was one thing to dabble in such activities behind closed doors, it was different to announce to the world that you were a woman who loved women. People speculated about Jo and Fran's relationship, but there were only a few who knew the truth and those who didn't weren't bold enough to ask. Although she was not actively looking for a relationship, Dinah, like her aunt, was fully prepared to find a way to make it work if the right woman came along.

By early afternoon, Dinah was feeling like new. She dressed and picked up a brown wrapped parcel Jo must have dropped off in her room while she slept. Inside was the costume Curtis brought over for the performance she was doing that evening. After inspecting it for any alterations needed, she discovered a few feathers missing and wasn't sure if she could get replacements in time. She went to find Jo for assistance and found her in the kitchen with one of their regular boarders, Lee, a local drag performer. As she explained the situation with her costume, Lee suggested she try Rousseau's Fashion. He told her the owner had assisted him with many costume repairs and he would be happy to take her to the shop. She recalled passing the shop once but thought they were more than likely too pricey for her budget, so she never went in. With so little time to find what she needed, she didn't have any other option except to try them.

When they arrived, they were greeted by a fashionable, attractive older woman who seemed to glide from behind the counter and swept Lee into her arms. "*Ah, bon jour, mon ami.* How are you? I haven't seen you in months," she said.

"*Bon jour.* I'm well. I've been traveling. I just came back last week and I'm staying around the corner at Hampton Place," Lee told her.

"Celine will be so happy to see you. She's running a quick errand for me. She should be returning shortly. Now, tell me who this divine creature is," the woman said.

Dinah blushed as the woman slowly looked her over from head

to toe. Divine would not be how she would describe herself as she noticed how plainly she was dressed. She self-consciously reached up to smooth back her curls, thankful she had taken time to pin her hair before she had slept earlier.

"Madam Rousseau, I'd like you to meet Dinah Hampton. Her aunt owns the boardinghouse I stay at when I'm in town," Lee said.

Dinah held out her hand in greeting. "It's a pleasure to meet you, Ms. Rousseau."

"Oh my," Madam Rousseau said, accepting her hand. "Such a seductive voice. It's a pleasure to meet you as well, and please, call me Olivia." She took her time releasing Dinah's hand before turning back toward Lee, who winked at Dinah playfully.

"So, have you come for a visit or a costume repair?" Olivia asked Lee as she looped her arm through his and guided him to a sitting area.

"Both. I've come for a visit and Dinah has a feather emergency," Lee explained.

"Ah, you've come to the right place. Let me see the damage," Olivia said.

Dinah handed the carefully wrapped costume to Olivia.

"Oh my." Olivia frowned as she looked over the outfit.

"She's performing at the ball tonight," Lee said.

Olivia's eyes widened in surprise. "So, you're the dancer Lizzie has been drooling over and insisting we had to have at the ball."

"I don't know anyone named Lizzie. Everything was arranged through the owner of the club I dance for," Dinah told her.

"Is that the same person who gave you this dreadful piece of work?" she said, indicating the costume.

Dinah felt her face flush with embarrassment. "It's all I can afford under the circumstances."

Olivia reached over and patted Dinah's hand. "I didn't mean to offend you. It's just that a beautiful, and from what I hear, exceptionally talented performer such as yourself deserves to be clothed in the finest attire for your performances. Not to worry, I will take care of everything."

Dinah liked Olivia Rousseau. She could tell, despite the expensive jewelry, European fashion, and sophisticated air that she was very much down-to-earth.

"Thank you, Olivia."

"You're very welcome. I'll bring the costume to the house when I come to assist with setting up for the event."

Dinah nodded and she and Lee stood to leave. As they said their goodbyes the bell over the door jingled and the subtle scent of jasmine filled the room as a woman came in chattering away in a flurry of French. As she turned, Dinah's gaze met that of the woman who had entered and she felt as if she lost the ability to see anything but the breathtaking woman standing in front of her.

"My apologies, *Tante*. I didn't realize you were with customers." The woman spoke in English this time.

"That's all right, darling, look who's here," Olivia said, directing her attention to Lee.

"Oh! Lee, you're back! How was Chicago?" The woman set her bags down and hurried over to hug Lee.

Dinah found that she couldn't take her eyes from the new arrival. Her complexion was the creaminess of sweet milk with honey; her almond-shaped eyes resembled the gold color of a tiger's-eye gemstone. Full lips were a tempting red that had Dinah wondering if she wore lipstick or if they were naturally that color. Her body was full and shapely with curves that couldn't be hidden by the fashionable but shapeless dropped waist column dress she wore. Dinah was completely taken by her beauty and enchanting personality.

"Celine, dear, I'm so sorry to break up this happy reunion, but we have so much to do before tonight. You and Lee can catch up later. It was so good to see you again, *mon ami*." Olivia looped her arm through Lee's, leading him to the door.

Dinah hesitantly followed. She was torn between leaving and wanting to stay and talk to the woman she found herself so fascinated with.

Olivia grasped Dinah's hand, tearing her attention away from Celine. "It was most definitely a pleasure to meet you, Dinah." Olivia placed a kiss on Dinah's cheeks.

Dinah smiled. "Thank you, Olivia. I'll see you this evening."

As she followed Lee out the door, she glanced back hoping to catch another glimpse of Celine, but she had disappeared from view, leaving Dinah with nothing but her intoxicating scent teasing her unmercifully.

CHAPTER TWO

Celine gazed at herself in the mirror and could not believe she let her aunt talk her into attending this masquerade ball. If her mother knew where she was, she would die of shock. As far as her parents knew, Celine was spending the night at Aunt Olivia's home to keep her company, something she had done many times before. It was partially true. After all, she really was staying at her aunt's after their night of hedonism.

As if she had conjured her up with a thought, Aunt Olivia appeared behind her in the mirror. If she had not seen her getting dressed just moments before Celine would not have recognized her. She was dressed in a black tuxedo with a cream silk shirt, vest, and ascot and a black and cream domino eye mask. If it weren't for the tight, intricately twisted bun her hair was pulled back into, she could have easily been mistaken for any sophisticated Creole gentleman.

"Is something bothering you?" Aunt Olivia asked.

"I can't believe I'm doing this," Celine answered.

Aunt Olivia turned Celine around toward her. "Are you happy, *mon bijou*? Do you enjoy playing the grieving widow who shall never marry because of her great love for her misguided dead husband?"

"You know I don't, but if my parents knew the truth they would die of shame."

"If you insist on spending your life in this role you've taken on, how is one night of pleasure going to change it? Don't you think you deserve at least one night of freedom?"

Celine seriously considered what Aunt Olivia was saying. One night, that's all it was. After tonight, she would never do it again.

"You know what helps me get into the swing of things? I become someone else. Monsieur Olivier, at your service." Olivia performed a gentlemanly bow.

Celine chuckled. "Very fitting since that was grandfather's name."

Olivia shrugged indifferently. "I've been told I favor him quite a bit. Now." She turned Celine back toward the mirror. "Let's find the appropriate persona for you. When you look in the mirror, who do you see?"

Celine gazed at the image before her, trying to see herself as someone she just met. It wasn't difficult considering she had never worn a tuxedo before tonight. Olivia had designed Celine's tuxedo like her own except she had given Celine a soft golden silk shirt, vest, and ascot with a matching black and gold domino mask and tailored the suit to fit Celine's curves rather than hide them. Olivia had sculpted the front of Celine's hair into finger waves and pinned the rest back into a loose bun. The result was a delicate play of masculine femininity that Aunt Olivia told her female drag performers had spent years trying to perfect.

"Camil," Celine said.

Olivia nodded. "I like that, a name that could be given to a man or a woman."

"Exactly."

"Well, Camil, I'm going to go help greet the guests and give you some privacy to get to know your new persona." Olivia placed a soft kiss on her cheek before leaving.

Celine gazed one last time in the mirror, but this time it wasn't to critique why she was there. It was to put Celine to bed for the evening and bring Camil out to play.

Dinah sat in a guest room preparing to become Sable, the persona she performed under. She had been directed to this room by a tuxedo-clad Olivia, who she had not even recognized until she handed Dinah a box and, with a wink, told her that she was expecting her money's worth tonight.

Lee came in to help her dress.

"You look a little nervous. I know this isn't your first private party performance, so what's got you worked up?" he asked.

"Honestly, I don't know. I've been feeling a little off since this afternoon," Dinah admitted as she undressed.

"Could it be a certain someone's golden-eyed niece?" Lee teased. "She is breathtaking, isn't she?"

"Breathtaking? Lawd, child, you've been reading too much of that poetry you always have your nose buried in."

Dinah playfully tossed her blouse at him. "Would you please lay out my costume while I powder up?"

She stood naked before the mirror, patting her entire body with a special sparkling body powder that made her appear to shine iridescently under the lights as she danced.

"Would you mind doing my back?" she asked him, but there was no answer. She turned to find him staring at the box her costume was in.

"Please don't tell me she ruined it." Dinah joined Lee.

Expecting the worst, although she couldn't imagine her costume looking any cheaper than it already did, she was surprised to see what lay amongst the tissue paper in the box. It seemed Olivia didn't just replace the missing feathers. She made a whole new costume.

"Now that is what I would describe as breathtaking," Lee said in awe.

Dinah carefully picked up the brassiere-style top and found it was not the same costume she'd left Olivia. "I can't believe she did this for free. This leather is softer than anything I've ever felt, and the feathers are flawless."

She turned it over, shaking her head in amazement. "You can't even see where she sewed them in from the other side. It's like they came attached to the leather."

"That's not Miss Olivia's handiwork," Lee said.

"What do you mean?"

Lee took the top from her, turned it over, and gently lifted one of the feathers along the edge. "You see this?" He pointed to a small embroidered design beneath the cluster of feathers.

Dinah could just make out the letters "CM" intertwined amongst a swirl of curlicues.

"Celine Montré, Olivia's niece," he said. "Feathers are her specialty. She mostly designs hats and feather boas. I've never seen her do anything like this before."

Dinah took the top back. "To do this much work and detail in just a matter of hours is amazing," she said in awe.

"She's here tonight."

Dinah smirked. "Sable will have to remember to thank her for such a beautiful job."

"It's a masquerade, darling. How will you know who she is?" Dinah ran her thumb over the embroidered initials. "I'll know."

❖

Celine spent the first hour of the party at a corner table nursing a glass of wine and wondering when she would be able to make an escape. Her aunt had been right, this was much different from the masquerades she went to in New Orleans. She thought she could handle it, that taking a new name would make her braver, but she was wrong. Most of the guests were in drag with men in some of the finest gowns she had ever seen, and women dressed in elegant tuxedos with tails and carrying walking sticks, but there were those who chose to display their uninhibited side that evening by barely wearing any clothes at all. One very shapely woman wore a shimmering, sheer gown that left little to the imagination, while another wore a similar one that had well-placed patches of silk leaves sewn over the most revealing areas.

It wasn't just the provocative clothing that had Celine's senses in overdrive. The large formerly private mansion turned social club was dimly lit with low lights and scented candles that left her more light-headed than the wine did. Each of the four main rooms was decorated in an exotic theme focusing on Asia, India, Africa, and a French boudoir. It was an environment that beckoned hedonism and wild abandon, neither of which her cultured, Creole sensibilities were used to. She sat in the African-themed ballroom, watching everything from her little corner table in the back of the room, too afraid of getting up to venture out and join the other revelers. She almost jumped out of her seat when someone sat beside her before she realized it was her aunt.

"Too much for you?" Olivia asked.

Celine looked nervously around the room. "It is a bit over-whelming."

"What happened to the bold Camil?"

Celine gazed down at her glass of wine in embarrassment. "Camil seems to have completely abandoned me."

"I see. Well, you are more than welcome to retire to the room we used upstairs if you've had your fill."

Celine frowned. "Are you sure? After all my talk, I feel like such a coward."

Olivia waved her hand dismissively. "Nonsense. You've lasted longer than most newcomers."

"Thank you, *Tante*."

Just as Celine stood to leave, the lights in the room dimmed even more and music from the tuxedo clad all-female jazz band changed from a swing beat to a subtle, jungle drumbeat.

"It's too bad you're going to miss the entertainment," Olivia said.

An excited murmur traveled through the crowd as a spotlight shone just past where Celine and Olivia stood. It seemed every person in the room turned in Celine's direction, gazing at something behind her. As she turned to see what everyone was looking at, a pathway cleared for the cloaked figure of a woman entering the room from a nearby doorway. Celine watched as the figure drew closer and found herself mesmerized by how it seemed the woman floated, rather than walked, toward her. She halted just as she passed Celine and gazed back over her shoulder at her. Celine's breath caught in her throat as she saw the sparkle of deep brown eyes peering at her through a feathered mask. The very mask Olivia had asked her to make that afternoon but refused to say who it was for. She gazed down at the front of the cloak, knowing what lay beneath, the matching top and bottom of the feathered costume she had created. She found herself wanting to rip open the cloak to see the body of the woman who wore it. Her imagination had run wild wondering what this woman looked like as she worked on the costume, causing her to prick herself several times with the sewing needle. She had, quite literally, poured blood, sweat, and tears into the costume.

When she looked back up, the woman smiled seductively, turned away, and continued her spotlighted, slow, sexy stroll to the center of the room.

"She's known as Sable," Olivia whispered in Celine's ear. "We should move closer for a better view."

Celine didn't argue. She just let Olivia guide her through the crowd until they somehow ended up in front. The rhythmic drumming that had been playing during Sable's entrance stopped as she slowly shed her long cloak to the delight of her audience, but no one was more affected by her appearance than Celine. Sable's long, lithe, muscular dancer's body and dark pecan complexion shone iridescently in the light. The way the leather of the feathered brassiere and shorts cupped her breasts and behind so perfectly had Celine flushed with heat.

A lonely trumpet wail filled the now hushed room, and Sable began a slow, graceful dance in response. The rhythmic drums joined in once again, and her movements grew wilder, more seductive, as her body gyrated and swayed in a provocative dance that left every man and woman watching heated with desire. At the height of her dance she turned directly toward Celine. The trumpet stopped, leaving only the drum cadence in its wake. It played a slow jungle beat as Sable reached her arms toward Celine, beckoning her forward.

Celine had been watching the performance awestruck. Even with the mask covering most of her face, Sable's dark, exotic beauty could not be contained. Now it was calling to her like a siren's song. The drumbeat picked up, and Sable closed her eyes, wrapped her arms around herself, swaying to the beat, then looked back at Celine and beckoned to her once again. A memory niggled at Celine's mind, but before she could grasp it someone gently pushed her forward. With her gaze locked onto Sable's, she continued moving forward. Celine stood, center stage, gazing up at Sable, who stood a few inches taller than her. She was lost in the depth of Sable's brown eyes, no longer caring where she was or who was watching. All Celine knew was that she had to be near this seductress who had woven a spell around her that she couldn't, and didn't, want to break.

Sable moved close enough to Celine for their bodies to almost touch. There was nothing but a thin strip of air keeping them apart. Celine trembled as she felt Sable's hands travel up the front of her tuxedo jacket. Something in the back of Celine's mind told her this was wrong. This was not how a lady behaved, but the thought was shoved aside by something more primal. A physical hunger she had denied herself for far too long. That hunger became a need that refused to be denied, especially with this beautiful temptation sliding her warm hands beneath her jacket and up her back. When Celine reached up to touch Sable, she was left grasping air as Sable slipped away.

Sable smiled mischievously as the trumpet joined the drums again and she began another dance. No longer able to control her desire, as the drum beat in a steady cadence that seemed to match her heartbeat, Celine walked over, pulled Sable up against her body, grasped the back of her head, and brought Sable's lips down on her own in a kiss that left her stunned at her own boldness and drew an excited applause from their audience.

"We should probably give them a bow," Sable said breathlessly when their kiss ended.

Celine was thankful for the mask she wore as Sable took her hand and turned her toward the audience, who cheered and whistled even louder. Still dazed by what just occurred, Celine allowed Sable to guide her from the room. She caught a glimpse of Olivia's broad smile as they passed, and Celine wondered if Olivia had been in on what just happened. The loud applause became a dull roar as the door to the ballroom closed behind them. Celine continued to follow Sable, in spite of the alarm bells going off in her head warning her to just turn around and go back to the ballroom. Within a few moments, they were in Sable's dressing room where she finally released Celine's hand, then closed the door behind them.

Celine looked everywhere around the elegantly furnished room except at Sable. When she noticed the huge four-poster bed on the other side of the room, she realized that being alone with Sable might be a mistake. She turned to leave and found Sable blocking her way, watching her curiously.

"I…I better go," Celine said hesitantly.

"All right." Sable stepped aside with a grin.

"Thank you." Celine started to leave.

"One request before you leave?"

Celine looked back at Sable, who stood close enough for her to touch, which she ached to do.

"Would you mind helping me with my costume? It's difficult to unhook the top by myself, and I don't want to ruin this beautiful creation."

Celine's mouth went dry at the thought of helping Sable undress. She licked her lips and took a shaky breath as she hesitated in answering. Her hand was on the knob, all she had to do was turn it and make her escape, but something about this woman, this night, had her doing things she never imagined. Wasn't that her whole reason for coming to the masquerade? To do and experience things she had not been able to before?

"All right."

❖

Dinah couldn't help but smile as she turned her back toward Celine. Her performances as Sable were known to be risqué, but tonight's show felt different. She usually felt no connection with the people she pulled out of the audience to perform with. Whether they were men or women, it was just part of her act, but Celine was different. Something had clicked inside her the moment they laid eyes on each other in the shop that afternoon, something strange and exciting. It felt as if her life changed at that very moment. Then to find out that Celine not only did the beautiful work on her costume but that she was here tonight, it was as if fate was throwing them together. Who was she to fight fate? Dinah stood facing a full-length mirror. As she locked eyes with Celine, she could almost see the internal battle she fought with herself. Dinah understood that battle all too well.

Dinah studied the image of the two of them in the mirror. Celine dressed in masculine garb and domino mask and her in a feminine and skimpy feathered costume. A shiver of desire ran through her as Celine, without taking her eyes off their reflection, gently traced her fingertips up the small of Dinah's back to the clasp of her top. Celine easily found and unhooked the hidden clasp.

Dinah held the top in place over her breasts. "Thank you."

Celine's fingers still rested lightly on Dinah's back. "You're welcome."

Dinah held Celine's golden gaze for another moment, then turned to face her. She could still feel the heated imprint of Celine's fingers along her back and wondered how a woman she didn't even know could have such an intense effect on her.

"What's your name?" Dinah asked, wondering if she would keep to the anonymity of the evening.

Celine hesitated for a moment then smiled. "I thought the whole purpose of a masquerade was to remain anonymous."

"True. I was simply curious about the person who so boldly kissed me out there," Dinah said.

Celine's face flushed a shade darker. "I apologize for that. I don't know what came over me."

"No need for apologies. If I didn't enjoy it, you wouldn't be here right now."

"I've never done anything like that before."

"You've never kissed a woman? You could've fooled me."

"I've kissed a woman before, but it was very…innocent."

"This party is not for the innocent," Dinah said.

"I've noticed."

"Tell me, are you innocent, my mysterious kisser?"

"What do you think?"

"I think you are, but you don't want to be. I think that this," Dinah reached up with one hand to straighten Celine's ascot, "is your true self, and what's underneath is the masquerade."

"Is Sable also a fortune teller? Are you going to tell me what my future holds?"

"No, but I can tell you what the rest of this evening holds."

"What would that be?" Celine asked.

"You have two choices. You can stay in this room with me instead of going back out to the party or you can turn around, leave, and forever wonder what would've happened if you had stayed."

Their gazes held for a moment before Celine turned to sit on a nearby lounge chair. She removed her jacket, sat back, and put her feet up on the chair.

Dinah chuckled. Celine intrigued her more than any woman she had ever met before.

"You don't mind if I get undressed, do you?"

"Uh, no, not at all," Celine said hesitantly.

Dinah wasn't blind. She could tell by how Celine's boldness turned to nervousness that she was not the experienced woman she pretended to be, and that appealed to Dinah more than anything else. The idea of being the one to appease a hunger Celine so obviously craved intrigued her. She would see how far Celine was willing to take this opportunity. Without dropping her gaze from Celine's, Dinah slowly slid her top from her breasts and laid it carefully on the dressing table. She then reached down to remove the bottom of the costume. Celine's gaze wavered, barely holding on to Dinah's as the costume slipped past her hips and down her legs. When Dinah placed the feathered bottom with its matching top on the dressing table, she stood before Celine.

Dinah felt as if she were being physically caressed by Celine's heated gaze as her eyes traveled slowly down her face, to her breasts, down her belly, hesitating at the triangle of hair at the juncture of her thighs, and down the length of her legs.

"You were very thorough with the sparkling powder," Celine said.

"My performances sometimes call for less clothing than I wore tonight."

Celine raised a brow. "I didn't realize nude shows were legal at Harlem clubs."

Dinah moved slowly toward Celine. "They aren't. I take it you've never been to one of those shows."

Celine shook her head.

Dinah stopped directly in front of Celine. "Would you like to see what they do at one of those illegal shows?"

"Now? D-Don't you need music?"

Dinah began to sway her hips. "No."

Dinah enjoyed the way Celine watched as she ran her hands down along her own body as she moved to an imaginary song. Celine eased to the edge of the chair and reached for Dinah.

"Customers aren't allowed to touch during the show." Dinah slowed her movements to a subtle undulation.

Celine grasped Dinah's hips and pulled her close. "I'm not a customer."

Dinah gazed down at Celine, whose lips were just inches from her midsection. When Celine moved her head forward, Dinah sucked in a breath as Celine brushed her lips across her belly. Dinah trembled at the intense pleasure brought on by the soft kiss.

"That's definitely not allowed," Dinah said.

"Really? What about this?" Celine used the tip of her tongue to trace a circle around Dinah's navel.

"Mmm…that would get you removed from the premises."

"I guess I won't be coming to that show anytime soon."

Dinah reached down and began removing the pins that held the loose little bun at the back of Celine's head in place. When she was finished, she knelt before Celine, tangled her fingers in her hair, gently grasped her head, and brought it toward hers.

"Kiss me like you did out there," Dinah murmured against Celine's lips.

Celine obliged, grasping Dinah's hips tighter and pulling her body flush against her own. As the kiss grew more passionate, Celine's hands traveled up to grasp Dinah's head to deepen the kiss. Someone loudly clearing their throat halted their intimate moment.

"My apologies for interrupting, ladies, but they're looking for Sable to come join the party," Lee said from the doorway.

Both Celine and Dinah were breathing heavily as they rested their foreheads rested against each other.

"Please tell them I'll be down shortly," Dinah told him.

"Would you like me to stay and help you dress?" he asked with a bit of humor in his tone.

"No…thank you. I can handle it." Dinah wanted to throw something at him.

"I'll see you downstairs." Lee closed the door as he left.

"They're waiting for you," Celine said.

"I know." Dinah untangled her fingers from Celine's hair and smoothed it back.

Celine stood and helped Dinah stand as well. "I'll go so you can get ready."

Dinah placed a soft kiss on Celine's lips. "You know you don't have to."

"I can't keep Sable from her adoring fans," Celine said.

Dinah grinned. "Are you an adoring fan?"

"Most definitely." Celine briefly kissed Dinah, then grabbed her jacket to leave.

"Aren't you glad you decided to stay?" Dinah asked.

Celine turned back, her golden eyes turning molten with passion. "Most definitely."

❖

Celine took a few moments to stop by the room she and Olivia had dressed in to try to calm her racing heart and make herself look as presentable as possible before heading downstairs to find her aunt. As she removed her mask and tried to put her hair into some semblance of what it was before Dinah had run her fingers through it, she gazed at her flushed face in the mirror.

"Who are you?" she asked her reflection.

She recognized her face but not the bold woman she had been just moments before. The mask had given her a sense of freedom she had not expected. Camil had come back, allowing her to do and say things she never would have as herself. Her face became heated as she remembered the beautiful sight of Sable standing naked in the middle of the room, body sparkling from the powder, and her full soft lips slightly swollen from their passionate foreplay. Celine's body reacted to the memory with the most delicious feelings. She closed her eyes, willing her body to calm down, then placed her mask back on. With one last look in the mirror, she knew she would never forget this night for as long as she lived. Celine found Olivia still in the room where Sable's performance had taken place.

"Ah, there you are. I was about to send a search party out for you. I was worried when you disappeared after your little performance with Sable," Olivia said.

"I was feeling rather odd, so I went upstairs to lie down," Celine said.

Olivia gave her a knowing look. "I see. Well, you might want to get that tuxedo cleaned first thing in the morning. You must have lain in a bed of powder. You're all sparkly."

Although Celine felt her face heat in a blush, she didn't feel the least bit of embarrassment. She felt more alive than she had ever felt before, and the woman she had to thank for it entered the room in a round of applause. She still wore her feathered mask but had exchanged the rest of the costume for a sheer floor-length chocolate brown robe cut daringly low in the front with a large peacock design in the back. Celine couldn't help but smile because she had picked the robe herself from her aunt's inventory when she completed the costume. Seeing Sable in the beautiful robe, she couldn't imagine anyone else wearing it. Celine also knew that she had to see Sable again. She didn't know how, but she had to find a way.

CHAPTER THREE

Celine walked around in a daze for a week after the masquerade. She had visions of the mysterious Sable clouding her mind. Her distraction had her mixing up orders and redoing sewing work that she could normally do with her eyes closed.

"Celine, you've seemed a bit distracted all day. Is everything all right?" Olivia asked. It was the end of the day and they were closing the shop.

"Everything is fine," Celine said.

"Maybe you've just been working too hard. Why don't you stay home and relax tomorrow?"

Celine looked at her in surprise. "But it's Saturday, our busiest day of the week."

"*N'importe quoi!*" Olivia waved dismissively. "I can get Simone to come in and help. You deserve it. Your hats brought in far more profit than I would have expected since you began helping me. Go treat yourself to something nice, on me." Olivia handed her a larger sum of money than she normally received for her weekly pay.

Celine hugged her. "Thank you, *Tante.*"

Celine couldn't remember the last time she just relaxed and enjoyed her day. When she wasn't at the shop, she was attending a church or social event with her mother. To be able to just take a leisurely day to sleep in late, have her hair professionally done instead of fighting with the thick mass herself, and pick up a few books she wanted to read would be a real treat. Since most of the establishments she frequented closed the same time as their shop, she was never able to visit any of them. Maybe a day off would also help rid her of the distracting images of the dark beauty she had been thinking about all week.

After the masquerade had ended, she realized trying to find a way to see Sable again might not be the best idea. What happened that night was something she could not allow to happen again. One night, that was all it was supposed to be. One night to experience the freedom Paul had offered her so many times before he died. She would keep the memories of that night locked away in the back of her mind, never to be experienced again. The thought of that made her sad, but it was something she knew had to be done. Tomorrow she would take the break Olivia offered and make a pointed effort to get herself back to the normalcy of her life before Sable had danced her way into it.

Dinah stretched and moaned in pleasure as she slowly awakened from enjoying not only a full night's sleep for the first time in months, but also the sensual dream she had of a golden-eyed, masked woman. A woman she had been dying to see all week but couldn't find the time to do so until today. As a matter of fact, Dinah had done something she had never done before, she called in sick to work last night, which was why she was able to sleep in late today. She was not the least bit worried about what horrible Nurse Porter had to say about it. Dinah found out yesterday that after two days of interviews at Harlem Hospital, she had been accepted onto the nursing staff.

She didn't know how she managed to work her usual overnight shift, come home in just enough time to shower, change, eat, and be bright-eyed for the interviews, but she did it. By the time she got home she was too exhausted to do anything but sleep until it was time to leave for her next shift once again, so her plan to drop by Rousseau's Fashions to thank Olivia for her costume, and hopefully see Celine again, was set aside. After hearing the good news from the head nurse at Harlem Hospital, Dinah decided that taking the day off and completing that task was the perfect way to celebrate.

Dinah took her time getting ready. She dressed carefully in one of her best day dresses and removed the pins from her hair that she had asked her aunt to hot comb and pin curl before she went to bed last night, all so that she would look her best when she saw Celine. She headed downstairs where her aunt, Fran, and Lee were sitting in the living room talking. As soon as she entered, Lee whistled in admiration.

"My, my, where are we going all draped down?" he said.

"I have to run some errands," Dinah said.

"Would one of those errands happen to be a certain dress shop?" Lee asked.

Dinah avoided Aunt Jo's curious gaze by turning to check her reflection in a nearby mirror.

"Maybe. I do have to stop by and thank Olivia for her assistance with my costume." Dinah picked an imaginary piece of lint from her dress.

"You mean that fancy place with the French name? I think I'll come with you," Jo said.

"What on earth for?" Fran asked.

Jo joined Dinah at the mirror, completely ignoring her gaze, and smoothed back her hair.

"I was talking to Geraldine at church about her hat and she told me she got it from that place and that they aren't that expensive."

"You haven't bought a new hat in years," Fran said.

"Exactly, that's why I need another one. The one I have is getting rather worn. Give me a minute to grab my purse," Jo said.

"Fran?" Dinah pleaded at Jo's exit.

Fran shrugged. "When I see that look in her eyes, I've got about as much control over her as a runaway train."

Dinah gave Lee a withering glare.

He looked very much like a puppy that got caught snatching food. "Sorry."

"Ready?" Jo asked cheerfully when she came back into the room.

Dinah pasted on a smile. "Yes."

They strolled quietly along the street for a few minutes until Dinah couldn't hold back any longer.

"Aunt Jo, you know as well as I do you couldn't care less about getting a new hat. I've offered several times to replace the one you have, and you turned me down. So why are you really going with me?"

Jo's mouth quirked upward. "I want to see this woman who's got you floating around like you're on a cloud."

"Has it been that obvious?" Dinah asked.

Jo nudged her in the side with her elbow. "Only to someone who knows you as well as I do."

"It probably doesn't hurt that you've got a gossip like Lee living in the house. He told you what happened at the party, didn't he?"

Jo shrugged. "Not everything, just the good parts."

"Remind me not to tell him any secrets."

When they arrived at Rousseau's, nervous butterflies took flight in

Dinah's stomach in anticipation of seeing Celine. To her surprise, they weren't greeted by Celine or Olivia.

"*Bon jour*. Welcome to Rousseau's. How may I help you?"

"Hello, is Miss Rousseau in?" Dinah asked the young woman.

"Yes, Madam Rousseau is in the back. I will get her for you."

"I take it she's not the one you were coming to see," Jo said.

"No, that's not Celine."

The woman reentered followed by Olivia, looking as sophisticatedly beautiful as ever.

"Ah, *ma chérie*, you didn't tell me it's the beautiful Sable calling on me," Olivia said.

The young woman looked confused for a moment. "I'm sorry, madame, but she did not tell me who she was."

Olivia turned back toward the woman and gently brushed her fingertips across her cheek. "You have to remember to ask who is visiting the shop in case they are particularly important clientele, and Ms. Hampton is especially important. Now, why don't you go upstairs and fix us some lunch." Olivia placed a soft kiss on the woman's temple.

The young woman nodded, gazing adoringly up at Olivia before practically floating out of the room.

Olivia came around the counter and pulled Dinah into an embrace. "Hello, Dinah. Your beauty is always such a pleasure to see."

Dinah returned the embrace. "Hello, Olivia."

Olivia released her and smiled at Jo. "Now, let me guess, this must be your aunt, Josephine. I see the resemblance."

Dinah was surprised at the smitten expression on Jo's face. It seemed no one was immune to Olivia Rousseau's charm.

"Yes, this is Josephine Hampton. Aunt Jo, this is Olivia Rousseau."

"It's a pleasure to meet you, Josephine." Olivia offered her hand to Jo.

"Likewise. You can just call me Jo." She seemed to have recovered from her initial reaction to Olivia.

Olivia wrinkled her nose. "No, I like Josephine. It rolls off the tongue so well. Someone as beautiful as you should not be called such a manly name."

Jo laughed. "I see Lee wasn't exaggerating when he described you. I think you and I are going to get along fine."

Olivia gave Jo a wink. "I hope so. Now, what can I do for you ladies?"

"I came to thank you for my beautiful costume. It was much more than I expected," Dinah said.

"It was nothing. As I said, someone as talented as you deserved something better. It was well worth any effort to see you perform that night. Besides, it's my niece you should really be thanking. She's the one who did the work."

"Is she here?" Dinah asked.

"No. She's been working so hard I gave her the day off."

"Oh." Dinah didn't hide her disappointment. "Well, please tell her I said thank you."

"I will. Is there anything else I can do for you?"

"Yes," Jo answered. "I'd like to see some hats."

"I have the perfect one for you in the back." Olivia left the room, leaving them alone in the store.

Dinah gazed at her aunt curiously.

"What?" Jo asked. "I said I was coming with you to get a hat, and that's just what I'm going to do."

"A hat, huh?"

"Child, Olivia Rousseau is more woman than I could handle even if I were interested. I wouldn't leave Fran for anything in the world, and judging from what we saw, I'm too old for her."

"Do you want me to wait for you?"

"No, go finish running your errands."

"All right, I'll see you later." She placed an affectionate kiss on Jo's cheek, then waved to Olivia on the way out as she came from the back room with a large hat box.

Celine gazed at herself in the mirror and nodded in appreciation. "Thank you so much, Sissy. I can never get the curls the way you do," she said to the woman who had just finished styling her hair.

"No need to thank me, honey. You know I love doin' your hair. You got that good grade of hair that makes my job easier. Not like the usual nappy-headed women that come up in here wantin' to look like those girls from the Cotton Club. I keep tellin' them I'm a hairdresser, not a miracle worker," Sissy said.

"Well, thank you all the same," Celine said.

As much as she enjoyed coming to the salon for a little pampering, she hated the attention she received because of her hair. It reminded her of the color class distinction she thought she had left in the South. Good hair, light skin, just a couple of the things that were outward signs of your status and gave Whites and darker Negroes alike a reason to sneer at you.

Looking down into her purse as she left the shop, Celine bumped into someone walking by.

She quickly looked up into a familiar face. "Oh, sorry."

"That's all right." The woman stepped aside to let Celine pass.

"Thank you." Celine realized she was the woman who came into the shop the afternoon of the masquerade.

"You look very familiar," the woman said.

"I believe you came into my aunt's shop, Rousseau's Fashions, about a week ago," Celine answered.

"Oh, yes, with Lee. I don't think we were introduced. I'm Dinah Hampton." She offered her hand in greeting.

Celine took Dinah's hand. "Hello, Dinah, I'm Celine Montré."

There was something else familiar about this woman, but Celine couldn't place it. Realizing she was holding Dinah's hand a little longer than appropriate, she slid her hand from Dinah's warm grasp.

"Well, it was nice meeting you, Celine."

"You too. I hope we see you in the shop again soon," Celine said, still bewildered by the feeling that she met this woman someplace other than Rousseau's.

"Oh, I'll definitely be coming by again," Dinah said.

Celine stood in a daze for a moment, not sure what to do next. The familiarity of the woman was too much to ignore. She sucked in a breath as the pieces started falling into place. Dinah Hampton had come into the shop with Lee the day of the masquerade. The day her aunt asked her to create the costume that ended up being on the dancer at the masquerade, the dancer with the warm, soft hands and sensuous mouth that she had gotten to know quite intimately that night. Celine slowly turned, but Dinah had disappeared. She looked frantically around, but Dinah was nowhere in sight. She could have gone into any one of the shops along the street. Did she recognize her, Celine wondered? She couldn't have. It would be impossible for someone to realize she was the same woman dressed in her feminine attire from the one who had been in men's clothing wearing a domino mask that night.

Images of Dinah's nude body and their passionate kisses flooded Celine's mind. She had promised herself that night would not happen again, but it was all she had been thinking about for a week now, and those memories were showing no signs of fading anytime soon. When she finished her errands and arrived home, her mother gave her a message from her aunt asking if she would like to go with her to one of her friend's card games. Celine smiled and immediately called her aunt to accept the invitation. "Card game" was their code for going to dinner and dancing in Jungle Alley. She needed the distraction to get her mind off Dinah Hampton's dark beauty.

❖

Later that night, Olivia took Celine to a club they had not been to before. It wasn't as upscale as the Bamboo Inn, where they usually went, but it was still classier than a few of the others nearby.

"I see you're in one of your adventurous moods," Celine said.

"I've been here a few times before." Olivia managed to get them seated fairly close to the stage.

Shortly after their arrival, they were joined by several of Olivia's friends. By the time the entertainment started they had their own little party going, and Celine was feeling more relaxed than she had in a long time.

The owner of the nightclub, Curtis Flynn, came out to introduce "Flynn's Follies," and Celine thought he exemplified the slick club owner with his smooth voice, charming smile, tailored suit, and shrewd look in his eyes that made you hesitant to trust him. The dancers came out to perform, and unlike the sepia and tan colored dancers of the Cotton Club chorus line, Flynn's Follies dancers were of the darker hues, ranging from caramel to ebony. Although she had never seen them perform, Celine had a feeling that the Cotton Club's dancers were far more sedate in their shows than Flynn's. Every act was performed with a seductively wild abandon that had the audience entranced. It reminded her of Sable's performance at the masquerade.

Thinking of that night caused a flutter of excitement in Celine's belly. She was fairly sure that Sable and the woman she met that afternoon were one and the same. There was no mistaking those deep brown eyes and luscious mouth. The question Celine had to answer was could she truly put Dinah Hampton and their passionate moment out of her mind enough to not want to experience it again? As if in answer to her question, a familiar drumbeat interrupted her thoughts. Her eyes widened in surprise as a cloaked figure made her way to the stage and the audience applauded excitedly. It was as if she were reliving the performance from the masquerade all over again.

Celine narrowed her eyes at Olivia. "I'm assuming this is why you chose to come here tonight instead of our usual place."

Olivia grinned. "You enjoyed her performance so much the first time I thought you might like to see it again."

"Mm-hmm," Celine said doubtfully.

She turned back to watch the woman she had been dreaming about for a week weave her seductive spell once again. It wasn't the exact performance the infamous Sable had done at the masquerade, but it was just as effective in arousing desires Celine had tried so hard to hold back.

❖

After her performance, Dinah stood in her dressing room beaming at her reflection in the mirror as the costume assistant helped her undress. Before every performance, she liked to watch a few of the previous entertainers to gauge the crowd's mood for that evening. During the opening performance she spotted a particularly lively table near the stage. It was Celine's group.

Dinah remembered passing by the salon earlier that day and spotting Celine through the window. Once again, chance had thrown her and Celine into each other's path at the least expected moment. Noting that Celine's appointment was finishing up, Dinah decided to stay out of sight until she left the shop. As soon as she saw Celine heading for the door, she purposely stepped into her path. Dinah also made sure to keep the conversation brief, to give Celine just enough time to possibly recognize her before walking away and ducking into the shop next door.

She knew exactly when Celine put the pieces together, and her excitement soared as she watched Celine search frantically around for her. Fortunately, a window display in the shop she had ducked into had hidden Dinah from Celine's view. Afterward, she spent the rest of the afternoon gliding happily through her day filled with thoughts of seeing Celine again. That opportunity had come tonight when their gazes met for a moment as Dinah exited the stage after her performance. She saw her desire mirrored in Celine's bright eyes. She was going to have to make a point of stopping by Celine's table first when she went out to mingle with the customers.

The costume assistant left, and Dinah sat at her dressing table carefully reapplying her makeup so that she looked good when she saw Celine. There was a knock at the door and, thinking it was the assistant with her next outfit, she told whoever it was to come in. She looked at the mirror as the door slowly opened and Celine stood in the doorway. Neither said a word as their eyes locked in the mirror and Celine walked into the dressing room, closing the door behind her. Dinah stood, watching Celine's reflection as she came up behind her. Except for the absence of their masquerade garb, their image in the mirror was the same as it had been that night, Celine standing behind her with their gazes locked.

"You knew who I was that night, didn't you?" Celine asked.

Dinah turned to face Celine. "Yes."

"Did my aunt have anything to do with what happened?"

Dinah didn't hear a hint of anger or accusation in her tone, just genuine curiosity. "No. I hope you're not angry with me."

"Not angry, just curious," Celine said.

"About?" Dinah reached up to run a finger along Celine's delicate jaw line.

"You," Celine said breathlessly.

"What can I do to help you appease your curiosity?"

"Tell me why I can't stop thinking about you? Tell me how a glance from you can set me on fire?"

Dinah ran the pad of her thumb across Celine's full lips. "Those are questions I've been trying to answer since I first saw you at your aunt's shop."

Celine's eyes fluttered closed and she shuddered in response to the intimate touch.

Dinah brought her hand up to the nape of Celine's neck and pulled her close. "What would you do if I were as bold as you were the night of the masquerade and kissed you?"

Celine didn't respond. Their lips were so close Dinah could feel Celine's soft breath mingling with her own. Then a curt knock, and the dressing room door flying open halted them from going any further.

Celine stepped away, keeping her back to the door, as Dinah struggled to close her dressing robe.

"Curtis, how many times do I need to ask you to stop coming in here without my permission?" Dinah asked angrily.

Curtis, the club's owner, stood in the doorway looking from one of them to the other, "How many times do I need to remind you that this is MY joint and I don't need permission to do anything in MY joint. You've got a room full of people waiting to see you, so unless you can pay me for the time you're wasting in here instead of being on the floor making me money, I suggest you get out there."

Dinah hated Curtis Flynn. If she didn't need the money she would have quit right then and there.

"I'll be out in five minutes," she said through clenched teeth.

"Three, not a minute longer." He sent a final glance at Celine's back before leaving.

Dinah looked at Celine. "Are you all right?"

"Seems we keep getting interrupted. Maybe somebody is trying to tell us something."

"What, that we need to find a more private place to meet?" Dinah joked.

"Not exactly what I was thinking."

"Celine, if someone thinks we shouldn't be together, then why do we keep getting thrown together like this? Why do we have the feelings we do for each other?"

Celine didn't answer. Dinah took her hands.

"Meet me tomorrow, anywhere, you pick the place. We'll talk and if you still feel like what's happening between us shouldn't happen, then we'll never speak again," Dinah said.

Another knock on the door interrupted them again. This time it was Dinah's dresser letting her know she had two minutes.

"Okay. Meet me at the shop tomorrow at one. It's closed on Sundays and my aunt spends the afternoon at our house, so we'll have some privacy." Celine hesitantly released Dinah's hands and turned to leave.

"Celine."

"Yes."

Dinah walked over to her and placed a soft kiss on her lips. "See you tomorrow."

Celine nodded and left the dressing room.

❖

After the club closed, Dinah stopped by Curtis's office to pick up her pay. She hoped Lenny, the club's manager, was there instead of Curtis. After he had barged in on her and Celine, he had watched her like a hawk the rest of the night. She also caught him watching Celine and Olivia's table just as intently. Dinah hoped he would let the incident drop, but she had a feeling he wasn't going to. Curtis Flynn was the type of man who loved knowing other people's secrets. Knowing secrets was what kept his bootleg business afloat while his competition was being shut down all around him. As Dinah drew closer to the office, she could hear Lenny talking and sighed with relief, but it was short-lived when she realized he was talking to Curtis.

"Well, if it isn't our star. We were just talking about you," Curtis said.

"Curtis, I'm too tired for your foolishness. Can I just get my money and go home?" Dinah asked.

Curtis's gaze narrowed on Dinah. "Go handle that business I told you about," he said to Lenny without taking his eyes off Dinah.

Lenny nodded, then headed toward the door. He gave Dinah a warning look as he passed by. When she looked back at Curtis, he was watching her intently.

"You seem to be getting a little too uppity lately. Maybe it's time for Sable to retire and one of the other girls to take over as featured dancer. Cora and Ruth have been eyeing your spot for some time."

There was no hint of his usual smug expression, so Dinah knew he was serious.

"I'm sorry. It's just been a long day." She hoped the apology would be enough to appease his anger.

His eyes narrowed again, as if trying to peer right through her. Dinah knew that look all too well. She had seen him give it to others who had pushed him one step too far. She never had it turned on her until now.

"Don't forget who pulled you out of that rat-infested juke joint down the block where you were nothing but a hootchy-kootchy girl," he said.

"I'm sorry, Curtis." She tried sounding more sincere this time.

His smug expression returned as he came around his desk toward her. He gently grasped her chin and raised her head.

"You're my moneymaker, Di. I would truly hate to lose you, but don't try me like that again."

Dinah nodded in agreement, hoping he didn't see the cold disgust she felt for him. Curtis gazed at her for a few moments, then released her chin.

He reached back to pick up an envelope off his desk. "There's a little something extra in there for entertaining the table of the mayor's brother-in-law tonight. It should keep them off our backs a little while longer."

"Thank you." Dinah took the envelope and turned to leave.

"By the way, congratulations on getting the job at Harlem Hospital."

That stopped her short. She hadn't told anyone but her aunt and Fran about the job.

"Thank you," she said before hesitantly leaving the office.

Curtis knowing about her new job could only mean one thing—he had one of his thugs watching her. The thought of that brought a chill down her spine and had her wondering what he was up to.

CHAPTER FOUR

Celine sat in the window seat of her family's sitting room gazing out the window but only seeing the image of Dinah's beautiful body shimmering before her. She could think of nothing else but her seductive smile, smooth pecan skin, and soft curves. Images that sent butterflies fluttering in her belly. Celine's intense attraction to Dinah frightened and thrilled her all at once. Society said that what she was feeling was wrong, but her heart and body said otherwise. It felt as natural to her as being a woman when she was with Dinah. As if she could finally be herself and stop hiding behind the mourning widow's mask she had been holding on to for the past year. Celine finally understood what her husband had been trying to tell her for so many years. Although she couldn't see herself risking her life the way Paul had when he fell in love with Robert Cole, she could understand how the feelings of their forbidden affair could be so addictive.

"Celine?"

Celine jumped at the sound of her mother's voice. She had been so lost in her own thoughts she had not heard her enter the room.

"Yes, Maman," she answered.

"What's wrong? Are you coming down with something?" her mother said in concern.

"I'm fine." Celine gave her a reassuring smile.

She could see the doubt on her mother's face. She also knew that her mother was not one to pry and believed that if there was something she needed to know she would be told in due time. Celine was grateful for that because she didn't think her mother would really want to know what had Celine so distracted.

"Well, your aunt should be here any minute, so why don't we get the tea and cards set up for our game."

Celine nodded and assisted her mother with the task of preparing for their weekly game of gin rummy. The activity helped pass the time and kept her mind from its current distraction. Aunt Olivia arrived shortly after, and by the end of their game, the time had flown by. If she didn't leave within the next few moments, she would be late meeting Dinah. Olivia and her mother moved from the card table to sit and finish the embroidery they were working on. Celine searched the room as if she were looking for something.

With a frustrated sigh, she grabbed her purse and hat. "Mother, I have to run back to the shop. I left the book I've been reading there."

"Are you sure? Did you look in your room?" her mother asked.

"No, I'm sure I left it there. I was reading it in the back room while I ate lunch the other day."

"Will you be back in time for dinner? Your father is bringing a guest," her mother said.

"Yes," she assured her before rushing from the room.

A quick glance in Olivia's direction as she was leaving told Celine that she didn't believe her excuse about the book. Although she trusted her aunt, Celine couldn't bring herself to tell her about meeting Dinah. She wasn't sure where she was going with this newfound friendship and felt the need to keep it to herself until she did.

Celine arrived at the shop a few minutes past one o'clock. She didn't know if she should have been relieved or disappointed that Dinah wasn't there yet. Maybe she changed her mind. Celine straightened up her hat display and went to the back room to get the book she had purposely left behind the previous night when she and Olivia had returned from Flynn's. As she headed back to the front of the shop, she heard a soft knock on the door. Her nerves went awry when she saw Dinah's silhouette through the mostly sheer curtain. She stared at the door, fighting the urge to let Dinah think she wasn't there. In that moment's hesitation, Dinah disappeared, which jolted Celine into action. She rushed to the door, hurriedly unlocked, and yanked it open. Dinah was halfway down the block when Celine called her name. Dinah turned and slowly walked back. Without a word, Celine stepped aside to allow Dinah to pass, then closed and locked the door behind her.

"I thought you might have changed your mind," Dinah said.

"I almost did," Celine admitted guiltily.

"Me too. That's why I'm late."

"Why?"

Dinah shrugged. "Probably for the same reason you almost did. I'm not sure where this is taking us or even if we should find out."

Celine felt a sense of relief at Dinah's admission. It helped to calm her nerves to know that Dinah was as unsure as she was.

"Why don't we go up to my aunt's apartment?"

Dinah nodded and followed Celine to the back room and up a stairway to the second floor. Once they entered the apartment, Celine knew there was no turning back for her. She had no choice but to figure out how Dinah was going to fit into her life, or she would spend the rest of it wondering and regretting.

Dinah gazed around Olivia's apartment. "This looks just the way I imagined it would. Just like Olivia, sophisticated and fashionable, yet warm and comfortable."

"Yes, my aunt always hated the stuffy, overdone drawing rooms in New Orleans. She said you should be able to breathe and be fashionable at the same time."

"She's definitely a Renaissance woman. I'm sure she was never one to wear a corset, was she?" Dinah asked.

Celine chuckled. "No, and she was the scandal of the family because of it."

"What about you? Are you a Renaissance woman?"

"Unfortunately, despite how much I've tried, I'm painfully conservative. Would you like a glass of wine?"

"Yes, whatever you have will be fine."

Celine poured them both glasses while Dinah took a seat on the sofa. Celine handed her a glass and joined her.

"Thank you." Dinah took a sip of the wine and settled back into the plush cushions.

"Have you always lived in Harlem?"

"No. I came here a little over three years ago. My family is from Alabama, including my aunt, who came up twenty years ago. Good jobs for us are hard to find down there, so after I finished nursing school my aunt suggested I come up North where there were more opportunities. It hasn't been easy, but it's been better than if I would have stayed in Alabama."

"So, dancing is not your only job?"

"No, nursing doesn't pay as well for Negro nurses as it does for Whites, so by the time I send money back home to my mother and sister, then pay Aunt Jo for room and board, I don't have much left over to save for a place of my own. I want to get a brownstone and bring my mother and sister up here. That's why I dance for Flynn's Follies."

"That's very commendable of you."

"It's the least I could do. After my father died, my mother had to take on twice the workload doing other people's laundry to take care of me and my sister. I want to get her out of that life before she's too old to enjoy what life she has left. What about you? What brought you to Harlem?"

Celine gazed down at her glass of wine, contemplating what to say. The same story she always told about the forlorn widow too heart-broken to stay in New Orleans after her husband's death, or the truth? She gazed back up at Dinah, who patiently waited for her to answer. Celine decided that if she was going to tell anyone the real story, it would be Dinah. She had a feeling Dinah would understand and not judge.

"We left New Orleans to escape a family scandal," she began.

She told Dinah about her and Paul's friendship, marriage agreement, his secret separate life that she was too afraid to join him in, how it eventually led to his death, and the scandal that followed. With each bit of the story revealed, she felt as if the heavy burden of carrying such secrets was being lifted from her shoulders. It was helpful that Dinah listened without the look of disgust, scorn, or condemnation she expected if she had told her story to any of her acquaintances in the social circle her family was in. The sympathy she saw in Dinah's expression had Celine on the verge of tears. Dinah took the wineglass from Celine's trembling fingers and set it on the coffee table then moved closer to her on the sofa.

Dinah wrapped her arms around Celine. "Let it go."

Celine hesitated for just a moment before giving in to the tears. Dinah held her tightly as her body shook with sobs of unreleased grief and frustration.

"I'm sorry," Celine said when her tears finally ceased. "I'm not usually so emotional."

Dinah tenderly stroked Celine's hair. "Isn't it time you allowed yourself to lean on someone else for a change?"

Celine laid her head on Dinah's shoulder and buried her face in the curve of Dinah's neck, softly brushing her lips across Dinah's skin. Celine turned slightly, placing soft kisses along Dinah's neck, jawline, and up toward her ear. When Celine softly nipped her earlobe, Dinah turned toward Celine and gently grasped her face for a passionate, heated kiss.

"Every time you kiss me, I feel like I'm drowning in liquid fire," Celine said breathlessly.

"Is that good or bad?" Dinah traced the pad of her thumb along Celine's jawline.

"Both," Celine answered with a shudder of desire. "It feels too good, which frightens me a little."

"I don't ever want you to be frightened of me," Dinah said. "We don't have to go any further than this moment. I'll leave if that's what you want."

"Stay," Celine said without hesitation. She was tired of denying herself out of fear.

"Are you sure?"

Celine stood, grasped Dinah's hand, and led her to a bedroom.

"I have to tell you, my husband and I never consummated our marriage. It was one of the reasons we chose to marry. We didn't want to be forced to be intimate with people who weren't of our choosing."

"Are you saying you're still a virgin?" Dinah asked in surprise.

"Yes," Celine nervously admitted.

"I won't force you to do anything you don't want to do."

"Thank you," Celine said with relief.

Celine released Dinah's hand and walked toward the bed. She began to unbutton her dress, but her fingers shook too much for her to properly grasp the small pearl buttons.

"Let me," Dinah said.

Dinah deftly unbuttoned the top of her dress, then slid the sleeves off Celine's shoulders and down her arms. Goose bumps prickled along Celine's skin as Dinah's fingers brushed along her arms.

"Are you cold?" Dinah asked.

Celine shook her head. She was far from cold. Her body was beginning to feel as if it were on fire.

"May I finish undressing you?" Dinah asked.

Celine nodded, and Dinah slid the dress down her hips and knelt at her feet to help step out of it. Without standing, she laid the dress on a nearby chair and sat back on her heels to look up at Celine. Celine wore nothing but her undergarments, a lightweight semi-laced, step-in satin corset with lace trim, and ribbon garters holding up a pair of sheer silk stockings. Dinah ran her hands along the outside of Celine's leg from her ankle to her knee. Celine sucked in a shuddering breath. Her reaction spurred Dinah on, and she continued running her hands up Celine's legs until she reached the garter clips of her corset, taking her time to unfasten each one and gliding the stocking down Celine's leg. Dinah gently lifted each of Celine's feet up and out of the silky material. She laid both stockings over Celine's dress on the chair, then looked up at Celine once again.

"You are so beautiful," Dinah said.

Celine's face heated with a blush. "Thank you."

"You've never been told you're beautiful?"

"Not by someone who made me feel the way you do," Celine answered.

"How do I make you feel?"

"Like I want to stay in this room with you, shut away from the outside world, for as long as I can."

Dinah stood and grasped Celine's face for a kiss, then descended from her lips in a heated trail down her neck to the flushed mounds of her breasts peeking over the top of the lace corset. Celine bit her lip and moaned. Heat radiated throughout her body until she felt as if she were about to burst into flames.

"Please," she begged, not sure exactly what she was asking for.

Dinah pulled away from Celine just enough to be able to remove the rest of her undergarments, then quickly undressed as well. She sat on the edge of the bed and reached a hand toward Celine.

"Come here," she told her softly.

Celine's heart pounded faster at the sight of the beautiful body she had seen in her dreams every night since the masquerade. Her hands itched to touch Dinah's smooth, dark skin, and run along her soft curves. Knowing she was moments from doing so sent her nervousness scattering to the wind, replaced by intense arousal.

Celine stood before Dinah, who spread her legs to bring Celine's body closer to hers. Dinah pulled Celine into her embrace, laying her head upon her breasts as Celine wrapped her arms around Dinah's shoulders. They held each other that way for a few moments, Celine enjoying the softness and warmth of Dinah's body against hers. Dinah began placing soft kisses upon Celine's breasts, working her way down to gently pull a nipple into the warmth of her mouth. The tip of Dinah's tongue flicked across Celine's nipple in a steady rhythm that shot fireworks of pleasure throughout Celine's body. Celine's head fell back as she moaned and dug her fingertips into Dinah's shoulders passionately. When Dinah shifted to give her other breast the same sensual treatment, Celine thought she would explode from the heat surging through her body. Celine whimpered as Dinah left her breast and peppered kisses back up toward her neck.

Dinah's lips brushed along Celine's. "Join me on the bed," she whispered.

Celine didn't hesitate to do as Dinah requested. She no longer worried about what others would say if they knew of her attraction to women, if what she and Dinah were doing was wrong, or even if she would make it home in time for dinner as she had promised her mother. The only thing that mattered to Celine in that moment was the pleasure she was receiving from Dinah. Celine lay down and Dinah knelt above her.

"I only want to give you pleasure, so if I touch you in any way that doesn't, don't be afraid to stop me."

Celine nodded. She enjoyed the way Dinah hesitated for a moment to admire her before leaning down and giving Celine another dizzying kiss. Celine was bombarded with physical sensations she never thought were possible as Dinah kissed and stroked her from her head to her toes, bypassing the one part of her body that Celine felt the most sinful sensations pulsing from. She moaned and trembled from the pleasurable torture Dinah was assaulting her with.

Dinah slid her body up the length of Celine's and once again took her nipple into her mouth while her long fingers glided over the wet opening between her thighs. Celine cried out and arched her back in response to the intimate stroking. She had pleasured herself in a similar way many times, but it never brought on the intensity of pressure that was building in the center of her womanhood at that moment. She whimpered and moaned as pleasure built to an unimaginable peak that left her teetering on the edge before tipping her over into a pool of white-hot release that rushed over her like nothing she had ever experienced before. Celine's hips rose off the bed and she cried out as wave after wave of pleasure washed over her.

Celine lay trembling from aftershocks when Dinah whispered seductively into her ear, "I want to taste you."

She met Dinah's passion-darkened gaze and nodded in response. Dinah kissed a path down her lower body and gently spread her legs wider and settled down between them. Recalling the night Paul had brought home the two women for her birthday when they had played voyeur, Celine knew what was coming next, but knowing didn't come close to experiencing such an intimate act. Dinah's warm breath tickled the curls at the juncture of Celine's thighs, and her eyes widened in surprise at the pleasure that vibrated through her body. She had a moment's hesitation, and then Dinah began to trace the outline of her womanhood with the tip of her tongue.

All reasonable thought flew from Celine's mind, and she grasped the bedding to steady her suddenly dizzying world. Rising on her forearms, she gazed down the length of her body and locked eyes with Dinah. She watched in fascination as Dinah pleasured her in the most scandalous way imaginable with her tongue. She prolonged the moment with teasing licks and kisses, gently taking the hardened nub that lay within the folds of her womanly lips into her mouth and flicking it with the tip of her tongue until Celine squirmed and moaned passionately. Dinah grasped Celine's hips, pulled her closer, and delved her tongue into the slick wet heat of Celine's lips.

Celine's head fell back, her moans turning to whimpering pants as Dinah's tongue stroked in and out, seeming to reach the very point of where she most ached for fulfillment. Her inner walls throbbed and contracted until the pressure was too much for Celine to hold back. A molten heat had begun to gather at the point where Dinah's tongue stroked her and built to a raging inferno when her release came upon her. Like a volcano, her body felt as if it were exploding from the inside out, and she had no control once it began. She heard Dinah moan and felt her body trembling in the same way hers had just done. As she lay trying to still her racing heart, Celine felt as weak and boneless as a rag doll. Dinah's head lay resting on her thigh, then she moved up the length of Celine's body and pulled her into the warmth of her embrace. Celine cuddled close and rested her head on Dina's shoulder.

"Are you all right?" Dinah asked.

"Yes. I just never knew it could be so…overwhelming," Celine answered breathlessly.

"I didn't either," Dinah admitted.

"But there have been other women, haven't there?" Celine asked.

Dinah shifted so that she could see Celine's face. "Yes, but I didn't feel with them the way I feel with you."

Dinah reached up to smooth an errant curl away from Celine's cheek. "What am I going to do about you, Celine?" she asked.

Celine placed a kiss on the palm of Dinah's hand as it rested on her cheek. "Let me give you the same pleasure you gave me."

"Being here like this with you gives me pleasure."

Celine closed the distance that separated their lips and kissed Dinah with such slow, aching passion that Dinah moaned in what sounded like regret when Celine ended the kiss, left her embrace, and knelt beside her on the bed.

"Since the night of the masquerade all I could think of was your body and how much I wished I could explore it at my leisure," Celine said.

"Here's your chance," Dinah said seductively.

Celine smiled and moved to straddle Dinah's thighs. Dinah reached up to touch her, but Celine stopped her.

Celine laid Dinah's arms at her side. "It's my turn," she said.

Celine's touch was tentative as she began to caress Dinah, softly gliding her fingertips from Dinah's shoulders to the tops of her breasts. Dinah moaned as Celine grasped her breasts and gently massaged. Celine leaned forward, took one of Dinah's nipples into her mouth, and gently teased it with her tongue until it stood aching and pebble hard. By the time Celine finished giving Dinah's other breast the same loving attention and began to kiss and lick her way down Dinah's body, Dinah was moving and arching passionately.

When Celine reached the hidden treasure at the juncture of Dinah's thighs, she delved her tongue between Dinah's womanly lips, tasting and exploring, until Dinah's moans were intermingled with passionate pants. Dinah reached down and tangled her fingers within Celine's thick curls and her hips rose off the bed as her pleasure reached its peak. The orgasm that rocked Dinah's body almost had Celine bucking off the bed. Celine's hands tightened on her hips as she rode out the tidal wave with her.

As the trembling in Dinah's body eased, Celine moved up to lie beside her. Dinah took Celine into her arms once again and kissed her until they were both breathless. Afterward they lay quietly, arms and legs entangled, holding each other tightly. Celine didn't want this moment to end, but she knew it had to.

Dinah brushed her lips across Celine's brow. "It's getting late. You should be getting back." She seemed to have read Celine's thoughts.

Celine tightened her arms around Dinah. "Can't we just stay here for a little while longer?"

"We could, if you don't mind your family worrying over where you are and deciding to come looking for you. From what you've told me, I don't think they would be very understanding about finding their daughter in bed with another woman. If I were a man and they found us together it would be different. Widows are given certain allowances with what they do behind closed doors as long as they keep up a certain appearance in public. But this is different, this is considered unnatural."

"Is this all I'll have?" Celine asked. "Lying to my family for a few stolen hours of passion?"

"If that's all you want, then yes, that's all you'll have," Dinah answered.

Celine gazed up at her with tears in her eyes. "Is there any other way? You said yourself that this is considered unnatural. A relationship like ours will never be accepted by society or any church."

"Some women like us have found a way to make it work."

"Someone you know?" Celine asked.

"My aunt, Josephine, and her business partner, Fran, have been living as lovers for over twenty years."

Celine's eyes widened in surprise. "Twenty years? How is that possible?"

"They don't feel the need to shout it from the rooftops. To everyone outside, they're two old spinsters running a boardinghouse. Most of their boarders are entertainers, writers, and artists who are more open-minded or share similar lifestyles. The few that are none of those either choose not to see what's right in front of them or Aunt Jo and Fran make sure that they're careful about how they act around them," Dinah explained. "Aunt Jo told me it's more common than you think. There are women like her and Fran who appear to be just two older women living together to keep each other company or help to make ends meet. Then there are the women who go even further by appearing to be just an ordinary couple, like your parents, but one of them is living as a man."

Celine recalled some of the women she had met at the masquerade that she would never have known were women if her aunt had not told her otherwise.

"What are you thinking about?" Dinah asked.

"What it would be like to live as a man. About how free I felt dressed as a man the night of the masquerade. Being able to love a woman openly and freely."

Dinah chuckled. "Well, I don't think you would be able to get away with it as easy as you might think, especially with these curves." Dinah ran her hands along the curve of Celine's behind. "And as exciting as it may seem, it's a hard life. The constant worrying that you'll be found out, the lies and secrets, and even being cut off from your family because they either won't accept you or you couldn't take the chance of them finding out and telling your secret. It's not the glamour and glitz of the drag balls, Celine."

"No, I guess that was a bit naïve of me to think it was. If it's such a difficult life, why do these women choose it? Why don't they choose to live like your aunt and Fran?"

"I think it's because they don't know of any other way to be and live their lives, but I think someone who lives that life will be able to answer that better than I can." With a deep shaky breath, Dinah gently untangled her limbs from Celine's.

"It's getting late. We should go," Dinah said.

Celine nodded in agreement and they climbed out of the bed and began to dress. Dinah was dressed much quicker than Celine.

"I'll go clean up in the other room while you finish dressing." She turned and left the bedroom before waiting for a reply.

Celine watched her go and knew she should say something to let Dinah know how she felt about what they had just shared, but there were so many thoughts running through her mind that she didn't know where to begin. She dressed as quickly as possible, then took a few more moments to try to get her wild curls in some semblance of what they looked like when she left to meet Dinah. When Celine finished, she found Dinah in the other room gazing out the window looking as forlorn as she felt. She wrapped her arms around her waist and laid her cheek against Dinah's back. Celine felt the tension ease from Dinah's body. It gave her hope that Dinah didn't regret their time together. Celine almost cried out in relief as Dinah turned and wrapped her arms around her.

Celine gazed up Dinah. "What do we do now?"

"Do you want to be together again?" Dinah asked, sounding hopeful.

"Yes," Celine answered without hesitation. "But how? I certainly can't conveniently forget a book at the shop every Sunday."

"No, I guess that would look suspicious. I'll think of a way."

"All right, I trust you." Celine placed a soft kiss on Dinah's lips.

Dinah gently grasped Celine's face in her hands. "Do you?"

"With my heart," she said before Dinah brought her lips down on hers for a lingering kiss that left her aching for more.

"We'll never leave if we keep this up," Dinah said.

"Would that be so bad?"

Although the question was asked in jest, Celine searched Dinah's eyes for an answer. An answer she was not even sure she was ready to hear, at least not right now while she was still discovering who she really was. As if Dinah knew she wasn't ready, she simply placed another soft kiss on her lips, and Celine allowed her to lead her toward the door without an answer.

CHAPTER FIVE

Celine arrived home just as her mother and aunt were setting the table for dinner.

"There you are. You left hours ago. I was just about to send your father out looking for you," her mother said.

"I'm sorry, Maman. I decided to finish some work while I was there." Celine surprised herself with how easily the lie came.

"You work too hard when you don't need to," her mother lovingly reprimanded her. "Why don't you finish setting the table, then collect your father and our guest from the study."

Guilt began to eat at her in response to the look of concern on her mother's face. "Yes, Maman."

Her mother left the room, but Olivia stayed behind.

"Did you find your book?" she asked.

Celine almost dropped a plate in response to the question. She had been so caught up in her goodbye to Dinah that she had forgotten the book on the counter in the shop.

"I must have left it behind when I finished working." She avoided Olivia's gaze as she set the table.

"By the way, did I tell you Dinah's aunt invited me to dinner on Wednesday? I thought you might like to join me."

Celine's heartbeat sped up. She and Dinah thought it might take some time to plan to see each other again, and here her aunt was giving them the opportunity to do so much sooner than they expected. It was as if Olivia knew, but she couldn't, Celine thought. She finally gazed up to meet her eyes. Was it that obvious?

As if in answer, Olivia placed a loving kiss on her cheek, then whispered, "I was you once." With a conspiratorial wink, she left Celine alone in shocked silence.

It was all Celine could do to hold back the tears of relief that threatened to fall for the third time that day. First Dinah's, now her aunt's quiet understanding became too much to take in all at once. She took a deep breath, wiped away her tears before her mother saw them, and finished her task. When everything was properly set, she made her way to her father's study.

"Ah, there's our long-lost daughter. Your mother was about to send out a search party for you," her father teased. "Does she know you're here?"

Celine placed a kiss on her father's cheek. "Yes, Papa, she sent me to tell you dinner is ready."

He nodded. "Celine, I would like you to meet Julien Durand. He is our new manager at the tailor shop."

Celine turned toward their guest. Dressed in a very well-fitted light wool gray suit, Mr. Durand was an attractive man.

Celine accepted his offered hand. "A pleasure to meet you, Mr. Durand."

"Please, call me Julien, and the pleasure is all mine." He bent slightly and placed a gentlemanly kiss on the back of her hand before releasing it.

"The Durands are a very prominent Creole business family from Baton Rouge," her father said proudly.

"Your father flatters me." Julien looked embarrassed by her father's pride. "I'm a descendent of a very resourceful Frenchman who left Paris when his father, a fabrics manufacturer, squandered away most of their family's fortune making a bad investment decision with some untrustworthy men. He managed to save their family name by purchasing a ship and bringing a warehouse of fabrics he was able to steal away before the debtors got to them and opened a successful business in Baton Rouge. During his first trip to New Orleans, he discovered the quadroon balls and thus began the darker lineage of the Durand family. Not much different from most of the Louisiana Colored Creole community."

Celine liked Julien's modesty. It was a refreshing change from the snobbery of the well-to-do Creoles she had grown up around who couldn't introduce themselves without laying out the lineage of their family to prove their importance. If you could not trace your family back to a wealthy French nobleman, then you were not worthy enough to travel in their society.

Dinner was a much livelier affair than usual due to Julien's attendance. It had been some time since they had socialized with someone from Louisiana, so the poor man was bombarded with questions of the latest social and political news from home. Their conversations slid from English to French to Creole within a matter of moments. Celine found Julien to be polite, charming, and very much the Creole gentleman. All of which had her mother in true hostess form. Celine had not seen her so animated since they had been in Harlem. It was obvious her father was also quite taken with Julien. He told stories of his apprenticeships with some of the finest tailors and fabric manufacturers in Europe. Her father proudly bragged of the letters of reference Julien had presented him with when he answered the advertisement her father had placed in the Negro newspapers. The only person who seemed to not be moved by Julien's easy charm was her aunt, who was surprisingly quiet throughout dinner. After dinner, they moved to the parlor to have tea and dessert.

"So, Mr. Durand, with such a successful family business in Baton Rouge, what brought you to Harlem to work as a tailor?" Olivia asked.

Although the question was politely asked, Celine knew her aunt better than that. Her pleasant smile did not reach her eyes. Celine realized that her aunt didn't like Julien. Knowing this gave her pause in her own opinion of him.

Julien shrugged. "I am the youngest of five children, all but one of which are boys. I decided making my own way was much more appealing than fighting for my siblings' crumbs. With everything I've heard of Harlem, I thought what better place to start anew."

"But wouldn't your family's name and business afford you more advanced opportunities closer to New Orleans or Baton Rouge?" Olivia asked. "With all of your apprenticeship experience I can't imagine you not starting your own business rather than managing someone else's."

For a moment, Celine saw something shift in Julien's polite expression. Something unsettling, but it happened so quickly she couldn't be sure what she had actually witnessed.

"Madam Rousseau, I am not one of those privileged men who choose to live life on their father's fortune and reputation. I choose to carve my own niche in the family's success," Julien answered.

"I see," Olivia said skeptically.

"Well, I think we have questioned Julien enough for the night." Celine's father directed an annoyed gaze at her aunt.

Julien stood. "Thank you again for inviting me to dinner with your lovely family," he said to her father.

"It has been a pleasure to have you, and you have a standing invitation to join us any time," her mother said.

"Since I am new to the area with no family to call my own, I may just take you up on that, Madame Broussard. Your warm hospitality reminds me so much of my own mother." His compliment brought a surprising blush to her mother's face.

He then turned toward Celine, grasped her hand, and placed a soft kiss on her knuckles. "It was truly a pleasure to meet such a charming and beautiful woman," he said.

Celine smiled pleasantly. "Thank you, Julien. I wish you much success in your new life here in Harlem."

Julien held her hand and gazed at her a moment longer, then turned toward her aunt. "Madam Rousseau," he simply said and turned to follow her father to the door.

"Such a charming young man, don't you think, Celine?" her mother said.

Almost too charming, she thought but said instead, "Very much so."

Her mother gazed at her expectantly. When Celine said nothing further her mother frowned, then picked up the tea tray and headed for the kitchen.

"What was that all about?" Celine asked Olivia.

Olivia patted her shoulder sympathetically. "Walk me out?"

Celine waited as Olivia gathered her purse and shawl then walked her out to the end of their walkway.

Olivia turned to her with a scowl. "Your mother would be very upset if she knew what I'm about to tell you, but she already knows that I believe what she is doing is wrong."

"What is she doing?" Celine asked.

"The moment your father told her about Julien Durand, she had her sights set on him to be your next husband."

"What!" Celine said in disbelief.

"Your mother believes that you've been in mourning long enough and that it is high time you remarried. I still can't believe that in this day and age she believes a woman is nothing without a husband and children to take care of."

"I have no interest in marrying Julien or any other man."

"Well, Lanie believes you just haven't found the right man to help rid you of your memories of what Paul did to you."

Celine groaned in frustration. "I thought I was past having to live my life according to my parents' ideals."

Olivia grasped her hands. "You are a grown woman, my beautiful niece. You may live whatever life you choose. Whether you choose to never marry again and live a life of independence or to remarry and have a family, I will support you, but do it because you choose to, not as an obligation to your family."

"Thank you, *Tante*. What would I do without you?"

"I can't imagine." Olivia pulled her into a tight embrace before turning to leave.

Celine watched her until she turned the corner out of sight, then she headed back into the house. She found her mother still in the kitchen cleaning up from their dinner. Celine picked up a dishtowel and began to dry the dishes her mother had washed and set on the counter. They worked together in companionable silence.

"Are you happy, Celine?" her mother asked once the last dish was dried and put away.

"Yes, I am," Celine answered without hesitation. Thoughts of her afternoon with Dinah came to mind. "Happier than I've been in a very long time."

"But what about your dream of marriage and children?"

"Maman, please sit." She drew her mother to the small table in the kitchen.

Once they were seated, Celine took her mother's hands in hers. "Marriage and children were never my dream. They were your and Papa's dream for me. Paul and I married to make you and his parents happy. Neither of us wanted to be forced to marry someone we didn't know because it was our duty."

Her mother smiled. "We all knew that, and we were thrilled by the decision because we knew that despite it, you two loved each other. What happened was regretful, but you can still find a way to move on."

"By marrying again?"

"Olivia told you, didn't she?"

"Whether she did or not doesn't matter. What matters is that I don't want to marry again. I'm happy with my life the way it is."

"I knew you spending so much time with your aunt would do this to you," her mother said sadly.

"The only thing that being with *Tante* Olivia has done is made me realize that I've spent my life trying to be what you, Papa, and our community expected me to be. I never allowed myself to be who I wanted to be or do what I wanted to do."

"What are you doing now that you cannot do if you were married?" her mother asked in confusion.

"Live, Maman. By my own terms, not by what I'm expected to do as a wife and mother. I love going into the shop every day, helping *Tante*, and creating something beautiful with my own two hands. I love the freedom I have that I wouldn't if I were married. I want to enjoy this time right now, maybe even travel if I so choose. Unless someone comes along who is accepting of my independence, marriage is not something I want."

Her mother pulled her hands from Celine's grasp. "I see."

Celine hated seeing the hurt and disappointment her words brought to her mother's eyes, but she knew that if she wasn't honest about how she felt and continued the masquerade her mother was asking her to, she would eventually just give up and allow self-pity to swallow her whole.

"Maman, please try to understand," Celine said.

Her mother stood. "It's been a long day, I'm going to bed now." She avoided Celine's gaze as she left the kitchen.

Dinah stood in the kitchen helping Aunt Jo prepare dinner. Jo had mentioned they would have guests, but she had been so distracted with thoughts of Celine that she hadn't thought to ask who their guests were. Dinah had not seen or spoken to Celine in several days. She had wanted to stop by the shop, but they were usually closed by the time she got off work, so she planned to write her a note this evening and drop it off at the shop on her way into work in the morning.

"Child, you're going to lose a finger if you don't pay attention to what you're doing," Jo said.

Dinah shook herself out of her reverie and looked down to notice she had sliced the loaf of bread she had been cutting down to the nub of crust at the very end. "I'm sorry, Aunt Jo." She laid down the knife and placed the bread in a small basket.

"No sense in asking what's got you so distracted."

"I've never felt like this before, Aunt Jo. It's making me crazy that I haven't been able to see or talk to her. I don't know if she's regretting what happened and never wants to see me or if she's going through the same confusion."

Jo gazed at her in understanding. "Love isn't easy, and especially the kind of love you and Celine want."

"You and Fran have made it work all these years."

Jo smiled, but there was a touch of sadness in her eyes. "Yes, but we've also lost a lot. The acceptance from her family, raising a family of our own, living openly. Choosing this life meant never having any of that."

"Those are sacrifices I'm willing to make."

"But is Celine? Her life was much different than yours. You told me she was widowed. I'm sure that whoever her husband was, their parents had it all arranged before she could walk. Women like her were raised to believe that all their life required was marrying the right man from the right family and having children. Creoles are really strict about keeping their bloodlines from being mixed or disappearing because their children fall in love with somebody outside of their approval."

The doubt Dinah had managed to tuck away into her subconscious peeked through at her aunt's words. Things with Celine had happened so quickly that she hadn't really thought it through. Even when Celine explained that she had married Paul to avoid being forced to marry a stranger, Dinah didn't think it would affect them being together. But now, she realized that as much as Celine might want to be with Dinah, pressure from her family might have her changing her mind. Just the thought of that happening made her heart ache. Dinah was now feeling desperate for a way to see Celine and find out what she was thinking. She couldn't bear laying her heart out any more than she already had with a woman who may walk away sooner or later.

"Aunt Jo, I need to run out." Dinah brusquely cleaned her hands on her apron as she took it off and hurried out of the kitchen.

"Whatever it is, it can't wait until after dinner?" her aunt called.

"I won't be long," Dinah shouted back.

"Whoa! Where's the fire?" Fran asked as Dinah almost collided with her in the entryway.

"I'm sorry, Fran, I need to—" Dinah's hurried explanation was cut short by the unexpected sight of Celine and Olivia following behind Fran.

"I'm sure you know our guests." Fran grinned.

Seeing Celine standing there caused Dinah to forget how to speak. She couldn't believe she was here, in her home.

"Cat got your tongue, girl? Here." Fran handed Dinah a covered dish. "Why don't you take that in the kitchen to your aunt."

Dinah absently took the dish from Fran but didn't move. So many questions were running through her head. As if reading her mind, Celine answered one of them.

"Your aunt was kind enough to invite my aunt to dinner, and she asked me to join her. I hope that was all right."

"It's more than all right. It's nice to see you again, Olivia," Dinah said, never taking her eyes from Celine's.

"You too," Olivia said, her tone laced with humor.

Dinah gazed longingly at Celine for another moment, then abruptly turned back toward the kitchen. Jo was placing glasses of lemonade on a tray when she walked in.

"You knew she was coming, didn't you?"

"Thought you might appreciate a little help moving things along."

Dinah placed the dish on the counter and threw her arms around Jo's waist. "Have I told you how much I love you?"

Still holding a glass, Jo wrapped her free arm around Dinah and placed a motherly kiss on her forehead. "I love you too. Now, why don't you take this tray of lemonade to our guests and I'll be out shortly."

Dinah smoothed her clothes and hair as much as she could and did as Jo asked. When she entered the parlor, Celine was looking at family pictures Jo had displayed on the mantelpiece above the fireplace and turned toward Dinah as she entered. The captivating smile she gave Dinah took her breath away. She was so lost in Celine's beauty that she couldn't move.

Celine walked toward her. "May I help?" She indicated the tray Dinah had completely forgotten was in her hands.

"Oh, no, I have it," Dinah said, willing her feet to move.

Celine nodded and allowed Dinah to walk ahead of her. Dinah placed the tray on a low table that was in the center of a circle of a pair of comfortable sofas and several chairs, then handed glasses to their guests and Fran.

"Aunt Jo will be joining us in a bit. Is there anything else I can get you?" she asked Celine and Olivia.

"Yes, you can sit down and relax. We are all open and free here, so there is no need to tiptoe around in fear of being found out," Olivia said.

Dinah looked to Celine for confirmation.

Celine looked a little embarrassed. "It's very difficult to keep anything from my aunt."

Before Dinah could respond, Jo entered the parlor.

"Just a few more minutes and dinner will be ready. Until then I thought I'd bring out something to hold you all over." She set a small tray on the table beside the lemonade that held about a dozen small items that Dinah had not seen when she was helping to prepare dinner.

"Olivia, I haven't seen canapés like this since we quit our jobs as a hotel maids," Jo said. "And they even taste better than the ones their fancy French chef made."

"Ah, *mademoiselle*, you flatter me," Olivia said appreciatively.

"It's a French specialty," Celine explained, offering one to Dinah. "This one has smoked salmon, crème fraîche, and cucumber on a small wedge of toast."

Dinah popped the canapé into her mouth and chewed slowly, surprised by the delicious blend of flavors in the small bite.

"Well, I'll be damned." Fran picked up her second one. "Never thought I'd be eating fancy French food and liking it."

Olivia chuckled. "I'm glad you like them. I thought that since we're all becoming such good friends, I would bring something that represented our family."

"Thank you," Jo said. "And speaking of your family, this must be your niece, Celine."

"Yes," Olivia said, "I don't know where my manners have gone. Josephine, may I introduce you to Celine Montré."

Celine offered her hand in greeting. "It's a pleasure to meet you, Miss Hampton."

"You too, Celine. I see why my Dinah is so taken with you," Jo teased.

Dinah's face flushed heatedly in embarrassment. She saw that Celine experienced the same reaction. Her aunt had never been one to not speak her mind.

"Why don't we head to the dining room? Dinner should be ready," Jo said.

While the others left the room, Dinah grasped Celine's hand and pulled her toward her. Their gazes held, communicating more than words could say.

"Your aunt knows?" Dinah said.

"I think she knew before I did."

"I've missed you."

Celine took a step closer to Dinah. "I've missed you too. You're all I can think about."

Dinah grasped Celine's other hand. "If what happened…what is happening…between us is a lot to accept right now just tell me and I'll—"

Celine's soft, full lips were on Dinah's, cutting short whatever she was going to say. The kiss was so achingly tender it filled Dinah's heart with joy. The spell was broken by the sound of her aunt calling them from the dining room. They ended their kiss slowly.

A moment passed before Dinah took a step back. "We better go in before my aunt comes looking for us." Dinah took Celine's hand and led her to the dining room.

"We thought it might do you two some good to be together without worrying about having to hide what you're feeling," Jo said.

"Also, to offer some sage advice from a few old ladies." Celine's aunt gave them a wink.

"This is not an easy life," Jo said, "especially when your family wants another life for you."

Dinah knew the comment was directed at Celine. From the look of guilt Dinah saw on Celine's face she must have realized it also. Dinah looked over at her aunt in annoyance.

Jo met her gaze. "Don't give me that look, child. We're all family here. There's no need to be all closed-mouth about this. The sooner you get things out in the open, the better."

"Josephine is right," Olivia said, looking at Celine from across the table. "I was the oldest and it was expected of me to marry first. For several years, our parents despaired ever finding a match for me. I found fault with every prospective husband they paraded before me. They finally gave up when rumors that I was having an affair with the son of a French aristocrat began to circulate, a rumor I had conveniently started." She grinned mischievously.

"The rumor assisted with deterring any further interested suitors as well as to prove to my young aristocrat's family, who worried their son's predilection for young Negro boys would deny them heirs, that there might be hope for him to marry after all. To my parents' relief, I accepted an apprenticeship under a family friend who was a seamstress traveling to France. I was no longer a worry for them, able to live the life I chose, and they were able to focus their attention on your mother, who was more than happy to fulfill her role as a dutiful daughter. Unfortunately, as the only child, you don't have the option of having a younger sister to carry the burden that you don't wish to. If you continue down the road I and these wonderful ladies have chosen," Olivia said, indicating Jo and Fran, "sooner or later, you will have to choose between breaking your parents' hearts to be with a woman you will never be able to love openly or breaking the heart of the woman you love to fulfill your familial obligations to your parents."

"Could you live with making Celine choose?" Jo asked Dinah. "I love Fran with all my heart, but I'll live the rest of my life feeling some guilt over knowing her choosing to be with me is the reason her family won't have anything to do with her." Wordlessly, Fran reached over and grasped Jo's hand.

"Why are you doing this?" Dinah asked. "I thought you wanted us to be together. You practically threw Celine at me at the masquerade," she said to Olivia, then looked at Jo. "And you're always telling me to follow my heart and that we can't always help who the Lord chooses for us to love. Now you all sound like you're trying to prevent us from deciding to be together."

Celine grasped Dinah's hand. "They're not trying to keep us from being together, they're trying to help us realize what we'll be facing if we decide to be together. They want us to be sure we're ready for such a life…if I'm ready for such a life."

Dinah squeezed Celine's hand. "I haven't asked you to choose," she said gently. "All I've asked is that we take this one step at a time and see where it leads us."

"And if it leads us to having to make a choice?"

"We'll deal with that road when we come to it," Dinah said.

"Dinah, we only said what we said because we love you both and don't want to see either of you get hurt," Jo said.

"I understand you're trying to help, but we know what we're doing. You don't have to worry about us."

There was a tense moment of silence before Fran picked up her fork and said, "I don't know about you all, but I've been waiting all day for that peach cobbler sitting in the kitchen, so if we're done advising the young folks I'm gonna go ahead and finish eating so I can have some."

With the tension broken and chuckles all around the table over Fran's enthusiastic eating, everyone else followed suit. Although the remainder of the meal was spent discussing Dinah's new job at Harlem Hospital and other topics, what their aunts said weighed heavily on Dinah's heart.

After dinner, Dinah decided to give Celine a tour of the boardinghouse. They ended the tour on the floor where Dinah occupied her own suite of rooms consisting of a small sitting room, bedroom, and private bathroom.

"Why do I have the feeling this grand tour was just to get me up here alone?" Celine said.

"Because it was." Dinah pulled Celine into her arms. "Mmm… You feel so good."

Celine relaxed into Dinah's embrace and rested her head on her shoulder with a contented sigh. "I feel so safe in your arms. I never thought that could be possible with another woman."

Dinah lowered her head to place a soft kiss on Celine's lips. "I wish I could undress you, climb into bed, and feel your body lying against mine all night, but it will have to wait until we have more time and privacy. We better head back down," Dinah said.

Celine nodded in agreement and clasped Dinah's hand as she reached for the doorknob.

"Wait," Celine said.

Dinah turned a questioning gaze back to Celine.

"I want to see you after your show on Friday. Will you meet me at my aunt's apartment?" Celine asked.

Dinah was thrilled. "Yes." She pulled Celine toward her for one last quick kiss before opening the door and leading her back downstairs to rejoin the dinner party.

CHAPTER SIX

Dinah walked into Flynn's Place feeling like she was floating on air. She had managed to get another of the club's popular dancers to cover for her second performance that evening so that she could leave early to surprise Celine, who wasn't expecting her until late in the evening. Dinah had decided it was time for Celine to see the Harlem nightlife she preferred to inhabit because it gave her more freedom to be herself and let loose. The anticipation of what the evening held had her filled with nervous excitement.

"I hope that smile is for me," Dinah heard a male voice say as she entered her dressing room.

She saw Curtis lounging on the settee in the room.

"Can I help you, Curtis?" She walked past him to her dressing table.

"Is that the way you greet the man who keeps you from living on the streets?"

Dinah was tired of his trying to put himself in the role of her savior. "Just because you took me out of that dive I was working in before doesn't mean I owe you my life. I had a roof over my head before you and will continue to do so after."

Curtis snorted. "You mean that boardinghouse your bulldagger aunt owns? I could have that place shut down tomorrow and your aunt and her little friend locked away for what they're doing. Then where would you be? I'll tell you where, crawling to your ol' boy Curtis, but I won't be as nice as I was before. You're gonna have to spend a little more time on your knees giving me what I want before I help you."

Dinah had been putting up with his arrogance all this time because she only had herself to worry about, but threatening her aunt was a whole different matter.

She met his hard gaze with her own. "Don't you EVER threaten my aunt again, Curtis. If anything happens to her or Fran you will see a side of me you never knew, and don't want to know, exists."

Their standoff lasted for a moment, then Curtis pasted on a crocodile smile and shrugged indifferently. "I didn't come in here to get you all upset before your performance tonight. I just wanted you to know Cora came to me about her covering for you tonight and I think it's a good idea."

Dinah eyed Curtis warily. "What's the catch?"

"Why's there gotta be a catch? I can't be nice? You've been working hard and deserve some time off."

Dinah trusted Curtis about as far as she could throw him. He was up to something and she had a sneaking suspicion that it involved her.

"Thank you," she said hesitantly.

Curtis nodded, then turned to leave the dressing room but stopped just before exiting. "Oh, almost forgot, I'm gonna need you to be available for a private party tomorrow night. Be here at six," he said, leaving without waiting for her reply.

Dinah slumped into the chair at her dressing table, gazing dejectedly at herself in the mirror. Nothing was ever easy with Curtis. She knew the moment he came into the club where she was working as a hootchy-kootchy girl that he was trouble. His conked hair, pretty face, expensive suits, and charm didn't fool her one bit into thinking he was a legitimate club owner, but he was offering her the same amount of money to be a headliner a few nights a week in his club that she made in a week at her nursing job. The fact that his club was strictly look but no touch didn't hurt either. It wasn't until a month after she had been a part of Flynn's Follies that he told her one of those nights included entertaining at private parties when requested. She had been furious until she found out that it was strictly dancing or playing hostess and that she could keep whatever tips she made. He always sent one of his hard-boiled guys with her to the more risqué parties to make sure his don't touch policy was enforced.

Other than the masquerade, the parties she had performed at lately had been with a crowd she didn't like being associated with. Curtis was trying to rise among the ranks of the gangsters he worked for and was doing whatever he could to impress them, including providing entertainment for them on and off the stage. Dinah knew he only used willing girls for the off-stage entertainment, but she was no longer sure where she stood with Curtis. He was up to something, and Dinah knew that whatever it was would put her in a dangerous position. She needed to get out from under his thumb before that happened. It meant sacrificing the extra money she was making, but she would scrub floors before she allowed herself to get roped in by whatever Curtis had planned.

Once Dinah finished her performance and spent the half hour Curtis insisted she provide on the floor greeting and chatting with customers, she couldn't get home fast enough to freshen up and meet Celine. She wanted to look her best so she re-curled her hair, then changed into her favorite party outfit, a short sleeve, open neck, golden-colored button-down dress that was fitted in the waist and flared loosely at the hips to her knees. The dress was perfect for dancing, and to finish it off, she pinned a matching gold silk flower into her hair above her ear, nodding with approval at her image in the mirror. The color of her dress made her complexion glow and the style of the dress complemented her figure.

She left the house excited for the evening to begin. When she arrived at Olivia's apartment, she was met by the young woman who greeted her and her aunt when she last visited the shop.

"*Bon jour,* Miss Dinah. Miss Celine wasn't expecting you so early. She is finishing up in the shop, but you are welcome to wait up in the apartment."

Dinah was just about to ask if she could go see Celine in the shop when Olivia called down from the top of the stairway. "Who's at the door, Simone?"

"It's Miss Dinah, madam," she answered.

"Well, for heaven's sake, let her in," Olivia said.

"*Oui,* madam. Please come in." Simone stepped aside to let Dinah in.

Olivia waited at the top of the stairs. "Ah, my little minx, you're early. Anxious to get your evening started?"

"I was hoping to take Celine to a friend's party. I didn't know she would still be working this late."

Olivia grasped Dinah's hand, kissed her affectionately on the cheek, and led her to the sofa. "Come and sit with me. Simone will go and collect Celine." She gave a quick nod to Simone.

Olivia watched Simone leave through the door that led to the shop and sighed. "She's a bit flighty but such an eager lover. I'm not getting any younger, so I must take what I can get."

Dinah laughed at Olivia's boldness. "You're a very beautiful and vibrant woman. I can't imagine you having any trouble finding companionship."

"Oh, how you flatter me, but alas, you are taken. I was ready to snatch you up the moment you walked into the shop with Lee, but as soon as I saw how you and Celine looked at each other I knew I didn't have a chance."

The door to the apartment flew open, and Celine entered looking flushed and out of breath.

"I…didn't expect…you so…early," she said breathlessly to Dinah.

"I asked one of the other girls to cover my second performance for me. I thought maybe you'd like to go to a party."

"I'm not quite dressed for a party." Celine self-consciously tried to smooth the wrinkles from the front of her dress.

Dinah looked over Celine admiringly. "You'd look good in a burlap sack."

Celine's eyebrow quirked with humor. "I think I can find something better than a burlap sack. I leave clothes here just in case I work late and have to stay overnight. Give me a few moments and I'll be right out." She hurried past Dinah into the guest room.

She stopped just outside the door and turned back as if remembering something. "I almost forgot, *Tante*, Simone will be right up. She offered to clean up for me so that I could get ready."

"That's fine, darling. I'll keep Dinah entertained for you."

Celine gazed Dinah's way, flashed her a bright, happy smile, and then closed the bedroom door.

"I haven't seen Celine this happy since she came up from New Orleans. And it's all because of you. Thank you," Olivia said.

"She makes me happy also," Dinah said.

"It's rare to find that kind of happiness with women like us. Like your aunt Josephine, you must find a way to hold on to it before it slips through your fingers."

Dinah could tell that Olivia spoke from experience. The sadness in her eyes kept Dinah from asking what happened, but it was replaced by Olivia's usual carefree expression.

"You will make sure Celine enjoys herself tonight? She led such a quiet life with no real enjoyment before she moved here. I've tried to get her out as much as possible, but I know she's still not allowing herself to be free when we do go out. I think you're just what she needs to shed that final layer of propriety and allow herself to enjoy life."

Dinah smiled to herself as she remembered how Celine had no

problem shedding her propriety when they were in this very apartment not that long ago. "I think she'll have a good time tonight. It's almost impossible to go to one of my friend's parties and not enjoy it."

"Wonderful, then I have no problem with leaving her safely in your hands for the evening."

When Celine returned, Dinah couldn't help but feel like she was the luckiest woman alive to have caught Celine's attention. Celine wore a sleeveless peacock-blue drop-waist dress with a multilayered scarf skirt that came just to her knees. The top had a V-neckline that dipped modestly to just above her cleavage in front and daringly midway down in back. She wore a felt cloche-style hat with a long peacock feather that perched jauntily over her right ear, and she carried a fringed black shawl. She held herself with such grace and elegance that Dinah knew she would be beaming with pride to have such a beautiful woman on her arm.

"You look fabulous, darling," Olivia said.

Celine gazed nervously at Dinah. "I wasn't sure what to wear. Will this be acceptable?"

"It's perfect," Dinah said. She took the shawl from Celine, who turned toward a mirror nearby to adjust her hat.

"Is that one of your designs?" Dinah asked, trying to fight the temptation to place her lips at the soft curve of her shoulder blades exposed by the opening in the back of the dress.

"Yes, it's one of the first I made." Celine smoothed the feather with the tip of her finger so that it curved perfectly to the hat's curve.

Dinah placed the shawl over her shoulders. As she slid her hands down the length of Celine's arms, their eyes met in the mirror in a brief heated gaze that left no doubt that they were thinking the same thing.

"We better get going," Dinah said, slowly stepping back from Celine.

"Celine, stay out as late as you like. Dinah, feel free to stay here if it's too late for you to walk home. Simone can help me open the shop tomorrow, so you two just enjoy yourselves," Olivia said.

Dinah thought it was adorable when Celine blushed in response.

"Good night, *Tante*," Celine said.

"Your aunt is a very interesting woman," Dinah said.

"Is that a nice way of saying she's eccentric?"

"If we were all eccentric like her, this would be a much better world."

"Very true. I'm going to do just as she suggested and enjoy myself this evening. I'm so tired of tea and card parties with vapid women. Tonight, I shed the pitiful widow's mask and begin enjoying life as a vibrant, independent woman." Celine gave a determined nod.

Dinah linked her arm through Celine's. "In that case, Ms. Montré, let's go have us some fun."

❖

Celine and Dinah strolled along 125th Street amongst the hustle and bustle of others all decked out in their finest fashions for a Friday night in Harlem. They drew some attention and comments from a group of men they passed.

"Woo-hoo! Check out the chassis on that Sheba!" one of them said to Celine.

"I don't deal in coal, but I'll make an exception for you, baby!" a second said to Dinah in reference to her dark complexion.

"Aw hell, I'm not picky, as fine as they are, I'll be both their daddy!" a third one replied.

Celine and Dinah acknowledged the men with friendly smiles but continued on their way in spite of the moans of disappointment from their admirers. As they approached a brownstone a few blocks away, Celine saw three women and a man sitting on the steps laughing boisterously. It wasn't until they reached the group that Celine, noticing the outline of breasts under the stylish men's suit, realized the fourth wasn't a man at all. They greeted Dinah and Celine with friendly waves. Dinah did the introductions. The first was a pretty petite blonde named Dotty who reminded Celine of a Kewpie doll, dressed in a daringly low-cut flapper style dress. She mumbled an inaudible greeting to Celine while gazing longingly at Dinah, who moved on to introduce her to the tall, statuesque Claudine, who Celine had mistaken for a man. Claude, as she preferred to be called, was about Celine's complexion with short black hair styled in finger waves. The last woman, also dressed in a flapper style dress that was more subdued than Dotty's, was named Lilly. She was a curvaceous dark-skinned beauty who surely turned male and female heads alike. As she spoke in greeting, her voice had a soft cat-like purr quality that mesmerized Celine, who flushed in embarrassment when she realized she was staring as Lilly patiently waited for her to respond.

Claude laughed. "Looks like ol' Lil has hooked another one."

Celine gazed at Dinah guiltily.

"Wait until you hear her sing." Dinah gave her a wink. "Why are you all sitting out here? The party can't be over already."

"No, we just couldn't take Big T's howling anymore," Claude complained.

"She still mooning over Roxy?" Dinah said.

"Yeah, and Roxy is playing her like a fiddle. That girl is no more a bulldagger than I'm a chorus girl," Claude said.

All but Celine laughed at Claude's comparison. Claude gazed at her more intently, then smiled.

"You're new, aren't you? First trip out the closet?" Claude asked Celine.

When Celine only gazed at her in confusion, Claude nodded as if Celine had answered her question.

"You better keep this little beauty by your side tonight, Dinah. Philly is here and she's on the prowl for some fresh meat," Lilly said.

Celine could feel Dinah tense beside her at Lilly's warning. She instinctively grasped Dinah's hand in support. Dinah looked tenderly at her and gave her hand a gentle squeeze.

"We're going to head on in. See you all later." Dinah led Celine up the steps.

"It was a pleasure meeting all of you," Celine said, not missing the indignant gaze from Dotty as they passed her. "Is there anything I should know about Dotty?" Celine asked.

Dinah turned to Celine. "Dotty has wanted more than a friendship since we met. I've always told her I wasn't interested. Then, about a year ago, I got very drunk and lonely one night and woke up next to Dotty with no recollection of what happened," she answered, looking very embarrassed by the admission. "I told her it was a mistake, and I haven't made that same mistake since."

"Well, judging by the looks I was getting, she still wants more," Celine said.

"I'm sorry about that. I thought she'd moved on because I've seen her with other women."

"Has she seen you with other women?"

"No, what few women I've been with since her have been behind closed doors. This is the first time I've introduced them to a woman I'm seeing."

"Oh," Celine said in surprise.

Dinah raised a hand to stroke Celine's cheek. "Who wouldn't want to show you off?"

Celine blushed, not used to public displays of affection, even if it was in a semi-dark alcove.

"Now, let's go in so I can continue to show you off," Dinah teased.

The sound of piano music and laughter greeted them as they neared the door to the first-floor apartment. It was open so Celine allowed Dinah to lead her in. There were about a dozen people in the apartment, some lounging on low settees and piles of throw pillows spread around the room while others surrounded a grand piano being played by a well-known tuxedo-clad female blues singer Celine had seen perform at the Clam House. They were greeted by a tall, elegant woman dressed in a flowing afghan and matching head wrap.

"Dinah, darling, I'm so glad you could make it." She grasped Dinah's hands and placed a kiss on both her cheeks. She had a fair complexion and there was a hint of an accent that Celine thought might be Caribbean.

"You know I'd never miss one of your parties, Helene," Dinah told her. "I hope you don't mind that I brought my friend Celine."

"The more the merrier." Helene gave her a warm smile, grasping Celine's hands in her own and greeting her with the same double kiss. "Welcome to my home," Helene said to Celine in Creole.

Celine responded back in Creole. "Thank you, are you Creole?"

Helene's smile widened. "Yes, I knew I recognized a fellow Creole. My parents brought me here right off the boat from Haiti when I was a child. If I detect the dialect correctly, you're from New Orleans?" She responded back in English.

"Yes," Celine said, gazing at their host curiously.

"Helene is a linguist. She speaks several languages, travels around the world as an interpreter for foreign dignitaries, and teaches English in her spare time," Dinah explained.

"What an interesting life you must lead," Celine said in fascination.

Helene waved her hand dismissively. "I do what I must to live the way I like to live. Now, come, you must meet the rest of our colorful group of companions." She placed Celine's arm through the crook of her own and led her farther into the room.

By the time Celine was introduced to the other guests, she couldn't help but be in awe at this eclectic group of musicians, dancers, artists and writers, some just as famous in Harlem as their musical entertainment, who were Dinah's circle of friends and acquaintances. She also felt herself falling even more for Dinah as she openly staked her claim on Celine with her hand resting casually but possessively at the small of her back during the introductions. As they approached the last guest, she could practically feel the tension rolling off Dinah. Celine realized that this must be the woman they called Philly that Claude had warned them about. Like Claude, she was dressed in a men's style pinstriped suit, but that's where the similarities ended because she would never be mistaken for a man with her voluptuous figure. If anything, the cut of the suit emphasized her womanly curves. With her perfectly coifed dark brown bobbed hair, smooth olive complexion, and manicured painted nails, she was not trying to hide the fact that she was very much a woman, and a beautiful one at that. The woman's slow, appreciative perusal of Celine as they approached was obvious and made her feel uncomfortable.

"Dinah Hampton, it's been a while." Philly offered a hand in greeting.

Dinah hesitantly accepted it. "I had no idea you were in town."

"I hadn't planned to be, but Big T called me crying about Roxy. I had to come and check on my little sister," she said.

Celine found it amusing for someone to call the woman she had met moments ago named Big T their little sister. Big T was twice as wide and almost a foot taller than Philly.

"I see you saved the best introduction for last. I'm Antonia Manucci, but everybody calls me Philly." Philly held her hand out to Celine, not waiting for Dinah to introduce them.

Celine took the offered hand, ignoring the temptation to pull her own hand back when Philly bent over to place a soft kiss on the back of it. "Nice to meet you, Philly, I'm Celine Montré." Philly's intense gaze bored into Celine as her lips lingered just a second longer than was appropriate.

"And it's definitely a pleasure to meet you, Celine." Philly slowly released Celine's hand from her firm grasp.

Celine had no time to respond as Dinah's hand settled once again on the small of her back and began to steer her past Philly.

"Helene has a great cook. Why don't we grab some food before it's all gone?"

Dinah's long strides and the insistent pressure of her hand pressing on Celine's back had her hurrying to keep up. As soon as they crossed the threshold of the dining room, Celine came to an abrupt halt, causing Dinah to almost trip into the food-laden banquet table. She turned and gazed at Celine in confusion.

"The food can wait. Tell me why you're in such a hurry to get away from Philly. Is she another past lover?" Celine asked, hoping she didn't sound jealous.

Dinah looked disgusted at the thought. "No, I'm not one of Philly's conquests."

"Well, there's obviously something between you two. If I'm going to be caught in the middle of it, I need to know what it is," Celine said.

Dinah took Celine's hand, leading her into another room off the dining room.

"This is a popular room during Helene's parties, so we only have a few moments to talk. I didn't want anyone overhearing us," Dinah said.

It was a beautiful enclosed garden sanctuary filled with all manner of exotic flowers, hidden alcoves, and cushioned stone benches that Celine would have loved to explore, but this was not the time, so she brought her full attention back to Dinah.

"Only a very few people know Philly's history and that we used to work together as hootchy-kootchy dancers at a sleazy nightclub. We were good friends until she fell for a woman named Jenny who was using her to get to me. I wasn't the least bit interested in Jenny. She flirted and threw herself at me every chance she got. When I tried to tell Philly what was going on she didn't believe me, especially when Jenny cried that I was the one coming on to her. Philly chose Jenny over our friendship, and it seemed, for a while, that Jenny chose Philly over pursuing something that would never happen," Dinah explained.

"Then Curtis Flynn offered me a job at his nightclub, and I took it. On my last night at the club, Jenny decided to pay me a visit hoping that I had changed my mind about her since I wouldn't be working with Philly anymore. She didn't know that Philly had followed her and that she was listening outside the door, but I had seen her briefly in the mirror and decided I'd prove once and for all that Jenny wasn't as innocent as she appeared. I asked Jenny about her and Philly, and she told me she didn't love Philly, that she was just a distraction until I came to my senses. I called to Philly outside the door asking if she'd heard, and as soon as Jenny saw her step fully into the doorway she changed her tune back to being the victim, only this time Philly wasn't buying it and kicked Jenny to the curb. Unfortunately, it still didn't make her any less angry with me. After that we ended up at some of the same parties, and if any woman showed the slightest bit of interest in me Philly would make it her mission to try to seduce them away. It didn't really bother me before because I never developed anything more than a physical attraction for anyone, until now."

"And you're worried that Philly is going to try to seduce me away from you," Celine said in understanding.

Dinah nodded, looking away from Celine.

Celine gently turned Dinah's face back to her. "You don't ever have to worry about that happening. I'm yours and I'm not interested in Philly." She followed up her declaration with a soul-stirring kiss that she hoped would leave no doubt in Dinah's mind that she meant what she said.

"We better join the rest of the party before we start something we can't finish," Dinah said.

"Only if you promise to relax and enjoy the rest of the night without worrying about ex-lovers and scorned friends," Celine said.

❖

Philly strolled over to Dinah. "She's a natural."

Dinah turned a narrowed gaze on Philly. "Stay away from her, Philly. She's not interested in your games."

Philly chuckled. "You warned her about me? Shouldn't that be for her to say?"

"She said it to me and I'm saying it to you. You made your point about Jenny, now let it go."

"You still think this is about Jenny? I don't give a damn about that two-bit whore," Philly said indifferently.

Dinah's anger turned to confusion.

"You really don't know, do you?" Philly asked.

"Know what?" Dinah said warily.

"Until you walked into Jungle Jim's Lounge, I was the headliner, the one who brought all the customers in because Jim's watered-down bootleg liquor sure wasn't what did it. Then here you come, straight off the bus from Bama, shimmying that ass like you were born to it and I was shoved to the background like some unwanted penny."

"The background? All I did was open for you. You were still the headliner up until I left Jungle," Dinah said.

Philly gave a derisive laugh. "Dinah, you can't still be that naïve to genuinely believe that. Yeah, Jim billed you as the opening act, but everybody knew that you were the draw. I guess you were too wrapped up with that nursing gig to even notice what was really going on. I knew it was just a matter of time before he pushed me into the background, so I went to Curtis Flynn and told him I was interested in working for him at his new club. I invited him to the Jungle to see my act."

Dinah's eyes widened in surprise.

"Yeah, you stole my gig," Philly said.

"I didn't know," Dinah said. "If you had just said something, I would've asked Curtis to hire you as well."

"You know, Dinah, that's priceless. I honestly believe you would've tried to help me 'cause your country Bama ass didn't know any better. I also believed you when you told me you weren't interested in Jenny, but the fact is, she still wanted you despite everything I did for her. The fact that I couldn't live up to the fantasy she had built up of you in that ditzy little head of hers hurt my pride. In the end you took my act, my girl, and my way out of that hellhole of a club and I couldn't just let it go. The most ironic thing about this is that you had no idea. I let you believe it had to do with Jenny because it suited my needs."

"Why are you telling me all of this now?" Dinah asked.

"Cause, once again, it suits my needs," Philly answered cryptically.

"Your needs? From what I hear, you don't NEED anything. You left Jungle shortly after I did, have a stable of dancers and working girls, and run a profitable business out of Philadelphia and Atlantic City with a girl of your own in every town from there to here to keep you satisfied for the rest of your life. I'm still in Harlem working two jobs and living with my aunt. What could I possibly have that you would need?"

Philly looked over at Celine.

"What I want, Dinah Hampton," Philly said, turning back to her, "is to take away what you covet."

"With a woman I told you isn't interested in you?"

Philly shrugged. "For now."

"I told you to stay away from her, Philly," Dinah said through gritted teeth.

Philly began to walk away, then turned back as if remembering something. "By the way, how are things at Flynn's? I hear there are some management changes coming down the road."

"I wouldn't know. I don't get involved in Curtis's business affairs," Dinah said.

Philly nodded. "Still the same old Dinah. Do your job and go about your business." Philly left the party with Big T in tow.

CHAPTER SEVEN

Hours later, as the party began to reach its peak, a laughing and slightly inebriated Celine flopped down onto the floor pillows Dinah had been lounging on and laid her head on Dinah's shoulder.

Dinah placed a kiss on the top of Celine's head. "Having fun?"

Celine nodded. "I think too much fun. You better get me home while I can still walk a straight line."

Dinah chuckled. "Helene said we're more than welcome to stay in one of her rooms upstairs if you don't want to leave."

"That's kind of her, but I want you all to myself in my own bed. Well, the bed I use at Aunt Olivia's." She placed a soft kiss on Dinah's cheek.

The kiss was tame, but the look in Celine's eyes was filled with a hunger that had nothing to do with food. It was enough to propel Dinah up off the pillows, gently pulling Celine up with her. They made their way toward Helene to say their goodbyes.

"Leaving so soon?" Helene asked.

"Yes, I had a wonderful time and thought it best to leave while I still had my wits about me," Celine said.

"I understand. Thank you for coming, and I hope you'll accept my invitation to come for tea soon. I think you'll enjoy it much more than those teas you and your mother attend up on the Row," Helene said.

"I will be here." Celine embraced Helene affectionately.

Helene turned to Dinah. "And you, my friend, must not let Antonia steal your joy. She feeds off other people's misery because she has no joy of her own. Take her power away by denying her the ability to affect you."

"You were always the wise one of our little group. I'll take your sage advice and chew on it a bit," Dinah said.

Dinah and Helene embraced, and then she and Celine said a general farewell to everyone else before heading out of the apartment. Once they were outside, Dinah looped Celine's arm through hers to help steady Celine's slow, careful steps as they strolled back to her aunt's apartment.

"Your friends are all so wonderful," Celine said. "I admire their carefree spirits. They remind me of Paul. He wasn't afraid to enjoy life to the fullest, even when he had to hold so much of himself back to keep others from knowing his true desires."

"You still miss him, don't you?" Dinah asked.

"Yes, but not as a husband, because we never truly lived as a husband and wife should. What I miss is my closest and dearest friend. There was nothing I couldn't tell Paul. He loved me no matter what, and I loved him just the same."

"Maybe you'll find that kind of love again," Dinah said hopefully.

Celine gazed up at her with a smile. "Maybe I will."

They strolled quietly along for a bit. "I think if we had stayed at the party for a while longer, I would have liked to go into the secret garden room," Celine said.

"I guess you found out why it's so popular."

"Yes, I saw a few guests pairing up and heading toward the room shortly before we left. I asked Helene about it and she told me what the room was used for."

"You really would have wanted to go there?"

Celine seemed to seriously contemplate her answer. "Maybe not the garden itself but possibly the room attached that Helene told me about," she admitted with a blush.

"Ah, the voyeur room."

"That doesn't surprise you?"

"No. Not after what you told me about the books your husband gave you and his last birthday gift to you. If you're interested, Helene also has private parties for select guests. I'm sure she won't mind if I brought you to one."

Celine slowed their pace and looked up at Dinah in surprise. "You would do that for me?"

"Yes, if it would make you happy," Dinah said.

Dinah was charmed by the beaming look of happiness on Celine's face as their step picked up again.

❖

When they arrived at Olivia's, Celine and Dinah quietly entered the apartment and went straight to Celine's room. It had not been a week since their first intimate encounter together, but Celine felt as if it had been months. They hurriedly undressed each other and tumbled onto the bed in a passionate embrace. Celine didn't know if it was the wine or the carefree atmosphere of the party that made her feel so uninhibited, but she found herself wanting to be the one in control. Wanting to do to Dinah all the things she had seen and read about in the scandalous books that Paul had brought home to her. She had destroyed those books after his death, but she had looked at them so often she could remember every picture as vividly as the first time she had seen them.

Celine explored, touched, and tasted Dinah from head to toe. When she turned Dinah over for the most sensual of massages, then lifted her hips to taste her from behind, she reveled in seeing Dinah bury her face in the pillow to keep from waking Olivia, and possibly the entire neighborhood, with her passionate moans. Celine sensuously slid her body up the length of Dinah, straddling her round behind, and laid her head on Dinah's back, listening to the thumping of her heartbeat.

"I hope that was all right. That I wasn't too bold," Celine said, feeling her face suddenly flush in embarrassment. "Talking about Paul's gifts had me wanting to do all the things I had read about and watched the women he brought home do."

"That was wonderful," Dinah murmured.

"I'm so glad to hear that because it will probably happen again." Celine yawned.

As she started to drift off to sleep, she felt Dinah shift just enough to gently ease Celine off her back and cover them both with a blanket before pulling her close within the circle of her arms.

She couldn't be sure, but she thought she heard Dinah whisper, "I love you," before she completely gave in to sleep.

❖

Celine awoke to bright sunshine and the sound of traffic and voices filtering in through the open window. It took a moment for her mind to clear and remember where she was. Her scandalous behavior from the previous night came back to her in a rush and brought a hot blush to her face. She slowly glanced beside her to find she was alone in bed and wondered if her boldness had been too much and sent Dinah running for the hills. When she sat up, a light pounding began at the back of her head and worked its way to the front in a steady rhythm. One too many glasses of wine, she thought, burying her head in her hands with a loud moan.

"Good morning, sleeping beauty," Dinah said.

Celine peeked through her fingers to find a smiling Dinah standing in the doorway with a tray of covered dishes and teacups and dressed in one of Celine's robes. The soft pink made Dinah's rich, dark complexion even more delectable, and despite the pounding in her head, the sight made Celine ache for more of what they did last night.

"Good morning. I thought you left," she said.

"I can't think of any other place I'd rather be." Dinah set the tray on one of the bedside tables and leaned over to kiss Celine. She then pressed heated kisses along Celine's jawline and nuzzled her neck. "How's your head?"

"My head?" Celine asked distractedly.

"I thought you might be suffering from a little too much wine last night." Dinah nibbled along Celine's ear.

"Oh…it seems…to be better…now."

"That's too bad. Nurse Hampton was hoping to personally nurse you back to health, but since you're feeling better…" Dinah stood to leave.

"No, wait." Celine flopped back onto the pillows with a dramatic moan. "I suddenly feel another headache coming on, Nurse Hampton."

With a mock look of concern, Dinah pressed a hand to her chest. "Oh my, I guess I better stay after all."

They laughed, then Dinah sat on the bed and uncovered one of the dishes on the tray. Celine was delighted to see that it was her favorite, beignets. Dinah tore off a piece of one, added some sweet cream butter, and offered it to Celine.

"Your aunt kindly left these for us and told me that I was to make sure you didn't feel the need to rush downstairs to work because she and Simone had everything in hand," Dinah told her.

"Waking up late, lounging, and being fed breakfast in bed…It feels so decadent," Celine said.

"I could get used to it, especially if it meant waking up next to you." Dinah's playful gaze darkened with intensity.

Celine's heart skipped a beat as the thought of waking up beside this intelligent, fascinating, and beautiful woman every morning took hold in her mind. "I can't imagine waking up beside anyone else."

Dinah gently took hold of Celine's face. "Could you really do that? Spend the rest of your life with a woman? Risk your reputation, your family's acceptance, the chance to have children of your own, to be branded as a bulldagger and dyke, to be with another woman?"

Celine met Dinah's suddenly serious gaze with her own. "If it's the woman sitting before me. The woman who has turned what I thought was a shameful secret into something beautiful, the answer is yes."

Doubt shone in Dinah's eyes. "Our aunts were right. This is not an easy life, Celine. The secrecy, the lies, the fear of being caught." Dinah's hands slid from Celine's face down to grasp her hands. "This is not the life for someone like you."

"Someone like me?" Celine tensed. "What do you mean someone like me?"

Dinah stood and went over to gaze out the window for a moment, then turned back to Celine.

"A spoiled woman who has never experienced a day of hardship in her life. The kind of woman who should be at home being primped and pampered by maids instead of sleeping with them. The kind of woman who should be living in a big house married to a doctor and bearing him pretty little light-skinned children to brag about," she said bitterly.

Celine didn't understand Dinah's sudden mood change. "Why are you saying such horrible things?" She threw the bed sheet aside and marched over to Dinah.

"You hypocrite! I would never have thought you, of all people, would put me in such a clichéd box. Do you think it was easy spending my whole life lying to everyone? Being married ten years to a person I had no passion for? Watching him leave me night after night to live out a life I could only dream of because of that damn box society had put me in? It may not be the hardship you're talking about, but it was a hardship just the same." Celine wiped away tears of disappointment.

She turned her back on Dinah and wrapped her arms around herself hoping to stave off the sudden chill that had nothing to do with the open window. "I thought you were different, Dinah. I thought I'd finally found someone to love honestly and wholeheartedly, but I guess I was wrong."

"You love me?" Dinah asked hesitantly.

"Does it matter?" Celine said.

Dinah wrapped her arms around Celine's waist, and laid her cheek against her hair.

"If you truly mean it, then yes, it does because I love you. I couldn't bear to lose you if we started a life together only for you to change your mind when everything I described begins to happen."

Celine turned within Dinah's embrace, untied the robe she wore, and wrapped her arms around Dinah's waist. "I love the way our bodies fit so well together. I love the way you look at me when you think I'm not paying attention. I love the way you make me feel like I'm the only woman in the room. I love the way I know I can be myself with you." She stood on tiptoe to place a kiss on Dinah's lips. "I love you, Dinah Hampton, and nothing, not my reputation, my family, or name-calling will change that."

Dinah took Celine's face in her hands. "I didn't mean those things I said about the kind of woman you are. I've just never felt this way about any woman before, and I didn't want to allow myself to get my hopes up that you would, or could, ever feel the same way about me."

"This is all new to me as well, so why don't we just take it one day at a time and fight whatever battles come our way when the time comes." Celine said.

"All right." Dinah lowered her head toward Celine's, putting all her love into the kiss she placed upon her lips.

What little clothing Dinah wore was shed and breakfast was forgotten on the bedside table as they made love once again.

It was another two hours before Celine managed to make her way down to the shop.

"My apologies, *Tante*," Celine said.

"No need to apologize, you had a late night," Olivia said.

Celine blushed, grabbing the appointment book to avoid Olivia's knowing gaze.

Olivia gently grasped her chin and lifted her head up. "*Mon bijou*, there is no need to be embarrassed or ashamed of what you have done. There is nothing wrong with experiencing life and love to the fullest if it's for the right reasons and no one is looking to harm anyone. Now, Simone is making some deliveries and then visiting her brother, and I am going to give myself the rest of the afternoon off to enjoy a glass of wine, an interesting book, and a long nap." She paced a motherly kiss on Celine's forehead.

"Thank you, *Tante*."

Celine watched Olivia gather a few things and head for the back stairwell. Her aunt had become such a bright light in her life since she had moved here, and she treasured every bit of advice and encouragement Olivia handed down to her. A calming sense of contentment warmed her then she glanced down at the appointment book and her eyes widened in surprise.

"*Tante*?"

Olivia turned from the doorway. "Yes."

"You made an appointment for me just after closing?" Celine asked, trying not to sound as worried as she felt.

"Yes. She's one of our special clients who's just come back to town and stopped by earlier. She's throwing a party and has some special requests I thought could use your talents. Was that all right? I can get a message to her to reschedule if you have plans."

"No, no, it's fine," Celine said.

"Are you sure?"

Celine gave her a tentative smile. "Yes. You go and relax. I'll take care of it."

"All right, but do not hesitate to buzz if you need me," she said, indicating the buzzer beside the stairwell that rang up to the apartment.

"I will."

Olivia gazed at her for a moment longer, nodded, then turned and left. Celine looked back down at the name written in her aunt's bold script, hoping her sudden anxiety would be for nothing.

❖

The shop closed at five, which came a lot sooner than Celine expected. She locked the door and began cleaning and rearranging displays to pass the time until her after-hours client arrived. At the appointed time, there was a knock on the shop door. Celine's heart beat frantically in her chest as she peered through the curtain to see Philly standing outside. She took a deep breath then opened the door.

"Good evening, Celine," Philly said.

Celine pasted on her best service smile. "Good evening, Philly. Please, come in." She stepped aside to let Philly pass.

"Thank you," Philly said.

As she passed by, Philly's arm brushed along Celine's breasts and her face flushed in shock as her nipples hardened in response.

She turned away from Philly to close the door, hoping Philly wouldn't notice the effect the accidental touch caused. When she turned back around, the sly grin on Philly's face told her not only did she notice but that the brush probably wasn't accidental.

"My apologies for the last-minute appointment. I hope I'm not keeping you from anything," Philly said.

"No." Celine walked a wide berth around Philly to stand behind the counter. She wanted to put as much distance between them as possible. "My aunt mentioned you had some special requests for a party?"

"Yes, I need a set of peekaboo feather fans, and I heard you're the best person in Harlem to go to for them."

As Philly slowly approached the counter, Celine could practically feel Philly's eyes on her body like fingers stroking along as she looked at Celine from head to toe. Once again, Celine's body betrayed her as she felt a spark of attraction begin to light for the beautiful woman. Philly was dressed in a similar suit to the one she had worn to Helene's party. Her hair was slicked and molded back into finger waves, showcasing the soft feminine features of her face. She reminded Celine of someone, but she couldn't recall who it might be. She was trying to focus her attention on trying to curb the physical attraction she didn't want to have for Philly, so she reached under the counter for her design sketchbook. Locating some sketches of fans she had recently sold to a club owner in the Village, she turned the book so that Philly could see the sketches.

Philly flipped through the pages as she gazed down at the book. "You did all of these sketches yourself?"

Celine was relieved by Philly's question as she felt on safer ground discussing her work. "Yes, it's the best way for anyone wanting to purchase a fan to see what it may look like. I use colored pencils to show the texture and variety. Do you see any styles you like?" Celine asked.

"All of them," Philly answered with a flirtatious grin.

Celine pulled her sketch book from under Philly's hands, closed it shut, and glared at her.

"What are you really here for? It's obvious it's not to purchase fans," Celine said.

Philly gave her a bemused grin. "I truly do need fans for the entertainment at my party. I figured I'd hit two birds with one stone. Get my fans and see you again." Philly leaned on the counter, slid her hand across it, and stroked her finger across the back of Celine's hand.

Celine snatched her hand away as if she had been burned. "I can help with the fans, but that's all I can do for you."

Philly stood. "I'll take the large white ones with the ostrich feathers. They'll look good next to the smooth, dark skin of the dancer."

Celine pulled a pad out from under the counter. "When would you need them ready?"

"Two weeks from today."

"Will you be sending someone to pick them up or should we have them delivered?"

"I was hoping you would deliver them yourself." Philly slid an envelope across the counter to Celine. "I'd love for you to come to the party."

Celine looked down at the envelope and then up at Philly with a shake of her head. "I don't think that would be a good idea. I'll have them delivered."

Philly left the envelope on the counter. "If you change your mind you won't regret it, and I promise you a night you'll never forget." She winked and ran her tongue across her lips sensuously.

Celine gasped and backed away from the counter. The clicking of heels against floor had both of them looking toward the doorway to the back of the shop where Olivia, to Celine's relief, came through the door.

"Ah, Antonia, you're still here. I hope Celine was able to assist you with your request," Olivia said.

"Madam Rousseau, your niece was just as charmingly helpful as you always are." Philly took Olivia's hand and gallantly pressed a kiss to her knuckles.

Olivia patted Philly's cheek. "Save that charm for someone who doesn't know any better."

Philly's lips turned down into a dramatic pout. "I see immunity to my charm must run in the family."

Olivia raised an arched brow in amusement. "I'm guessing my niece didn't fall so easily under your spell."

Celine gave Olivia a tentative smile. "We were just discussing delivery arrangements when Philly invited me to her party. I politely declined."

"Oh, but we must go," Olivia said. "Antonia's parties are not to be missed. The entertainment, the food, the atmosphere, it's all pure decadence. Something she obviously learned from her years living in New Orleans."

"You lived in New Orleans?" Celine asked.

"Only for a short time. I stayed with an uncle. He would throw these private parties and I was part of the entertainment," Philly said.

"Wh-when were you there?" Celine asked.

"From mid twenty-two to late twenty-four." Philly said.

Vivid images from a night long ago paraded across Celine's mind. Eyes so similar to Philly's beckoned her. The possibility of what that meant caused her legs to weaken. She reached out and grabbed the counter for support.

Olivia reached out to steady her. "Is there something wrong, Celine?"

"No, I think I'm just tired." She attempted a tremulous smile to reassure her aunt.

Philly's eyes narrowed on Celine, studying her intently. "You know, I never forget a face. Especially one as lovely as yours. We've met before Helene's party, haven't we? Aren't you originally from New Orleans?"

"It's getting late, Antonia." Olivia walked around the counter and steered Philly toward the door. "Since you and Celine have discussed all the necessary arrangements, we'll be closing shop for the night." Olivia unlocked and opened the door for Philly to leave.

Philly gazed back at Celine. "I look forward to seeing you at my party," she said in parting.

Celine hadn't realized she was holding her breath until it whooshed out of her in a dizzying sigh.

Olivia turned and gazed at Celine curiously. "Is she right, Celine? Have you two met before?"

Celine found she could not tear her eyes away from the door as she was flooded with a memory of her and Paul, wearing masks, watching two women lying on a bed, their bodies entwined in a passionate embrace, kissing and touching in ways Celine had never imagined. One of the women, with her soft curves, long, thick dark hair, and full, tempting lips had given her many pleasurable fantasies before Dinah had brought those fantasies to life. She didn't want to believe that the woman from so long ago might very well be the woman Dinah worried would try to seduce Celine as payback for how she felt Dinah had wronged her.

"We didn't quite meet," Celine said, going on to explain how she might know Philly. "Do you think she remembered?"

"If you wore a mask, I don't see how she would," Olivia said.

"That's what I was thinking." Celine wanted so much to believe it, especially since it was obvious Philly had set her sights on seducing Celine to get back at Dinah. Her attraction to Philly further complicated the matter. The last thing Celine needed was Philly knowing that the attraction for her began on that night almost two years ago.

CHAPTER EIGHT

Dinah arrived at Flynn's with thoughts of Celine and their night together on her mind. She had begun to think she would never find the kind of love Aunt Jo had, but now with Celine in her life she believed it was finally within reach. She made her way to her dressing room to get ready for the night's show and was surprised to find Curtis once again waiting for her.

"Well, well, look who finally decided to honor us with her presence," he said.

"I'm only a few minutes late, Curtis, besides, I'm usually the first dancer here and the last one to leave." Dinah tried not to let the smug expression on his face worry her.

"True, which is why I'll let it slide because I'm going to need you to be at your best tonight. The private party I told you about is to introduce some people to my new business partner," Curtis said.

Dinah made it a point to not get involved in Curtis's business dealings. She came to the club, did her job, and left. She didn't want any part of his legal, or illegal, activities and he knew it. She stopped unpacking her costume and turned toward him.

"I thought this was a customer's private party. You know how I feel about entertaining your business associates privately. That's what you have Cora and Lucy for."

"These people are too important to have Cora or Lucy work. I need my best act, and that's you."

"We had an agreement, Curtis," Dinah said angrily.

Curtis stepped toward her. "There's going to be some changes around here, Dinah. No more special treatment. Everybody works when and where I say they work, and until your contract with me ends, that goes for you also." He now stood directly before her, his face inches from hers. "Now, unless you have a thousand to buy out your contract, I suggest you get ready and be out on the floor in thirty minutes," he said with a look Dinah knew meant he was deadly serious.

She had five hundred, but it was the money she was saving to bring her mother and sister up north and get them settled. She couldn't sacrifice that for having to entertain what was probably Curtis's bootlegging associates. All she was doing was dancing and playing hostess. There was nothing illegal in that even if the people she was entertaining were criminals. Without another word, she turned her back on Curtis and finished laying out her costume.

"By the way, I found out something very interesting today," Curtis said.

She stiffened as she felt him move up behind her. "As much as I'd love to find out what that was, I really do need to get ready," she said.

"Oh, I think you can take a moment to hear this." He rested his hands on her hips possessively.

"I was at my tailor's earlier today and overheard a conversation between him and his new manager. It seems that my tailor is pleased about his widowed daughter being courted by the manager. He's hoping they'll be married by this time next year."

"And why is this of interest to me?" Dinah asked, using all her willpower not to move away from Curtis's touch because she knew it would anger him.

He always did just enough to make her uncomfortable but had never taken it past that point until now, when she felt his face come up beside hers and his lips brush along her ear as he said quietly, "Oh, did I forget to mention who the daughter is? It's your little friend who you've been spending a lot of time with lately. How do you think Ms. Montré's family and beau would feel if they found out their properly raised Creole daughter and future wife spent last night in the arms of another woman?"

Dinah struggled to turn around, but Curtis wrapped his arms around her waist. They felt like bands of steel holding her in place in front of him.

"I'll give you one week with her before you stop seeing her completely. If you don't, then her dirty little secret gets back to her family," he said.

Dinah's vision blurred with tears of anger. "Why are you doing this, Curtis?"

"I've wanted you from the moment I saw you at Jungle Jim's. I hired you, made you my star attraction because I wanted you to see what it would be like to be First Lady of Flynn's. To be number one at the club and in my life, but despite all that, you've barely given me a glance except to pick up your pay and cringe every time I touch you. Then to add insult to injury, I find out you prefer fucking a dame over me," he said angrily in her ear.

"So, if you want things to stay the way they are, to keep your place as the headline attraction, to not have to work another private party again, and keep your bulldagger friend's family from finding out about her," Curtis loosened his hold and his hands traveled along her waist to her hips, grinding the bulge in his pants against her behind, "then you'll walk out of her life and take your place beside me."

"Uh, boss, they're arriving," a male voice said from the doorway of Dinah's dressing room.

"Thanks, Lenny." Curtis stepped away from Dinah and checked his image in her mirror before walking toward the door. "Make sure she doesn't go anywhere but the stage," he told his club manager as he left.

Dinah stood shaking from fear and rage. She had to sit down before her legs gave out from under her. As she gazed up into the mirror, she caught the unexpected sympathy in Lenny's eyes.

"We all got our secrets, Dinah," he said before closing the door to stand guard on the other side.

Dinah wiped the tears from her eyes and went about the automatic mechanics of getting ready for her performance, all the while racking her brain over what Curtis told her about Celine having a beau. Was it a lie used to manipulate her, or was Celine the one who lied? They had not planned to see each other until the following weekend, but Dinah had to find a way to talk to her sooner. She couldn't bear the thought of having to give her up because of Curtis's threats, but she also couldn't believe Celine would lie to her about having a man in her life. She had to find a way to get through this party and her performances tonight while also fighting the urge to get up, walk out, and go convince Celine to leave town with her. Then she remembered Lenny was outside the door just to make sure she didn't do that. There was no help there. It was obvious that whatever secrets Curtis had on Lenny would override the sympathy he felt for her. Dinah decided she would go see Celine in the morning. In the meantime, she put the finishing touches on her makeup and left her dressing room with Lenny trailing close behind until she reached the curtain at the back of the stage.

Dinah gazed back at him over her shoulder. "You can relax, Lenny. I'm not going anywhere."

He held her gaze for a moment, then nodded and walked away. She signaled to the stagehand that she was ready, and the orchestra took up the familiar jungle rhythm. She took a deep calming breath and decided to just let the music take over. No worrying about Curtis, just the rhythm and the memories it now evoked of the night she met Celine. After her introduction, Dinah stepped out onto the stage with no care of who was in the audience. She danced for Celine, losing herself in the hypnotic music. When her performance was over, she stood in her closing pose, breathing heavily, the shimmering powder she wore glistening even more from a light sheen of perspiration. There was silence for a moment followed by the scraping of chairs and applause from the small group of people in the audience. Celine bowed then hurried backstage to change into the gown she wore for greeting the guests. When she arrived at her dressing room, Lenny was waiting with a large box.

He handed the box to Dinah. "Boss says you should wear this." Then he left.

Dinah carried the box into her dressing room and hesitantly opened it. Inside was a white beaded flapper dress with a rounded neckline in front and a deep V-neckline in back that stopped just short of the crack of her behind with three rows of beads draped across. It was obvious she would have to go without undergarments. If she weren't afraid of what Curtis would do to Celine she would have walked out. Instead, she freshened up, put the dress on, and went back out with her head held high. She refused to let Curtis break her. As she neared the long table that had been set up for the small group at the foot of the stage, Curtis stood, a huge, satisfied, grin splitting his face. All Dinah felt like doing at that moment was slapping it right off, but she put on her most charming smile and took the hand he held out to her.

"Gentlemen and lady." He pulled her to stand beside him and wrapped a possessive arm around her waist. "May I introduce you to the extraordinary Sable."

Everyone stood and applauded, and it was then that Dinah noticed the woman at the other end of the table. Her smile faltered as Philly tipped an imaginary hat her way.

"That was an inspiring performance, Miss Sable. May I buy you a drink?" an older White gentleman asked.

Dinah pulled her attention away from Philly. "It's just Sable," she said, acknowledging the man. "As wonderful as a drink would be right now, I'm sure Mr. Flynn would prefer to have me sober and ready for tonight's performances."

"Then maybe some other night when you're shift is over. Of course, with Mr. Flynn's permission," he said, not wanting to offend Curtis in case she was his girl.

Curtis smiled in that charming, snake oil salesman way that Sable had seen so many times before. "Lou, with all the business you send my way, I couldn't possible say no to one drink with Sable."

Lou looked as if he'd just won the lottery instead of the opportunity to buy Dinah a drink. By the way his eyes practically undressed her, Dinah had a feeling that a drink wasn't the only thing he had in mind.

"In the meantime, why don't I have Dinah get you all refills? I have a special punch I was keeping on reserve for just such an occasion as this," Curtis said, then turned to Dinah. "Tell Frank to give you eight glasses of the special." His hand slid across the bare skin of her back as she turned away.

It took everything she had not to shudder in disgust at Curtis's obvious show of possession. He wanted them all to think Dinah was his in every way, and it filled her with even more loathing for him. She could feel the sweaty imprint of his hand, as well as the hot stares that followed her bare back as she walked away. She gave Frank the order and waited as he pulled a bottle of hooch from out of a secret compartment under the bar. She gazed up at the mirror behind the bar and noticed Philly coming her way.

"Surprised to see me?" Philly said.

"Should I be?" Dinah asked.

Philly shrugged. "I asked Curtis not tell you I'd be here. I mentioned we were acquainted and that I wanted to surprise you."

After the encounter with her and Curtis earlier, Dinah just didn't have the patience to play games with Philly. "What are you doing here, Philly?"

"Good, he didn't tell you. Well, let me have the pleasure of telling you that you now work for me as well as Curtis," Philly said smugly.

Dinah's eyes widened. "You're his new business partner?"

"For now," Philly said.

Before Dinah could respond Curtis called to her wondering what was taking so long with the drinks. She picked up the tray and turned back to find that Philly was already making her way back to the table. Dinah wondered how it was possible that such a beautiful day could have gone so wrong. She made her way over to the group, silently praying for the strength not to take the tray and smash it over Curtis's head. Once she served everyone their drinks, she hoped Curtis would be finished with her and allow her to leave, but luck was not with her tonight. He insisted she stay nearby in case they needed anything, so she sat at the bar with Frank until the meeting was over. Then he had her standing between him and Philly at the entrance as they bid farewell to their departing guests. The last to leave was the gentleman Curtis had called Lou. He shook hands with both Philly and Curtis, then turned back to her and took her hand in both of his.

"It's been a pleasure having your beauty grace us this evening, Sable. I will be back to see your performance soon, and I hope you will allow me that drink." The charm in his tone didn't hide the lecherous look in his eyes.

Philly answered for her. "I'm sure we can find a way to make that happen, Lou."

Lou nodded happily in agreement. "Until then, Sable," he said.

As soon as the door closed behind him, Dinah turned on Philly. "I don't give a damn if you're Curtis's partner or not, I'm not one of your whores in your stable that you can just pimp out to whoever you want!"

"Dinah won't be part of those changes," Curtis said from behind her.

"It's not unusual for a club owner to have a headliner to entertain VIPs," Philly said. "She doesn't have to sleep with them, just get them to spend their money on her in drinks."

"I don't drink on performance nights," Dinah said.

"You won't be doing the drinking, he will. We'll serve you iced tea instead of whisky. You play tipsy and the customer isn't any wiser."

"And if they expect more than that?" Curtis asked.

"She tells them that as your girl she's off-limits, then I set them up with one of my girls who'll take them backstage to handle other matters."

Curtis nodded. "I like it. Dinah reels them in and you cook them up."

Dinah gazed at both as if they were crazy. "Did either of you not hear me? I will not be pimped out!"

"How is what you do after every performance, walking the floor and greeting and thanking the customers, any different than what we're talking about doing?"

"I'm not conning them out of their money. I'm not going to do it!" Dinah said angrily. She couldn't believe Curtis was considering going along with this idea.

Curtis's expression turned serious. "You seem to be under the impression that you have a choice in the matter," he said to her in a deadly calm manner. "While you're working for me you will do whatever I tell you to do without question. The only choices you have are what Philly is suggesting, working in her stables until your contract is up, or paying me the money to get out of it."

Dinah felt her body grow hot with rage. They had backed her into a corner she found difficult to escape. As distasteful as what they wanted her to do was, she couldn't just quit. Her nursing job alone would never make her enough money to buy a place and bring her family up north to live. Unless you were the sepia-toned beauties of the Cotton Club, it was hard finding other dancing gigs, especially since Curtis paid her twice as much as her fellow dancers. In the beginning, it was because he wanted her in his bed, but she ended up earning every penny he paid her by bringing in the majority of his big spending customers and hiring her out for requests to perform at private parties. She truly felt as if she didn't have a choice, not one that would maintain her dignity and save her mother and sister from a life of poverty in the rural South. She decided she would scrape and save as much as she could over the next few months for whatever she needed to pay her contract out as well as take her aunt up on her offer to help with her mother and sister. At least she would be done with scum like Curtis and Philly for good. Now if she could only figure out what to do about Celine.

Celine knelt in the garden of her home pruning the rosebushes she and her mother had cut from their solarium in New Orleans and transplanted shortly after they arrived in Harlem. It had flourished since then, blooming even stronger and more beautiful than it had before. Celine felt like that rosebush, as if she had also grown stronger since coming to Harlem. Working for her aunt allowed her to find her independence as well as do something she enjoyed. Being with Dinah gave her the courage to be herself and to genuinely love someone.

Standing up to her mother freed her of the burden of guilt she had been carrying since the circumstances surrounding Paul's death drove them from their life and home in New Orleans. It also made her realize that the only way she would truly be able to live the life she chose was if she moved out from under her parents' smothering wings. She knew they wouldn't like it, but it was something she had to do.

Unbeknownst to her parents, she had more than enough money to live comfortably. Paul had put the substantial amount of money her parents had given them as a wedding gift in a separate account just for her. He had also given her a generous weekly allowance to take care of their household and her social needs. Since it was just the two of them, the household expenses didn't amount to much, and since she didn't socialize like he did, she barely spent any of the money, allowing it to accumulate over the ten years of their marriage in the same account the wedding money had been placed in. She found out shortly before they left New Orleans that Paul had left her a large inheritance made from various investments that she knew nothing about. Lastly, the salary her aunt paid her was added to her accumulating fortune. There was nothing keeping her from going out on her own. She felt an overwhelming happiness at the thought of Dinah being there to wake up next to every morning and fall asleep cuddled up with every night.

The sound of voices brought her out of her musing. She recognized her mother's but not the male voice that accompanied it. A moment later, the door opened, and Julien Durand came out to the garden.

"*Bonjour, madame*, I hope I'm not disturbing you," he said in greeting.

Celine stood. "Hello, Julien. Please excuse my appearance. I wasn't expecting visitors today." She removed her gardening gloves and attempted to smooth back the wild tendrils that had escaped from the loose bun she had pulled her hair into.

Julien looked her over appreciatively. "There is nothing to excuse. You are even more beautiful than the last time I saw you. You seem to have a glow about you. Being outdoors must agree with you."

Celine smiled, not at the compliment but at thoughts of who really had her glowing so happily.

"Thank you. May I offer you something to drink?"

"No, your mother was kind enough to give me a glass of sweet tea before I came out to see you."

"You're here to see me?"

"Yes, I would like to take you to dinner, with your father's permission, of course," Julien said.

"Julien, there is no need to ask my father's permission. Despite living under my parents' roof, I am not some young innocent girl who requires permission from her parents or a chaperone to go out."

Julien smiled. "Old habits from a lifetime of training," he said. "In that case, Celine, would you care to join me for dinner sometime this week?"

"While I'm flattered, I must decline," Celine said.

"Is this week not a good time? We could always go next week," Julien offered.

Celine hid her annoyance. She had hoped her conversation with her mother would have been communicated with her father, who would have deterred Julien from courting her, but that didn't seem to be the case.

"Julien, while I am sure you are very nice, I am not interested in seeing anyone."

Julien nodded. "I understand. You must have loved your husband very much to still be mourning him."

Celine considered for just a moment falling back on that old excuse to deter interested men, but she was tired of hiding behind the lie.

"Yes, I did love Paul very much, but that isn't why I'm not interested in suitors. Paul and I married at a young age. I never had a chance to truly experience life, so I would very much like to do that now. I'm enjoying the freedom I have to do as I please, going in to work with my aunt in her shop, attending parties with friends, and meeting new people."

"And you can't have all of that with a suitor?" he asked.

Celine raised an eyebrow. "Julien, you and I both know that with our upbringing you would not be happy with a woman who is determined to have her own life outside of her time with you unless it had to do with tea socials and knitting circles."

"You believe me to be so shallow?"

"I don't know you well enough to make that assumption, but I do know how traditional men in our community are, and what they want is a good, dutiful, Creole-raised wife. If you're looking for a wife, then you will not find her here."

"And if I'm just looking for a dinner companion with no other motives but to enjoy each other's company?"

The look he gave Celine was one she had seen before from men who assumed that her widowhood offered the promise of promiscuity. It annoyed her greatly, and she was just about to say so when someone clearing their throat interrupted them. To Celine's surprise, Dinah stood in the doorway.

"I hope I'm not interrupting." Dinah's smile didn't quite reach her eyes as she looked at Julien.

"Not at all, what a surprise." Celine walked over and grasped her hands.

"I'm sorry to drop by unexpectedly like this, but I needed to speak with you," Dinah said.

Celine didn't miss the worry in Dinah's eyes. "Don't be silly. You're welcome here anytime." She gave Dinah's hand a squeeze of reassurance.

Celine turned back to Julien, still clasping one of Dinah's hands in her own. "Will you give us a moment please, Julien?"

Julien glanced briefly at their clasped hands and then Celine's face. "Yes, of course. I'm sure we can finish our conversation later since your father invited me to dinner again tonight," he said.

Dinah and Celine moved from the doorway so that he could enter the house. He stopped to glance once more at Dinah. "Have we met before?"

"I don't think so," Dinah said.

"Dinah, this is Julien Durand. He works for my father. Julien, this is my friend Dinah Hampton," Celine said.

Dinah offered her free hand to Julien. "Nice to meet you, Mr. Durand."

"It's a pleasure to meet you as well, Miss Hampton. I have the strongest feeling we've met someplace." Julien looked once more down at Dinah's and Celine's clasped hands.

"I'm sure I would remember if we had," Dinah said.

Julien nodded, then turned his attention to Celine with a charming smile. "I will see you inside."

"What brings you here on a Sunday afternoon? Did you miss me?" Celine led Dinah to a stone bench in the garden.

"I always miss you. It's taking all my willpower not to grab you up into my arms and kiss you silly."

"I feel the same way. Did you really need to speak with me or was it just an excuse to see me?"

Dinah frowned. "As much as I love seeing you, I actually came to speak with you about something I heard."

"I can tell by your expression that it wasn't something good."

Dinah took a deep breath before speaking. "Curtis knows about us. He must have had me followed."

"Followed? Why would he do something like that?"

"Celine, the club isn't the only business Curtis deals in. His other businesses are the kind that could either get him arrested or killed, so he does whatever he can to protect his investments. Since I'm a major part of the club's income, I guess he felt the need to keep an eye on me."

"Are you involved in any of his other businesses?" Celine asked in concern.

"No. I'm just a performer at his club," Dinah reassured her.

"But you're not just any performer, Dinah, or he wouldn't feel the need to have you followed. There's something more to it."

Dinah's gaze fell to their clasped hands. "He wants me, Celine, and he feels threatened by our relationship. It must have started the night you came to the club with your aunt and he walked in on us in my dressing room."

"Are you...are we...in danger?"

Dinah raised her gaze to meet Celine's. "Not physically, but he's threatening to tell your family about us if I don't stop seeing you."

Celine quickly glanced at the house. "It won't be much of threat if I decide to tell them myself."

"You can't! There's no telling what your parents will do. Are you sure you want to take the chance of losing them?"

Celine reached up to stroke Dinah's cheek. "I told you yesterday that I love you and that we'll fight any battles that come our way together. Consider this our first battle."

Dinah stood and paced anxiously in front of Celine. "If we defy Curtis, if we decide to continue this relationship, this will be more than a simple battle." She looked down at Celine. "This will be an all-out war."

Celine stood. "I'll tell my family, which will take what little power he has away. If they decide to shun me, it will hurt but I'll survive. I have already spoken to my aunt about the idea of moving in with her, and she's more than happy to have me. There's nothing Curtis can do after that."

"He'll still have me," Dinah said sadly. "I have several months on my contract with Flynn's Follies. He knows I can't afford to quit and will use that to find a way to manipulate us."

"There's no way for you to get out of the contract?"

"Yes. I could buy it out for a thousand dollars. I have half of that saved up to get a place and bring my mother and sister up from Alabama. I can't risk them for that, Celine."

Celine grasped Dinah's hands. "I can give you the money! I have more than enough. You can buy out your contract, and I can give you whatever else you need to bring your family up here."

Dinah gazed at Celine in disbelief. "You have that kind of money?"

"Yes." Celine grinned.

"You would do that for me?"

"Yes, because ultimately it would be for us."

Dinah sat down. Celine watched various emotions play over Dinah's face. First, hopeful excitement followed by a look of defeat as she lowered her head.

"It might not work," Dinah said.

"Of course it will. If he wants to tell my family, we'll just beat him to it. He wants money, we'll give it to him."

"You don't know Curtis. I've never witnessed it, but I've heard about the things he's done to people who crossed him. He wants me too much to let me go that easily."

Celine frowned. "You said there was no physical threat."

"There isn't, but Curtis is too confident he's got us backed into a corner to do anything but what he asks. Losing me means not only losing money for the club, but it will also hurt his pride, which will back him into a corner. Curtis backed into a corner is like a wild animal that will claw its way out, no matter what's in its path, and leave a bloody trail on the way."

Celine crossed her arms. "What do you want to do?"

"I don't want to lose you. I also don't want to put you in the middle of this," Dinah said.

Celine sat beside Dinah. "I don't want to lose you either, and you're not putting me in the middle. I'm stepping in with both feet." She smiled to reassure Dinah.

"Promise me something," Dinah said.

"Anything."

"That you'll walk away if this doesn't work." Dinah halted Celine, who was about to protest. "Just until my contract has ended, and I can leave without him holding that over my head."

Celine hesitated in answering. "I promise."

"Thank you." Dinah let out a breath. "I'll offer Curtis the money first. I don't want you to tell your parents anything if you don't have to."

"Eventually, I will have to tell them something. I realize we can't be together openly, but I don't want to go through my life deceiving my parents no matter how upset they get about it. I've lived a life of deception long enough with my family."

"You may want to reconsider that declaration. I don't know your parents other than the brief introduction to your mother when I arrived, but judging by the subtle look of distaste on her face when I mentioned I was a friend of yours, I don't see that going well at all."

Celine felt her face flush in embarrassment. "I have to apologize for that. My mother is very much a social and racial classist."

"In other words, my dark skin and unfashionable dress offended her."

Celine placed her hand on Dinah's cheek. "You're beautiful to me, and that's all that matters."

Dinah placed her hand over Celine's as she turned her head to place a kiss on her palm. Celine closed her eyes in contentment.

"If your family wasn't nearby, I'd lay you down and make love to you right here on this bench." Dinah gave her a sexy smile.

"Celine," her mother called, announcing herself as she approached the doorway to the garden.

Dinah released Celine's hand and slid to the other side of the bench just as Celine's mother came into view.

"Yes, Maman," Celine answered.

"Will your…friend…being staying for dinner?" her mother asked with a tight smile.

"Will you stay for dinner?"

Dinah shook her head. "No, but thank you."

"Well, it was nice to meet you…"

"Dinah," Celine said, annoyed by the obvious look of relief on her mother's face.

"Yes, well, it was nice to meet you. We hope you'll visit again soon. Celine, you should get cleaned up. Dinner will be ready shortly." She turned and went back into the house.

Celine shook her head. "Again, I apologize."

Dinah chuckled. "I'm from deep in the heart of Alabama. I've dealt with worse."

"That doesn't make it right."

"True, but it makes for thick skin," Dinah gave her a wink. "There's one other thing before I go."

"What is it?"

"Curtis hinted that you were being courted by someone who worked for your father. Can I assume he's referring to Julien Durand?"

Celine ran her hand down her face in frustration. "How is it possible for him to know so much about what is going on?"

"He goes to your father to have his suits tailored. Is it true?"

Celine wondered if that was jealousy she heard in Dinah's tone. "Yes, Julien works with my father. No, I'm not seeing him, despite my parents' manipulations."

"I wouldn't blame you if you were interested in him. He's a looker," Dinah teased her.

Celine grasped Dinah's hand. "I'm not looking at anyone but you."

Dinah gave Celine's hand a gentle squeeze then stood. "I better go. The longer I sit here, the more I want to touch you."

"That is exactly why I need to move out from under my parents' roof. I have to be so restricted here." Celine walked with Dinah into the house.

"Dinah, what a surprise!" Olivia stood in the kitchen helping Celine's mother.

She grasped Dinah by the shoulders and placed a kiss on both of her cheeks. "I didn't know you were here. You are staying for dinner, of course."

Celine saw true affection between them.

"As much as I'd like to, my aunt is expecting me," Dinah said.

"Well, I'm sure Celine's probably already extended an open invitation for you to join us the next Sunday you're available, but if she has not, then I shall. You don't mind, do you, Lanie," Olivia stated rather than asked, drawing a brief look of irritation from Celine's mother before she pasted on her best hostess smile.

"Of course not. Celine is welcome to invite any of her friends over for dinner," her mother replied with little sincerity.

"Excellent, then it's settled." Olivia gave them a conspiratorial wink. "And we'll finally have a fourth for cards."

"I'll walk you out." Celine looped her arm through Dinah's and led her out of the kitchen.

"Will you really come for dinner soon?" Celine asked as she opened the door for Dinah to leave.

"If you would like me to."

"I'd love you to."

"I can't promise anything until I've spoken to Curtis about what we discussed but know that I will be here the first chance I get."

Celine wanted so much to pull Dinah into her arms to rid her of the worry in her face.

"Get word to me as soon as you can."

Dinah nodded and turned to leave.

Celine stood in the open doorway watching Dinah walk down the steps. Dinah turned back and mouthed the words "I love you" then hurried down the street.

Celine closed the door and turned to find Julien watching her from the doorway of her father's study. She turned away and made her way toward the stairs. He laid his hand atop hers on the banister to halt her.

"It seems your dearly departed husband wasn't the only one with tastes that ran toward the debauched." He smirked.

Celine gazed down to gather her thoughts then calmly looked back up. "You will remove your hand immediately."

Julien ignored her. "You let that darkie touch you, yet you look at one of your own with such disgust? Do your parents know their little Creole princess prefers cunt?"

Celine was more shocked by Julien's lust-filled gaze than what he said, but she managed to keep a cool head. She moved to snatch her hand from beneath his, but he was faster as he grabbed her wrist and moved close enough to the stairs that only the width of the banister separated them.

"I know of a place that has parties where we could both indulge in quite a bit of pleasure." He licked his lips suggestively.

Celine narrowed an angry gaze on him. "You have less than a minute to release me before I scream bloody murder and bring everyone in this house running to find out what's going on. At that point you can kiss your job with my father goodbye."

"And if I tell them about your scandalous affair with that black whore that just left here?"

First Curtis Flynn and now Julien. She was tired of the threats and hiding in the proverbial closet like some scared mouse. "Tell them," she said nonchalantly. "Shout it to the rafters if you like, I couldn't care less. But you better decide what's more important, revealing what you think my dirty little secret is or your job, because the moment you spew such nonsense to my father, with no proof, you will be tossed out like yesterday's garbage."

Their gazes held for a moment. Her father calling Julien's name from his study brought an end to their showdown.

Julien abruptly released Celine's wrist. "I'll be right there, sir." He watched Celine intently before turning away.

Celine watched him close the study door and breathed a heavy sigh of relief. As she made her way upstairs, she could only hope she was not wrong in thinking Julien wanted his job more than he wanted her. She also hoped that this would deter him from paying her any unwanted attention from now on.

Unfortunately, their encounter didn't have the desired effect on Julien as Celine had hoped. Although she was sure he hadn't, and probably wouldn't, tell her parents of his suspicions about her and Dinah, his surreptitious glances her way throughout dinner told her he was just as interested in her as he was before.

After dinner, Celine helped her mother carry coffee and dessert into the parlor and announced that she would pass on dessert and bade everyone good night. She could no longer watch Julien fawning over her parents, especially since Olivia had made her escape as soon as dinner was over and left Celine with no one to talk to.

"Celine, a moment of your time before you go," Julien said.

Celine turned slowly back to him, trying to keep a pleasant look on her face.

"I have two tickets for the latest show at the Lincoln Theater for this Friday and was wondering if you would like to accompany me."

Celine noticed her mother fidgeting anxiously with her napkin and wanted to slap the smug grin off Julien's face.

"I think that sounds like a fine idea. I'm sure she would love to go, wouldn't you, Celine?" her father answered for her. "You've been working far too hard. You should get out more and enjoy yourself with folks your own age."

Despite the look of fatherly concern, she could tell by his tone that it was more of a father's command than a suggestion. The look in his eyes said he would not tolerate an argument from her in this matter, and that was when she realized it was his idea. He had probably given Julien the tickets with the insistence that he take her. She might be a grown woman on the verge of thirty, but she still lived under her parents' roof. Out of respect for them and the guilt she still felt over what they had given up after the scandal, she agreed to the date with Julien, then brusquely wished them good night once again and left the room, barely holding her simmering anger in check. She didn't appreciate her parents interfering and manipulating her life the way they were. As soon as she arrived at the shop in the morning, she would arrange to stay with her aunt sooner rather than later.

CHAPTER NINE

Flynn's was closed on Mondays, but Dinah knew Curtis would be there anyway, so that was her first stop after leaving work. She had been up most of the night trying to figure out the best way to approach Curtis with the ideas Celine had. She would not tell him they were Celine's. She didn't want to get her any more involved than she already was. Dinah decided to offer him the money to buy out her contract first. Having Celine tell her parents about their relationship would be a last resort. She only hoped his greed would overrule his pride.

She entered the club through the back door as always and was surprised to find two huge suit wearing men standing right inside the entrance.

One of them stepped directly in her path. "We're closed."

"I'm one of the performers," she said, wondering why Curtis suddenly needed these goons guarding the door.

Goon number two turned away from a stack of boxes he was checking and picked up a clipboard. "Which one?"

"Sable," she said, using her stage name.

He gazed back down at the list and nodded. "She's good," he said to goon number one, who had been blocking her path while ogling her from head to toe.

He sneered. "I bet she is."

"You know Philly don't like us messing around with the girls," goon number two said.

Goon number one snorted in derision. "That's cuz she wants 'em all to herself."

"Ours is not to reason why, ours is but to do or die," goon number two said thoughtfully.

Goon number one turned a confused gaze on him. "What the hell mumbo jumbo shit you talkin' 'bout now?"

Goon number two shook his head. "Try picking up a book sometimes, you uneducated ape, and let the lady through."

"Who you callin' an ape?" goon number one mumbled as he stepped out of Dinah's way.

She nodded in appreciation at the more intelligent goon. "Thank you."

He tipped an imaginary hat at her, then turned back toward the boxes he had been going through when she came in.

As Dinah made her way to Curtis's office, she saw workmen everywhere and heard the banging of hammers and scraping of a saw. She knew this had to be Philly's doing because the performers and staff at the club had been asking Curtis to make repairs for some time. It was amazing that only a couple of the stage crew got hurt considering rafters were hanging by a nail and the stage itself felt like it would collapse underneath the weight of the band and dancers any day now. If that was the case, it would only be a matter of time before Philly found a way to ease Curtis out. There were stories of her doing just that at many of the businesses along the East Coast that she already had her hand in. Her previous partners had either "retired" or disappeared altogether. Curtis had to know of Philly's reputation and was either too stupid or too cocky to think she would do the same to him. Dinah just hoped she was able to get out before Philly completely took over.

When she arrived at Curtis's office, she found Philly sitting behind his desk and him leaning over, showing her his books.

Curtis gazed up at her entrance. "Dinah, what are you doing here?"

"Curtis, I'd like to speak to you," she gave Philly a quick glance, "alone."

Curtis came around to lean against the edge of his desk. "The only time you come to my office is to talk business, and since Philly is a part of this business now, whatever you have to say I'm sure you can say it in front of her."

Dinah hesitated. She didn't want Philly involved in this conversation. "I want to talk to you about releasing me from my contract."

"I already told you the only way that will happen is if you buy it out. You have the money to do that?"

Dinah took a deep breath before answering. "Yes."

Curtis narrowed his eyes suspiciously. "You have a thousand dollars?"

"I can get it." Dinah hoped he took the offer without question so she could get away from him and the club for good.

"Nursing at that hospital paying that well?" Philly asked.

Dinah ignored Philly, keeping her attention on Curtis. She could practically see the dollar signs running through his head.

"Ask her where she's getting the money from," Philly said.

Curtis gazed back at her in annoyance. "I don't care where it's coming from. That'll go a long way toward upgrading our hooch inventory."

Philly settled back in the chair with an air of casualness. "Yeah, it would, but I think you'll be more interested in where she's getting the money from than you think."

Curtis turned a suspicious gaze on Dinah. "Where are you getting the money from?"

"My aunt Jo," Dinah said.

"If your aunt had that kind of money you wouldn't be working here in the first place," he said.

Dinah had hoped to make this easy and it would've been if Philly hadn't been there. "Curtis, do you want the money or not?" She hoped she didn't sound as anxious as she felt, which was more for Celine's sake than her own.

Curtis's gaze narrowed and his jaw clenched tightly. "It's the Creole princess, isn't it? She's trying to buy my silence by buying out your contract, isn't she?"

"Does it matter?" Dinah asked in frustration.

Curtis looked at her pointedly. "I want fifteen hundred to release you from your contract and five hundred to keep my mouth shut about you two."

Dinah looked from him to Philly and wanted to smack the smug, satisfied look off her face. "You don't have to do this, Curtis. You could just take the thousand and let me walk away."

"How much do you think you're worth to her?" Curtis asked.

"Slavery was abolished over sixty years ago," Dinah said angrily.

Curtis roughly grabbed her face. "You know, Dinah, you need to learn when to shut up because that mouth is gonna get you hurt."

"Curtis," Philly said, drawing his name out as if she were warning off a child from misbehaving.

To Dinah's surprise, he backed off and looked toward Philly, who had strolled over to where they stood. She put herself between them and placed an arm along both of their shoulders.

"I'm sure we can come to a reasonable agreement. Curtis, why don't you give me a moment with Dinah? Sometimes a woman's touch is all that's needed to straighten out misunderstandings."

Curtis briefly looked at Dinah before leaving. That's when Dinah knew that it would only be a matter of months before Philly had full control. She gazed back at Philly, who watched her intently as she leaned back and propped a hip against Curtis's desk. Seeing the stubborn glint in Philly's eyes made Dinah realize that she would make this difficult. Dinah turned to leave.

"Giving up so easily?" Philly said mockingly.

Dinah stopped but didn't turn around. "You and I have nothing to talk about."

"I'll make a deal with you."

Dinah turned around. "My deal is the thousand, take it or leave it."

Philly shrugged. "I don't want or need your money."

"Then what do you want?"

"Celine."

Dinah's fists clinched at her sides. "She's not mine to give."

"True, she's not your property, but she is yours in other ways, and I want those other ways."

"What do you mean?" Dinah knew what Philly was suggesting, she had to hear it anyway.

"I'm sure you can figure that one out, but if you'd like me to spell it out, I will." Philly placed her hands in her trouser pockets. "I don't care about Celine's heart or even her mind, I just want some time to explore that lush body you so obviously enjoy."

Dinah's eyes widened in disbelief. "You're doing all of this because you want Celine?"

"No. I'm doing all of this because *you* want Celine. Want her so bad that you're willing to risk Curtis's wrath to be with her. I want a piece of that action to see what all the fuss is about."

Dinah took a step toward Philly and was confronted by the sharp tip of a switchblade.

"I was hoping we could talk about this like two civilized women and not resort to violence like the animals men tend to be," Philly warned her softly.

Dinah didn't move any closer, but she didn't back away either, meeting Philly's gaze over the switchblade.

"What makes you think Celine even wants you?"

Philly closed the switchblade and set it on the desk instead of back in her pocket. "I don't. But what I do know is that it's obvious she'll do anything to help you. You want out of your contract? You want Curtis to keep his mouth shut about your affair? You tell her the only way to do that is to spend one night with me. That's all I'm asking." Philly turned back to sit in Curtis's chair.

"Of course, you'll still have to give Curtis the money," she continued, "because this little deal will be struck between me, you, and Celine without his knowledge. I'll convince him he'd be better off just taking the money and letting you go than trying to milk Celine for all she's worth."

Dinah looked at the blade Philly left sitting on the edge of the desk. For a moment, she considered lunging for it and sticking it into Philly's cold heart, but it wouldn't be worth spending the rest of her life in prison.

"I'll stop seeing Celine and work until my contract ends before I'd even think about telling her about your deal."

"The choice is yours." Philly returned her attention to the account ledger.

Dinah assumed their conversation was over and turned to leave.

"Oh, by the way, since you'll obviously be continuing at Flynn's there will be some changes. You'll be the VIP entertainment, which means after your regular sets you'll also be entertaining our VIP customers in our new private lounge being constructed backstage. I'm sure you saw the workers on your way in. They should be finished by the end of the week. I wouldn't plan on being home before dawn most Friday and Saturday nights if I were you."

Dinah's grip tightened painfully on the door handle. Her eyes clouded with tears of anger and frustration as she jerked the door open and hurried out of the club.

❖

It had been a long, busy day and Celine was relieved when her aunt told her it was time to close shop. After she locked the door and turned out the lights, she joined Olivia in the sewing room to help clean up.

"*Tante*, I'd like to take you up on your offer to stay here until I'm able to acquire a place of my own," Celine said.

Olivia smiled affectionately. "Of course, I adore having you here. Would this have anything to do with Dinah?"

Celine felt her face heat in a blush. "Yes. But I also think it's time I started living my own life and not the one my parents would like me to live."

Olivia frowned. "Are they still attempting to push that horrid Julien Durand on you?"

Celine rolled her eyes. "Yes. Papa has insisted I accompany Julien to the theater this Friday."

"Even after what you told your mother?"

"I believe it was the very reason Papa was so adamant about my spending time with Julien as well as more people my own age and less time at the shop."

"Well, we'll solve that problem by moving you in this week, and by the time Friday comes around you won't have to keep your date with Durand."

"No, I gave my word, *Tante*. I'll speak with Maman and Papa this week about moving in with you and inform Julien on Friday that we will not be seeing each other after that night." Celine gathered her hat and purse to prepare to leave.

"Is there something more going on?"

Celine hesitated. She was tempted to tell her about Curtis Flynn's and Julien's threats, but she didn't want to involve her in anything that she and Dinah could handle on their own.

"No. I will see you tomorrow." She gave her a hug in departing.

Celine made sure the shop door was locked, then put her keys in her purse and stepped away from the door. She was startled by a figure standing in the shadows.

"I didn't mean to frighten you," Dinah said as she stepped out of the alley beside the shop. "By the time I got here the door was locked, so I figured I'd wait for you."

"Why are you skulking in the shadows? You know we would've let you in."

"I needed to talk to you. I didn't want to take the chance of your aunt overhearing."

Even in the fading daylight, Celine could see by the look on Dinah's face that something was wrong. "Why don't we go to the boardinghouse since it's nearby."

They walked the few blocks in silence. When they arrived, Dinah hesitated at the bottom of the front steps. "Would you mind if we sat outside?"

"No, not at all," Celine said.

They sat side by side on the steps.

Dinah looked down at her lap. "I spoke with Curtis today."

"I take it that it didn't go well."

"No." Dinah gave Celine the details of her confrontation with both Curtis and Philly.

By the time Dinah finished, Celine found that she felt almost the same intense anger for Curtis that she had felt for Robert Cole when he lied about Paul to save his own reputation.

"I told her I'd work my contract out before I'd put you in that position."

Celine shook her head. "You can't do that. It'll only be a matter of time before they decide to start offering you up to the highest bidder."

Dinah finally lifted her gaze to Celine. "You can't possibly be thinking about her offer."

"I won't let them turn you into what they're threatening to turn you into, Dinah."

"And I won't let that woman lay one finger on you," Dinah said vehemently.

"It's the lesser of two evils," Celine tried to reason. "One night with Philly compared to months of whoring you out to complete strangers."

"I won't let it come to that!"

"Dinah, I'm not as naïve as you may think I am. I know what kind of man Curtis is. I've heard the rumors about him. You know just as well as I do what he's capable of."

Although Dinah knew Celine was right, it didn't make it any easier for her to accept. Celine grasped Dinah's hand.

"It's one night, Dinah."

Dinah knew Philly. She couldn't help but believe otherwise. "Philly can be quite persuasive."

"What are you saying?"

"Can you honestly tell me you don't find her attractive? That there's not something seductive about her? Hell, I find her attractive and I don't even like her. You're a passionate woman who's only had one lover in her entire adult life, you can't tell me you're not the least bit curious to explore with other women now that you've had a taste of what it's like."

Celine released her grasp on Dinah's hand. "After everything I said to you the other day. After admitting how much I care for you, you think I could be so easily swayed by sex?" Despite knowing Dinah was closer to the truth than she was willing to admit, Celine was hurt by Dinah's accusations.

Dinah ran her hand down her face in frustration. "I would hope you wouldn't be, but you can't predict what will happen when that moment comes."

Neither spoke for a moment. It was enough time for Dinah's words to cause Celine doubt.

"Promise me something," Dinah said.

"Anything."

"If we go through with this…if *you* go through with this…you won't let it go too far? If Philly becomes too demanding, you'll end it. You won't let her manipulate you into a situation that could put you in danger."

Celine grasped Dinah's hands, wanting so much to reassure her of her love. "I promise."

Their gazes held for a moment, and despite her promise, Celine could still see the doubt and worry in Dinah's eyes.

Dinah eased her hands from Celine's. "You better go."

Celine stood and hesitantly made her way down the stairs. She wanted so much to stay with Dinah. To never have to walk away like this again. To not have to worry about her parents or people like Curtis, Philly, and Julien. She had only gone a few steps when she turned back to find Dinah no longer sitting on the stairs. The soft click of the door being shut gave Celine a strange sense of finality. As if Dinah wasn't just closing the door to her home but also to her heart.

To Celine's relief, Dinah hadn't closed the door to her heart. She still found a way to reach out to Celine since they didn't think it would be safe for them to continue seeing each other until she spoke with Curtis. Dinah found ways to drop little notes at the shop for Celine. They communicated daily that way, and it comforted her get those notes and be able write her back. Dinah's notes were filled with so much tenderness, humor, and sometimes, even quotes of poetry or sonnets from some of her favorite books. Celine felt as if she were being courted in the oldest fashion of ways, it was completely endearing.

Besides reading Dinah's notes, Celine spent the time planning her move to her aunt's place and how best to approach the conversation with her parents. She was going to wait until after her night out with Julien, then tell them during Sunday dinner while Olivia was there. Once she told them, she would leave that very night. She had already packed most of her belongings. It was a plan that left her feeling a sense of sadness and excitement all at once. She would finally be able to live her life on her own terms and not worry about what her parents would say, but it also meant breaking her parents' hearts. Something she would have to accept if she wanted to be happy.

Sunday dinner arrived, and they gathered around the table which, to Celine's chagrin, included Julien. She had hoped her cold demeanor during their evening out that Friday would have deterred him from continuing his pursuit of her. If not, she was sure her moving out would drive the point of her disinterest home because he wouldn't have the leverage he believed he had by threatening to tell her parents about the relationship he assumed she had with Dinah.

"You've barely touched your food, Celine. Are you not feeling well?" her mother asked in concern.

"I'm not that hungry," Celine said.

"Unless you've been eating at the shop, I have barely seen you eat much of anything lately. You are working her too hard, Olivia," her mother said. "You might want to start searching for another shop girl, because I am sure once Celine and Julien are married, she will be too busy making a home and starting a family to work."

Celine looked from her mother's clueless expression to her father's stern countenance, then met Julien's smug expression and ended on her aunt's look of shock. She turned back to her mother, who continued daintily cutting her food and trying to avoid Celine's gaze.

"Maman, I don't know where you got the idea that Julien and I are getting married, but let me assure you that we are not."

Celine's father sighed and laid his fork on his plate. "I was hoping we could have this conversation after dinner."

"There is no conversation to be had, Papa. I'm not marrying Julien." She tried to remain calm.

"Celine, I understand you loved Paul and his death was difficult for you, but it's time to move on with your life," her father said.

"I have moved on and I'm enjoying my life just the way it is. I don't need a husband to do that."

"Julien has expressed his affection for you," her father continued as if she hadn't spoken, "and your mother and I have decided that it is time for you to marry again."

"*You've* decided?" Celine said.

"Yes, and we could not have chosen a better man than Julien if we had handpicked him ourselves," her father said.

"Then you and Maman may marry him!"

"Celine!" her mother said.

"You're *telling* me to marry a man I've known for only a few weeks, as if I have no say in the matter, and expect me to just go along without protest?"

"What we expect is that you be respectful of your mother and me and conduct yourself with proper decorum," her father said. "You should consider yourself fortunate that we even gave you the opportunity to meet and get to know him. In most arranged marriages the young women are not even given the opportunity to meet their intended. From what I can see and what Julien has told me, you two seem to get along quite well."

Celine narrowed her gaze at Julien, who sat across from her looking very much like the cat that ate the canary. She could either call him out for the conniving liar that he was or take this opportunity to tell them she was leaving. She met her father's expectant gaze.

"Papa, I love you and Maman and I know how much you sacrificed in leaving our home and life in New Orleans because of the circumstances of Paul's death. I've carried that guilt and burden for too long, trying my best to be the dutiful daughter you expect me to be, but in this I cannot. I don't want to marry Julien, and I don't plan on marrying anyone else in the future. For the first time in my life I'm living for me, no longer under the shadow of Paul's death or a daughter's guilt, and I plan on continuing to live for me from this point on, which is why I've chosen to move in with *Tante* Olivia."

"You will do no such thing! We won't allow it!" her mother shouted.

"Maman, I am a grown woman. You no longer have the right to tell me how to live my life. I'm already packed and plan to leave this very night."

"You enjoy breaking my heart, don't you?" Celine's mother wailed, her eyes shining with unshed tears.

"Oh, Lanie, stop the dramatics," Olivia said in annoyance.

Her mother turned an angry glare on Olivia. "This is all your fault! You and that sinful life you live. I knew Celine should not have gone to work for you, but Francois insisted it would keep her mind off her grief."

She turned her glare on Celine's father. "Well, all we have done is push our daughter right into her clutches to steal her away from us and a respectable life."

Celine's father ignored her mother's histrionics and looked at her. "Your mother and I have sacrificed our reputation and livelihood for you, and you choose to repay that by turning your back on us?"

"Papa I'm not turning my back on you. I'm choosing to live my life the way I want. I don't wish to be married again, especially to a man I barely know. This is 1925, Papa, not 1905."

"If you leave this house tonight, I will no longer support you financially. You will be on your own," Celine's father said, and then went back to eating his dinner as if the conversation was done.

Celine looked at her father pleadingly; he ignored her. She looked once again at her mother, who silently watched her anxiously. When her gaze landed on Julien's smug expression, she stood to leave.

"Papa, I didn't stay here with you and Maman because I didn't have the means to support myself or was too grief-stricken to find another husband. I stayed because I felt responsible for you having to choose to uproot your life and leave New Orleans. With the money I saved while married to Paul, the large inheritance he left me from investments neither his father nor you knew about, and the money I make selling my hats, I am more than capable of taking care of myself for a very long time, so you can keep your money because I don't need it." She walked out the dining room.

"Francois, you're not going to let her leave, are you?" she heard her mother say.

"Lanie, she has made her choice," her father said.

Celine made her way upstairs to bring the few things she was taking with her downstairs and met Olivia in the foyer.

Olivia gave her a tight hug. "I will get us a taxi while you say your goodbyes."

Celine gazed back at the closed study door where she heard her father and Julien talking then toward the dining room where her mother's cries drifted out to her. "No, let's just go." She picked up her valises and headed for the door.

She hated leaving this way, but prolonging her departure to say a goodbye that would only turn into another bitter argument was not worth it. She left her parents' home with no regrets and a nervous excitement for this new chapter in her life.

CHAPTER TEN

That night, Celine unpacked as much as she could fit into her new home at Olivia's apartment before she called it a night. She brought only the clothing she had accumulated since moving to Harlem and a trunk full of personal items she had brought up from New Orleans. She sat on the bed, opened the trunk, and saw her wedding album. She took it out and opened it to the first photo that was taken just after the ceremony. She gazed wistfully at the photo of her and Paul smiling happily at one another. It truly had been a happy day for both, despite the reason they had chosen to marry.

Celine ran a finger along the image of Paul's face. "I truly wish I had your counsel right now."

She heard the telephone ring but knew Olivia would answer it. A moment later, she heard Olivia call her name. Celine set the album back in the trunk and went out to the other room.

"Who could that be? No one knows I'm here yet."

Olivia smiled. "It's Dinah."

Celine rushed to take the telephone. "Dinah?"

"Hi," Dinah answered. "Is this a good time? I'm not calling you too late, am I?"

"Yes, it's fine." Celine sat and curled up in the chair next to the table the telephone was on and waved happily to Olivia as she left the room.

"How did you know I was here?"

"I didn't. I was calling hoping your aunt could get a message to you and she told me you had moved in already."

Celine sighed. "Yes, I decided not to prolong the inevitable and left my parents' home earlier this evening."

"How did that go?"

"Not good. They were trying to push me into marrying Julien, and I told them no. They didn't give me any other choice but to leave."

"I'm sorry to hear that. Are you all right? You sound sad."

"I am, but only because of the fight we had before I left. My father said he would disown me."

Dinah gasped. "Why? Because you wouldn't marry Julien?"

"I don't think it's so much about marrying Julien as it is about them believing that being independent and on my own is not a respectable way for their daughter to live."

"I'm sorry," Dinah said.

"There's no need to feel sorry. It's better for everyone this way. Now, why did you call?"

"Oh, that. I wanted to know if you were up for some adventure tonight."

"And what does this adventure entail?"

"It's a surprise. Can you be ready for me to swing by and collect you at nine?"

Celine could feel the excitement she heard in Dinah's voice. "Yes. How should I dress for this adventure?"

"Nothing dressy. It's a casual gathering."

"All right. I'll see you in an hour."

At precisely nine o'clock, Dinah rang the buzzer to Celine's apartment. As she waited for someone to answer she began to have second thoughts about where she was taking Celine. She hadn't planned on seeing her this soon, but Dinah found she couldn't stay away much longer. Especially knowing that any day now Celine would be sharing Philly's bed. Knowing Philly, it would happen sooner rather than later, and Dinah had no doubt Philly would make sure she knew when it would be happening. It made Dinah anxious, so she was relieved when Helene sent word that she was having one of her private gatherings. Since Celine had expressed interest in attending one after Helene's last party, Dinah thought it would be the perfect excuse to see her again. Now, standing outside Celine's door, she no longer felt so confident about the idea. As she heard someone coming down the steps, she tried to think of something else she could do with Celine this late on a Sunday night, but nothing came to her by the time Celine opened the door. She stood before Dinah looking as beautiful as ever dressed in a white blouse with a lace ruffled button front and mid-length gathered sleeves with the same lace at the cuffs, an A-line black skirt with white pinstripes, silk stockings, and black open toe patent leather pumps.

Dinah chuckled. "I guess we had the same look in mind," she said, indicating her similar attire but with a solid burgundy skirt and matching shoes.

Celine frowned. "I didn't even notice. I could go up and change."

"Don't be ridiculous. Besides, I don't think anyone will be paying much attention to what we're wearing anyway." Dinah offered Celine her arm. "Shall we?"

Celine gazed at her curiously before sliding her arm through Dinah's. "Would you mind telling me where we're going that no one will be paying attention to our clothes?"

A mischievous look came into Dinah's eyes as they walked along the quiet street. Sunday evenings held no trace of the wild night life Fridays and Saturdays drew along Harlem's 125th Street. Sunday night was a ghost town after everyone spent their morning in church repenting for the sins they committed on the previous nights.

"Remember when you asked if I would take you to one of Helene's private parties?" Dinah asked.

Celine gasped. "We're going there now?"

"Yes, unless you changed your mind." Dinah watched nervously as Celine chewed her lip in thoughtful consideration before she looked at Dinah with excited anticipation.

"No, I haven't changed my mind. I just hadn't expected it to be so soon."

Dinah blew out a breath in relief. "She's going to be traveling out of the country soon and decided to have one last party before her trip."

Celine chewed nervously on her lip again.

"Celine, if you don't want to go, we don't have to. I just thought since Helene doesn't know when she'll be returning it would be the perfect opportunity for you to go. I sprang this on you out of the blue, so if you're not ready, I completely understand."

Celine looked hesitant. "It's not that I don't want to go, it's that I'm not sure what I'm supposed to do when I get there."

"Whatever you want to do. If you want to watch, then we'll watch. If you want to participate, we'll do that. If you decide it's all too much for you, then we'll leave. I won't push you into anything that makes you uncomfortable."

Celine looked relieved. "All right."

Dinah was suddenly filled with a nervous anticipation. She wanted to help Celine explore her sexuality and be the one to introduce her to anything that piqued her curiosity, but she was also afraid that all of this might be too much too soon. Celine was so much more than she could've imagined and the last thing Dinah wanted to do was scare her off.

"This is late for you. Don't you have to work in the morning?" Celine asked.

"No, I work a double in a couple of days so I'm off tomorrow."

"Well, that worked out well for tonight." Celine gave Dinah a sexy smile. "Would you be inclined to stay over with me?"

Dinah placed a kiss on Celine's temple. "If that's what you want."

"Yes, it is."

Knowing Celine wanted her enough to ask her to stay over made Dinah's heart skip a beat. She couldn't help the happy smile as they strolled the rest of the way to Helene's in companionable silence.

Celine's nerves almost got the better of her as they arrived at Helene's home. Unlike the first time she was there when music and laughter drifted out of open windows and people gathered on the front steps, it was quiet enough to hear the sound of low jazz music drifting through the closed curtains, and the only thing lounging on the steps was a black and white cat blinking lazily up at them as they passed. Dinah stopped and turned toward her when they reached the top step.

"At any point you feel uncomfortable with what's going on, you tell me, and we'll leave immediately. Helene and I will completely understand."

"I will."

Dinah nodded then rang the bell. The door was opened by one of Helene's maids, who greeted them pleasantly when she recognized Dinah. She stepped aside to let them in, then locked the door behind them, proof that this was obviously not the open house party from last time where anyone looking for good music, food, and company could stroll in. Looking around as they entered, Celine could see why. Instead of guests dressed to the nines in party attire, they lounged on the sofas, chairs, and floor cushions barely dressed, if at all. Even Helene greeted them in a sheer dressing gown with nothing but pair of silk drawers underneath.

"Ah, you made it!" Helene hugged and gave both a kiss on the cheek.

She took Celine's hands. "My dear Celine, I'm so glad to see you again. Since I was told you may be joining us tonight, I already notified the other guests that you are new to our little soiree and that you are with Dinah, which means you are off-limits unless you and Dinah initiate a coupling. Please feel free to eat, drink, and explore to your heart's, or body's, pleasure."

Celine tried looking everywhere but at Helene's heavy dark breasts and hardened nipples showing through the sheer material.

"Now, I must get back to a particularly handsome jazz musician and his wife, but you are in excellent hands with Dinah, as she has not only attended but also helped me host several of these little gatherings." Helene blew them both kisses and hurried off.

"Would you like to get a drink?" Dinah asked.

"Yes, please," Celine said, knowing she would need something to help her relax. She was not used to seeing so much naked flesh other than when she took a customer's measurements. Even then they kept their undergarments on.

Celine allowed Dinah to lead her into the dining room where, thankfully, the clothed guests had gathered.

"Dinah! Celine!" someone called from across the room.

Dinah's friend Claude was set up at the bar in the role as bartender. They went over and Celine was pulled into an embrace so tight she was lifted off the ground.

"Welcome to the family, beautiful," Claude said.

Celine felt the heat of blush on her face. "Thank you."

"We haven't seen Dinah at one of these soirees in quite some time. You must be pretty special to get her back out again."

"Claude," Dinah said in warning.

Claude chuckled and held her hands up in surrender. "Sorry, it's just good to see you out and about again. What can I get you ladies? I don't know how Helene manages to keep a full bar even with the slack Prohibition laws in New York, but she's got everything."

"I'll take a gin and club soda," Celine said, wanting something stronger than wine.

Dinah looked at her in amusement. "Make that two."

"Two gin rickeys coming right up."

Once Claude made their drinks, they thanked her and found a pair of empty chairs nearby. Celine sipped her drink and tried to calm the butterflies in her belly.

Now that they were sitting down and she was able to gaze around the room, Celine noticed many looks directed at her. Even people who stopped to say hello to Dinah spent more time staring and grinning at her than Dinah.

"How are you feeling so far?" Dinah asked.

"Like an exotic bird in a cage. I was fine until I noticed the glances and whispers my way."

Dinah placed her hand on Celine's thigh and gave it a gentle squeeze. "You're a new, and beautiful, face. They're simply curious. Don't worry. Like Helene said, they won't approach unless you, or we, initiate it."

"Is that why so many people have stopped to speak to you on their way out to the garden? To try to gauge our interest in more than a friendly chat?"

"Yes, and the fact that I haven't been to one of these in some time."

Celine looked at her curiously. "Why is that?"

Dinah shrugged. "My hours at my previous nursing position and working for Curtis didn't lend me much free time to do anything but eat and sleep."

"You must have been very popular, especially if you hosted as well."

Dinah nodded. "It was a confusing time in my life. Trying to figure out if I was like my aunt or if I just hadn't been with the right man, the fiancé I left behind in Alabama. Then I met Claude and Lilly while we were all working at Jungle Jim's and they brought me to one of these parties to try to help me figure out what I wanted. Coming here gave me the freedom to explore, and since I was in no rush to settle down with anyone, I enjoyed it to the fullest. As much as I hate to say it, I think Curtis coming along kept me from getting addicted to all of this. Once I started working private parties for him, I had to stop coming to these parties. I don't regret having experienced it. In a strange way, these parties helped me discover who I was and what I wanted."

Celine stared down into her glass. "That sounds so much like what happened with Paul. He wanted to include me because he thought it would help me in the same way."

Dinah took her hand. "And now? Are you still afraid?"

Celine looked around the room and was met with looks of curiosity, friendly smiles, and admiring glances. There was no judgment. Like Paul, these people didn't take life or their pleasure for granted. They were open and affectionate with one another in a way Celine had rarely seen or experienced growing up. She wanted to feel the same freedom Paul and Dinah felt embracing their own pleasure.

"No, I'm not afraid, not with you by my side."

Dinah ran the pad of her thumb softly across Celine's lips. "Good. Tell me what you would like to do now."

"You mentioned there were rooms we could watch from." She wasn't ready to be the center of attention.

"Yes."

Dinah gave her an encouraging smile, took her hand, and led her to a hidden panel in the wall beside the doorway to Helene's indoor garden. As they made their way down a corridor softly lit by candle sconces rather than electric lights, Celine noticed they passed curtained alcoves along the way. From what she could tell, there were only six of them, and all but one had the curtains closed. Celine assumed that meant they were occupied. She followed Dinah into the last alcove. It had two wide cushioned chairs that faced a window looking out into one of the garden alcoves she had briefly seen at Helene's last party. On the other side of the window were two nude women lounging on a blanket surrounded by large throw pillows, feeding each other fruit in a seductive manner.

Both women were attractive with lush, curvaceous figures that would make the goddess Venus burn with envy. One had a smooth, dark brown complexion, and the other was just a shade lighter than Celine. She found herself comparing the contrast to her and Dinah, and her body flushed with pleasure.

"Can they see us as well?" Celine whispered.

"No, it's a one-way mirror. We can see them, but all they see is their own image as long as there's no light shining from our side."

"So, the curtain isn't just for privacy. It keeps light from showing through."

Dinah nodded. "Exactly. Here, sit." She pointed toward the chairs.

They sat and Celine watched in fascination as the darker woman took a bite of her strawberry, then gently rubbed the uneaten half of the fruit over each of her lover's nipples until they were as red and looked as juicy as the remainder of berry she was then fed. The woman who had spread the berry juice on her nipples took one into her mouth, and Celine's mouth watered when the woman whose nipples were being devoured gasped and arched her back passionately.

"Do they know someone is watching?" Celine asked, finding it difficult to tear her eyes away from the erotic scene playing out in front of her.

"If they noticed the light behind the mirror disappear when we closed the curtain, they probably do. These alcoves, on both sides of the mirror, were specially created for voyeurs and exhibitionists."

"So, they enjoy being watched?"

"That's part of the pleasure."

As the women's kisses and caresses became more intimate, Celine's mind was thrown back to the night Paul brought two women home for her entertainment, which had her thinking about the one who sensually haunted her dreams at night. The one who might very well have been Philly. Her mind began to play tricks on her, and the image beyond the mirror turned into something that both shocked and sent a thrill of pleasure through her most intimate area. The two strangers blurred into images of Dinah and Philly. Her past and present shimmered in a vision before her, and she felt like Alice peering into a scandalous looking glass. Celine became aroused, and a need like she'd never felt before made her body tremble. She turned toward Dinah to see if she was just as affected by the women as she was. She saw Dinah's eyes darkened with arousal, but it was directed at her and not the other women. Celine leaned over the arms of the chairs toward Dinah, who met her halfway for a heated kiss.

"Come here," Dinah said, her voice husky with passion.

Celine took one last look toward the window and saw that the shimmering image of Dinah and Philly had turned back to the strangers on the other side of the glass. They were in a position that allowed them to feast on each other's sexes hungrily, and Celine's drawers became wet with arousal. She turned back, straddled Dinah's lap, and leaned in to cover her lips with her own. Dinah's hands settled on Celine's hips as they devoured each other's lips. Their kiss continued even as Dinah slid her hands up around Celine's waist and began unbuttoning her blouse. Once Dinah's task was accomplished, she slid Celine's blouse and brassiere straps down her shoulders and arms until Celine's breasts were free of their constraints. Celine couldn't stop the cry of pleasure that escaped when Dinah took one of her nipples into her mouth and flicked her tongue back and forth until the nipple stood erect and aching pleasurably as she also massaged her other breast.

"I don't need strawberries to enjoy the taste of you," Dinah said before she paid equal attention to Celine's other nipple.

Celine writhed in Dinah's lap as the sound of faint moans could be heard from the other side of the mirror. Celine turned her head to look behind her and was greeted by the sight of the darker skinned woman facing the mirror while she was straddled over her lover's face buried between her thighs. It felt to Celine as if the woman was looking directly at her as she practically ground her sex against her lover's mouth while cupping and massaging her own breasts.

"Stand up and turn around," Dinah told her.

Celine did as she was told, watching the play of ecstasy on the face of the woman they were watching. Celine sighed when Dinah slid her hands up her legs, pushing her skirt up as she did so. When Celine's skirt was gathered around her hips, Dinah eased her back onto her lap so that she was facing the mirror. Dinah reached around and spread Celine's legs, then moved the lacy trim of her drawers aside. When Dinah's fingers slipped past the briefs and two of them delved into her wetness, Celine thought the loud moan that followed surely had not come from her. As Dinah's fingers stroked in and out and she heard the sound repeated, she could no longer deny it was her and didn't care. She closed her eyes and allowed herself to get lost in what Dinah's strong and long fingers were doing to her. Celine relaxed back against Dinah, laid her head back on her shoulder, and thrust her hips toward Dinah's fingers. As Dinah's thumb massaged the nub at the juncture of Celine's thighs, her fingers continued to plunge into her, and she brought her other hand up to tweak her nipples. All of this was Celine's undoing. Her orgasm hit her like a tidal wave.

"Dinah!" Celine called out as her body tightened then shook from the intense pleasure pulsating through her.

Celine opened her eyes for just a moment to see the two women lying with their fingers frantically working between each other's thighs as they also cried out from their own orgasms. Celine closed her eyes again and let the aftershock tremors run their course as Dinah gently stroked her to ease her out of her pleasure. With a shuddering sigh, Celine placed her hand over Dinah's wrist to still her.

"As pleasurable as this has been, I'd much rather continue this in the comfort of my bed," Celine said breathlessly.

Dinah placed a kiss along her temple. "I agree."

Celine was grateful when Dinah helped her to stand and get her clothes back into some semblance of order because her legs and mind were mush at the moment. She caught movement out the corner of her eye and saw that the two women on the other side of the mirror were putting on dressing robes and gathering their bowl of fruit and champagne. Before they walked away, both ladies knocked on the mirror and blew kisses toward it before a final wave in parting.

Celine felt her face heat in a blush. "Do you think they'll know it was us on the other side?"

Dinah took Celine's hand and gave it a gentle squeeze of reassurance. "I doubt it, unless they recognize your moans from talking to you," she teased her.

Celine's face grew even hotter. "Maybe we could just hide in here until everyone leaves."

Dinah took Celine's face in her hands. "Celine, don't ever be embarrassed about your passion, especially with me."

"It's not having enjoyed it that causes embarrassment, it's having others know about it. I've been a private person for so long it's a difficult habit to break."

"Take comfort in knowing that everyone at this party is here for the same reason, to express themselves and connect with others through pleasure. They won't be judging you for doing the same." Dinah placed a soft kiss on Celine's lips.

Celine knew Dinah was right. Once again, she was reminded of Paul. He had told her something similar many times in his attempts to get her to join him when he attended such parties. She was surprised to hear how common they were in New Orleans as well as other cities. Paul told her that since the end of World War I Americans had become more hedonistic and brought these parties over from Europe. Now she stood in a curtained alcove with her body still tingling from the pleasure of having finally experienced the sexual freedom he spoke of.

Celine smiled at Dinah. "I think Paul would have truly liked you."

Dinah returned the smile. "If you loved him then I'm sure I would have liked him as well. Now, are you ready to go?"

Celine nodded. As they passed the other curtained areas, she could hear sounds of passion from the other voyeurs. It sent a thrill of pleasure through her and made her even more impatient to get Dinah home to her bed. As if reading her mind, Dinah made quick work of their goodbyes and they were on their way back to Celine's apartment in no time.

❖

"You're awfully quiet," Dinah said, worried that Celine had not spoken since they left Helene's. "Are you regretting having gone to the party?"

"No." Celine reassured her. "In the beginning, it was a shock to what prudish sensibilities I seem to be holding on to, but with your help, I quickly got over it and enjoyed myself."

"Then you're all right?"

Celine squeezed Dinah's arm that was looped through hers as they walked. "I'm fine. I've just been thinking of Paul and I'm hesitant to talk to you about him."

"Why? He was an important part of your life. From what you've told me, he would have loved that you went to the party."

"That's what I was thinking about. He tried for years to get me to explore this life with him and I said no too many times to count. Now, here I am, after only knowing you for just a few weeks, not only attending but somewhat participating."

Dinah understood. "It feels like you've betrayed him."

Celine nodded. "He was such a wonderful and kind husband. He was never demanding and had asked so little of me during our marriage."

"Celine, I'm sure he understood and is probably cheering you on from up above." Dinah was relieved to see the worry leave Celine's face.

"You are so good to me, Dinah."

"I can't wait to get you home to show you how good I really am." Dinah gave her a wink.

When they arrived at the apartment and hurried upstairs to Celine's bedroom, Dinah was glad she had decided to take Celine to the party. Not only had she managed to get Celine to open sexually but also emotionally. Dinah felt it would be a great opportunity to be a little bolder with their lovemaking. They undressed and fell into each other's arms in the bed, kissing and caressing each other as hungrily as the women they had watched through the mirror.

"Do you trust me?" Dinah asked.

Celine nodded. "With all my heart."

Dinah's own heart soared at Celine's declaration. "Stay right there."

Dinah hopped off the bed and retrieved Celine's silk stockings. "Ready for more adventure?"

Celine looked curiously at the stockings in her hands. "Are you planning to dress me?"

Dinah chuckled. "Put your arms above your head."

Celine did as she was told, and Dinah climbed back onto the bed and straddled her. "I'm not going to hurt you."

"I know."

Dinah gave her a lingering kiss, then sat up and grasped Celine's right hand, raising it slightly above her head, and tied her to the headboard with one of Celine's stockings.

"Is that too tight?"

Celine watched her curiously. "No."

Dinah nodded then did the same with Celine's other arm. "I want you to just lie back and enjoy. Tonight is all about your pleasure." She ran her fingers from Celine's wrist, down her arm, and over her breast until she reached and tweaked her nipple.

Celine's eyes darkened with desire. "I'm not even allowed to touch you?"

Dinah gave her a mischievous smile. "No." She replaced her fingers with her mouth on Celine's nipples.

Dinah wasn't only thinking of Celine's pleasure. She wanted to make sure that after Celine spent the night with Philly, she would know what she had to come back to. She knew that love had more to do with an emotional connection than it did a sexual one, but when it came to Philly's expertise in all things physical, Dinah felt she would have a hard time competing. Celine knew she loved her, but Dinah had to make sure that Celine also knew how much she desired her. She spent the rest of the might making damn sure there would be no doubt in Celine's mind about that.

❖

Dinah dedicated last night to making sure Celine knew how much she desired her and decided to make the rest of the week about showing her how much she cared for her. When she finished her shift at the hospital, she went home, freshened up, then went by the shop to take Celine out for the evening to dinner, a movie, a gathering of her artist and entertainment friends, and even spending one evening at the boarding house simply cuddling and talking. She gifted Celine with flowers and books of sonnets and wrote her little notes she would drop off at the shop on her way into work.

Dinah had never been in love before, so this was all new to her. Celine was something special, and Dinah knew she couldn't treat her like one of her casual flings. While she hoped spending all this time with Celine would prove to her that Dinah was serious about them, she realized that it made her feel something she had never felt before with anyone, jealousy at the thought of Celine and Philly together. She almost told Celine to call it off, but as much as she hated her doing it, Celine's sacrifice meant Dinah would be free and they could begin their life together. Once in a while, a small voice in her head told her this was wrong, that it would blow up in her face, but she shushed it by reminding herself that Celine made the decision to take Philly's offer, Dinah hadn't forced her. Once it was all over, Philly and Curtis would be out of their lives forever.

CHAPTER ELEVEN

Celine spent the next several days working tirelessly on the burlesque fans for Philly's party at the end of the week. The morning of the party, she awoke with the realization that she had not heard from Philly since she sent her the note accepting her invitation, or coercion as Celine thought of it, to spend the evening with her. She made her way out of her room to find Olivia setting the table for breakfast.

"Ah, *mon bijou*, I knew you would be up early. Do you still have much to do on the fans?" Olivia set out a platter of beignets and honey butter, Celine's favorites.

Celine yawned. "No, they're finished. I just need to wrap and prepare them for delivery."

"I'm so glad you're going to the party. As hard as you've been working this week, you have earned some time to enjoy yourself. Will Dinah be meeting you there?"

Celine paused in the act of spreading butter onto her beignet, wondering if she should tell Olivia about what was going on, but decided against it. Olivia's protectiveness would have her wanting to take Curtis and Philly head-on. Celine didn't want to put her in that situation.

"No, she has to work tonight." Celine avoided Olivia's steady gaze.

"I see. Well, then you and I will make a day of it. We'll close the shop early, go into Manhattan, buy something daring for you to wear, treat ourselves to dinner at a nice restaurant, then come back here to have Simone do something extravagant to our hair," Olivia said.

Celine couldn't help but smile at Olivia's enthusiasm. "I have plenty of clothes, and you own a boutique, *Tante*. I certainly don't need to buy a new dress to wear."

"True, but I can tell you need cheering up. Nothing cheers up a woman up more than shopping."

"It has been some time since just the two of us spent the day outside of the shop together."

"*Excellente!*" Olivia exclaimed happily. "Then let us finish our breakfast and begin our day!"

❖

At Philly's home, a four-story brownstone in the Striver's Row area of Harlem, Dinah sat in one of the guest rooms staring at her reflection in the mirror seriously considering packing up and heading back to Alabama, but the thought of leaving Celine behind swept that idea right from her mind. She would continue to endure Philly's manipulations until she knew for certain whether Celine still wanted her after their night together. Philly had made it a point to pull Dinah aside before she left Flynn's in the early morning hours to tell her she had received a note from Celine accepting her invitation to spend an evening with her. Dinah's hand had itched to slap the smug expression from Philly's face. She had secretly hoped Celine wouldn't do it and couldn't help but worry how this would affect their relationship. She worried that Celine would be ashamed and not want to see her again, which she would accept, or that her inexperience would have her falling for Philly, which Dinah couldn't bear to think about.

Dinah had chosen not to ask Celine when their planned night would happen because it was torture enough knowing it was going to happen at all. She also knew Philly would not be silent about it. She would more than likely enjoy supplying Dinah with every detail of the night.

With a heavy heart, she went about the process of getting ready for her performance. She had arrived at the club only to be told she and a few of the other dancers were going to be part of the entertainment for Philly's party. They were greeted by Philly's houseman, shown to a guest room they would be sharing as their dressing room, and told to be ready to perform in two hours. Dinah's fellow dancers had been dressed a half hour ago and were appeasing their curiosity about their new boss by wandering around the large home. Dinah declined their invitation to go with them. She knew enough about Philly to last her a lifetime and just wanted this evening to end sooner rather than later.

Making some final adjustments to what little she was given to wear—sheer silk panties with a cluster of diamond-shaped crystals sewn into the front to discreetly cover the V-area at the juncture of her thighs and a set of crystal pasties to cover her nipples. She was told by Philly's houseman she would be reprising a fan dance she did at the lounge where they used to work. She'd told him she didn't have the costume or fans. He had told her everything was taken care of and waiting in the guest room. Dinah walked over to the bed where the fans were lying, picked them up, and practiced manipulating the heavy fans when something at the base of one of them caught her attention. Upon closer inspection, she saw the familiar embroidered initials and Dinah's heart skipped a beat. She thought Philly had insisted she be part of the entertainment for her private party to torture her, but now she realized what the real reason was. This was going to be the night Philly planned with Celine, and she wanted to make sure Dinah had a front row seat to the show.

When Olivia and Celine arrived at Philly's home sometime after nine in the evening, the party was already in full swing.

Olivia gazed around the opulently decorated foyer. "I see Antonia has done well for herself. She always threw fabulously decadent parties with barely a penny. I can't wait to see what she has planned with the obvious wealth she gained while away. Shall we venture farther into the lioness den to see what awaits us?" Olivia slipped her arm through Celine's and urged her forward.

They made their way through the crowded foyer into the main room which opened to three other rooms equally filled with loud, laughing, and drinking party revelers. Although a band played in the main room where guests danced and mingled, Celine noticed one of the rooms had a large number of boisterous guests and two big, serious looking, tuxedo-clad men standing just outside the doorway.

Following her gaze, Olivia leaned toward her and whispered, "That would be where she serves her private reserve of libations."

"I'll remember to avoid that room," Celine said.

"Wise choice. Antonia's reserve is not for the faint of heart. She has it secreted in from the Bahamas."

Celine gazed at Olivia in surprise. "Pray tell how you know so much about Philly's private dealings, *Tante*?"

"As I am sure you are realizing, my dear Celine, Harlem is not a place for the innocent or faint of heart. To become the successful businesswoman that I am I have had to deal with some unsavory clientele and business deals along way. That is all I shall say about it."

Celine placed an affectionate kiss on Olivia's cheek. "I hadn't realized moving in with you would be such an adventure."

"Ms. Rousseau, Ms. Montré," a deep male voice said.

Celine and Olivia turned to find a tall, slim, tuxedo-clad gentleman standing nearby. Celine would have assumed he was just another one of the men Philly had for security if it weren't for his bobbed and finger-waved hair and the tastefully done makeup on his smooth, caramel complexion.

"Ms. Manucci would like you to join her for a drink if you'll please follow me." He walked past them without waiting for a reply.

Olivia gazed curiously at her, then followed the man's retreating figure, pulling Celine along by the hand. They were led into the room Celine had just said she was going to avoid. He took them to a small table in the corner where Philly sat casually smoking a thin brown cigarette. She was dressed in a white tuxedo with a black vest, bow tie, and patent leather shoes. Her hair was sculpted to her head in shiny, perfectly coifed finger waves, and her lips curled up into a sexy crooked grin as she saw them approaching. It was a look that Celine had seen many times in her dreams about the seductive woman in New Orleans.

Celine realized the dress she had chosen during their shopping expedition might not have been a good idea. It was a sleeveless layered dress with a sheer overlay and clear beaded fringe. The neckline dipped just low enough to give a tempting view of her breasts. At Olivia's urging, she put a light rouge on her cheeks and a tastefully red lipstick on her lips. The way Philly licked her lips when her gaze fell on Celine's had her regretting that as well. Philly stubbed her cigarette in the astray beside her and stood when they reached her table.

She offered a hand to Olivia. "Madam Rousseau, it is a pleasure to have your grace and beauty appear at one of my little soirees once again."

Olivia laughed. "Antonia, your flirtations have no bounds."

"When I'm lucky enough to be graced with such beauty I can't help it."

Olivia snorted in an unladylike fashion. "Save it for the young birds who don't know any better," Olivia said.

Philly turned her attention to Celine, whose hand she grasped and brought to her lips where she placed a soft kiss. "I'm enchanted by your beauty, Madame Celine," Philly said in perfect French.

Celine felt the heat of a blush at Philly's compliment and got annoyed at her body's betrayal.

She slid her hand from Philly's grasp. "I delivered the fans earlier this afternoon. I hope you had a chance to look them over."

"I have not, but I'm sure they're fine. After all, I know talent when I see it, and I have no reason to doubt you do very satisfying work."

"Yes, well, they should hold up nicely for the performance tonight. You're welcome to stop by the shop next week to pay the balance on them."

"The performances start in about a half hour. Until then, why don't I get you ladies something to quench your thirst." Philly signaled one of the many scantily clad ladies circulating through the party.

A moment later, two ornate glasses filled with an orange colored beverage were set before Olivia and Celine. Assuming it was some type of fruit juice, Celine took a large sip and went into a brief coughing fit that made her eyes water.

Philly offered Celine her handkerchief. "I take it that was your first taste of Barbadian rum punch."

Celine snatched the handkerchief from Philly and dabbed at her eyes.

"Much smoother than I've recently had, but I believe your bartender may need to be less generous with your rum unless you want your guests passed out on your floor before the night is even half over." Olivia took a sip and swallowed smoothly.

"Ah, Madam Rousseau, you were always a connoisseur of my inventory. I will be sure to mention it to my bartender." Philly stood and offered Celine a hand. "In the meantime, may I borrow your niece? We have a transaction to complete."

Celine hesitated in taking Philly's hand, turning to Olivia in a panic.

"My niece is a grown woman. She does not need my permission to do anything. Unless, of course, she's not comfortable and requires my interference." Olivia gave her a look of suspicion.

"I can assure you, Celine will be perfectly safe with me," she said smoothly.

As Philly waited patiently for her to take her offered hand, Celine wondered what would happen if she just turned and left. Then she remembered why she was here and took Philly's hand in defeat. "I'll return shortly, *Tante*."

Philly led Celine through the crowded room, stopping to speak to guests along the way, with a possessive hand placed on her lower back. Celine didn't know most of the guests, but the ones she did, the ones she knew from the shop or met at Helene's party, gazed at her curiously or with a look of disappointment. The disappointment from Dinah's friends Claude and Lilly was the most difficult to accept. Especially when Philly stopped to speak with Helene. Celine could barely meet her gaze without a flush of shame heating her face.

"You've done well for yourself," Helene said to Philly. "Rumor has it you're staying in town and partnering with Curtis Flynn."

"Not a rumor. Curtis had a business deal go bad and needed someone to bail him out. Fortunately, I was there to catch him before he fell," Philly said.

"I bet you were. Celine, I've been meaning to call on you to schedule that tea you promised." Celine looked up at Helene. Instead of disappointment, Celine's gaze was met with worry in Helene's eyes. "Why don't we meet tomorrow around two?"

Celine felt the itch of tears as she nodded to Helene. "I would like that."

"Excellent." Helene grasped Celine's hands and placed an affectionate kiss on both cheeks. "I'm here if you need me," she whispered before walking away.

Fortunately for Celine, that was the last person Philly decided to stop and chat with before leading Celine to her study. Once they were inside, Celine walked toward a large oak desk, keeping her back to Philly. When she heard the door shut and the click of the lock, she felt like a cornered mouse with no way out. Philly came up behind her, placed her hands onto Celine's hips, and pressed the front of her body along Celine's back. She made no other move nor spoke for a full minute, causing Celine's already jangled nerves to become even more distraught. She could not stop the trembling that took over her body as she felt the warmth of Philly's breath caress the nape of her neck. She closed her eyes as she felt the softness of Philly's lips press a kiss just below her right earlobe. To Celine's horror, when the tip of Philly's tongue snaked out to trace the outline of her ear, her body no longer trembled from nerves but from arousal.

"There's no need to be nervous. I won't hurt you. I just want to bring you pleasure," Philly whispered seductively in Celine's ear.

Celine turned to Philly, which she realized may have been a mistake as Philly stood so close that their lips almost met as she maneuvered in the small space between Philly and the desk.

"Is this how you want to do this?" Celine asked angrily. "Here and now with a house full of people? Is your plan to get back at Dinah by shaming me in front of everyone as I leave your office with all eyes on me knowing what went on here?"

Philly nonchalantly stepped away and went to the other side of her desk. "No." She opened a drawer, pulled out an envelope, and came back around to Celine.

"I simply wanted to pay you the remaining balance for the fans since I was not here to accept the delivery earlier today." Philly held the envelope out to Celine, looking as if she were offended by the accusation.

Celine wanted to slap the look from her face. She chose to take the envelope instead, folding it and placing it in her purse.

"Aren't you going to count it?" Philly asked.

"I'm sure it's all there, and I don't want to keep you from your party any longer than necessary." Celine wanted to escape as quickly as possible before people began to talk more than they probably already were.

Philly moved to unlock and open the door to allow Celine to leave, but before she could cross the threshold Philly grasped her elbow.

"Tsk, tsk, little birdy, there will be no flying away from me tonight. You promised me the entire night, and I plan to take as much as I can. You will stay by my side for the entire evening, as my companion. You will do this by pulling out all those social tricks you learned in your *Gens de Couleur* upbringing to be the sparkling hostess for me." The look Philly gave her said she would not tolerate an argument from Celine.

"What about my aunt? Am I supposed to just ignore her all night?" Celine asked, not willing to be the docile participant Philly seemed to want her to be.

"I don't care what you have to tell her, but you will do this, and if she insists on following along beside you the entire night that's fine as well, but understand this, Celine," Philly's grasp tightened on her arm, "you will not be leaving here tonight with her."

Philly released Celine's elbow and placed her palm on the small of her back with a pleasant smile pasted back on her face. "Now, we need to hurry, or we'll miss the show," she said.

"Celine," Olivia called as they entered a ballroom where all the guests had gathered. Celine practically collapsed with relief at the sight of Olivia.

"Ah, Madam Rousseau, would you like to sit with us for the show?" Philly asked courteously as they made their way to the front row of seats facing the middle of the room.

Once Philly ensured Celine and Olivia were seated, she left them to speak with the band.

As soon as Philly was out of earshot Olivia leaned toward her and whispered, "What is going on, Celine?"

When Celine turned toward Olivia, she could barely keep her tears in check. "I will be staying here with Philly tonight."

"Celine, I will not allow that woman to force you into anything you don't want to do. I have dealt with Phillys in the past, male and female. Tell me what she has over you and I will take care of it."

"*Tante*, this is the only way Dinah and I can be together."

"Does Dinah know about this?"

Celine nodded. "She didn't want me to do it, but if I don't, she'll be forced into doing things for Curtis Flynn and Philly that I can't bear to even think about."

Olivia grasped her hands and placed a soft kiss on her forehead. "Maybe your mother was right. I have led you into a life of debauchery," she said sadly.

Celine squeezed Olivia's hands. "No, you have led me to a love I will sacrifice anything to keep. I'm doing this willingly." She pasted on an encouraging smile to ease Olivia's concerns.

Just as Olivia was about to speak again the lights went down and spotlights brightened the center of the floor where Philly stood.

"This conversation is not finished," Olivia said, not releasing Celine's hand.

As Philly thanked everyone for attending and regaled her guests with what entertainment she had in store for them, Celine watched Philly, trying to find something about her that would help her keep her unfaithful body in check, but all she could see was the masked temptress reaching out to her from the bed in her guest room. *It's just one night*, she told herself. One night to purge that image from her memory forever so that she could spend the rest of her life with the woman she loved. After her speech, Philly sat beside her, placing her arm along the back of Celine's chair and a possessive hand along the nape of her neck. There would be no mistaking their relationship for anyone who happened to gaze their way in the dimly lit room.

The first performance was a reading from a writer Celine had met at Helene's party. Richard Bruce Nugent was well-known within the Harlem artistic community for not only his writing but also for his openness about his sexuality. Celine had spoken with him at length and thought he was not only talented but brave for having the confidence to live in his truth. Something she was hoping to be able to do with Dinah by her side. After Nugent's reading there were singers, drag performers, chorus girls, and finally the band leader announced the much-anticipated fan dancer. The spotlights went down, there was a hush in the crowd, and the band went into a rendition of Bessie Smith's "Careless Love." When the spotlights flashed back on, there was a lone figure in the center of the floor hidden behind the two enormous white ostrich feather fans Celine had created. The dancer shook the fans lightly as she seductively bounced to the tune. The only thing visible was her bare feet. The fans separated slightly to reveal the dancer's face, and the audience applauded enthusiastically, all but Celine, who gazed angrily over at Philly. Philly grinned smugly back at her.

"How are you enjoying the entertainment?" Philly asked.

"You're sadistic."

Philly leaned over and whispered in Celine's ear, "Only if you want me to be," then placed a kiss on her temple.

Celine's gaze went directly to the performer, but she realized that with the spotlight Dinah would not be able to see the audience clearly. She watched Dinah's performance, all the while aching to run out onto the floor, grab her hand, and take her someplace no one would find them. During the entire time she watched the performance Philly's fingertips traced up and down her spine, her open back dress giving Philly easy access to the exposed flesh. Once again, her body betrayed her by reacting to the combination of Dinah's near nakedness and Philly's fingernails gently grazing what, she had recently learned while making love to Dinah, was an erotically sensitive area of her body. Her nipples hardened and strained against her brassiere, and she barely restrained herself from squirming in her seat as a pleasurable throb grew at the juncture of her thighs.

❖

Dinah's performance ended, the lights came up and, as if some instinct told her where they were sitting, she looked directly at Celine and Philly. Dinah flinched as if the sight of Philly's hands on Celine and the wanton expression on Celine's face had physically struck her. She looked away, bowed to the audience and, with as much dignity as she could muster, walked instead of ran from the room. She barely made it to the dressing room before the tears sprang free. She sat in the chair at the dressing table, laid her head in her hands, and wept as her heart shattered. The other dancers had gone out to mingle with the guests, so she was alone until she felt soft hands on her shoulders and the familiar scent of Olivia's jasmine perfume. She turned and wept in her arms.

"Shh, we will find a way out of this," Olivia said.

Dinah gazed up at her. "She told you?"

Olivia removed a handkerchief from the bodice of her dress and wiped Dinah's tears. "She told me enough to know that you both are being manipulated by Philly and Curtis for their own selfish needs and that my niece is going to be the one left damaged by it all," she said angrily.

"Are you so sure about that?"

"What are you saying?" Olivia asked.

"You didn't see what I saw when the lights came up," Dinah said angrily. "She didn't look too put out. She looked like she was enjoying Philly's touch."

"How dare you doubt Celine's love for you after everything she sacrificed to be with you, and is planning to do tonight, to keep you safe."

Dinah hung her head shamefully. "What if it's not enough? What if Philly is able to make her forget what we have?"

"Do you believe Celine is so fickle that she would let passion rule her heart?" Olivia asked. She grasped Dinah's hands. "I'm going to do something I've never done, and that is betray my niece's confidence."

Olivia told Dinah how Celine knew Philly and that neither of them were sure if Philly remembered as well.

Dinah frowned. "You're telling me Celine has always been attracted to this mystery woman and now that same woman is trying to seduce her? If Philly does know who Celine is, it would explain her obsession with her. If she doesn't know and finds out, there is no way she is going to let Celine go without a fight."

Olivia looked worried. "You know Philly just as well as I do. She doesn't fight fair."

Dinah grabbed her bag, pulling out the flapper dress she was told to wear, and hurriedly began changing her clothes. "We have to get Celine out of here," she said in a panic.

"Dinah, we can't. This will happen whether we want it or not. We are in Philly's home. She can hold Dinah here against her will without repercussion considering the amount of money she has spent keeping the authorities looking the other way with her business dealings. It's better that we let her think we are cooperating for now. After we get Celine home tomorrow, we will work on a way to get you both out of this predicament safely."

Dinah sat dejectedly back into the chair. "I know you're right. It doesn't make it easier knowing she's going to have to spend the night in that woman's clutches."

Olivia stood, pulling Dinah up with her. "Get dressed and play your part just as Celine has to play hers. The longer we sit in here commiserating about the situation, the longer Celine is left alone with that woman parading her around like some prized trophy. She needs to see us strong and supportive. Can you manage it?"

A knock on the door interrupted them.

"Hey, Dinah, it's Big T. Philly wants to know why you ain't out on the floor."

Dinah nodded in agreement with Olivia. "I'll be right out," she answered.

Olivia gave Dinah a hug, then left her to finish getting dressed.

CHAPTER TWELVE

Despite what was to come once the party ended, Celine played her role well. She stayed close to Philly, smiling, charming, and being the entertaining hostess, her mother raised her to be. Ten years of living a life of deception with Paul had taught her well. The difference was that at the end of the night she and Philly wouldn't be retiring to their own beds. She was going to have to share a bed, and more, with Philly. As much as her heart and mind wanted to run in the other direction, her body ached from all the teasing caresses Philly had been feeding her growing passion throughout the night. Even having her heart break at seeing Dinah work the rooms with the other dancers to entertain Philly's guests didn't stop her body from missing the warmth of Philly's hand at the small of her back when she removed it to greet someone or to get them drinks. She and Dinah were only able to engage in brief glances at each other before Philly whisked her away in the other direction. Even in those brief moments, she could see the pain in Dinah's eyes.

Fortunately, Olivia stayed by her side the entire time, which annoyed Philly a few times when she tried leading Celine to a dark alcove for more than a discreet touch here and there, but as helpful as it was, the night had to come to an end at some point. It was half past midnight and the party was still going full swing when Philly announced that she was retiring for the evening but everyone was welcome to stay as long as they liked or until the cops came to shut them down. Either way, her staff would take good care of them. Celine turned a panic-stricken gaze to Olivia.

"Antonia, I would like to have Celine walk me out, if you don't mind," Olivia said pleasantly.

Philly, in the middle of giving her staff instructions, nodded and released Celine's hand. Celine and Olivia went to the foyer together.

Neither missed how closely they were watched by Big T standing at the door.

Olivia faced her and grasped her hands. "Do not allow yourself to feel guilty about tonight, do you understand me? I spoke with Dinah and she's fine. Don't worry about her, just get through tonight. Tomorrow we will figure out what to do next," she said in French in case anyone overheard them.

Celine pulled Olivia into a fierce hug. "*Merci, Tante.*"

"Thank you for coming, Madam Rousseau." Philly walked into the foyer and placed her hand possessively onto Celine's back.

With a pleasant look on her face, Olivia offered Philly a hand. Philly took it and winced as Olivia tightened her grip. "If you lay one hand on my niece other than with affection, you will regret it." Her pleasant demeanor never wavered, but the threat in her gaze was obvious.

"I'm not into abusing women, Olivia. My girls are all treated well."

Olivia released Philly's hand and accepted her wrap from the coat check girl. "That's the thing, Antonia, Celine is not one of 'your girls.' Remember that," she said before walking out the door Big T held open for her.

Celine watched her aunt proudly. She sometimes forgot that underneath all Olivia's sophisticated feminine wiles lay a dangerous woman. Celine was the only one in her family who knew Olivia's years in Paris were not all spent making dresses and enjoying French pastries in fancy parlors. Olivia struggled to make ends meet and had to do things to survive that would make her prudish mother burn with embarrassment. To this day Olivia carried a stiletto on her at all times in a special garter knife holder she made. Celine asked her once if she had used it on anyone, Olivia told her yes but wouldn't say what happened to the other person or persons.

"I see you find that amusing." Philly looked annoyed.

"Not at all. I just know not to underestimate my aunt. Shall we get this evening over with?" Celine turned toward the stairs as if she knew where she was going. She assumed, after being throughout the entire downstairs, that Philly's sleeping rooms were on the next level of the brownstone.

Philly caught up with her. "If I'd known you were so anxious to bed me, we could've skipped the whole party and gone right up," she said.

"Don't flatter yourself. I just want this over." Celine hesitated as Philly bypassed the second floor and continued up.

"The first floor is the main entertaining area, the second is for guests, and the third is my personal domain." She held open the first door they reached for Celine.

Celine tried to appear confident, but her nerves took over as she entered the large bedroom. There was a sitting area in front of a fireplace, a wardrobe and dresser and two doors. One looked like it led to a private bathroom and the other to a dressing room. Most of the room was taken up by the largest bed Celine had ever seen. It could easily fit four adults. Next to the bed was a nightstand that held a platter of fruit, a bottle of champagne, and two glasses. Philly poured the champagne in the glasses and brought them over to the sitting area where Celine retreated, trying to avoid the oversize bed for as long as possible. She had avoided drinking much alcohol, wanting to keep her senses about her, but after seeing the bed she gladly accepted the glass of champagne from Philly, drinking the liquid courage down.

Philly chuckled. "Whoa, slow down." She took a sip from her own glass, then placed it on a nearby end table to take her jacket off.

Philly sat on the sofa and patted the cushion beside her. "Sit with me."

Celine took a steadying breath and sat down.

"Turn your back to me."

Celine did as she was told and was awarded with the gentle caress of Philly's fingers once again along her spine. A moment later, Philly began to knead and massage the muscles along her shoulders and neck. When her thumbs kneaded up and down along either side of her spine, she moaned. Realizing the passionate sound came from her made her tense up once again.

Philly continued her manipulations. "There's nothing wrong with feeling pleasure from someone else's touch, Celine."

Celine couldn't respond as the tip of Philly's tongue replaced her fingers as she created a heated trail along the nape of Celine's neck and down her spine. Celine squirmed and arched her back as her body finally gave up and succumbed to the pleasure.

"You're so tense. I imagine sitting bent over a sewing machine for hours can do that. You know, this would feel much better if you were lying down." She stood and offered Celine a hand.

Celine sat quietly listening to the internal battle her heart and body waged. In the end, her heart won, but not in the way she would have expected. She was here to free Dinah from Philly's and Curtis's machinations. Her lustful body might betray her, but her heart still belonged to Dinah, and nothing Philly did tonight would take that away. Celine stood, let her dress fall to her hips, wiggled her way out of it, and accepted Philly's hand.

"May I undress you?" Philly asked.

"Now you're asking permission for something?" Celine said.

Philly quirked a brow. "Would you prefer I rip those lacy undergarments from your body? I would hate to ruin such expensive items."

Celine frowned. "I'll do it."

Philly shrugged and began taking off her own clothes as Celine turned her back to her and removed her undergarments. By the time Celine turned back around, Philly was undressed and climbing into her bed. She lay down and offered a hand to Celine. Celine's breath hitched, and she placed a hand to her chest, shaking her head. Philly gazed at her curiously, then her eyes widened in recognition and she sat up in the bed staring in disbelief at Celine.

Philly climbed out of the bed and stood in front of Celine. "It's you! It was you that night in the mask watching with your husband as Val and I fucked for your entertainment."

Celine shook her head in denial. Philly hurried over to a trunk sitting at the end of the bed. She opened it and pulled out a feather mask, an exact replica to the one Celine had worn that night.

Philly held the mask out to Celine. "Put it on."

Celine's fingers trembled lightly as she took the mask from Philly and put it on.

"I'll be damned, it is you. You knew when I came into your shop the night after we met, didn't you?"

Celine nodded.

Philly removed the mask, threw it aside, and took Celine's face gently in her hands. "Do you know I have thought about you constantly since that night? Wondered who you were. If your husband would call on us again to give me the chance to initiate you into the world of Sapphic love. I had the mask made just so I could have women who resembled you wear it when I took them to my bed. Now here we are." Philly ran her hands from Celine's face down to grasp her hands and led her to the bed. "Have you thought about me since then? Of course you have, or you wouldn't have recognized me. Is that why you agreed to this tonight? You were curious?"

Celine finally found the ability to speak. "No, it's not. I agreed because I love Dinah and I won't stand by as you and Curtis manipulate her into something horrible. The fact that I was already attracted to you makes it easier. Like taking a little sugar with medicine to make it more palatable."

Philly grinned. "So, I'm the sugar?"

Celine wanted to slap Philly for turning her meaning around. Philly leaned forward and pressed her lips to Celine's. Celine didn't respond right away, but it didn't stop Philly. She plundered Celine's mouth expertly. Celine gave in, opening her lips to allow Philly's tongue access. Philly managed to distract Celine enough to get them both onto the bed. She straddled Celine as she continued to kiss her with passionate abandon. When Philly ended the kiss, Celine whimpered until Philly began making a heated trail along her throat to her breast and then wrapped her lips around Celine's hardened nipple.

Philly bombarded her with sensual sensations that had her moaning, whimpering, and squirming beneath her. She shifted just enough to be able to slide her fingers down to the juncture of Celine's thighs and slide them into her slick opening as she wrapped her lips around her other nipple. Celine moaned and thrust her hips toward Philly's fingers.

"Mmmm...so wet." Philly pressed her thumb against the nub of pleasure between her legs and delved two fingers deeper within Celine's walls.

Celine cried out as Philly gently removed her fingers. "Look at me, Celine."

"I want to taste you. Do you want me to taste you?" Philly slid her fingers back into Celine and slowly stroked in and out.

Celine threw her head back, moaning in response.

Philly halted her fingers. "That's not an answer, Celine. I want to hear you say it."

"Oh yes, please, I want you to taste me," Celine begged as she spread her legs for Philly.

Philly smiled triumphantly, settled herself between Celine's legs, lowered her head, and moaned. When Philly dipped her tongue into Celine and explored her inner lips the same way she had explored her lips with their passionate kiss, Celine's hips rose off the bed and she grabbed the bedspread to keep from flying off. Philly greedily feasted as she reached up and gently pinched Celine's swollen clitoris between her thumb and index finger. Philly sucked and licked until Celine was shuddering beneath her.

Philly slid up alongside Celine as her body trembled from the aftereffects of her orgasm, and Celine turned away from her.

Philly gently turned her back around. "No, my little flower, there will be no shame tonight, only pleasure. There is no need to be embarrassed with me." Philly spoke in whispered French.

Tears blurred Celine's vision. "But I love Dinah."

"The body and the heart aren't always in agreement," Philly said, proving her words by dipping her head to capture Celine's nipples once again.

Celine's body came alive under Philly's sensual ministrations. Celine buried her fingers in Philly's hair as she left one nipple to pay homage to the other before rising above Celine and capturing her gaze.

"You are so beautiful. Let me make love to you…" Philly continued in whispered French against her lips. "Let me please you…" She placed another kiss along Celine's neck. "I cannot force you to enjoy our time together, but since you are here, you might as well," Philly said before devouring Celine's mouth once again.

"I have something special for you." Philly leaned over to open a small chest on her nightstand.

Celine's eyes widened in surprise as she sat up and watched Philly strap a harness around her hips and thighs. She recognized the contraption from the books Paul had given her. When Philly was done, a rubber dildo protruded from between her legs. Celine had seen various pictures of how women used them on one another and realized that Philly planned to use it with her. Celine was both shocked and curious at the same time.

"I…" She swallowed loudly. "I've never been with a man before."

"You and your husband never made love?"

Celine gazed down, fidgeting with the blanket covering the bed. "Our marriage was for appearances only."

Philly gently grasped Celine's chin, lifting her face to meet her eyes. "As I said, I won't force you to do anything. All I want is to give you pleasure."

Celine saw the sincerity in Philly's eyes and, for a moment, wondered if she told Philly that her pleasure was to leave now would she let her go. As if reading her mind, Philly's gaze hardened.

"I will not force you to do anything you don't want to, but you promised me the whole night and you will stay the whole night, whether we continue with this or not."

Celine gazed down at the phallus cradled between Philly's muscular thighs, remembering a picture of a woman sitting atop another wearing a strap-on like Philly's. The woman on top's head was thrown back in pure abandon as she grasped her own breasts while she rode her lover. That night, Celine had one of her most erotically vivid dreams ever of being the woman who rode with such abandon. She reached out and was just able to grasp the entire width, which left about a half inch of space that kept her fingers from meeting around the other side and was about seven inches in length. It was a smooth ebony black with a bulbous head.

"Will it hurt?" she asked Philly.

"There might be some discomfort in the beginning since you've never been penetrated," Philly answered breathlessly as Celine continued to stroke.

Hesitantly, Celine lay back and met Philly's smoky gaze. "I promised I would be yours for a night…"

Philly looked pleased. "There's no rush." She lay between Celine's legs and let the head of the dildo rest at the juncture of Celine's thighs, then leaned forward and pressed her lips upon Celine's.

"Kiss me, Celine, touch me like you've wanted to since we first laid eyes on each other," Philly whispered against Celine's lips.

The slight pressure of the hard rubber against her clit, Philly's seductive talk, and the pleasure she had given her just moments ago brought Celine's arousal back to the forefront. She grasped Philly by the head and kissed her just as passionately as Philly had done. The longer they kissed, the more Philly shifted and caused the dildo to stroke along Celine's sex. She opened her legs and felt the bulbous head of the dildo rub fully along her lips. The friction caused her sex to throb. She moaned into Philly's mouth.

Philly responded by kissing and licking her way down Celine's body until she lay between her thighs. Within moments, Celine was moaning and whimpering for relief, but instead of giving her the release she wanted, Philly slid back up along her body, stopping to lavish attention on each breast.

"Are you ready for me?" Philly whispered.

Celine, overcome with aching desire, nodded, didn't care what Philly did as long as she gave her the relief her body was craving. It wasn't until she felt Philly's fingers sink into her wetness, then be replaced by the bulbous rubber head of the dildo that she realized what Philly was asking if she was ready for.

Celine tensed. "Relax," Philly said, then took command of her lips once again.

When Celine felt the head of the dildo slip inside her, Philly stopped but continued to overwhelm her with kissing. The sensation of the bulbous head within her was strange to Celine, but as Philly allowed her time to get adjusted, the partial fullness had her inner walls craving more. Philly continued her assault on her lips, then there was a dull pressure as Philly thrust the remainder of the dildo within her, but it was forgotten as the fullness brought on a whole new pleasure Celine didn't think she could experience. Once again, Philly gave her time to adjust to the penetration, but Celine didn't need it. She began moving her hips, and Philly met her thrusts in a sensual rhythm as old as time. When Celine felt her orgasm coming, she pushed on Philly's chest.

"I want to ride you," she said breathlessly.

"Whatever you want, *ma fleur*." Philly eased the dildo out of Celine and then lay on her back. She held the dildo steady as Celine straddled her hips.

Celine slowly lowered herself onto the dildo, moaning with pleasure as the position brought on a whole new set of sensations. She gazed down at Philly, who watched her in awe, and Celine felt that sense of abandon the woman in the photo must have felt. She kept eye contact with Philly as she grasped her breasts, squeezing and massaging the tender nipples.

Philly grasped Celine's hips and met each of her thrusts passionately. As Celine threw her head back and her body tensed for a few seconds as her orgasm crashed through, Philly cried out and her body bucked beneath Celine's.

Both of them lay panting breathlessly for a few moments before Celine slowly rose, climbed off Philly, and lay on the bed with her back to her. Celine curled into a ball, hugging herself, and cried. A moment later Philly curled herself around Celine and held her as she cried herself to sleep.

CHAPTER THIRTEEN

Celine woke momentarily confused about her surroundings, then memories of the previous night came crashing down on her. She scrambled to sit up, pulling the covers up around her to hide her nakedness. She gazed around the room to find that she was alone. Had Philly got what she wanted and left her to find her own way out? She closed her eyes hoping to shut out the wanton things she had done with Philly.

"Ah, you're awake."

Celine opened her eyes to find Philly coming from the bathroom. She sat beside her on the edge of the bed.

"Good morning, *ma fleur*." Philly took Celine's hand and placed a soft kiss on her knuckles.

"I thought you might like a nice warm bath after last night's activities. I ran one for you. There are towels and a dressing robe in there as well. Why don't you go freshen up and I'll get us something to eat," Philly said, before rising and heading out of the room.

Philly had run her bath, was getting her food, and had looked at her with such tenderness that Celine wasn't sure if she was still asleep and dreaming or if Philly had suddenly become another person. Wanting to leave as soon as possible, Celine didn't linger on the thought and shifted to get of out bed. It was then that she noticed the slight soreness between her legs and the light flakes of dried blood on her inner thigh. Tears sprang to her eyes as she remembered that she had allowed Philly to take her virginity, something she had not even let Paul do when he suggested they consummate their marriage on their wedding night. She could tell just by the look on his face that it would not have been the most pleasant thing to do, but he would have done it if she had wanted to. She most certainly had not wanted to, so they had spent the evening gossiping about their wedding guests and eating leftover wedding cake.

She made her way to the bathroom, climbed into the tub, and sank down into the steaming water. She hugged her legs to her chest, laid her head on her knees, and let the tears glide down her face and drip into the bath water. The tears had her remembering how tenderly Philly had held her as she cried last night, trying to comfort her with soothing touches and cooing to her in French and Italian. She had a difficult time reconciling the domineering heartless woman she had been from the moment they met with the tender and soft one from last night and this morning. Celine knew a few tender moments did not mean that Philly could be trusted or that she could let her guard down around her. Philly was an expert manipulator. Celine took a deep breath, wiped the tears from her face, grabbed the cloth and soap sitting on a table beside the tub, and vigorously tried to scrub away the physical, and not so physical, evidence of last night from her body.

When she was finished with her bath and had managed to tame her wild locks, she put on the thin silk robe Philly had left her and marched out of the bathroom ready to battle her way out of this nightmare to go home. She came out of the bathroom to find Philly setting up a coffee service, fruit, and pastries in the seating area in front of the fireplace.

"There you are. I thought maybe you had tried to climb out the window," Philly said.

Celine gazed at her in awe. Even dressed in the male attire she wore all the time and with her constant malicious grin, Philly was a beautiful woman, but seeing her with softened features, a teasing smile, and dressed in a similar robe, it was like looking at a totally different woman. One Celine found her body reacting to, which made her even more anxious to leave. She saw her dress hanging over the back of a chair and headed toward it.

"Leaving so soon?" Philly asked.

Celine struggled to zip the back of the dress. "I gave you what you wanted. I'm assuming I'm free to leave."

"Yes, of course you are. I had just hoped we could enjoy some breakfast, but if you insist on going you might want these."

Celine looked up to find Philly holding one of Celine's dresses, a pair of shoes, and undergarments.

"Your aunt had them brought over a short time ago. I assume she wanted to save you the embarrassment of making your way home in last night's attire."

"Thank you." Celine took the clothes and went back into the bathroom to get dressed. She came out to find Philly munching on a pastry and reading a newspaper.

"Are you sure I can't tempt you with a croissant? My cook is a wizard in the kitchen."

Celine didn't know what to make of Philly's sudden change in demeanor. "No, I just want to leave."

Philly put her pastry and the newspaper down, walked over to Celine, and took her hands. "Last night was wonderful. I hope you enjoyed yourself as well."

Celine slid her hands from Philly's grasp. "Are we done here? Will you and Curtis leave Dinah alone now?"

Philly's soft smile slid from her face, and she flinched as if Celine had slapped her. She turned her back to Celine and went back to where her pastry and the newspaper lay. "Dinah is safe and free to do as she pleases as soon as she pays Curtis what she owes him."

Celine sighed with relief. "Thank you."

"My driver is waiting downstairs to take you home." Philly still had her back to Celine.

"That's kind of you. Thank you." Celine suddenly felt guilty for her brusque dismissal of Philly's question about last night, but her guilt was replaced by anger at the reason she was there at all. With one last look toward the large bed, Celine walked out of the room.

Celine felt as if the drive home would never end. When they arrived, she didn't bother waiting for the driver to come around and open the door. She thanked him and was out of the car before he opened his own door. Celine rushed to the side entrance and was greeted by Olivia, who must have been watching out the window awaiting her arrival. She ran immediately into Olivia's warm embrace, crying more tears than she thought she ever had.

"There, there…let it all out," Olivia soothed her.

After a few moments, Celine took a deep, shaky breath. She allowed Olivia to guide her upstairs to the apartment where she sat forlornly on the sofa.

"Let me get you some tea and we'll talk." Olivia placed a kiss on Celine's forehead and went to their small kitchen.

Celine took the moment to gather herself enough to be able to talk. It would be an uncomfortable conversation, but one she needed to have to figure out how she could still be with Dinah after what she had done.

Thinking about the night once again started a fresh batch of tears that ran down her face as Olivia came back in and handed her a cup of tea.

"I put a little extra courage in there for you." Olivia sat beside her and gently wiped the tears from her face.

Celine took a sip and tasted more whiskey than tea. She drank it all, letting it burn its way down her throat and spread throughout her chest.

"Did she hurt you?" Olivia asked in concern.

Celine shook her head.

"Would you rather not talk about it?"

Celine hesitated in responding. "I'm so ashamed." She stared tearfully down into the empty cup grasped tightly in her hands.

"You have nothing to be ashamed of. You did the only thing you thought you could do to help Dinah. There is no shame in that kind of love."

"It's not the shame of having done it, it's that I enjoyed it. How could I profess to love Dinah, then become the wanton woman I was with Philly last night?"

Olivia took the teacup from her before it shattered within her death grip and grasped her hands. "My dear sweet Celine, the Rousseau women are deeply passionate. Once that passion has been unleashed it's like a dam that has broken with no way of stopping the flow. While I was living in Paris, like you, I fell deeply in love with my first lover, but she knew eventually she would not be enough for me. I argued, but she was right. After just a few months together, I was craving more. She brought in other lovers and we spent a year sharing our bed with many people, men and women, but our love remained as strong as it did when we first professed it to each other." Olivia gazed off at a memory only she could see.

"What happened?" Celine asked.

A look of sadness came over Olivia's face. "She became sick and I lost her."

"Oh, *Tante*, I'm so sorry," Celine said.

"Yes, well, what I'm trying to tell you is that there is no shame in feeling passion for someone else while still being able to love another. Not everyone is made to be with one person their entire lives."

"My mother would disagree with you on that."

Olivia snorted. "Your mother is not the saint she makes herself out to be, but that is not my story to tell. You've had one lover your entire adult life. You've never experienced anything else, so there is bound to be some curiosity and attraction for another. Especially for someone like Philly, who you have fantasized about for years."

"I thought I could do this and purge her from my system, but all it seemed to do was open up a floodgate of feelings that I don't know what to do with. I genuinely love Dinah and I feel just as passionate for her now as I did before last night, but with Philly, I felt a wild abandon I have never experienced with Dinah. I…"

"You what?"

Celine took a deep breath. "I gave Philly my virginity. I gave her what I should've given Paul all those years ago but neither of us had the courage to do."

Olivia looked confused for a moment then realization hit her. "She penetrated you?"

"Yes," Celine answered quietly.

"But she didn't hurt you?"

Judging by the angry look on Olivia's face, Celine suddenly regretted being so open about what happened. "No. She told me I didn't have to do anything I didn't want to do. Paul had given me books and pictures that showed women using a dildo on one another, and memories of how those images made me feel…" Celine found it difficult to go on. "Afterward, I felt so ashamed and guilty I curled up and cried. Philly held me until I cried myself to sleep. Then, when I woke up this morning, she had drawn me a bath and brought us breakfast. I just wanted to leave and did so as soon as I was dressed. She even arranged for her personal driver to bring me home."

"Does Philly know who you are?" Olivia asked.

"She didn't until last night."

"And how did she react?"

"She admitted that she had thought about me…or that woman… for years. Hoping that she would be invited back to perform for us. To entertain me privately."

Olivia now looked worried. "What about your arrangement? Has she released Dinah from any further obligation to her and Curtis?"

"She said Dinah was free to do as she pleased."

"That's all that happened?"

Celine's tears began again. "Wasn't that enough?"

Olivia pulled her into a tight embrace, then pulled away and took Celine's face in her hands. "I'm sure Dinah will be here as quickly as she can, and you can't let her see you this way." She smoothed a lock of hair from Celine's face. "Go get some rest and I'll wake you when she gets here."

Celine nodded. "Thank you, *Tante*." She placed a kiss on Olivia's cheek and went to her bedroom.

Dinah had been lying in bed staring at the ceiling for an hour before she finally decided to get up. She tried to prolong it because getting up meant she would have to go see Celine, and she wasn't sure how she felt about that. There was no doubt that she loved her, especially after what she did last night to help her. She just wasn't sure if she was ready to accept the truth of what she saw last night in Celine's eyes with each caress and touch of Philly's fingers along the open back of her dress. Dinah had seen that same look as she touched and caressed Celine, and she never imagined she would have to witness it from another person's hands. She left the party as soon as she heard Philly had taken Celine upstairs. There was no need for her to stay, and she was grateful when Big T didn't try to stop her. After washing up and putting on the first thing she grabbed out of her closet, Dinah slowly made her way downstairs. She trudged into the kitchen and flopped into a chair at the table.

"Child, what are you doing up already? I thought for sure that you would sleep in after coming in so late last night," Aunt Jo said.

"Good morning, Aunt Jo. I couldn't sleep." Dinah yawned.

Jo always kept a pot of coffee warm on the stove for their boarders. She poured a cup and set it in front of Dinah.

"Well, since you're up, you can help me with some chores. Fran isn't feeling well, so I don't want her to worry about trying to get anything done today."

Dinah looked at the clock in the hall and started to protest. After all, it was already ten in the morning, and Celine had to be back home by now. She should be going to see her, but fear and doubt kept her from doing so. What if Celine was still with Philly? What if she chose to be with Philly instead of her? What if she took one look at Celine and realized it would be too heartbreaking to be with her after she spent the night with Philly?

"Whatever you need," Dinah said.

Jo placed a plate of biscuits with sliced ham in front of her and gave her a kiss atop her head. "You eat a little something and I'll get the toolbox."

Dinah gazed down at the plate of food and felt her stomach knot. She pushed the plate away and got up to get another cup of coffee. As she sipped at the brew, she gazed at the phone on the wall. Maybe if she heard Celine's voice, she could rid herself of the nagging concern wracking her heart and mind. Before she could change her mind, she picked up the phone and had the operator connect her to Olivia's shop.

"*Bon jour*, Rousseau Fashions, how may I help you?"

Dinah almost sighed with relief at hearing Olivia's voice instead of Celine's, then instantly felt guilty for it.

"Hello, Olivia, it's Dinah. May I speak with Celine?"

"Good morning, she's still sleeping," Olivia said.

Dinah was glad to hear Celine had come home already. "Is she... is she, all right?"

Dinah's heart skipped a beat at the silence on the other end of the line. "Olivia..."

"She is struggling," Olivia said.

"Should I come over now?"

"No, give her time. Why don't you come for dinner this evening, around five?"

Dinah felt the knot in her stomach wind even tighter. "I'll be there."

"Dinah, be assured, she loves you very much," Olivia told her.

Tears sprung to Dinah's eyes. "Please tell her I love her too," she said, then hung up the phone.

Dinah leaned against the wall by the phone and silently wept. For what, she wasn't sure. Anger at being the reason for Celine doing what she did, fear at possibly losing Celine, or sadness over what her life had come to? She wiped away her tears when Jo returned.

"Did you talk to her?" she asked.

"No, she's still sleeping."

Jo handed Dinah a handkerchief from her pocket. "Something you should also be doing."

"No, I need to keep busy. Olivia told me to come by for dinner. Maybe I'll lie down for a bit before that." Dinah took the toolbox from Jo. "Until then, what needs to be done?"

❖

Celine woke and, for a moment, blissfully forgot about her night with Philly, but just as quickly the memories and guilt came crashing down on her like a wave slamming onto the shore. The sound of feminine laughter drifted up to her from the shop, and she gazed over at the clock on the mantel to find that it was already noon. She climbed out of bed, dressed, and rushed out of her bedroom.

"Ah, Miss Celine," Simone greeted her. "Your aunt asked me to fix you something to eat when you awoke and to let you know that you have the day off."

"The day off?" Celine said.

"*Oui*, she said, and I quote, 'I do not care how you spend the day, but it will not be cooped up in the shop ruminating about last night,'" Simone said. "Now, I have made you some beignets and prepared a bowl of strawberries with cream." Simone placed a plate of pastries and a bowl of fruit on the table.

Celine was dejected that she wouldn't be able to keep herself busy in the shop. "I'm not really hungry."

Simone pouted. "Well, I suggest you try to eat, or I will be forced to follow her other instructions, and that would not be pleasant."

"What in instructions would those be?"

Simone her arms over her modest bosom. "To tie you to the chair and feed you myself."

Knowing how devoted Simone was to Olivia, Celine had no doubt that Simone would do just as Olivia instructed, so she sat down and, after her first bite of beignet, realized she did have an appetite after all. After two beignets and the whole bowl of strawberries and cream, she thanked Simone, who had sat on the sofa watching her closely to make sure she ate. Celine cleaned the powdered sugar from her hands and clothes and made her way down to the shop.

"I'm only going to speak with my aunt," she said in response to Simone's warning gaze.

Simone nodded and gave her a dismissive wave.

"You look refreshed," Olivia said.

"I do feel a bit less worn than I did earlier," Celine admitted.

Olivia brushed a bit of powdered sugar from Celine's cheek. "Amazing what a bit of sleep and beignets will do for the constitution."

Celine smiled. "It was either eat or get into a wrestling match with your French poodle upstairs."

Olivia chuckled. "Well, since I could not be up there to make sure you took care of yourself, I had to send the next best thing."

"Dinah hasn't come to see me?"

"No, but she called earlier. I told her you were still asleep and invited her over for dinner so that you can talk. In the meantime, I think you both need to take the day to do something other than worry about each other, Curtis, and Philly. Her aunt agreed."

Celine gazed at her suspiciously. "You and Dinah's aunt are now conspiring on our behalf?"

"I'm offended," Olivia said in mock offense. "We are not conspiring, we are looking after our nieces' well-being."

"Mm-hmm," Celine said doubtfully.

"What will you do on this unexpected day off?"

"I ran into Helene at the party last night and she invited me to tea today. I'll call her and ask if she would like to do lunch instead."

"Excellent. Helene is a wonderful lunch companion. You will be in good hands."

"I wasn't aware you and Helene knew each other."

A secretive smile played across Olivia's lips. "We're old friends."

Celine gazed at Olivia curiously. "And why didn't you mention it when you knew we met?"

"There are some things, my dear niece, that I choose to keep close to myself, *c'est la vie*." Olivia gave a soft pat to Celine's cheek. "Now, run along, but be sure to be back by five."

Celine shook her head in amazement. She could only hope to have as many adventures and secrets as Olivia had in her life. As she made her way to Helene's home an hour later, Celine tried not to think about the not-so-secret part of her life last night or what she would say to Dinah when she admitted to enjoying it.

"Ah, *bienvenue, mon ami*." Helene greeted Celine with a kiss on both cheeks.

Celine warmed at the affectionate welcome. "Thank you for having me. My aunt has banned me from the shop for the day, and I was at a loss what to do, so here I am."

Helene looped her arm through Celine's and led her into the dining room. "You are welcome here any time."

They sat across from each other at one end of the large dining table.

"Now, tell me how you ended up in Philly's clutches?" Helene asked as she poured them both glasses of wine.

Celine took a sip, then told Helene the whole sordid tale of her arrangement with Philly.

"Unbelievable! So, she blackmailed you into her bed," Helene said angrily.

Celine gazed up nervously at the maid who served them their lunch. The maid continued as if she had not heard anything that had just been discussed.

"Don't worry about the staff, they are very discreet," Helene said, correctly reading Celine's worried expression. "So how did you leave things with her this morning?"

Celine realized that although she had confirmed Dinah was safe, she had not made it clear to Philly that what happened would not happen again.

Helene read her expression and reached across the table to take her hand. "You didn't truly end it with her."

Celine shook her head. "No, I was more worried about Dinah's safety."

Helene gave Celine's hand a comforting pat, then settled back in her seat and began eating her food. "From what I could see last night, Philly will not let you go so easily. I fear even if you had made it clear that you would not continue with an intimate relationship, she would still have it set in her mind that you are hers. It was obvious to anyone in attendance last night that she had staked her claim on you."

Celine gazed down at the bowl of gumbo and lost her appetite. "Everyone, including Dinah."

"Here is the most difficult question, did you enjoy your time with Philly?" Helene asked.

Celine found it difficult to admit that she had. "Before last night, the only woman I had ever been intimate with was Dinah. I fantasized, but I never imagined love with another woman could be so wonderful." Celine took a moment to form her thoughts. "But with Philly, it was different. I didn't even recognize the woman I was with her."

Helene nodded. "With Dinah, it's passion from the heart. With Philly, it's passion based on a purely physical level. Sometimes that physical passion can overwhelm you and cloud the heart."

"What I feel for Dinah is truly love."

"Have you spoken to her today?"

Celine stirred her gumbo distractedly. "No, she's supposed to come over for dinner this evening so that we can talk."

"Good. You must find a way, together, to deter Philly. If she's able to drive a wedge between you, then she will hammer at it until she gets what she wants, and what she wants, my dear friend, is you."

CHAPTER FOURTEEN

Dinah stood outside the side entrance that led to the apartment above Olivia's shop trying to get up enough nerve to ring the bell. She gazed down at the rum cake Jo had insisted she bring because, no matter what, you never went to someone's house for dinner empty-handed. Dinah hadn't cared about the niceties, she just wanted to see Celine to not only find out if she was all right but if they were all right.

She was just about to ring the bell when the door opened.

"Miss Dinah." Simone gave her a welcoming smile. "Miss Celine is waiting for you." She stepped aside to allow Dinah to pass.

"Have a wonderful evening and I hope all works out for you," Simone said before leaving.

Did everyone know about last night? Dinah slowly climbed the stairs toward the apartment where the delicious aroma of food drifted down to her. She knocked on the door and waited nervously for Celine to answer.

Olivia greeted her with a hug. "Right on time and bearing gifts, I see."

"My aunt's rum cake." Dinah handed the platter to her.

"Oh, how wonderful! I'll put it in the kitchen until we're ready for dessert. Come in, Celine is freshening up. I'll get you a nice glass of wine. You look like you could use it," Olivia said.

"Thank you." Dinah felt disappointment and relief warring with each other at the delay in seeing Celine.

She walked over to the front window that looked out over 125th Street. The street was quiet and practically empty except for a car parked on the other side that she hadn't noticed upon her arrival. She recognized Philly's driver leaning casually on the hood as his gaze met hers. Anger and jealousy heated her blood when he tipped his hat to her.

"He's been there off and on for most of the afternoon," Olivia said from beside her as she handed Dinah a glass filled with wine.

Dinah took it and gulped half the glass down.

"You might want to slow down. You two have a lot to discuss, and I'm sure you'll want a clear head to do it," Olivia said.

"I could use one of those as well," Celine said from behind them.

"I'll get us both a glass." Olivia gave Dinah's arm a reassuring squeeze as she walked away.

Dinah turned and didn't know what she expected to see when she saw Celine, but it wasn't the calm and poised presence that stood before her. Dinah had practically worried herself sick about what Celine might have gone through with Philly and how it would change things between them. Celine looked rested and not the least bit worried about anything, which made Dinah not only a little angry but even more concerned. Neither said a word as they waited for Olivia to return.

Olivia handed Celine a glass, then held hers up. "To the belief that love conquers all." She tapped her glass to each of theirs in a toast.

"I'm going to check on dinner while you two talk. I don't care who talks first, as long as someone does. This silence will solve nothing," Olivia said before leaving them alone again.

Dinah looked guiltily into her wine, as if the answers she sought could be found there.

"How are you?" Celine asked, breaking the uncomfortable silence.

Dinah looked over Celine from head to toe before meeting her eyes once again. "I'm fine. I should be asking you that. Did she hurt you?"

"No, not physically."

Dinah didn't miss the brief look of sadness in Celine's eyes before she looked away. She took her wineglass from her, set both glasses on the coffee table, then took Celine's face in her hands. "Look at me, Celine."

Celine looked up again and her eyes sparkled with unshed tears. "I'm so sorry," she said.

Dinah pulled her into her arms. "You have nothing to be sorry for. I should be apologizing to you for being the reason you had to do it in the first place." She held Celine for a few moments as she silently cried, then Celine stepped out of her embrace.

She started to speak, but Olivia interrupted.

"Dinner is ready. You should both eat something, then I'll go to my room to read so you can talk privately." Olivia set a platter of rolls on the small dining table and went back into the kitchen.

"I should probably help her," Celine said.

Dinah watched her leave the room and had the feeling that she would not like what she was going to hear tonight and preferred to skip dinner altogether just to get the conversation out of the way sooner. Olivia and Celine returned with the rest of their dinner, and they all sat down. It was a quiet and strained affair, and Dinah barely tasted any of the food she ate. She was relieved when it was over. She helped Celine and Olivia clean up, then bid Olivia good night as she left them alone as promised. Dinah sat on the sofa and there was an awkward moment of silence as she waited for Celine to join her, but Celine stood on the threshold of the kitchen and living room, looking as nervous as a skittish cat ready to bolt at the slightest sound.

"Celine, talk to me," Dinah pleaded.

Celine moved over to the window and gazed out. She tensed, and Dinah knew Philly's man was still out there watching the apartment.

"You're no longer obligated to Philly and Curtis. Tomorrow, I'll provide you with the money to pay your contract out and you can leave that life behind without a worry," Celine said.

Dinah knew she should have felt relief from Celine's announcement, but her heart ached at the sadness in her voice. She walked over, wrapped her arms around Celine's waist, and placed a kiss on her temple. Celine relaxed within her arms and Dinah felt a little better.

"If that's true, then why do I get the feeling that you have more to tell me?" Dinah asked.

"You know I love you, don't you?"

This time it was Dinah who tensed. "Yes."

Celine grasped Dinah's hand and led her to the sofa. They sat down, and this time when Dinah met Celine's eyes, she saw how tired she really was.

"Before I tell you what happened with Philly last night, I need to tell you about something that happened before I left New Orleans," Celine said.

Dinah nodded and waited patiently for Celine to speak.

"You already know about the scandalous books and photos Paul used to give me to encourage me to explore my attraction to women and the time he brought women home to entertain me, but all I had the nerve to do was watch from behind a mask," Celine said, nervously picking at a string on her dress.

"Yes." Dinah knew where Celine was going with this. She was trying to tell her how she knew Philly, but Olivia had already told her. Since Olivia had broken Celine's confidence to tell Dinah that information, Dinah thought it would be best not to mention to Celine that she already knew.

"Well, one of the women piqued my interest very much. It was obvious that this woman was genuine in her passion for other women in how attentive she was with her lover and how much she seemed to enjoy what the other woman did to her. At one point, I could no longer hold back my own desire and touched myself as the women made love. The woman who I found myself attracted to locked eyes with me as she was being pleasured and reached out for me to join her, but I couldn't bring myself to do it and continued to only watch as her body flushed and arched in her release, which brought me to my own release."

The scene Celine described played like a moving picture in Dinah's mind and, to her surprise, she found herself getting aroused at the image of Celine pleasuring herself while watching Philly with another woman.

Celine continued. "Not long after that night is when Paul met Robert and we no longer spent evenings like that together, but I found myself fantasizing about the woman and had been considering asking Paul how I could find her so that I could see her privately, but then he was killed and our lives were turned upside down."

Dinah wiped away the tears that fell along Celine's cheeks. "You don't have to talk about this if it causes you pain."

Celine shook her head and looked so sad it broke Dinah's heart. "Yes, I do, because I found out that the woman in New Orleans that night is Philly. I realized it the night she came into the shop to order the fans you used for your performance at her party."

"Did Philly recognize you?" Dinah asked.

"No, she didn't recognize me until last night, right before we..." Celine hesitated then stood and went over to a cart that held a decanter of dark liquid. She poured a small amount in a glass and drank it down. "Right before we were intimate."

"Did she use the information to force you to do anything you didn't want to?" Dinah hoped that was what made Celine pour herself another glass.

"No, everything I did last night I did willingly and derived unexpected pleasure from," Celine said quietly.

Dinah had to tamp down a flare of jealousy that rose at the thought of Philly seeing a side of Celine that she thought she would be the only woman to see. She stood, took the glass from Celine, and set it on the cart before taking her hands. "Celine, I don't want you to feel any guilt over anything that happened last night. It was one night that you don't ever have to repeat. We can be together now. Philly and Curtis will be a thing of the past."

"I don't think Philly is going to give up that easily."

Dinah knew she was referring to Philly having her watched. "You don't have to worry about her bothering you again. I'll take care of it."

When their eyes met, Dinah was relieved to see the tenderness she hoped still resided in Celine's heart after last night. As if knowing she needed reassurance that they would be fine, Celine led Dinah to her bedroom. As soon as the door was closed, Dinah pulled Celine into her arms and poured her whole heart into the kiss she gave her. She was exhilarated when Celine returned the kiss with just as much feeling. Their clothes were off in a matter of moments, and Dinah was thrilled to feel the silky warmth of Celine's skin against her own, to run her hands over Celine's voluptuous curves, to taste the proof of Celine's desire and to hear her moans of pleasure. Then a thought came unbidden to her mind: Philly had explored these same curves, had tasted Celine, and had made her moan.

Were her moans for Philly as passionate as her moans were for Dinah? Had Philly made Celine whimper her name the same way she said Dinah's name? Dinah tried to block the doubts and jealousy that reared their ugly heads, but it was difficult. She mounted Celine, slid a finger into her slick opening, and felt Celine tense beneath her. She looked down at Celine and saw a look of regret mingled with arousal, and she knew in that moment that Philly had taken far more than a night away from Celine.

Dinah shook her head as Celine started to speak. She didn't want to hear any apologies or excuses, she just wanted what they had back. Celine's unspoken words were buried in the onslaught of kisses Dinah gave her as she slid another finger inside her and stroked her clit with her thumb. Dinah devoured Celine's moans as if they were her only source of food and delved her fingers in and out of her as if she could drive everything Philly had done from her body. Dinah was not gentle with her lovemaking, and Celine met every thrust of Dinah's fingers with a frantic desperation that matched her own. When Celine's thigh pressed into Dinah's clit and she felt that familiar tension within Celine's body that told her she had reached her climax, Dinah also let go and climaxed with her. Afterward, Dinah gently removed her fingers and lay beside her.

"Dinah…"

"Shh. You don't need to say anything. It's behind us." Dinah felt her heart breaking.

❖

Celine woke, and the warmth of Dinah's body curled around hers made her want to stay in bed forever. She listened to the sound of Dinah's soft breathing as she remembered last night's lovemaking. It was as if they desperately needed to reassure each other that what happened with Philly didn't matter, but when Dinah's fingers entered her, Celine couldn't help but think about Philly. She had willingly given Philly something she had not earned the right to have. Celine had no idea if Dinah used a dildo. She also had not even given something like that a thought until Philly. Philly had even given her the opportunity to say no, but Celine had allowed her arousal and curiosity to make the decision for her. Her heart ached remembering the look on Dinah's face when she must have realized why Celine had hesitated once she entered her. She knew then that she had broken Dinah's heart and would do whatever it took to make it whole again.

She turned to face Dinah and found her already awake. "Good morning." She placed a soft kiss on Dinah's lips.

Dinah smiled sleepily. "Good morning."

Celine slid her hand down into the patch of hair at the juncture of Dinah's thighs and the treasure buried beneath.

Dinah moaned in response, then stilled Celine's hands. "As much as I would love to play around in bed with you all day, some of us have to work for a living."

Celine groaned as she watched Dinah slip from the bed and search for her clothes. "You could always come live here and let me take care of you the rest of our lives."

"I happen to like going to work every day despite having to depend on the income to live, so thank you but no thank you," Dinah said.

Celine didn't miss the irritated tone in her voice. She got out of bed, put her robe on, and walked over to Dinah. "I didn't mean to offend you. I was only teasing."

Dinah pulled Celine into an embrace. "I know. I haven't gotten much sleep this weekend, so I'm afraid I'm not in the best of moods." She let go and continued to dress.

Celine sat on the bed and watched her. Dinah did look tired, but she also looked sad and Celine knew she was the cause of that sadness. Once Dinah was dressed, Celine walked her out. Before Dinah could leave, Celine grasped her hand and turned her around.

"I love you," Celine said.

Dinah pulled Celine into her arms. "I love you too." She kissed Celine in a way that gave her no doubt that she meant it.

Celine headed back upstairs to start her day. Olivia was exiting her bedroom just as she entered the apartment.

"Good morning, *mon bijou*, has Dinah left without breakfast?" Olivia asked.

Celine followed Olivia into the kitchen. "Yes, she had to go to work, and I'm sure she wanted to go home and freshen up before she did."

"And all is well?" Olivia asked with a side glance.

Celine thought for a moment about last night and how she and Dinah left each other this morning. "No."

"Let's chat." Olivia handed her a cup of tea and sat across from her. "What did you tell her?"

"Everything. Well, most of it, but I think she may have guessed what I didn't say."

"I see. The only thing to do now is to try to move forward."

"And what if she can't? What if I can't?" Celine wiped angrily at a tear that escaped. She was tired of crying. When did she become so emotional?

Olivia shrugged. "What choice do you have? You either move forward with each other or separately, but either way time will not stand still waiting for you."

Celine knew Olivia was right, but she couldn't imagine moving forward without Dinah.

"I came out after you went to bed last night and noticed Philly's watchdog had finally left," Olivia said.

"I hadn't even bothered to check this morning. Hopefully, he reported back to her that Dinah stayed the night, and she'll leave it at that."

Olivia looked doubtful, but Celine didn't want to think about having to deal with Philly insisting on a repeat of their night together. It would only make things more difficult for her and Dinah to move forward in their life together. Celine refused to give up on that life and planned to go see Dinah tonight not only to give her the money for Curtis but also to reassure Dinah that nothing that happened with Philly changed how she felt about her.

❖

That afternoon as Celine worked on a hat in the work room of the shop, the bell above the door signaled someone had entered. Her aunt had gone to lunch with a friend, so Celine was the only one there.

"I'll be right with you," Celine called out.

"Take your time," a woman's voice responded.

Celine quickly set aside her work and made her way to out to the front. "My apologies for keeping you waiting..." She was stopped in her tracks by the sight of Philly leaning casually on the counter "What are you doing here?"

Philly placed a large bouquet of flowers on the counter and bowed as if she were making an offering. "I come bearing gifts."

"I don't want your gifts, Philly. What happened the other night will not happen again."

Philly flinched at Celine's tone, but she kept her smile and continued. "Have dinner with me."

"No," Celine said. She crossed her arms over her chest, determined not to fall for Philly's charm.

Philly slowly approached her, hands held out in supplication, as if she were trying to coax a frightened kitten from the corner. "Just dinner, nothing more."

"Nothing is ever that simple with you, Philly."

Philly stopped within reach of Celine, grasped her arms, and unfolded them from their stiff position. She held Celine's hands gently within hers. "I want to apologize for what I put you through. I shouldn't have used you to get back at Dinah, I know that now. It wasn't fair to put you in that position."

Celine was surprised at Philly's apology. Regret was the last thing she imagined Philly would have. She wasn't quite sure how to respond.

"A nice dinner in a public place, and then I'll bring you straight home," Philly said.

"I can't." Celine slid her hands from Philly's grasp and went behind the counter where she tentatively ran her fingers over the roses Philly had left there.

Philly followed her but stayed on the other side of the counter. "I'm not trying to get between you and Dinah, Celine. I would just like a couple of hours of your time."

Philly ran her fingers over the flowers as well, brushing Celine's hand in the process. Celine's breath hitched, then she snatched her hand away.

"This isn't some scheme to get me in bed again. Just dinner?" Celine asked.

Philly crisscrossed a finger over her heart. "Cross my heart."

"We can go to dinner, but I will meet you at the restaurant."

Philly raised her hands in surrender. "Fair enough. If you have a pen and paper, I can give you the address of the restaurant."

Celine retrieved what Philly asked for and slid it across the counter to her.

"Do you like Italian food?" Philly asked as she wrote.

"Yes."

Philly handed her the paper and pen. "Excellent, one of my cousins owns a restaurant in the Village. Will six o'clock on Friday work for you?"

"Yes, that's fine."

"Until then." Before turning to leave, Philly tipped her hat at Celine, looking far too pleased with herself.

Celine stared at the door for several minutes after Philly left wondering what the hell was wrong with her and what she had just agreed to. She didn't recognize the woman she became around Philly. How could she possibly claim she loved Dinah while she had the most erotic thoughts and feelings about another woman? There was no doubt in her mind that what she felt for Philly had less to do with the fantasies of the masked woman she had held on to all this time and more to do with carnal lust. A physical desire that seemed to override all good sense. She had lain with Philly one night, then with Dinah the next, and found that she still desired Philly.

Celine sat on the stool behind the counter and wiped away tears of confusion. She had to pull herself together before Olivia returned. She would tell her about the dinner but she knew she couldn't tell Dinah and cause her any more worry than she already felt about the whole situation. Fortunately, there would be no need to lie to Dinah about her whereabouts as that would be her final night working a private party for Curtis before she left that life. Celine had gone to the bank shortly after Dinah left in the morning to withdraw the money Dinah owed Curtis. The bright spot Celine saw in all of this was that once Dinah was done with Curtis and Philly, they would have more time together and less time for her to worry about her attraction to Philly. A few loudly chattering ladies entered, interrupting Celine's thoughts and she was relieved to have the distraction.

When Olivia returned from lunch and saw the roses Celine had placed in a vase at the end of the counter, she asked if she missed anything. Celine didn't mention Philly's visit, but she did tell her that the flowers were from Philly and had been delivered to the shop on her behalf. It wasn't an outright lie but more a lie by omission. Later that evening, as she sat across from Olivia eating dinner, her main concern was how to make it clear to Philly that she wanted nothing more to do with her after their dinner, even though she could still feel the soft brush of Philly's fingers across her hands and couldn't help but remember how they felt skimming along her nude body. Celine felt her face flush with heat at the thought.

"What has you blushing so profusely?" Olivia asked.

Celine blushed even more, feeling as if she had just been caught in a compromising situation. "I wasn't completely honest with you earlier. Philly delivered the flowers personally and asked me to have dinner with her."

Olivia only gazed at her curiously. "What did you tell her?"

Celine hesitated in answering, lowering her gaze to her plate. "I told her I would go."

"I see." Olivia went back to eating her dinner.

Celine looked up at her, not sure what response she expected, but she'd thought it would be more opinionated than that. "You have no opinion on it?"

"Should I?" Olivia said.

"So, you approve of me going to dinner with Philly?"

"Celine, I'm not your parents. This is your life. How you choose to live it and who you choose to spend your time with doesn't require my approval."

Celine was at a loss as to what to say. There was a tone in her aunt's voice that could've been disapproval, but she wasn't sure. Did she want Olivia's approval or for her to talk her out of going? Thinking further on it, she realized she wanted the latter. She could have simply turned Philly down, told her she was no longer interested in any further contact with her, ended it right then and there, but she didn't. Why, suddenly, couldn't she make a rational decision when it came to Philly?

"I…I'm at a loss as to what to do about Philly and would appreciate your advice on the matter," Celine hesitantly admitted.

Olivia seemed to seriously consider her response before speaking. She set her dinner aside and looked at Celine with sympathy. "I can only imagine being in your shoes right now. With that in mind, I can only advise you as to what I would do if I were. If I were you, I would nip whatever this is with Philly in the bud if you want to be with Dinah. If you continue this way you will cause yourself further confusion, give Philly permission to continue her pursuit of you, and cause Dinah heartbreak."

Celine knew Olivia was right. "I'll cancel dinner with Philly."

"Is that what you truly want to do?" Olivia asked.

"I honestly don't know what I want." Celine ran her hand through her hair. "Actually, I think I want too much. The love I have for Dinah is what I've wanted to spend a lifetime sharing with someone. The purely physical desire I have with Philly is what I craved for so long during my marriage to Paul that I practically became obsessed with the fantasy of it."

"Can you not have love and desire with Dinah?"

"The passion and love with Dinah is so pure and simple that I feel like the uninhibited woman I am with Philly would dirty it somehow."

Olivia reached across the table and took Celine's hand. "Have you spoken to Dinah about this?"

Celine shook her head. "I don't know if I can. She already seems so hurt by what happened between Philly and me that to admit to her that I still have such carnal feelings for Philly would be like throwing salt into the wound."

"I understand that, but you made the decision to go through with your night with Philly to help her. You will need to talk about it at some point or it will cause more harm than good and your sacrifice will have been for naught."

Celine threw her head back and groaned. "You're right, of course."

Olivia pat Celine's hand and stood. "I usually am." She picked up both of their plates.

Celine chuckled and helped her clean up dinner, then decided to do something she hoped she wouldn't regret.

"I'm going to go talk to Dinah," Celine said.

Olivia nodded. "Good idea."

Celine seriously hoped it was a good idea.

CHAPTER FIFTEEN

Dinah was helping her aunt clean up after dinner when Fran came in and told her Celine was there to see her. She felt happy and relieved. She didn't like the way she had left things with Celine that morning.

Fran shooed her out of the kitchen. "Go, I'll finish helping Jo."

"Thank you." Dinah gave Fran a quick peck on the cheek and hurried from the kitchen.

Celine stood in the middle of the parlor wringing her hands nervously. When she looked up at Dinah her eyes shone brightly with unshed tears. Dinah immediately pulled her into her arms and held her as she softly cried.

"What's wrong? What's happened?" Dinah asked.

"I needed to talk to you," Celine said.

Dinah led Celine over to the sofa to sit down. Celine pulled a handkerchief from her purse to dab at her face. Even with a puffy face and red eyes, Celine was still beautiful.

"Are Olivia and your parents all right?" Dinah asked.

Celine sniffed. "They're fine. It's me. I think I made a mistake and thought it was important for us to talk about it."

Dinah felt a tightness in her chest. She just knew Celine was here to break it off with her. Dinah felt as if she had ruined things between them and wouldn't blame Celine for not wanting to see her again.

"All right, what happened?" Dinah asked.

"Philly came to see me today. She wants to take me to dinner to apologize for using me to get back at you. She says she realizes how wrong that was and feels bad about it."

Dinah snorted in derision. "Philly has never been sorry for anything a day in her life. I'm assuming you turned her down."

Celine averted her gaze. "I told her I would go. She promised that it would be only dinner, nothing more."

Dinah felt as if she had been punched in the chest. She drew in a slow steady breath. "And you believe her? After everything she's done, do you actually believe that's all she wants? Philly has never done anything that wouldn't benefit Philly."

Celine stood and began pacing in front of Dinah. "You don't think I thought about that? That she could be up to something?" She stopped and looked at Dinah pleadingly. "That's why I'm here. I need to understand how I could love you and, after all her scheming and manipulations, still fall for Philly's games."

Dinah could hear the anguish in Celine's tone and see the indecision in her eyes. She began her pacing again.

"What is wrong with me that I could be so fickle?" she said in despair.

Dinah stood and made Celine stop her pacing to look at her. "Celine, there's nothing wrong with you. You're confused. You aren't the first woman Philly has twisted up like this and probably won't be the last. I should've never let you spend the night with her."

"Dinah, I don't regret doing it. I would do it all over again if it meant your freedom. I just don't know how to handle all of this. It's like I have everything I could want in you, yet I still want more."

"Is that more Philly? Do you have feelings for her?" Dinah wasn't sure if she wanted to know the answer, but she had to ask.

"No, not like I have for you. I truly love you. I lust after Philly. It's like I'm a different woman with her than I am with you."

"How? What's keeping you from being that way with me? Is it me? Do I not satisfy you?"

Celine stroked Dinah's cheek. "Oh, Dinah, you're a wonderful and generous lover. I know I don't have much to compare it to, but I can't imagine anyone being so loving in bed."

"Then what is it? What does Philly do for you that I don't?" Dinah tried to control her rising frustration. Celine was still new to all of this and needed patience to help her understand what she was going through, not jealousy and anger.

"It's not what Philly does for me but how I am with her that's different than I am with you. I feel like I need to hold back with you because I don't want to disgust you or push you away because I'm too wanton."

Dinah grinned at Celine. "I took you to a sex party, which I used to help host. Do you really think there's anything I would think was too wanton?"

A blush crept across Celine's cheeks. "I guess not."

Dinah took Celine's face in her hands. "Celine, don't ever feel embarrassed or ashamed to share anything with me. All I want is to please you and make you happy. If we have to go to more of Helene's gatherings to do so, then we will." She gave Celine a soft kiss that made her ache for more.

"Would it be too scandalous if we went to your room right now?" Celine whispered, her blush darkening.

Dinah grinned. "Probably, but I don't think anyone will notice."

She took Celine's hand and led her to her room. Once they were there, Dinah was filled with a hunger for Celine like she had never felt before. They began to make love and suddenly thoughts of Philly clouded her passion. She tried to shake it off, tried to lose herself in desire, but Celine's admission that she still desired Philly held her back. She moved off Celine and buried her face in her hands.

Celine knelt beside her. "What's wrong?"

"I don't know if I can do this. I can't help but see you with Philly." Dinah felt tears of frustration gathering in her eyes. She took Celine's face in her hands. "I love you, Celine. More than I ever thought I could love anybody, but it hurts to know you were with her. It hurts to know I sent you into her arms and now you're torn between wanting both of us and it's my fault."

Celine's eyes filled with tears. "What are you saying?"

Dinah took a deep, shaky breath. "I need time. I need to be able to touch you without wondering if you enjoyed Philly's touch more than mine. If you're thinking about her while you're with me."

Celine covered her mouth, muffling the sound of a cry, and left Dinah's bed. Dinah could only watch as Celine dressed, with tears streaming down her cheeks, then headed toward the door.

"I'll give you all the time you need. I'm so sorry, Dinah. I only wanted to help you so that we could be together, and all I've done is driven us apart."

Dinah had no experience with a love like she felt for Celine. She had kept her relationships with other women on a friendly or purely sexual basis. These feelings of jealousy and doubt were new to her, and she didn't know how to handle them overwhelming her usual clear thinking as they were presently doing. She made no move to stop

Celine from leaving. Once the door closed behind her, Dinah grabbed one of her pillows, buried her face in it, and wept as her heart shattered.

❖

During the long taxi ride downtown to meet Philly, Celine worried that she was making a mistake, especially after what happened with Dinah the last time they were together. It had been a week but tears still clouded her vision every time she thought about how heartbroken and vulnerable Dinah looked as she left. Celine had stood outside Dinah's room for a moment, considering going back in to convince her that she had nothing to worry about with Philly. That they could find a way, together, to get past this, but the sound of muffled crying had stopped her. Besides, what could Celine do to make Dinah stop seeing what she herself couldn't stop envisioning more than she cared to? She and Philly together.

Celine arrived at the restaurant and took a moment to gather her nerve before walking into the little bistro-style place. Philly waved to her from a table that sat right in the middle of the restaurant and stood as she approached.

"You look lovely tonight," Philly said.

"Thank you. You do as well," Celine said. "It's nice to see you in something other than a suit."

"Thank you. Would you like some wine?" She indicated the bottle in an ice bucket beside the table.

"Yes, please." Celine hoped Philly didn't notice the nervous shake to her fingers as she picked up her glass. "I've never been this far downtown before."

Philly grinned. "I'm not surprised. Most people who come to the Village are looking for more risqué entertainment that they can't find uptown."

"And what kind of entertainment would that be?"

Philly signaled the waiter over. "Why don't we order first. I'll tell you all about it. Maybe, if you're feeling bold this evening, we can visit one of my favorite establishments for after-dinner drinks."

"I don't want to be out too late."

"I understand. Just one drink and then I'll personally escort you home."

Celine shook her head. "You don't have to do that. I'll be happy to take a taxi back home."

"I won't hear of it. Besides, it's difficult to get a taxi down here and I wouldn't feel comfortable having you wandering around looking for one."

"All right. Thank you."

Philly nodded. "Good. Now, the food here is excellent. There's no official menu, as it changes nightly, so our waiter will tell us what's available tonight. Does that work for you?"

"Yes." Celine was not used to this courteous and attentive version of Philly. She had been given a peek of it the morning after their night together, but that was nothing compared to the full version sitting across from her now. It was disconcerting.

Philly nodded at the waiter to indicate he could proceed. As they listened to him, Philly refilled Celine's glass before she could protest. She needed her wits about her to get through this. They ordered their food and Celine sipped at her wine as she looked around the restaurant, which was growing more crowded by the minute.

"This looks like a very popular establishment," Celine said.

"Frankie does well for herself. Since she does most of the cooking, you have to get here early or there will be a line out the door and you'll still have to wait at least an hour for your food once you finally get seated. Believe me when I say it's well worth the wait."

"I take it you come here a lot."

Philly nodded. "I like to support family whenever I can."

"I assumed Big T was the only family you had here. I thought you were from Philadelphia."

"Philadelphia was where I grew up. Like you, I was born in Louisiana. Baton Rouge, to be exact."

Celine's eyes widened at that revelation. "My father's family is from Baton Rouge."

"Really? Unfortunately, I wasn't there for long. My mother moved us up North shortly after I was born. A certain shipping magnate's family wasn't too happy to find out about his quadroon mistress and illegitimate child."

"Oh, I'm sorry." Celine looked away, embarrassed.

Philly chuckled. "Why are you sorry? It wasn't your family that ran us out of town. I'm not ashamed of my past. My mother did what she had to do to survive. I'm sure you know, back then, quadroon balls were the only way many Colored women in New Orleans were able to escape a life of poverty and degradation. Most children from those relationships grew up to be very well taken care of. I wasn't so lucky. My father was killed just weeks before I was born."

"Is your mother still in Philadelphia?"

Philly poured her more wine. "No, she died when I was sixteen years old. I've been on my own ever since."

"Judging by what I've seen, you've done quite well for yourself."

"So, what brought you to Harlem? If I remember correctly, you and your husband were doing well for yourselves," Philly said.

Celine took a sip of her win, giving herself a moment to decide whether to tell Philly about Paul. Dinah had been the only person she had shared her story with.

Philly must have noticed her hesitation. "I'm sorry. I didn't mean to pry."

"No need to apologize. My story isn't so simple."

"Another man who was thinking with what was between his legs instead of his ears?" Philly said.

Celine giggled, then frowned at herself. She better get some food in her before she got too far into her cups.

"Paul was in love. Sometimes love makes you do things you never thought you would do." Celine looked pointedly at Philly.

"Touché."

Their food was brought out and conversation was halted for them to eat.

"This is divine," Celine said.

"I'm glad you're enjoying it."

Celine looked at Philly's plate, then up at her. "Why aren't you eating?"

"I'm enjoying watching you."

Celine felt her face heat with a blush and she avoided looking at Philly. Philly asked Celine about her childhood, how she started making hats, and if she planned to open her own shop one day. When Celine asked about her work, Philly told her how she got her start in dancing and all that followed.

"I came back to New York to find a business to invest in and then I'll probably head back down to Atlantic City at the end of the year," Philly said.

"So, this isn't a permanent trip?"

"Not unless there's something, or someone, that keeps me here." The look Philly gave Celine said far more than words could have.

To Celine's relief, they were interrupted by the waiter clearing his throat.

"Will you be ordering dessert, Miss Manucci?" he asked.

Celine took a sip of wine. Was this still her second or third glass? She had lost track because Philly had kept refilling it before she could fully finish one.

"Yes, could you bring us a bowl of chocolate gelato with two spoons."

"I don't think I could eat another bite," Celine said.

"There's always room for gelato."

Their dinner was cleared, and the bowl of gelato Philly ordered was set between them.

Celine looked at it curiously. "It looks like ice cream."

Philly gasped dramatically and placed a hand over her chest as if she had been wounded. "My God, that's a sacrilege!"

Celine laughed. "My apologies, I didn't mean to offend."

Philly smiled, scooped a spoonful up, and offered it to Celine. "If this were ice cream, it would be the ice cream of the gods."

Celine allowed Philly to feed her, closed her eyes, and moaned in pleasure as she tasted the rich frozen dessert. When she opened her eyes again Philly watched her with eyes darkened with desire.

"More?" Philly offered.

Celine nodded, her lips parting in anticipation of another spoonful, and Philly obliged her. They shared the remainder of the dessert, and before their last spoonful, Philly had signaled the waiter to bring her the check. Philly stood, offered her arm to Celine, and they left the restaurant. They strolled along, Philly's driver slowly following in the street. They went about three blocks before Philly stopped at a brownstone with music drifting up from the lower entrance. There was no sign to tell what the building was, but it was obviously busy judging by the all the laughter and noise that could be heard when someone opened the door to leave.

"Are you ready for a little adventure?" Philly said.

Celine knew she should just go home, but the thought of another sleepless night of tears and worry wasn't appealing. "Yes."

Philly grinned, led Celine down the steps, and held the door open for her. A large, masculine dressed woman sat on a stool just inside the door and stood at their entrance.

"Philly! I heard you were in town." The woman grabbed Philly up into a hug so tight Celine had to release Philly's hand or she would have been pulled up along with her.

"Cat, you're gonna break a rib," Philly said.

Cat gently set Philly down. "I'm sorry, Philly. It's just so good to see you." Cat looked over at Celine appreciatively. "And who is this beautiful doll?"

Philly took Celine's hand and brought her up alongside her. "Cat Greene, I'd like you to meet Celine Montré."

"Ooh, sounds French. Boon joor," Cat said, taking Celine's free hand, bending over it, and placing a gentlemanly kiss on the back of it.

Celine held back a giggle. "*Bon jour*, Cat. It's nice to meet you."

Celine's face heated at the awkwardness of Cat staring at her as if she were transfixed. Philly had to snap her fingers in Cat's face to get her attention.

"Cat, did my shipment arrive?"

"Uh, yeah, Benjie has it behind the bar. We weren't expecting you so your table is being used, but I can clear it out if you like," Cat offered.

"No, we'll sit at the bar. Besides, the band sounds great tonight, so I think we'll be doing a little dancing if Celine is of the mind to shake a leg," Philly said.

Celine nodded excitedly. "Yes, I'd like that."

"Whatever the lady wants, the lady shall have." Philly winked.

Philly led Celine through the shimmying and shaking bodies on the dance floor toward the bar, where she ordered a bottle of the house special and soda water. The bartender set an unlabeled bottle on the counter with a bottle of soda water and two glasses and tipped her hat at Philly.

"On the house, boss," she said.

"Thanks, Benjie," Philly said.

Philly poured liquid from the unlabeled bottle into a glass, watered it down a bit with the soda water, and handed it to Celine, then poured a half a glass straight up for herself. Celine was about to drink hers when Philly halted her hand and leaned close to her ear to be heard over the music.

"That's pretty strong, take it slow."

Celine nodded and sipped at the beverage, and her eyes widened in shock as she went into a coughing fit. Philly took her glass and gently patted her on the back.

"What is that?" Celine wheezed out between coughs.

"Moonshine, my own recipe."

Celine's coughing stopped, but her face felt flushed. "Tastes like it would peel paint off a wall."

Philly laughed. "It probably could. Here, let me water it down a little more for you."

She poured more water in the glass and handed it back to Celine, who sipped it tentatively. "That's more tolerable."

The band went into a rendition of one of the newest jazz hits, "Sweet Georgia Brown," and Celine grabbed Philly's hand. "I believe you promised me a dance."

Philly let Celine lead her on to the floor. Celine began dancing the Lindy Hop right along with many of the other dancers on the floor. It wasn't a large space, but they made use of every bit of it as they shook, shimmied, and hopped around in wild joy. Before coming to Harlem, Celine's only experience with dancing was the sedate and stiff dances done at balls and cotillions. When she began going out to the clubs and bars with Olivia and her friends, she was introduced to a whole new world of joy and abandon and took to it like a fish to water.

After the band kept the crowd going with two more upbeat songs, they finally switched to a slow-tempo jazz song. Philly began to pull Celine close but she stepped back.

"I think I should be heading home now," Celine said.

Philly looked disappointed. "Of course. My driver should be right out front." She placed an arm around Celine's waist to guide her out of the club.

As soon as they exited, her driver spotted them and held open the car door for them. Philly helped Celine, then climbed in after her. Celine gazed out the window watching the scenery pass by trying to clear the slightly inebriated haze her mind was in. For just a moment, as Philly was pulling her into her arms, Celine wanted to give in and just let go, to lose herself in the mindless passion she knew waited for her in Philly's arms, but remembering Dinah sitting beautifully naked but looking so heartbroken on her bed kept her from doing so.

"You are so beautiful," Philly said in awe.

Celine turned to her with unshed tears pricking her eyes. "Philly, after tonight we can't see each other like this again. I can't do that to Dinah."

"Is that what you want?"

Celine lowered her gaze to her hands folded in her lap. "I know I love Dinah, and I can't bear to hurt her."

"I understand that, but is it what you want?" Philly reached over and gently lifted Celine's chin to meet her eyes.

Celine bit her lip. Why did she hesitate in answering Philly? It was a simple question, but she couldn't give a simple answer. Celine had spent her life like a princess locked away in a safe little tower of denial. Denying who she truly was, denying herself joy and passion, denying herself freedom. Since moving to Harlem, she had tasted all of that and didn't want to give it up. Philly was a long-awaited fantasy come to life, offering her the uninhibited passion she had denied herself for so long. Dinah was the love she had always wanted, offering her a passionate love she couldn't have with Paul. Both led her down a path she never believed was possible. The indecision lay in what ultimately those paths led to. With Philly there would be no love, just passion that would eventually come to an end because Celine believed passion without love could not be sustained. With Dinah, Celine wasn't sure if they would be able to work past how her night with Philly affected Dinah. She could barely touch Celine the other night, so where would that leave them? Love without the passion that Dinah had already shown her. As much as she loved Dinah, could she live that way now that she'd discovered that passion?

Philly took advantage of Celine's silence, leaning forward and pressing her lips to Celine's. Surprised by the kiss, Celine, tipsy and confused by the battle between her heart and body, didn't immediately pull away, so Philly did what she seemed to be a master at doing, overwhelmed Celine with passion. While she devoured Celine's lips, she attempted to unbutton her blouse. That brought Celine to her senses. She shoved Philly away and scooted as far into the corner of the seat as she could, holding her hands up in front of her like a shield to fend off any further advances.

"No! I can't do this!" Tears streamed down her face even as her body thrummed with desire.

Philly's eyes narrowed. "You want me, why are you fighting it?"

Celine could only shake her head because Philly was right. She did want her. Wanted her as much as she did the night Philly beckoned her from that guest room bed.

It took Celine a moment to realize that the car had stopped. They sat in front of the shop. The lights were out, and although there were plenty of people out and about, no one gave the car anything but a passing glance. Celine fled from the car before Philly's driver could open the door. She fled up the alleyway and refused to look back to see if Philly followed. With tears clouding her vision, she fumbled through her purse to find her keys and managed to get the door open without incident. She shut and locked it behind her and put her back to the door for extra measure in case Philly did follow her. After a few moments of silence from the other side of the door, she heard a motor starting and moving away in the distance. She hadn't realized she had been holding her breath until a shuddering sigh escaped at the sound of Philly's car leaving. She allowed the tears to fall but refused to give in to her body wanting to collapse in the stairwell. Climbing the stairs felt like climbing a mountain, and she sighed with relief when she reached the top. Celine placed the key in the lock and found the door unlocked. She walked into the apartment expecting to see Olivia but was surprised to find Dinah standing in the middle of the room with such a look of sadness that Celine almost turned around and fled.

Chapter Sixteen

"Dinah, I thought you were working tonight."

Dinah took one look at Celine's guilty expression and what had to be kiss-swollen lips and almost walked out of the apartment.

"I received the money you sent over and gave it to Curtis, then I told him I was done, so I thought I'd surprise you. I came to the shop and your aunt told me you had gone to dinner with Philly." Dinah tried to keep her tone calm despite wanting to scream.

Even though she was aware of Philly asking Celine to dinner, Dinah had hoped Celine wouldn't go. That maybe she had been wrong to doubt Celine's love and to be jealous of the passion she shared with Philly, but judging by the look on Dinah's face, that wasn't the case.

Celine looked around the apartment. "Where is my aunt?"

Dinah looked at Celine, silently begging her to tell her she was wrong to think the way she was. "She's in her room. When we saw Philly's car pull up, she thought it would be best to give us some time alone."

Celine closed her eyes and took a shaky breath before looking at Dinah again. "I met Philly for dinner to end things with us. To make sure she knew that I didn't want to see her anymore."

"And did you end things?"

"Yes."

"And that's all that happened? I've been waiting here for a few hours. Olivia said you had just left. Where have you been all this time?"

Dinah new she sounded like a jealous harpy, but she couldn't help it. All manner of thoughts about where Celine was and what she was doing had run through her head, and none of them were good.

Celine's face darkened with a blush. "We went to a club near the restaurant for a drink and dancing. If I had known you were waiting, I would have come straight back."

Dinah balled her hands into fists at her sides, she was trying extremely hard not to lose her temper. "So, you went to dinner to end things with her but still went dancing. You're telling me that's all that happened?"

"She kissed me in the car, but I stopped it from going further than that." Celine's eyes shone with tears.

"Did she force herself on you?" Dinah could feel her nails biting into her palms.

"It was just a kiss. Nothing more."

"Did you want it to be more?"

Celine shook her head, seeming to be at a loss for words.

Dinah let the tears that she had held back fall. "After everything, after I told you how I felt, you still wanted her?" Dinah didn't think it was possible to breathe with her chest aching the way it was.

Celine reached for Dinah. "Dinah—"

Dinah held up her hand to stop Celine from speaking. "If you lie to me, Celine, I swear I will not be responsible for my actions."

"Dinah, I wouldn't have let anything happen," Celine said feebly.

"Oh, I'm sorry, so you wanting to fuck her but not doing it makes it so much better," Dinah said, then marched past Celine toward the door.

Celine rushed ahead of her and blocked her exit. "Dinah, please, let me explain."

"Explain what, Celine? That this was all a lie? That I was just something to entertain you until something better came along?"

Celine grabbed Dinah's hands. "No, I love you. Philly has nothing to do with how I feel about you."

Dinah snatched her hands away and stepped back from Celine. "She has everything to do with how you feel about me. If you love me, Celine, then I should be enough for you, but obviously I'm not, or you wouldn't want Philly."

"I wouldn't have even been with Philly in the first place if I hadn't spent the night with her to help you," Celine said angrily.

Dinah's eyes widened. "So, it's my fault you almost let her fuck you in the back seat of her car with her driver right there?"

"Please don't use that vulgar term," Celine said.

Dinah gasped dramatically. "Oh, I'm sorry, is it hurting your genteel sensibilities? Well, what else would you call it? Did you make love to Philly?"

"I was happy simply being with you. With you, I felt free to be me and that I could live a life Paul and I could only dream of. With you, I was finally able to understand how Paul felt and how he would risk anything to be with the man he loved." Celine stalked away from Dinah and stared out the window. "I risked everything to be with you. I turned my back on my parents to be with you. I risked putting both of us in danger trying to go toe-to-toe paying off a gangster's contract on you." She turned back to Dinah. "I risked our love by sleeping with another woman to be with you, so you have no right to make me feel guilty for feelings I never expected to have as a result of it."

Dinah knew she was wrong for trying to make Celine feel as if the affair with Philly was what she wanted all along.

Tears slid down Dinah's cheeks. "I thought I could handle this. I thought we could just put what happened behind us and move on with our lives, but it's obvious that it's not that simple."

Celine held her hands out to Dinah beseechingly. "Dinah, please…"

Dinah shook her head and stepped out of Celine's reach. "I can't do this. I can't touch you, look at you, or even think of you without seeing you with Philly."

"But I love you. What happened with Philly is over," Celine said.

"I love you too, but I think you're wrong, and it wouldn't be fair to either of us to fool ourselves into thinking it is." Dinah turned away, walked out the door, possibly out of Celine's life, and it felt as if her world were crashing down around her.

As soon as the door closed behind Dinah, Celine collapsed into a heap on the floor and sobbed uncontrollably. A moment later, she felt arms circle around her as she was pulled into Olivia's comforting embrace. They sat on the floor for several minutes as Celine wept from the pain of her heart breaking and having caused Dinah's heartbreak as well. Before tonight she could have blamed everything on Philly's scheming, but what she did tonight could not be blamed on anyone but herself. In the back of her mind she knew Philly was probably scheming to seduce her and she still allowed it to happen. What did that say about her? What kind of woman did that make her?

When she finally cried all the tears she thought possible, Celine found she was too tired and weak to move.

"Come, *mon bijou.*" Olivia helped Celine up from the floor.

Celine allowed Olivia to guide her into her bedroom and assist her to undress. She climbed wearily into bed, and Olivia tucked her in and placed a soft kiss on her forehead as if she were a sickly child. Heartsick was more like it, Celine thought as she felt tears gather in her eyes once again when Olivia left the room. Just when she thought she had no more tears left, she quietly cried herself into a fitful sleep.

Celine peeked out from under her covers as Olivia breezed into her room, opening the curtains and windows to allow much-needed sunlight and fresh air into the room.

"Celine Montré, I will not allow you to wallow in self-pity any longer." Olivia stood over Celine's bed with her arms crossed and a glare that said she would not stand for any arguments saying otherwise.

Celine moaned and pulled the covers back over her face. Olivia immediately yanked them off her and the bed.

"It's been three days since you've done more than get out of that bed to relieve yourself."

Celine sat up in the bed. She realized that she was smelling a bit ripe and that her room was hot and musty from her being shut in.

Olivia headed toward the door. "Clean up and get dressed. I'll fix us some lunch and we can talk."

Celine gazed at her retreating figure in confusion. Lunch? She looked at the clock on her dresser and realized it was just after noon. She would have slept another whole day away if Olivia had not intervened. She dragged herself over to her dressing table and gazed at her reflection in the mirror. She barely recognized the frizzled-haired, puffy-eyed, pale woman who stared back at her.

"Is this what heartbreak looks like?" she said to her reflection.

Celine made her way to the bathroom, took a quick but much-needed bath, washed her hair, and brushed the mass of shoulder-length curls into a presentable chignon. Looking through her wardrobe, she shunned all the vibrant and fashionable outfits and settled on a gray skirt and white blouse to fit her drab mood. When she looked in the mirror again the only thing left was the dark circles under her eyes. Not caring enough to hide them with any makeup, she joined Olivia in the kitchen.

"Not quite what I was hoping for but much better," Olivia said when she entered the room and accepted the kiss Celine placed on her cheek.

Celine wrinkled her nose at the plate of eggs Olivia placed before her on the table. "I don't think I can stomach anything more than toast right now."

Olivia replaced the plate of eggs with a smaller plate of croissants and butter. Celine didn't bother with the butter. She just tore small pieces of the flaky bread off and ate it plain.

Olivia sat across from her with a cup of tea. "Would you like to talk about what happened?"

"Not really."

"Well, how about I talk, and you listen."

Celine's shoulders drooped in resignation. As much as she didn't want to hear what Olivia had to say, she knew that it would be something she probably needed to hear.

"What you did for Dinah was very admirable, but for a young woman in your position who is just learning to understand herself and her needs, it was also very foolish and was bound to lead to heartbreak." Olivia held up a hand to stop whatever protest she was about to make.

"I am not saying you were foolish. I'm saying you went into the situation naïvely because of your inexperience. You come from a passionate stock of women. Your mother included."

Olivia folded her hands in her lap. "I said I wouldn't tell your mother's story, but I will tell you that the life she led before your father came along would make me look tame in comparison. Our mother also shared a healthy sexual appetite and was not the least bit ashamed about it. What surprises me is that it took you so long to discover yours. It's too bad that you held yourself back from exploring like Paul did, or this might have ended a lot differently."

"Are you saying because of this, as you call it, 'appetite' that has been passed along to me, I won't be able to find love? I'm destined to be a slave to my cravings?"

Olivia grasped her hands across the table. "Not at all. I'm simply saying that you may need to take time to explore and discover who you really are and what you genuinely want before committing to someone. Your mother eventually found your father, and I..." Olivia trailed off, looking away.

Celine gazed at Olivia curiously. "Have you never found that someone to make you want to settle down to love?"

There was a look of sadness in Olivia's eyes. "Yes, but unfortunately, she was in the same situation you are, exploring who she was, and not in the same mind I was at the time."

"I'm sorry," Celine said sympathetically.

"Don't be. If you live long enough, sometimes life comes full circle and what you may have lost once could unexpectantly return to you again." Olivia gave her a secretive smile, then tried to look serious once again. "We're not talking about me. We're talking about your situation."

Celine hid her amusement at the surprising blush that came across Olivia's cheeks. She would have to remember to ask her about that later.

"So, what do you suggest I do?"

"You may not like what I have to suggest, but I think it would be best for everyone involved."

Celine looked at Olivia warily. "Just say it."

"It's obvious you feel something for Antonia." Olivia once again raised a hand to keep her from protesting. "Whether it's just physical or otherwise, they're feelings you can't so easily dismiss. You need to find out what they are before you can either fix things with Dinah or continue causing even more heartbreak."

Celine looked at Olivia as if she'd lost her senses. "You're encouraging me to be with Philly?" Celine couldn't bring herself to call Philly by her given name, as it would humanize her too much for Celine to continue thinking of her as the villain in all of this.

"I'm not encouraging you. I would prefer you to stay as far away from her as possible, but from what I can see, she represents something more to you than you're willing to admit, even to yourself. Until you know for sure that Antonia is nothing more than a passing fancy, you will not be able to move on."

As much as she didn't want to admit it, Celine could see the reasoning behind what Olivia was suggesting. "But what about Dinah?"

"Dinah has just as much to figure out as you do. To blame you for the consequences of the events she helped to bring about was unfair, and until she can clearly see and admit to her part in it, she won't be able to forgive you."

Celine thought about both Dinah and Philly, and the image she saw at Helene's party of the two women blurring into Dinah and Philly came to mind. They were both such complete opposites, yet they seemed to represent two parts of herself that she couldn't fight. Dinah represented the true love she had always wanted. Not that she and Paul didn't love each other. If anything, until Dinah, he was the only honest relationship she had in her life, but the lack of intimacy cheated them both out of a deeply loving relationship. She now realized that was probably what Paul thought he'd found with Robert and why he'd risked it all to be with him.

Philly, on the other hand, represented the part of Celine she had managed to keep in check despite the temptations Paul laid before her. Philly showed her the woman she could have been while Paul was alive. The woman who could have saved him from himself because maybe, just maybe, she would have been there the night he met Robert and could have stopped the tragedy before it even started.

The indecision of which woman Celine wanted lay in her deciding who she wanted to be. Did she want to be the woman who embraced a life filled with love and passion or a life filled with parties and mindless sex? Was Olivia correct? Had she not experienced enough of life to even make that decision? Dinah was her heart. Philly was her passion. Somehow, she had to figure out what was more important to her. She couldn't commit to a monogamous relationship with Dinah, or anyone, if she continued desiring passion from someone else.

❖

Dinah sat in the dining room at dinner with Jo, Fran, and a few of their boarders. She barely heard any of the conversations taking place around the table as she stared absentmindedly down at her untouched plate of food. It wasn't until Jo touched her shoulder that she acknowledged anyone.

"You have a visitor," Jo told her.

Dinah gazed up at her in uncertainty for a moment as she hadn't even heard the doorbell. With a tired sigh she pushed her plate away. "I'm not up to seeing anyone."

"Does that include me?" said a familiar voice.

Dinah turned toward the doorway and couldn't decide if she was more happy or angry to see Celine standing there gazing warily at her. All conversation halted as Dinah slowly stood and walked toward Celine.

She felt the pinprick of tears starting. "I don't know if I want to kiss you or strangle you."

"I would be happy if you just talked to me," Celine said.

Dinah looked her over and noticed the plain clothes she wore, the dark circles under her beautiful amber eyes, and the lack of sparkle in them. "I think I can manage that."

"I'm sorry to have interrupted your dinner."

Dinah shrugged. "I was finished anyway. Why don't we talk in my room?" Dinah moved past Celine, annoyed how her body reacted when their bodies brushed as she did so. She didn't even bother looking back to see if Celine followed.

As they climbed the stairs, she realized going to her room might not have been the best idea as she began thinking about wanting to kiss Celine rather than her earlier thought of strangling her. Once they stepped inside her room, Dinah closed the door. She would have preferred keeping it open but didn't want any of the boarders overhearing their conversation. She turned to Celine and really looked at her. Dinah's heart ached at how gaunt she had become since they had last seen each other.

"You look like I feel."

"I haven't been sleeping or eating well," Celine admitted.

Dinah sat on the edge of her bed. "Neither have I."

Celine hesitantly sat beside her. "What a fine pair we make."

Dinah felt a twinge of anger again. "Are we a pair?"

"That's what I'm here to figure out."

"What is there to figure out?" Dinah balled her hands in her lap trying to keep her temper in check. "You either want to be with me or you don't."

Celine blew out a frustrated breath. "It's not that simple for me, Dinah. You don't understand."

"Then help me understand."

Celine turned toward Dinah and grasped her hands. "When Paul and I were children we used to pretend we were married because I believe that even at that young age we knew we were different and that the only people who understood those differences were each other. As we grew older and realized what made us different would never be accepted, we promised to marry each other instead of allowing our parents to arrange marriages for us. Then we could be free to be who we were. We also, naïvely, promised to never put our relationship at risk by falling in love with someone else. Obviously, we had no more control over each other's hearts than we did our own bodies' cravings."

Celine sat quietly for a moment, as if gathering her thoughts, then continued. "I was so caught up in my fear of accepting who I was, the way Paul had accepted himself, that I wasn't there for him. I believe Paul thought that if I had shared the secret lifestyle he had so painstakingly maintained, it would have kept him from falling in love. It was selfish of me to leave him alone to navigate a life I had promised to share with him. Toward the end, I could see the disappointment that he tried so hard to hide because he didn't want to push me. Then, when I finally gave in on my birthday, it was too late." Celine's voice broke.

Dinah felt the pain she could hear in Celine's voice. She pulled her into her arms. "You don't have to talk about this."

Celine pulled away and stood. "Yes, I do," she said vehemently. "Not just for me but for the memory of Paul and for your love."

Celine paced silently in front of Dinah for a moment then stopped and knelt before her.

"Dinah, you are everything Paul and I wanted for each other and more. Being with you is like having my best friend back, but this time I can give you what I couldn't give to him. Not just my heart but all of me, body and soul."

"Celine, I'm not Paul," Dinah said in frustration.

"I know you're not Paul, that's not what I meant." Celine waved her hand dismissively. "I spent my entire marriage wishing Paul were a woman, one I could share the same life we had but that I would also be able to share a physical love with as well."

Celine took Dinah's face in her hands. "A woman like you."

Dinah took Celine's hands from her face to hold them in her lap. "You have me, Celine. I'm right here. You can have that life now. It may take some time, but I still love you. I can get past the thing with Philly."

Dinah saw the doubt in Celine's eyes, and it made her heart ache. As she said the words, she wasn't so sure she believed them either.

Celine released her hands and slowly stood again. "Can you, Dinah? I can't."

"What do you mean you can't?"

Celine began to speak then stopped and paced again. "My

attraction to Philly is more than a passing thing. I thought that it had to do with that night Paul brought her home for me, but it's more than that."

Dinah felt sick. "Do…do you love her?"

Celine shook her head. "No, I have no feelings like that for Philly. It's a physical passion I can't seem, or want, to deny. She makes me feel alive in a way I never allowed myself to feel before."

Dinah stood. "Let me make sure I'm understanding this. You're telling me you love me, that you want to be with me, but you also want to be with Philly?"

"Yes," Celine said in a quiet voice.

"Celine, I know women who share a life together but also openly share the beds of other lovers as well. I'm not a prude in thinking that I wouldn't share the woman I love if that's what makes her…us… happy." Dinah shook her head. "But not with the likes of Philly."

Celine gazed up at her with tears in her eyes. "I'm not asking you to share me with Philly. I'm asking you to give me time to figure out what this is with Philly for me to know if I can commit to being with you."

Dinah felt as if the very air had left her body. "You're choosing Philly over me?"

"I'm choosing me. I've lived my life too long for what others wanted of me. It's time for me to figure out what I want for me. Do I truly want to live a committed life of love or do I want to explore my passion?"

Celine reached for Dinah's hands, but Dinah stepped away. She understood what Celine was going through. She had gone through the same thing when she came to accept her love of women. But Philly. Of all the people Celine could be confused about, why did it have to be Philly? She wrapped her arms around herself and looked at Celine. God, she was beautiful, and she loved her like she had never loved another, but was she worth the risk? Worth waiting for? Dinah looked intently into Celine's eyes. Celine loved her too, she could see it in the way she was begging Dinah not to give up on her yet.

Dinah took Celine's hands and laid her forehead against Celine's. "She doesn't deserve you, but I understand." She led Celine to sit on the bed with her.

"Promise me you'll be careful. Philly is a selfish, dangerous woman whose only thought is for herself and her own pleasure. That's what you are right now. Something for her pleasure."

"Dinah—" Celine said, and Dinah placed a finger over Celine's lips.

"Let me say this," Dinah said. "When I first saw you walk into your aunt's shop in a whirlwind of French, sunshine, and a carefree smile, I was enchanted. All I wanted to do was bask in your beauty and light. When we met at the masquerade and you came to my room with me you made me feel more feminine and flirtatious with your bold teasing than I'd ever felt with anyone. Then, the first time we made love, your innocence and your passion had me hooked." Dinah placed a soft kiss on Celine's lips.

"But it was the night of Helene's first party that I fell completely in love with you." Dinah smiled at the memory. "Where I grew up, and even here in the North, women like you, with their fair complexions and lives of comfort and means, tend to be empty-headed, vapid, bougie paper dolls who looked down their noses at people like me. But you treated everyone you met that night, from the maids to the doctors, with equal respect. You managed to hold your own in every conversation whether it was about politics or the latest fashions. You're not just beautiful, you're also intelligent, kind, loving, with a passion for life that draws people like a moth to a flame."

Celine's face darkened with a blush. "Thank you."

"Celine, I'm telling you this so that you know I see, and want, you for who you are. Not for how good you'll look on my arm or what you'll do for me behind closed doors. I want you to remember that when Philly finally shows you her true colors and when the sparkle of the new diamond you are to her begins to dull, because she will, sooner or later, have to start seeing the person you are and not the trophy she can shine and put on a pedestal to show off."

Dinah hated the satisfaction she felt at the hesitation in Celine's eyes, but she had to make it perfectly clear to Celine what she was getting into and walking away from.

"I can't promise I'll still be waiting, but I can promise that I will be here if you ever need me for anything."

Tears sparkled in Celine's eyes. "I understand."

Dinah stroked Celine's face. "May I have one last request?"

Celine nodded.

"Stay with me tonight. We don't have to make love. I've missed you. I just want to hold you, talk to you, that's all."

Celine nodded. "Yes."

They both stood and silently undressed down to their undergarments. As Celine climbed into Dinah's bed, Dinah turned out the lights, then joined her. She pulled Celine into her arms as if afraid to let go.

"Tell me about your childhood," Celine said, her head tucked in the crook of Dinah's neck.

Dinah obliged her and they spent hours comparing stories of their vastly differently upbringings before Dinah heard Celine's light snores. Only then did she allow the tears to fall and the finality of what they shared to settle in before she to drifted off to sleep.

A few nights later Celine worked up the courage to visit Philly. Saying goodbye to Dinah after their last night together almost broke her, but she knew she couldn't commit to Dinah while she had feelings for someone else, even if they were just physical. It wasn't fair to her or Dinah. When she arrived at Philly's home she was shown to the parlor and paced nervously as she waited. Philly strode in dressed in black slacks, a partially unbuttoned white tuxedo shirt, and a black velvet smoking jacket. Celine found her casual combination of masculinity and femininity very sexy. It was as if Philly represented everything Celine had always wanted to be, bold and passionate without a care as to what anyone thought about her. Celine realized that maybe that's what drew her to Philly. She was the side of Celine that she was too afraid to set free.

"What a pleasant surprise," Philly said.

Celine didn't expect the genuine smile that greeted her. "Good evening, Antonia. I hope this isn't too late to drop by without having called first, but I didn't want to chance changing my mind," Celine said.

Philly's eyes widened. "Antonia, huh?"

Saying Philly's birth name was going to take some getting used to. "Under the circumstances, calling you Philly seemed…wrong."

Philly quirked a brow curiously. "Under what circumstances?"

"Can we sit?" Celine asked.

"Yes, of course. Please," Philly said, indicating the sofa in the room. "Can I get you a drink?"

"No, thank you. I don't plan to stay long. I have a taxi waiting."

"All right, what was so important that has you out here this late in the evening?"

Celine squared her shoulders. "As much as I've tried to fight it, there is no denying that there is something between us, and I would like to explore it to find out what, if anything, it may be."

"Excuse me?"

Celine gazed at her in annoyance. "Please don't make me repeat it. You heard what I said."

"What about Dinah?"

Celine looked down to smooth away a crease in her dress. "If we do this, we will not discuss Dinah." She looked back up at Philly intently. "If you want me, you can have me, but only if it's because of our mutual attraction and not because you want to get Dinah back for some imaginary slight you think she caused you."

"You're coming to me of your own free will?"

"Yes."

The look of uncertainty in Philly's face was almost amusing. As if she couldn't quite believe what Celine had said. She recovered quickly, though, when a cocky grin spread across her face.

"Will you accompany me to the theater on Wednesday evening? The Lafayette Players are doing a new play."

"Is it the one starring Evelyn Preer?" Celine said.

"Uh, I think so," Philly said noncommittally.

"My aunt and I have been wanting to go back to see the troupe perform since we saw their last Shakespeare performance."

"Then she's more than welcome to come along," Philly offered.

"No, I think just the two of us will be fine."

"Well then, it's a date. I will pick you up around six."

"That will be fine," Celine said, then stood. "My apologies for the unexpected visit."

Philly came to her, grasped her hands, and raised them to her lips. She placed a soft kiss on the backs of both hands. "No need to apologize. You're welcome in my home any time. Allow me to walk you out."

Celine nodded with a tentative smile.

"Good night, Celine. I look forward to seeing you on Wednesday."

"Good night, Antonia." Celine prayed this plan wouldn't backfire.

CHAPTER SEVENTEEN

"Are you sure you don't want me to tag along?" Olivia asked.

"Yes, I'm sure," Celine said. "How are Antonia and I going to get to know each other if you're running interference?"

"I just worry, that's all."

"*Tante*, this was all your idea."

Olivia frowned. "I know, and I'm beginning to regret it."

Celine pulled Olivia into an embrace. "You, as well as anyone, know I will not let anything happen that I don't want to happen. We're just going to a play. If I feel uncomfortable about a situation, I will leave immediately. I promise."

Olivia placed a kiss on her cheek before stepping out of her embrace. "I know. Have fun. I can't wait to hear all about the play."

"If it's as good as I hear it is, maybe I'll take you over the weekend."

Olivia smiled. "I'd like that."

The buzzer to the apartment rang and Celine took one last look in the mirror, then a deep breath, slowly blowing it out, to quell her nerves. Other than the dinner with Philly, Celine had only been out socializing with Dinah. It was going to be strange to be out and about with someone else, let alone someone as well-known as Philly. Thinking of Dinah almost had her changing her mind, but she knew this was for the best.

"I'll see you after the show," she told Olivia.

"You won't be staying over at Antonia's?" Olivia asked hesitantly.

"No. That's what got me into this predicament. If Philly... Antonia...and I have something more than passion, then we have to take the passion out of the equation for a bit."

Celine's aunt nodded in understanding. "Have fun anyway."

Celine gave her one last hug before heading down the stairs to meet Philly. When she opened the side door, Philly stood there looking incredibly attractive in a gray suit with a burgundy, gray, and black geometric designed tie. As usual, her masculine attire was tailored not to hide her feminine curves but to accentuate them. Her hair was styled in a pin curl bob that framed her beautiful face. Celine felt desire run through her at the sight of her.

"Good evening, Antonia. You look quite dapper this evening."

To Celine's surprise, even in the fading light, she could see Philly's face darken in a blush. "Thank you. You look as beautiful as always. Shall we go?" Philly offered her arm to Celine.

Celine took it and Philly escorted her to her waiting car where her driver stood holding the door open for them.

"Good evening, ma'am." He greeted her with a smile and a tip of his hat.

Celine returned the smile and climbed into the car.

"So, tell me about Antonia Manucci," Celine said.

Philly's full lips curved into a sexy grin. "I like it when you say my given name. I only let a select few people call me that, my family and your aunt, but they don't say it like you do."

The look Philly gave Celine made her nipples twinge in response. "And how do I say it?"

Philly shifted closer to Celine so that they were just a hand's width apart from each other. "Like you're the only person I want to hear say it. It makes me feel as if it were a caress rather than words you spoke."

Celine unconsciously licked her lips, and Philly's gaze darkened with desire. Her body ached to be touched by Philly again. "Kiss me," Celine commanded.

Philly didn't hesitate. Her lips were devouring Celine's before the words had time to float between them. Celine had chosen to wear her hair loose this evening, and when Philly's long, manicured fingers tangled amongst the curls at the back of her head to bring her closer, Celine moaned at the exquisite feeling that sent a throbbing need to her sex.

After a few moments, Celine tore her lips from Philly's. "No," she said breathlessly.

Philly breathed heavily as well. "Why?"

Celine scooted away from her and backed herself up against the door. "Because this can't be all that's between us."

"Why?" Philly asked again.

"Because if sex…passion…is the only thing between us, then that means all of this"—Celine waved her hands around in the air—"is for nothing."

Philly took one of Celine's hands. "Celine, it doesn't have to be. Who said we can't have a bit of fun outside the passion? Why can't we have both?"

Celine looked forlornly at Philly. "Because I don't love you."

Philly flinched as if she'd been slapped, and Celine felt guilty for her choice of words. "Antonia…I didn't mean…"

Philly smirked, but Celine could see the humor didn't reach her eyes. "Yes, you did. You still love Dinah, and I'm something just to pass the time until you can work it out."

"No, Antonia, please understand. Yes, I still love Dinah, but I also can't seem to stop wanting to be with you as well. It's what I told Dinah when I told her I need to see what's between you and me."

Philly's eyes widened in surprise. "You chose to be with me instead of Dinah?"

"Yes. What you make me feel is—"

"Lust," Philly said smugly.

Celine looked away guiltily, but Philly turned her back to meet her gaze. "I'll take whatever I can get."

"You don't want to be with someone who loves you?"

Philly chuckled. "From what I've seen, love is overrated. What we have is mutually beneficial. We're both passionate women with an obvious attraction to each other. I'll satisfy your hunger." Philly cornered Celine and gave her a scorching kiss, then pulled away with a quirked brow. "And you help me become more respectable."

Celine, still dazed from the kiss, looked at Philly in confusion. "Make you more respectable?"

Philly brushed the pad of her thumb across Celine's lips. "I don't want to be a hustler the rest of my life, Celine. I want people to see a respectable businesswoman like Madam CJ Walker. You can help me with that. Teach me how to hobnob with the socialites. You and your aunt's business is well-known and well-respected. If people see you take me seriously as a businesswoman, then so will they."

Celine reached up to halt Philly's teasing caresses. "Antonia, I've only been here a year. I don't have that kind of status in Harlem."

"But Rousseau's Fashions does, and you're a part of that."

Philly leaned forward and ran the tip of her tongue around Celine's lips, sending a tremble of desire through her.

"C'mon, Celine, think of all the fun we'll have." Philly trailed her tongue up along Celine's neck to her ear where she whispered, "I'm not asking you to love me, I'm offering you an opportunity to explore your pleasure in exchange for you making me look good. I'd say you're getting the better part of the deal."

Celine felt as if she understood what Eve felt as the snake seduced her into eating the forbidden fruit. The things Philly did with her tongue, the seductive way she whispered into Celine's ear, offering her the pleasure she had craved for so long—it was more than she could resist.

With a shuddering sigh, Celine said, "Yes."

"Thank you." Philly shifted to Celine's lips.

Celine placed her fingers between their lips. "The theater, remember? I don't want to show up looking ravished."

Philly placed the blocked kiss on Celine's fingertips. "All right." She grasped that same hand and moved back to her side of the seat, their hands clasped in the middle of the seat between them.

Upon arrival, they walked into the theater and Philly purchased their tickets at the box office. Celine had been to this theater several times. In fact, it was the only one she and her aunt went to. Besides the Lafayette Theater being the first desegregated theater in New York, they hosted big-name jazz musicians like Duke Ellington, and had an all-Negro players troupe that did plays ranging from popular Broadway hits like *Madame X* to classic Shakespeare plays.

Celine sat on the edge of her seat the entire play. At intermission they joined the other theater goers in the lobby to stretch their legs and quench their thirsts at one of the bars.

"Are you enjoying the show?" Philly asked Celine.

"Yes, thank you so much for bringing me. To see such a play, acted so well, with an all Negro cast is something I would've never imagined seeing until I moved here."

"Yeah, many folks in the South still think we can barely read, let alone memorize a script and act it out onstage in front of an audience."

"You also seem to be enjoying it," Celine said knowingly.

Philly chuckled. "I guess you figured out this isn't usually my cup of tea."

"Only when you looked a bit surprised at your own gasp when the murder happened."

"I'm more of a musical, variety act, or comedy woman."

Celine gazed at her curiously. "Then why did you bring me to this play?"

"Because I thought you would like something a little more intellectual."

Celine placed a hand on Philly's arm. "Philly, you don't have to change who you are. I would've enjoyed a musical or comedy play just as much as this."

"Now you tell me."

Celine gave her a teasing smile that turned into a frown as she noticed a familiar figure walking toward them.

"Well, well, if it isn't Ms. Montré."

"Julien." Celine didn't bother hiding her contempt.

Julien stood before them and gave Philly a cursory gaze before looking back at Celine with a knowing smirk. "I see your choice in companions has improved a bit, but still not quite what your parents would have expected from you."

"Who I spend my time with is none of my parents' or your business," Celine said.

He turned his gaze back to Philly. "As it's obvious Ms. Montré is not going to introduce us, allow me." He removed his companion's hand from his arm and offered his own hand to Philly. "Julien Durand, Miss…"

Philly hesitated before she slipped her hand into his. "Antonia Manucci, but most people call me Philly."

"Philly, what a strange name to give a woman," he said in amusement.

Celine watched as Julien and Philly stared each other down as if they were squaring off in a boxing ring. Something sounding like a mouse clearing its throat interrupted their stand-off and all eyes turned on the woman by Julien's side.

"Ah, my apologies," he said, grasping the young woman's elbow and bringing her forward. "Miss Manucci and Celine, I'd like you to meet my intended, Ruth Ann Frasier."

The petite woman smiled demurely and nodded in greeting. "How do you do?" she said in an almost childlike voice.

"A pleasure to meet you, Miss Frasier," Philly said.

"Your intended?" Celine gave the woman an incredulous stare, then recovered quickly enough to smile politely and say, "A pleasure, Miss Frasier."

Miss Frasier looked at Celine curiously for a moment. "A pleasure to make your acquaintances as well," she said, then reclaimed Julien's arm and gazed adoringly up at him. "Jules, I'm thirsty and I want to get something to drink before intermission is over."

Julien gave his fiancée an indulgent smile that didn't seem very genuine to Celine.

"Of course, my love." He turned to look back at them. "Enjoy the rest of your evening, ladies," Julien said.

"What was that all about?" Philly asked.

"Not too long ago Julien Durand was sniffing around my skirts looking for a bride, and he's already snagged another."

Philly quirked a brow. "Jealous?"

"No, good riddance to rubbish. All he was out for was my family's money and social standing. I have a feeling that if he's managed to find the same in Miss Frasier, she's in for a lifetime of heartache once she says, 'I do.'"

Philly's brow furrowed in thought. "The only Frasiers I know with money and a daughter of marrying age are a Dr. and Mrs. Alan Frasier. He frequents the VIP lounge at Flynn's."

"A doctor," Celine said. "That explains it. Not that Miss Frasier isn't a beautiful young lady, but men like Julien don't usually go for darker-hued women unless they're deeply in love or have something to benefit. I seriously doubt he's in love."

"Especially the way he looked at you," Philly said.

Celine shuddered. "Believe me when I say I want nothing to do with that man."

Celine took one last look in Julien's direction only to find him watching them just as intently as he supposedly listened to his fiancée's chattering. Their eyes locked and Celine gave him a look of warning. He simply smiled knowingly and nodded his head in acknowledgment. The lights flickered, notifying everyone that intermission was ending. Celine finished her drink, grasped Philly's empty glass, and handed them off to a passing waiter as they headed back in for the rest of the play.

❖

"That was a lot more enjoyable than I expected," Philly said.

"Yes, it was. Thank you for the wonderful evening."

Philly gave her a secretive smile. "It's not over yet."

"Antonia, I have to be up early tomorrow." Celine didn't want to have to make the decision whether to say no to spending the night with Philly because she knew no wouldn't be her answer judging by how quickly she succumbed to her lips in the car.

"You have to eat, don't you?"

Celine had been too nervous to eat an early supper before Philly picked her up. "I guess," she said hesitantly.

"Good."

When they made it out of the theater, the street was filled with the other theater goers mingling or waiting for their own cars.

"My driver is never going to make it through this throng." Philly gazed up and down the street looking for her car. "It's a beautiful night, why don't we walk."

"But what about your driver?"

Philly looked back at the theater and waved someone over. A moment later, a young theater page boy stood before them. "Can you do me a favor?" she asked the boy while pulling out her money clip and peeling off a bill large enough to make the boy nod eagerly.

"Yes, ma'am," he said.

"I need you to give someone a message for me." She described her car, her driver, and told the boy to let him know that they were walking and would meet him at their next destination. "When you give him the message, tell him Phil says to give you the twin to this."

If the boy's eyes had gotten any wider, they would have burst from his head. "Yes, ma'am!" Within seconds he was off, searching the line of cars waiting to pull up to the theater.

Celine gazed at Philly, somewhat surprised by her generosity. "That's probably more than he made in a week's wages."

Philly shrugged. "If he's working at that young an age, his family obviously needs the money. I've been there." Philly took Celine's hand and put her arm through her own, and they slowly worked their way through the mass of people.

Once they breached the crowd, they only passed a small number of people out and about. They strolled quietly along, giving Celine time to think. She slid a quick glance at Philly's profile. There was no doubt in her mind that Philly was a beautiful woman, but beauty alone wouldn't be enough for Celine to develop the kind of feelings they discussed on the drive to the theater. She ran through her mind what she knew about Philly so far. She could be kind when she chose to be, something Celine got to experience their first night together when she woke up the next morning to a bath and the offer of breakfast. She also saw it in the kindness she extended to the page boy just now. Philly also had business savvy with all the businesses she was invested in. Well, the way she did business could also be considered ruthless, which was one of the things that had Celine worried about being involved with her. She didn't want to be caught up in any of Philly's questionable business choices.

Celine remembered another part of their conversation in the car. Philly was trying to go legit and hoped Celine and Olivia could help her with that. Could she honestly say no to another Negro woman trying to better herself? There was one thing Celine knew she couldn't seem to say no to, and that was Philly's seductions. All Philly had to do was kiss her and whisper in her ear and she had Celine agreeing to an arrangement that she would have balked at just a month ago. The thought of the benefits Celine would get out of the arrangement made her face flush in arousal, and she hoped the evening darkness kept it hidden from Philly's view. They arrived at Small's Paradise, which was one of Celine's and Olivia's favorite night spots. Celine had a moment's hesitation.

"I'm not quite dressed for Small's," Celine said.

Philly looked her up and down. "You look fine to me. Besides, it's a weeknight. There won't be much of a crowd, and the food here is great."

Celine couldn't think of another excuse, so she just smiled and nodded, then entered the door Philly held open for her.

"Miss Celine," the maître d' said, greeting her. "I haven't seen you and Ms. Rousseau here in some time."

"Good evening, Tom. With the fall season coming we've been putting in some long hours, so we haven't been out much."

He gave Philly a curious glance. "Your usual table?" he asked.

Celine could see Philly's surprised expression from the corner of her vision. "Yes, that's fine."

He nodded and led them to a table near the bandstand. Once they were seated, Celine looked up to meet Philly's amused expression.

"You have your own table?" she asked.

"My aunt has a table," Celine said as she placed her attention on the supper menu.

"I'm impressed."

The waiter arrived, and Celine ordered the lobster salad while Philly ordered the sirloin, broiled lobster, and potatoes au gratin.

"You planning to eat all of that now?" Celine asked skeptically.

ANNE SHADE

"There are two things that I allow myself to indulge in that bring me true pleasure: food," Philly gave Celine a wicked grin, "and sex."

Celine blushed and gazed around them to tables nearby. Fortunately, there was no one sitting close enough to overhear them.

"Antonia, if we are going to do this, I'm going to ask that you not say such things while we're in public."

Philly's gaze narrowed. "Afraid of being seen as a bulldagger?"

Celine removed the napkin from her lap and shifted in her chair to stand. Philly reached across the table and gently grasped her hand.

"Celine, please don't go," she whispered, regret in her eyes.

Celine's body vibrated with anger. She hated that disgusting slang for women who loved women, especially when another woman like her used it. She pulled her hand from Philly's grasp.

"It has nothing to do with that word I hope to never hear you say around me again. You asked me to help you look more respectable. Such talk is not something a respectable woman would do in a public setting."

Philly seemed to think about what Celine said. "I apologize. I'm used to being around gangsters and gamblers who aren't too concerned with how they're looked at."

Celine sighed. "I'm not asking you to change who you are. I'm just suggesting you take the time to adjust to your environment. If you want to convince my aunt to help you, then you're going to have to prove you can comport yourself as someone other than a hustler or gangster."

"You're right. Thank you. I apologize again."

"It took me some time to adjust to the differences here in the North from what I was used to in the South. Although things here aren't perfect with the Jim Crow laws just as strict here as they are in the South, I don't have to worry about getting in trouble for looking a White person in the eye or speaking up for myself. My aunt was a big help with that, and I'm sure, between the two of us, we can separate Philly, the hustler, from Antonia, the businesswoman." Celine hoped that reassured Philly.

"Thank you." Philly's smile lit up her face.

Celine allowed herself to wonder what a genuine relationship with Philly would be like, but all she could see were passionate nights and nothing more. Sadly, when she looked at Philly, she could only feel what she felt that night a seductive masked woman came into her life and the night they spent together so many years later. It didn't help that her first introduction to Philly was through her revenge on Dinah. No matter how charming and attentive Philly could be, Celine wasn't sure if she could see past the schemer she first met, but she owed it to herself to find out.

❖

Celine gazed out the window just as Philly's car pulled up in front of the building. "She's here, *Tante.*"

Philly's driver got out and opened the door for her. Celine was surprised to see Philly wearing something other than her usual pinstriped suit. She wore ivory wide-leg pleated slacks, a tan tweed jacket with a matching vest, an ivory button-down shirt, a chocolate brown tie, and a chocolate brown derby jauntily sitting atop her head. She gazed up and waved at Celine as she made her way to the side entrance. Celine went downstairs and met her at the door.

Philly greeted her with a warm smile that shone in her eyes. "Good evening."

Celine met Philly's smile with one of her own. "Good evening. My aunt is still getting ready. Why don't you come up?"

Philly's expression changed to mock surprise. "You mean I've been deemed worthy to enter into the private abode?"

Celine crossed her arms and pretended to glare back at her. "On second thought…"

Philly raised her hands in surrender. "All right, all right." With a teasing grin, she bowed elegantly. "Please, lead the way, my lady."

Celine shook her head and led Philly up the stairs. They had become friends over the past few weeks they had spent together. Olivia had hesitantly agreed to assist Philly with trying to present herself less like a gangster and more like a serious businesswoman. She had only agreed because she thought helping Antonia become legitimate would help keep Celine away from her not-so-legitimate business ventures while they were seeing each other. The change in Philly's attire was at Olivia's insistence. She knew it would be pointless to try to get her in dresses, so she helped to soften her typical gangster attire. Philly had been spending her free evenings in the back room of the shop with Olivia like an eager student soaking up all she could learn from her teacher. At those times Celine had seen another side of Philly that had begun to soften her feelings toward her. She saw the young girl who lost her mother much too soon desperately yearning for that older female figure to look up to. Olivia introduced her to her fellow female business associates including businesswoman and patron of the arts A'Leila Walker, heiress of the Madame C.J. Walker empire, which had Philly floating on air for days.

This evening they were attending a dinner for Negro business owners hosted by W.E.B DuBois and the National Association for the Advancement of Colored People, an organization he helped start to assist in building and strengthening the Negro community.

"Would you like something to drink?" Celine asked when they reached the apartment.

Philly shook her head. "No, I'm too nervous."

"That's even more reason to have at least a sip of something," Olivia said. "Celine, why don't you pour us all a taste of the bottle Antonia brought the other day."

Celine smiled and went into the kitchen to retrieve three glasses and the bottle of rum Philly had given Olivia in appreciation for her help. She poured a small amount in each glass and brought them out to Olivia and Philly.

Celine's aunt touched her glass to each of theirs, then downed the liquid. "Shall we, ladies?" she said.

Celine and Philly looked at each other, and with a shrug, Philly downed her own glass, raising a brow in challenge at Celine. Celine met her challenge and managed to keep a straight face as the liquor burned its way down her throat and spread warmly throughout her chest.

"I'm impressed." She pressed a quick kiss on Celine's lips. "Shall we?" she said, repeating Olivia's words, and stepped aside to allow Celine to pass.

Celine shook her head. "You are such trouble."

Philly tried giving her a look of innocence that didn't quite hide the wicked gleam in her eyes. "Who, me?"

Celine smiled in amusement. A short time later they were off to their event. Celine watched Philly out the corner of her eye as Olivia instructed her about who to speak to at the dinner and the best way to approach them. It was still strange to Celine how she could be casually sitting in the car with Olivia and Philly talking business when just two nights ago Celine was passionately moaning in Philly's bed. Not all their time together was about the business of helping Philly go legit. Saturday evenings, long after the shop closed and Olivia went to bed,

Philly's driver picked Celine up and took her to Philly's home to wait for her to finish at the club. The housekeeper greeted her at the door with a glass of her favorite wine, the cook prepared her a light dinner, and then Celine made her way to Philly's bedroom. Once there, Celine found herself becoming someone she still didn't recognize after all these weeks.

There was always a platter of fruit and a bottle of champagne beside the bed. Celine always poured herself a glass and made her way to Philly's large dressing room. Philly had set aside a section of the room for Celine and filled it with an entire wardrobe of lacey, frilly, sheer, and scandalous lingerie she liked to see Celine in. Like a pampered concubine from some erotic novel, Celine would choose an outfit, lay it out near the dressing table, and then go to the bathroom for a leisurely soak in the bath. Afterward, she would come back to the dressing room and prepare herself for Philly's expert seduction, although she found herself being the seducer lately as she got more into her role. It was as if she could step outside herself to become the nameless wanton woman she had fantasized being for so long. Once she had primped and pampered herself, she would prop herself up in the bed to wait for Philly, who was never late.

As the clock struck one, Celine could hear Philly's car pull up, and within five minutes of arriving home, she was strolling through the bedroom door. She never came right to bed. She would give Celine a slow, passionate kiss and then head to the bathroom. She didn't like coming to bed smelling of cigarettes, alcohol, and the general variety of scents that came from working in a speakeasy. After her own quick primping and pampering, she joined Celine in bed and they spent the rest of the night, and sometimes part of the morning, indulging in pure carnal pleasures. Most of the time, as the sun was just peeking over the horizon, Celine would quietly slip out of a sleeping Philly's arms, clean herself up, change into the extra clothes she brought with her, and have Tony, who always seemed to be ready, drive her home.

This had been the extent of their relationship, the arrangement they struck up a month ago, business and sex, and although Philly seemed quite content with it, Celine found it had her thinking more of Dinah. When she and Philly were intimate, it was like a raging inferno that threatened to consume her, but with Dinah it was a slow burn of passion that filled her with warmth and love. She missed the companionship she and Dinah shared in and outside of the bedroom. The moments when they could simply just be together without words or touch, just the comfort of knowing the other was there. When they couldn't see each other for a day or two, instead of telephoning where prying ears could hear, Dinah would drop off notes for Celine before going into work telling her about her day or the goings-on at the boardinghouse. At that time, Dinah's free time had been limited between her nursing job and working for Curtis. Her taking the time out to write Celine made her treasure the notes that much more. There were none of those moments with Philly, who could barely sit still during a show, let alone sit through a whole conversation or just share a quiet moment. Celine knew that she would need to break it off with Philly sooner rather than later. With Philly seeming to bloom under Olivia's tutelage, Celine didn't think this would be a good idea for much longer.

When they arrived at Small's Paradise, where the dinner was being held, they were led to the second-floor balcony of the club, where many others were already gathering.

"Are we late?" Antonia asked in surprise.

"No, with such a popular event, the earlier you arrive, the better chance you have to speak with Mr. DuBois and his associates." Olivia pointed toward a man in the front of the room surrounded by a large cluster of the early arrivals.

"Is that why we're here early?" Philly asked.

"No, my aunt likes to arrive early at these events to claim the closest table to the door for a quick departure," Celine said.

Olivia wrinkled her nose in distaste. "These things can become such a bore sometimes."

Philly chuckled. "I can see why with all the stuffed shirts in the room."

"Unfortunately, most of those stuffed shirts will be the ones you need to charm if you want to get anywhere in this town," Olivia said. "Ah, I see the perfect table, come."

Celine and Philly dutifully followed her. Just as they reached the table, they were approached by the last person Celine wanted to see.

"Good evening, ladies." Julien greeted them with a slight bow.

"Mr. Durand, I had no idea you were a business owner."

Julien's friendly demeanor faltered just a bit at Olivia's condescending tone. "I hope to be someday soon. For now, I'm here with Mr. Broussard." He sent a quick glance in Celine's direction.

Celine's heart ached in her chest. The first couple of weeks after she had moved out, she had not gone back to her parents' home. She felt as if she would never be welcomed there again, but Olivia had continued to go for her afternoon card games with her mother. When her mother asked about Celine, to Celine's chagrin, Olivia told her mother how she felt. Surprisingly, Celine's mother said she was more than welcome to spend the afternoons with them, so Celine attended their tea and card games once again, but she would never stay for dinner, as her father refused to join them while she was there.

"He's here?" Celine asked.

"Yes, he's speaking with Mr. DuBois." Julien looked as if he enjoyed Celine's sudden discomfort.

Celine gazed over at the group in the front of the room and saw her father in conversation. Tears threatened to spring from her eyes as she noticed he looked thinner and grayer since she had last seen him. Even after the way he had treated her, she missed him terribly. Despite his old-fashioned ideas on the woman's place in society, her father was very much a supporter of advancing the race and was a stout supporter of W.E.B. Dubois and other members of the Black Elite. She should not have been surprised to see him at the dinner since he was also a prominent business owner in the community.

"We're just at the next table if you'd like to stop by. I'm sure he would love to see you," Julien said as if he hadn't been there the night her family fell apart.

"It's so sad to see him missing his only child, although he and your mother have become quite taken by my fiancée, so I'm sure that eases some of the heartache your leaving to live a life spent in the company of bulldaggers and gangsters has caused them." His tone sounded more like cruel sarcasm than concern for her father's well-being.

White-hot anger roared through Celine like a gas-lit flame and, as if of its own accord, her hand came up to slap the fake frown from Julien's freckled face but was stopped by Olivia. She saw movement to her right as Philly stepped forward to partially block Celine from Julien.

"Has anyone told your prissy little fiancée what a pompous, fortune hunting bastard her future husband is? Maybe I should have a chat with her father about two of the poor women in Baton Rouge and New Orleans that you left broke and destitute. That the real reason you're here is because you're a wanted man and that your family has disowned you," Philly said.

Celine watched as the haughty glare Julien had given Philly when she stepped forward slid from his face and his expression changed to outright fear. Her own eyes had widened in shock at the revelation.

Julien gazed nervously around them, then back at Philly. "I have no idea what you're talking about," he said unconvincingly.

"My uncle is Sebastian Lawrence. I'm sure you're familiar with him since, as it turns out, you owe him quite a sum of money." Philly gave him a mocking pout.

Julien's complexion went so pale his freckles stood out like ink splatters on paper. "What do you want?" he said in a desperate whisper.

Philly shrugged and stepped back to stand beside Celine. "I want you to leave Celine alone. If you see her on the street, cross it. If you see her at a restaurant or show, turn back the other way. If I see you anywhere within the vicinity of her, or even looking her way, losing your intended's fortune will be the least of your problems. I've managed to keep my uncle from sending one of his associates up here for a little visit, but one word from me and that won't be the case for long."

Julien looked at Celine, then quickly away as if he remembered Philly's threat about looking her way. He gave Philly a jerky nod in agreement.

Philly smiled pleasantly at him and offered her hand. "It was a pleasure to see you again, Mr. Durand."

Julien looked down at her hand as if it were a snake about to strike and walked a wide berth around them without another word.

"That was utterly delicious to watch," Olivia said.

Celine looked at Philly curiously. "How did you find all of that out?"

Philly looked Julien's way. "When you introduced us at the theater, I thought I recognized his name. I called my uncle, and he immediately knew who Julien was. It took a lot of convincing for him not to send one of his men up here and to let me handle the situation. I know men like Julien Durand well. I knew we would run into him again sooner or later and he would approach you, so I kept the information to myself until the opportunity introduced itself."

Celine gave Philly's hand a gentle squeeze. "Thank you."

"I would do anything to make sure you're happy."

The tender look Philly gave Celine in return made her realize that what she had been afraid of happening had happened, and waiting to break things off with Philly would be much harder than she anticipated.

CHAPTER EIGHTEEN

Celine arrived for her scheduled night with Philly to find her, instead of her housekeeper, greeting her with a glass of wine.

"Philly! What a surprise!" Celine said as Philly's housekeeper came forward and took her overnight bag.

Philly handed her the glass of wine. "A pleasant surprise, I hope."

Celine accepted the glass, then took a sip before answering. "Yes, of course."

"Good," Philly said, giving Celine a lingering kiss then took her hand to lead her directly to the stairs. "I know you usually have something light to eat before you head upstairs, but I thought it might be nice to share it in the privacy of the bedroom."

They entered Philly's bedroom, which was lit by candelabras placed along the perimeter of the room, and a picnic was set up before the lit fireplace.

"Here," she said, indicating the large throw pillows in front of the fireplace. "Sit, I'll get you more wine."

Celine was completely thrown. She had hoped she would have the usual time she spent preparing for Philly to gather the courage to do what she came here to do tonight. Well, it was probably best this way instead of prolonging it. Celine began to speak, but before she could, there was a knock on the door. Philly answered it to let her staff in with the food that had been prepared for them. Once they were finished, laid carefully out on the blanket in front of the fireplace were small trays of oysters and canapes, two cups of shrimp étouffée and a small tray of beignets, strawberries, and cream. Philly waited until the staff left, closed the door behind them, and knelt beside Celine. She poured them both more wine, then set the bottle in a nearby champagne bucket.

"This is so nice," Celine said quietly.

"You don't look very impressed by it," Philly said. She took Celine's hand. "Is something wrong, Celine?"

Celine slid her hand from Philly's grasp. "We can't continue this way, Antonia. It's not fair of me to keep seeing you knowing my feelings aren't the same as yours."

"How could you say our feelings aren't the same? Don't you enjoy when we go to dinner, shows, and dancing?"

"Yes, of course. You're an enjoyable companion, but—"

Antonia raised a hand to stop her from going further. "And nights like this?" she said, leaning forward and running the tip of her tongue along Celine's full lips. Celine felt a shiver of passion run through her body.

"Yes, nights like these are very enjoyable," Celine admitted breathlessly.

"Then there's nothing more to discuss. We had an agreement, and I'd say it's benefiting us both. That's all that matters. Now, let's eat."

Philly picked up an oyster and held it toward Celine's lips. "My cook made all your favorites." She waggled the oyster she held in front of Celine playfully.

Celine watched Philly for a moment, then opened her mouth to be fed. Philly slid the oyster between Celine's lips, then licked her own fingers when she was done. She fed Celine a taste of everything that was prepared until Celine shook her head.

"I usually don't eat this much when I come over so late," Celine admitted with a groan.

"Ah, well, I guess I better stop. Wouldn't want you so full you fall asleep on me," Philly teased. She stood and offered Celine a hand. "Your bath awaits, madame."

"My bath?"

"Yes, I was told you have a routine before I arrive home, and I'd like to stick to it, as it leads to such delightful things afterward." Philly wiggled her brows.

Celine laughed and took her hand. Philly led her to the bathroom where she poured bath oil into the partially filled tub and turned on the faucet to fill it the rest of the way. Rose-scented steam filled the bathroom as Philly turned to Celine and began to undress her.

"You do know I can undress myself," Celine said.

"Yes, but it's much more fun for me if I do it. I'm going to bathe you as well."

Celine shook her head and reached up to halt Philly from continuing to unbutton her blouse. "No, Antonia, that's too much."

Philly took Celine's face in her hands. "Celine, when was the last time you let someone do something just for you?"

"All right."

"Good." Philly gave her a quick kiss and finished undressing her, then led her over to the tub.

Celine stepped in and sank into the water with a contented sigh. Philly took off her robe and sat on the side of the tub. She picked up a sponge, soaped it up, then spent the next several minutes gently washing the day's worries from Celine's upper body. Philly dipped the sponge beneath the water, starting at Celine's feet and working her way up her legs until she reached the juncture of Celine's thighs.

Philly leaned forward and whispered against Celine's ear, "Open up for me, *ma fleur.*"

Celine did as she was asked, spreading her legs for Philly. Philly slid the sponge between Celine's thighs and worked it in a circular motion up toward the center of her womanhood but only brushed across it before moving directly to her other thigh with the same circular motions. She teased Celine that way, back and forth from one thigh to the other, with just a light brush across the folds of her sex. The water sloshed up the sides of the tub as Celine's hips strained to get closer with each pass of the sponge.

"Please," Celine moaned when Philly pressed the sponge against the nub of her desire.

"Well, since you asked so nicely." Philly set the sponge aside and replaced it with her fingers as she leaned over the side of the tub for better leverage.

When Philly slid two fingers into Celine's inner lips and swiped the pad of her thumb across her clitoris, Celine's hips almost came out of the tub. This time water did slosh over the sides and practically soaked Philly's top as she leaned in to kiss Celine while she drove her fingers deeply in and out of Celine's heated sex. Philly shifted just enough to climb into the tub with Celine, fully clothed, and continued pleasuring her. Celine's inner walls contracted around Philly's fingers as her orgasm rocked through her body. When her shudders turned to light tremors, Philly eased her fingers from Celine's slick opening and gave her a slow, sensuous kiss.

"We better get out of this tub before we catch a chill," Philly said.

Celine nodded and allowed Philly to help her from the tub. "I thought I had imagined you got into the tub with your clothes still on." Philly wrapped a large fluffy towel around Celine, then began to peel off her soaked pajamas. "It was a small sacrifice to pay to bring you pleasure."

She left her clothes in a wet heap on the floor, then took Celine's hand and led her back to the bedroom, grabbing a bottle of oil on the way.

"Lie down on your stomach," she told Celine.

Celine handed her the towel and lay on the bed. Philly tossed the towel aside and climbed onto the bed with Celine. She poured some of the oil onto her palm and rubbed her hands together to warm it up before kneading the oil into Celine's neck and working her way down her shoulders and back.

"Mmm…is that the same oil you poured in the bath?" Celine asked.

"Yes, it's rose oil. It's good for moisturizing your skin."

Celine moaned as Philly kneaded a particularly tight spot in her lower back. It wasn't long before the long day, the food, the warm, erotic bath and Philly's expert massage had her drifting off to a contented sleep.

❖

Celine awoke to find Philly splayed out on her stomach beside her with one of her arms draped across Celine's torso. Last night's activities, or lack of activities, came back to her. She must have been more tired than she thought to have fallen asleep so quickly. That Philly had simply let her do so without trying to coax her into sex said a lot about the seriousness of the situation. This agreement had gone beyond business and sex for Philly. Celine had known that when she came over last night with the intention of breaking it off, but Philly had managed to convince her that she and Celine were still in this for the same thing.

Celine gazed over at Philly as she slowly slid from under her arm. She fell off the bed in the process and lay on the floor for a moment before peeking up over the side of the bed. Philly still slept and Celine sighed with relief. She stood and tiptoed around the room to grab her bag before going into the bathroom to dress. The only thing she did to freshen up was run a comb through her hair. She picked up her clothes from a bench Philly had laid them across and shoved them into her bag. She tried being as quiet as possible as she tiptoed back out into the bedroom. How quickly she was able to leave the morning after their time together depended on how tired Philly was when she finally fell asleep. Sometimes she slept lightly and woke up at the slightest sounds. Those were the days Celine didn't make it back home until late morning because Philly wanted to continue the previous night's intimacies. Then there were days she slept deeply and soundly, and Celine had no problem leaving first thing in the morning. She hurried down the steps to find Tony waiting.

"Good morning, Ms. Montré." He gave her a friendly greeting.

Celine gave him a slight smile in return. "Good morning, Tony."

He grabbed his hat and opened the door for her. The car waited in front of the building, and Celine wondered again how Tony always managed to be ready no matter what time she left.

"Tony, how do you know when I'll be leaving? Do you sleep in the foyer?"

Tony smiled. "No, ma'am. I used to sleep on the sofa in the parlor but realized if I set my alarm clock for five in the morning I can usually make it to the foyer by six to catch you by six thirty, which is usually the earliest you leave."

"I see. Well, thank you for being so accommodating." She was a little embarrassed that he was so aware of the timing of her and Philly's nights together.

"You're welcome, Ms. Montré."

They rode the rest of the way in silence. When they pulled up to the front of the alley beside the shop, Celine exited the car and Tony began to get out as well, as it was his usual habit to make sure she made it into the apartment safely. Celine stopped him.

"As much as I appreciate it, Tony, there's no need to walk me all the way. I'll be fine."

Tony frowned. "Philly instructed me to make sure you get home safely."

"And you have. Besides, there's not much trouble I can get into from here to the door. I'll be fine, really," she reassured him.

Tony hesitated, looked down the alley, up and down both sides of the street, and gave a window washer working outside a shop across from the alley a suspicious glare before nodding.

"All right," he said, not sounding very sure of himself.

"Thank you. Go and enjoy the rest of your morning," Celine gave him a quick wave as she headed down the alley.

When she didn't hear the car leave, she knew he still watched her. When she got to her door and took out her keys, she gave him another wave. He nodded and pulled off. Celine stuck her key in the lock and heard footsteps rushing toward her. She looked up to find the window washer running toward her at an unbelievable speed for a man his size. It was a short distance from the sidewalk to the side door of the building so he was on her before she could either scream or get the door open. He shoved her back against the wall and placed a rough, calloused hand that smelled of tobacco over her mouth. She heard a car engine come up the alley and prayed it was Tony, but she didn't recognize the car that stopped in front of them.

"You scream, try to run or fight, I will gut you like a fish. You understand me?" the man said harshly as the tip of something sharp pressed against Celine's belly through her dress.

Celine's eyes widened and she nodded as best she could with her head pressed against the wall.

"Good." The back door of the car opened. "Get in," he said, stepping aside to block Celine from running down the alley and give her just enough room to get in the car.

Celine looked in the car and hesitated. Besides the driver and the man who had accosted her, there was a third man in the back seat who grabbed her arm and yanked her into the car. The first man slid in, trapping Celine between the two of them.

"What's going on? What do you want with me?" Celine asked him. "Ouch!" She felt the prick of a needle in her arm and turned to find her other kidnapper injecting her with something.

When he removed the needle, she yanked her arm from his grasp and rubbed the now tender area. A moment later, she felt a sense of wooziness. "What…" was all she could manage to say. Her last thought before everything went dark was why she hadn't found it suspicious that a window washer would be working that early on a Sunday morning.

❖

Celine slowly blinked her eyes open, confused for a moment as to why her vision was so blurred and her head was pounding. When her vision finally cleared, so did her memory. She had been kidnapped when she arrived home from Philly's and they had drugged her. She realized she was gagged, her arms were tied behind her, and her ankles were tied to the legs of the chair she sat in. She looked at her surroundings and found that she was alone in what seemed to be a one-room apartment that was partially being used for storage and, from the sight of the table and chairs and the stale scent of tobacco that permeated the room, possibly a break room for wherever she was. She listened intently and could hear traffic and voices drifting up from the window at her back. She was hoping she was still in Harlem.

Celine took a deep breath and blew it out through her nose to calm her racing heart. So far, all that she had endured was being drugged and tied up. She felt no other pain or aches other than the one in her head, and even that was subsiding. The only thing she could do was wait to see who had kidnapped her and why. Her wait wasn't long, as she heard voices past the door to the apartment. It opened and the first to enter was the man who had accosted her in the alley, followed by the one who had drugged her. She shot an angry glare at both since the gag kept her from speaking. Her eyes widened in shock as Curtis Flynn entered after them and closed the door behind him.

Curtis gave her a pleasant smile that didn't reach the hardness in his eyes. "Ms. Montré, it's a pleasure to finally meet you. I hope my associates weren't too rough with you."

Celine's shock was replaced by confusion and anger. "Why?" she tried to say past the gag.

Curtis frowned. "Oh, how rude of me. You can't speak with that gag in your pretty little mouth, can you?"

"I have to warn you, if you try to call out or scream, you will be shot," Curtis said.

Celine went cold when the man who drugged her pointed a gun at her. With surprisingly gentle hands, Curtis untied and untangled Celine's hair from the knot the gag had been tied in.

"There. Hopefully, we can chat without you causing any trouble."

Curtis picked up one of the other chairs and placed it in front of Celine where he sat down, crossed his legs, and clasped his hands in his lap. The pleasant look still held on his face, but it frightened rather than comforted Celine.

"Now, I'm sure you're wondering why I've gone to such lengths to bring you here. Well, it seems, Ms. Montré, you've become quite the thorn in my side. First, you steal away my best performer, which I could accept considering you did pay the asking price. What I can't accept is that now you're taking my main source of income from me by putting

ideas in my new business partner's pretty little head about going legit."
Curtis's smile slid from his face. He uncrossed his legs, leaned forward,
and roughly grabbed Celine's face.

"There is one thing I don't play with, Ms. Montré, my money, and
whatever you have between those thighs is taking money out of my
pockets." He squeezed her face painfully.

Celine whimpered, which seemed to snap Curtis out of his anger.
He released her and sat casually back in the chair pasting that pleasant
look back on.

"My apologies. I hope I didn't hurt you too bad. Back to why
you're here. You're going to help me get my club back from Philly. I've
been watching her and noticed that she's become extremely attached
to you. I'm hoping enough so that she'll trade the club for your life."

"My life?" Celine said, her body going cold with fear.

"Yes." Curtis stood and slid the chair up under the table. "I've
had a message delivered to Philly, which she should be receiving any
minute now, letting her know we have you and to meet us here at the
club within the hour."

"And if she doesn't show up?" Celine asked, afraid she already
knew the answer to that.

Curtis gave her a sad frown. "Let's just hope, for both your sakes,
that she does."

He turned without another word and left the room followed by his
two henchmen. She wasn't foolish enough to believe he would leave
the room unguarded, so she didn't even think about shouting for help
with the hopes that someone on the street would hear her through the
open window. All she could do was wait and hope that Philly cared
enough for her to give up the club.

❖

Dinah had just gotten home from a twenty-four-hour-shift and
was on her way to bed when someone began banging on the front door
calling her name. She opened the door to find Lenny from the club
standing on her doorstep looking frantically up and down the street
before he pushed past her into the foyer.

Dinah looked out the door, closed it, and turned to Lenny, who
was pacing and rubbing his hands up and down his pants leg. "Lenny,
what the hell is going on?"

"Dinah, something bad is about to go down, and you were the only person I could think of to go to," Lenny said.

His wide-eyed look and pacing made Dinah nervous. She stepped in his path and grabbed his shoulders to stop him. "Lenny, what are you talking about? Is this about Curtis? If it is, I don't want anything to do with any mess he's in."

"He's got your girl, Dinah."

"What girl? Lenny, you better start making some sense or leave." Dinah placed her hands on her hips to keep from slapping some sense into him.

Lenny wiped a big hand down his face and took a deep breath. He looked a little calmer, which calmed Dinah.

"Curtis found out Philly is trying to steal the club from him and brought a few of his runners in to help him get it back. He's had me keeping an eye on her, and I told him about how she's been seeing your girl, the Creole one from the shop."

Dinah shook her head. "None of this has anything to do with me, so I don't want to hear it." She opened the door for Lenny to leave.

"Curtis had your girl kidnapped to use as a trade for the club," Lenny said.

Dinah felt her whole body grow cold. "Curtis kidnapped Celine?"

Lenny nodded. "This morning. He had me deliver a message to Philly to meet him at the club. When I got back, I overheard him say that if Philly didn't show, he would either ransom Celine off to her family or sell her off to the highest bidder to recoup some of his losses and start over in Chicago. When I told him about your girl—"

"Her name is Celine," Dinah said angrily.

"Sorry. When I told him about Celine, I didn't think he would use her to get to Philly this way. I know you cared about her. I don't want to be responsible for anything happening to her. You been good to me, Dinah, despite me working for Curtis, so I thought you should know."

Dinah looked at Lenny with sympathy. Curtis had finally pushed Lenny to his limit. Dinah didn't hesitate in deciding what to do next.

Jo and Fran entered the foyer. "Dinah, what was all that racket?"

"Celine is in trouble and I have to go help her."

"What?" Jo looked between Dinah and Lenny in confusion.

Dinah tried to explain as quickly as possible and still make sense. She asked Jo and Fran to go see Olivia to make sure she was all right, then grabbed a pocketknife her aunt kept in a drawer in the foyer to open packages and made Lenny drive her to the club.

❖

Celine watched Curtis pace back and forth, looking as anxious as she felt about whether Philly would show up for her. Celine honestly didn't think she would considering how much trouble Philly had gone through to get Flynn's from Curtis. Two loud thumps out in the hall caught both of their attentions. Curtis quickly drew his gun out from under his jacket, walked up behind Celine, and pulled her out of her chair to stand in front of him. She felt a fear like she had never known as he pointed his gun toward her head.

"I know you're out there, Philly. Unless you want a bullet in your pretty little doll's head, open the door slowly and come in alone."

The door eased open and Philly walked cautiously into the room, gun in hand pointed in the direction of what Celine hoped was Curtis. "What do you want, Curtis?" Philly asked as she closed the door behind her.

"Did you really think I wouldn't figure out what you were trying to do? Trying to steal my club out from under me?" Curtis said angrily.

Philly sneered at him. "If you had the same head for managing this club as you did for running hooch, it wouldn't have been so easy to take it from you."

"I want it back. You're not taking all my hard work and turning it into one of those bougie places like Small's or the Cotton Club."

"And you think this is the way to get it back?"

"It's the most effective way. I could've gotten rid of you, but I'd rather not be on your uncle's hit list."

"I could just as easily kill you."

"And risk a stray bullet hitting her?" he said, tightening his grip around Celine's waist.

Celine whimpered in fear but something in Philly's eyes told her that she wouldn't let Curtis hurt her, so she tried to calm her racing heart.

"What do you want me to do?" Philly lowered her gun.

"There's a set of papers on the table over there. I had my suits draw them up. You sign the club over to me and we all leave here on our own two feet."

Philly walked forward to the table, picked up the papers, and looked them over.

"You're asking me to sign everything over to you without payment in return? I wiped your debt free and put my own money into the renovations." Philly shook her head.

"You get your dame back, or does she not matter as much as I thought?" he said.

Celine almost panicked until Philly looked at her. She saw nothing but tenderness in Philly's gaze and knew she would be all right. Philly placed her gun on the table, picked up a pen, and signed the papers. She stood and held the pen out to Curtis. Celine didn't think he'd let her go.

"Curtis, you need to sign the papers also. My gun is on the table. All I want is Celine safe," she said sincerely.

Curtis seemed to accept that. He lowered his gun and shifted Celine to his side as he moved toward Philly. What happened next seemed to move in slow motion for Celine. She and Curtis had barely taken a few steps when Philly, still holding out the pen with her right hand, picked up her gun with her left and pulled the trigger. Something warm and wet splattered Celine's face as Curtis, still holding her, took her down with him when he fell to the ground with a bullet between his eyes. Celine was too shocked to move as she stared up at the ceiling trying to blink away whatever was running down her face toward her eyes.

Philly came into her line of vision. "Are you all right?" she asked, frantically looking Celine over.

Celine looked wide eyed from Philly, to the gun in her hand, to Curtis lying dead beside her and shook her head. She sat up and scooted as far away from Philly as possible. Any other woman probably would have been hysterical at that moment, but to Celine's surprise she remained calm through the whole ordeal.

"Boss!" someone called from the hallway.

"We're good, see if you can find a blanket for Celine," Philly called back.

She holstered her gun, held her hands out in front of her, and slowly knelt before Celine. "Celine, it's all right. Let me untie you."

She continued with slow movements. Celine turned slightly so that Philly could reach around her back to untie her hands.

"Thank you," Celine said quietly, speaking for the first time since Philly arrived.

A knock on the door drew their attention.

"It's Diamond." A woman came in, handing Philly a blanket, followed by Tony. Both looked at Celine with concern.

"She looks to be physically all right, just in shock." Philly wrapped the blanket around Celine and helped her to stand. "Let's get you out of here." Philly led her to the door.

Celine suddenly stopped as everything that just happened settled into her head. She jerked free of Philly's arms, wrapping the blanket tightly around herself, and looked at Philly with horror.

"You shot him. With no regard to the fact that he had lowered his gun and I was standing right next to him…you just shot him," she said, trying to still the hysteria she heard rising in her voice.

"Celine, baby, I had to. He was going to hurt you. Probably kill us both once I signed the papers," Philly said, holding her hands out toward Celine in a plea for her to understand.

Celine shook her head. "All he wanted was his club, Philly. If he wanted to hurt me, he would have done it before you got here, but he didn't lay a violent hand toward me."

"Are you defending him after he had you kidnapped?" Philly said angrily.

"No, I'm saying you didn't have to kill him, especially with me standing right there. What if you had missed and hit me instead?"

"But I didn't. I knew what I was doing," Philly spoke to her as if she were speaking to a silly child.

Celine's shock and fear turned to anger at Philly's inability to understand how she had put Celine's life in jeopardy by taking the chance that Celine might have been hurt by her reckless action, or the fact that she had just shot someone in cold blood.

"Celine, please," Philly said, reaching for her once again.

Celine backed away and left Philly standing in the room. "Please take me home."

She heard footsteps behind her and didn't care whose they were, she just wanted to get out of there. She hurried down the stairs and had just reached the second-floor landing when she heard footsteps rushing up the stairs toward her. She hadn't realized how closely the others had followed her until she heard the click of guns behind her and was pulled back behind Tony. Whoever it was must have come within sight of the guns because the footsteps stopped.

❖

Lenny and Dinah pulled up behind Philly's car in the alley and heard a gunshot Dinah's stomach dropped, and she was hit with a wave of fear so intense that it threatened to root her to the spot. She jumped out of the car, knife in hand, ignoring Lenny's plea to wait and ran into the side entrance. Dinah briefly saw, and ignored, the pools of blood inside the door and at the foot of the staircase as she ran up the stairs without any regard to her own safety. All she could focus on was getting to Celine and killing anybody standing in her way as she gripped the handle of the pocketknife tightly in her palm. It wasn't until she encountered Philly and her driver pointing their guns at her that she realized how ineffective her weapon was, but fear for Celine overrode any fear for her own safety.

"Where's Celine?" she shouted.

"Dinah?" Celine said.

"Celine! Are you all right?"

"Are you going to shoot her in cold blood as well?" Celine said.

Philly flinched and lowered her gun, followed by Tony lowering his. Celine pushed past them and ran down the stairs into Dinah's arms. Celine held Dinah as if she were the last life preserver in a sinking ship.

Dinah separated them just enough to look Celine over. "Are you all right? Did he hurt you? Whose blood is this?" She took the edge of the blanket Celine was wrapped in and tried to clean her face.

"It's Curtis's," Celine said, her voice breaking. "She just shot him in cold blood, Dinah, with me standing right next to him."

Dinah looked up at Philly, who still stood on the landing with her people.

"Can you please just take me home?" Celine asked.

Dinah continued to glare at Philly with such rage it felt as if she could kill her, but Philly wasn't looking at her. She looked at Celine as if her heart were breaking. Celine must have gotten tired of waiting for Dinah. She turned away from them all and continued her descent down the staircase. Dinah followed her and came up short as Celine stopped to stare at Lenny standing at the bottom of the stairs with a gun lowered by his side.

Dinah slipped an arm around Celine's waist. "Lenny is with us."

Celine watched him warily as he turned and walked ahead of them toward the door. He held it open for them, and Celine leaned into Dinah as they left the club without being stopped.

CHAPTER NINETEEN

Dinah sat beside Celine's bed watching her sleep. She could barely keep her eyes open but found she couldn't sleep because she was afraid of waking up and finding Celine gone. She still couldn't believe Curtis would be stupid enough to push Philly into a corner like that. It was obvious he not only discounted Philly because she was a woman but underestimated the extent she would go to protect what was hers. Looking at Celine sleeping so fitfully, Dinah couldn't imagine having done any different if she'd been in Philly's shoes. She just hoped Celine recovered emotionally from the ordeal. She had been almost too calm during the ride home—not that Dinah expected her to be hysterical, but when she had asked her what happened, Celine had calmly explained what occurred from the moment she was taken up until Dinah had shown up. That was when she had finally asked how Dinah knew where she was. It was as if it hadn't dawned on her until then that Dinah had not been a part of the day's drama.

Dinah leaned forward and smoothed her hand over Celine's cheek as she whimpered in her sleep. She quieted at Dinah's touch and slowly blinked her eyes open.

"You're still here." Celine gave her a relieved smile.

"Did you think I would leave you before making sure you're all right?"

Celine moved to sit up and winced. Dinah stood and helped her, propping her pillows behind her.

"Your shoulders and arms are probably going to be sore for a while from the awkward angle they were tied behind your back," Dinah said.

"Thank you again for coming for me, but I wish you hadn't put yourself in jeopardy that way."

Dinah took Celine's hand. "I was more worried about you than myself."

Celine squeezed Dinah's hand. "That's my point. It would've been unbearable knowing I had been the cause of you getting hurt." She bit her lip and her eyes filled with tears. "Or worse."

Dinah sat beside Celine, pulling her into her arms. "There would have been no reason for Philly to hurt me. I think she knows how much I care about you and that I wouldn't do anything to harm you."

They sat that way for a few more moments, then there was a knock on the door right before Olivia opened it and peeked her head in.

"I thought I heard voices." She stepped fully into the room with a mug in her hand. "How's my brave niece doing?" Olivia handed Celine the steaming mug before sitting at the foot of the bed.

"I'm just happy to be home." Celine took a sip from the mug, then gave it a distasteful gaze.

Olivia smiled. "Fortified to help you rest. I told your mother you weren't feeling well, so we would be skipping tea and cards today."

Celine shook her head. "I still can't believe all that happened before noon."

"Since it was so early, I hadn't even realized you were missing. I just thought you were delayed at Antonia's," Olivia said; then, as if realizing what she'd just said, looked guiltily at Dinah. "If Josephine hadn't come over and told me what happened, I would have been clueless until it was too late."

Dinah tried not to think about where Celine had been coming from when she was taken by Curtis's men. This was not the time for jealousy. Celine was safe, and Curtis wouldn't be troubling any of them again. Dinah couldn't stop the yawn that overtook her. The long shift at work and the morning's drama were starting to take their toll on her.

Celine set her half-finished tea on the nightstand and turned to Dinah. "Go home, I'll be fine."

"No, I'm fine," Dinah said, another yawn making her a liar.

Celine smiled in understanding. "You can come back tomorrow, after we've both had some time to recover."

"She's in good hands," Olivia said.

Dinah sighed in resignation. "All right. I have the day off tomorrow, so I'll come by around noon and we can have lunch."

"I'd like that."

Dinah placed a soft kiss on her cheek and stood.

"I'll walk you out," Olivia said, standing as well.

Olivia closed Celine's door behind them. They walked together in mutual silence until they were in the stairway.

Dinah turned back to Olivia. "You'll call me if there's anything I can do for her?"

Olivia took her hands. "Yes. Right now, I think she needs to rest. As do you, from the look of it. Are you going to be all right getting home?"

Dinah managed to hold back another yawn. "Yes. Lenny insisted on sitting out front in case anyone unwelcome showed up."

"Please thank him for what he did," Olivia said, tears gathering in her eyes for the first time since Celine had returned home.

Dinah pulled her into an embrace. "I will."

Olivia took a deep breath, gave Dinah a quick squeeze, then released her. "We'll see you tomorrow."

Dinah nodded and made her way down the stairs. Lenny leaned against his car watching the building vigilantly. She climbed into the passenger's side and sat back against the seat with a sigh.

"Is Miss Celine all right?" Lenny asked.

"As well as can be expected, under the circumstances. She's putting on a brave face, but I can see the fear still in her eyes," Dinah said.

"Curtis was wrong for what he did, but he didn't deserve to be shot that way," Lenny said.

Celine told them how Philly had killed Curtis after he withdrew his own weapon. Dinah was simply happy Celine had found out about Philly's true colors now and not when she became even more involved with Philly and her dangerous life.

"What are you going to do now that Curtis is gone?" she asked Lenny.

Lenny smiled. "Go to Ohio. My sister, Mae, has been trying to get me to come up for years. Her husband has a repair shop. He wants me to come work with him."

Dinah looked at him in surprise. "You have a sister?"

Lenny chuckled. "Yep."

"You don't think Philly will want you continuing at the club now that Curtis is out of the way?"

Lenny shook his head. "Curtis liked to keep the secrets he had on people to himself so he could control them better. Besides, I'd rather be out of town when the news comes down that Curtis is dead and Philly is now in control of his businesses."

Dinah nodded in understanding. They pulled up in front of the boardinghouse and she turned toward him.

"Thank you again, Lenny," she said, pulling him into a hug.

Lenny hesitated for a moment, then wrapped his big arms around Dinah and squeezed her tightly before pulling away and looking bashfully down at the steering wheel. "Dinah, I hope you know I always liked you and hated the way Curtis treated you. I tried stepping up a couple of times, but you know how Curtis was," Lenny said apologetically.

Dinah nodded. "I understand. Just get to your sister safely and live a happy life," she said.

"You do the same. With Celine, I hope." He gave her a wink.

Dinah wasn't ready to think about that. "Only time will tell. Bye, Lenny."

"Bye, Dinah."

Dinah watched him leave with one final wave and headed into the house. She knew she wouldn't be getting to bed as quickly as she hoped because Jo and Fran were going to want to know what happened, but she was so relieved that Celine was safe and she would be seeing her tomorrow that she didn't care.

Celine knew she was dreaming, but it felt as real as if it were happening at that moment. Philly pulled the trigger and shot Curtis, except instead of him falling to the ground pulling Celine with him, Celine fell to the ground alone. She looked down and saw a dark red blotch blooming on her chest. It spread out until it soaked into her entire blouse. She looked up at Philly to ask why but found she had no voice. Philly stood over her, gun now pointed at her head, with a cruel twist to her mouth.

"You knew what you were getting into when you decided to choose sex with me over love with Dinah," Philly said.

Celine shook her head, still unable to speak.

"This is who I am, Celine. Is this what you want with your life?" Philly said.

"No," Celine managed to whisper.

"It's too late. Do you really think Dinah is going to want you now? That she could possibly still love someone so shallow?" Philly's grin spread across her face grotesquely. "You're mine now." She pulled the trigger again.

Celine awoke with a start, covered in sweat and shaking with fear. She clutched her chest and the front of her gown, crying out in relief when she didn't feel a gaping hole or see blood soaking her nightgown. She gazed around the darkness of her room and felt as if something dark and dangerous was lurking in every corner. She turned on her bedside lamp. The shadows receded in the room but not in her mind and heart. Was the Philly in her dream correct? Was she foolishly hoping Dinah would want her back after all this time? After whom she had chosen to be with and why?

Celine loved Dinah, never stopped loving her. The fact that Dinah had risked her life to come for Celine was proof that she still loved her as well. But would it be enough to get past Celine's decision to be with Philly? Her dream was right about one thing. She knew who Philly was when she got involved with her and foolishly thought she could change her. For what? Celine couldn't see a life with Philly. Whether she became a legitimate businesswoman or remained a gangster, she didn't love her and would never be able to overlook Philly shooting Curtis so coldly while there was also a chance of hitting Celine. A soft knock at her door interrupted her thoughts.

"Celine, *mon bijou*, are you all right?" Olivia asked from the other side of the door.

"Yes, *Tante*, come in," Celine said.

Olivia entered with a worried expression. "I heard you cry out."

"It was just a bad dream," Celine said.

"Move over," Olivia said, propping up Celine's pillows and sitting on the bed beside her. She put an arm around Celine's shoulder and pulled her close, holding her like she used to do whenever she came to visit while Celine was a little girl.

"Tell me about it," Olivia said.

Celine cuddled against Olivia, inhaling her lavender scent, and told her about her dream. "What do you think it means?" she asked after she finished, knowing Olivia would probably come to the same conclusion she had about its meaning.

"Dreams don't always have to mean something, but in this case,

I believe it's your subconscious trying to help you work through your feelings."

"Did I make a mistake in walking away from Dinah and getting involved with Philly? Was I being selfish in thinking of my own wants?" Celine asked.

"Since I was the one who suggested you explore your feelings for Antonia, no. I think you did what you thought was best for you at the time. You've spent so much time doing and being what everyone else has wanted you to do and be that you've never really done something for yourself. There is nothing wrong with being a little selfish if it leads you to finding out who you truly are and what you want for your life. Have you done that?"

Celine nodded. "I know being with Philly has made me realize how much I love Dinah. It's also shown me how much I denied myself out of fear of disappointing my parents."

"And what are you going to do with that knowledge?"

Celine thought quietly for a moment and felt tears gather in her eyes as she realized what she needed to do, once again, for herself. "As much as I love Dinah, I still don't think I'm ready to just settle down again, and it wouldn't be fair to ask Dinah to put her life on hold waiting for me to reach that point. I also know that I can't be with Philly either. The Philly I saw shoot Curtis so coldly is the one I've been turning a blind eye to these past weeks. It's the same woman who came back to town focused so much on revenge she was willing to sacrifice me as her pawn in doing so. I let myself forget that, but I can't anymore."

"Those are some tough lessons to have learned," Olivia said. "May I make a suggestion?"

"If it will help me figure out what to do next, I would love to hear it."

"You need to get away. You're not going to be able to do what you need to do for yourself if you're here amid all the people and situations that brought you to this point. Your parents, Antonia, and even Dinah. They all want something from you, and you are in no position to give any of them what they want."

Celine knew Olivia was right. "But where would I go? I won't go back to New Orleans."

"What about Paris? Haven't you said you've wanted to go there for some time and that you and Paul had even planned to travel there your next wedding anniversary?"

Paris? Celine and Paul had dreamed of going to Paris after listening to Olivia's stories about her time there. The beauty of the City of Lights and small provinces surrounding it. The acceptance and freedom of the Negro soldiers that stayed in France after the war rather than come back to a country that kept them under their boot heels with Jim Crow laws and segregation. Of course, those plans never came to be because of Paul's involvement with Robert, but that didn't mean she couldn't take the trip. She had the financial means and no longer had to answer to her parents.

As if she could hear the wheels turning in Celine's head, Olivia continued. "I could arrange for an apprenticeship with one of my friends there who is a clothing designer. You could continue to work and make your hats. You wouldn't have to worry about a place to stay, as I still have possession of the cottage in Montmartre that I lived in while I was there. It's within a community of Negro expatriate artists and entertainers that made a home for themselves there."

Celine's mind raced with the possibilities of taking time to find herself so far from everything and everyone here.

"What about you? I would hate to leave you here to run the shop alone."

"*Mon bijou*, I adore you, but I was running this shop perfectly fine before you arrived and will continue to do so after you're gone. Besides, I still have Simone."

"My apologies, *Tante*, I didn't mean to imply—"

"I know," Olivia interrupted her. "You were reaching for that one last excuse not to go, weren't you?"

Celine could hear the amusement in Olivia's voice. "Yes."

Olivia shifted so that she and Celine were facing each other. "Celine, go live the life you were meant to live, not the one you think you should live based on a society that wants nothing but to hold you back. Go enjoy the freedom that the unfortunate circumstances of Paul's death has given you. An unaccompanied beautiful, widowed woman has far less restrictions and more opportunities to live a gayer lifestyle than a married or single woman could. Take advantage of your situation. Life is too short not to."

Celine realized in that moment that she was more like Olivia than her mother. Like Olivia, she didn't feel like she was meant for a life with a husband and children and trying to be a proper society lady. When she finally did choose to settle down, it would be with the knowledge that she had no regrets in life and lived it to the fullest, the way she and Paul had always dreamed of doing.

"If I'm doing this, no one can know until after I'm gone. I couldn't bear it if anyone tried to stop me, especially Dinah or my parents. I'll write them each a letter for you to give to them."

"What about Antonia? I'm sure she'll come looking for you any day now to try to get you back."

Celine frowned. "I don't want her knowing where I am. Despite what happened yesterday, she deserves to be told why I don't want to see her anymore, but I don't think I can do that right now. Maybe in a couple of days."

Olivia nodded. "Do whatever you think is best. Now, when do you want to leave?"

"If I can get passage on a ship by the end of the week, I think that will be enough time to get things in order."

Olivia nodded in agreement. "Good. That will give me time to post telegrams to the friend I want to have you apprentice under and another to a friend who is taking care of the cottage for me so that she can have it readied for you."

Celine chuckled. "How many of these friends do you have, *Tante*?"

Olivia had a mischievous glint in her eye. "It depends on what kind of friend you are referring to. Just know that I will write to them all and you will be well looked after if you need anything while you're there."

Celine pulled Olivia into a tight hug. "Thank you, *Tante*, for being here when I needed you."

"You're the daughter I wish I had, *mon bijou*." Olivia sounded more emotional than Celine had ever heard her. "Now, you should get some rest." She pulled away and wiped at her eyes. "You have a lot to do this week to prepare, and we have to make sure you have just the right wardrobe for your travels."

They said their good nights and Celine was able to sleep without any further nightmares. The next morning, she remembered that Dinah was supposed to come by the shop and decided it would be best to cancel. She would ask Olivia to deliver her letter to Dinah after she boarded a ship and it was too late to turn back. Celine sat down and wrote letters to her parents and Dinah. Dinah's letter was the most difficult, but it was also the most important to her. Once that was done, she freshened up, dressed, and began her busy few days to prepare for her trip.

❖

There was one person Celine knew she needed to face in person. She made a visit to Flynn's, which proved to be more emotionally difficult than she thought as she remembered what happened the last time she was there.

"Celine, it's so good to see you. How are you?" Philly came around the desk with her hands extended in greeting but was stopped short by a shake of Celine's head.

"This isn't a social call, Philly," Celine said.

"What do I owe the pleasure of this visit?"

"I can't see you anymore. What happened with Curtis is more than I bargained for when we started spending time together."

"Celine, you can't blame me for Curtis kidnapping you. That was his own decision, I had nothing to do with it."

Celine shook her head in frustration. "You know damn well I'm not talking about the kidnapping."

Philly approached her slowly. "Celine, I am genuinely sorry you were put in the middle of that situation. I did what I thought I had to do to protect you."

Celine stepped away from Philly. "I thought I could look past who you were. To see you not as Philly the gangster but Antonia, the woman, but what I saw in your eyes when you shot Curtis made me realize that Philly will always be there, in the shadows, waiting to strike. I don't want to be around when that happens again."

"It won't happen again. I'm not a killer, Celine. I was protecting you…us. Curtis wouldn't have let us just walk away like that."

"He lowered his gun, Philly. It was obvious he thought things had been settled," Celine said.

"That was his second mistake. His first was underestimating me." The sneer on Philly's face proved Celine's point.

Celine shook her head. "Bye, Philly."

❖

It was a beautiful Saturday afternoon, yet Dinah sat in the parlor of the boardinghouse reading the same page of a novel that she had read twice already. She closed the book with a sigh and wondered why she was torturing herself this way. It had been several days since she had seen or spoken to Celine. When Celine had canceled their plans earlier in the week, she had told Dinah it was because she wasn't ready to go out in public after the ordeal she had gone through, and Dinah didn't blame her, but then when Dinah offered to come by just to spend time with her, Celine told her she wanted to be alone to deal with everything that had happened over the past couple of months. Dinah didn't try to reach out to her again, wanting to give her the time she needed. Finding that she couldn't wait any longer, Dinah planned to go see Celine after they closed the shop this evening.

She missed Celine. Although she was still heartbroken over how things turned out between them, she had to admit that she had only herself to blame. She was the one who brought Celine between her and Philly. She should've never told Celine about Philly's offer and just taken care of the situation herself, even if it meant getting further involved with the club's business than she wanted to. She knew that despite their contentious relationship, Curtis had still wanted her for himself and would've never let her become one of Philly's working girls. All she had been told to do was play hostess to their VIPs. Other than the long nights, it wasn't that difficult a job, but she had let Celine offer herself up to Philly like a sacrificial lamb just so she could be free of that life once and for all. She got what she wanted but lost Celine in the process. Celine had sacrificed her family, her reputation, and her body for Dinah, and what had Dinah given her in return? Accusations and anger.

Dinah understood why Celine had made the decision to be with Philly, but she also felt she should have fought harder to keep Celine in her life to prove that she loved her. Instead, Dinah had allowed her jealousy to control her and completely cut herself off from Celine while she was seeing Philly. Dinah was jolted out of her misery by the sound of the doorbell.

"I'll get it," her aunt shouted from the kitchen.

A moment later, Dinah heard Jo arguing with someone in the foyer. She went to see what the commotion was and was surprised to see Philly standing in the open doorway with Jo refusing to let her in.

"Philly, what are you doing here?" Dinah asked angrily.

"She's gone." Philly had a frantic look in her eyes.

It only took Dinah a moment to realize who she must be talking about. "What do you mean she's gone?"

"Do you want to have this conversation on your front stoop or are you going to let me in?"

Dinah met Jo's worried gaze and nodded. Jo stepped aside to allow Philly into the house, then closed the door but didn't leave the foyer. She stood beside Dinah with her arms crossed in front of her chest, watching Philly warily.

"I stopped by the shop to check on her, and Olivia told me she left town a couple of days ago," Philly said.

"She left town. Where did she go?"

"Olivia refused to tell me. I came here hoping you knew."

"If I did, do you really think I would tell you? You're probably the reason she left," Dinah said bitterly.

"Me!" Philly stepped toward Dinah and was blocked by Fran, who Dinah hadn't seen enter the foyer.

"It's all right, Fran," Dinah said. "Yes, you," Dinah stepped into Philly's space. "This is all your fault. You couldn't leave well enough alone. So busy trying to get revenge over something that never happened and not considering the people you're hurting along the way. Celine had nothing to do with what you think I did to you, yet you involved her anyway."

"Celine originally chose to get involved to save your ungrateful ass and what did you do? You let her. You pushed her into my bed, and I took full advantage of it. Obviously, you cared more about your self-preservation than her love."

Dinah had no response. What Philly said was the very thing Dinah had been chastising herself over just moments before her arrival. The truth of it hit her like a punch to the gut.

"Well, I don't know where she is. I haven't spoken to her since the day after the kidnapping."

Philly narrowed her eyes, looking at Dinah as if she could glean the truth in her words. As if satisfied with what she saw, Philly turned and left without another word. Jo closed the door behind Philly and turned back toward Dinah with a look of pity in her eyes.

"You didn't know?" she said.

Dinah shook her head with a sob. Jo pulled her into her arms and held her as she cried for what she lost due to her own foolish stubbornness. After a few moments, she stepped out of Jo's embrace and wiped her face with her sleeve.

"I have to go talk to Olivia and find out where she is," Dinah said.

"And if she doesn't want to tell you either?" Fran asked.

"I have to at least try. Philly was right, I barely put up a fight when Celine chose to be with her. This is all my fault."

Dinah felt as if the fifteen-minute walk to Rousseau's Fashions was the longest of her life. She rushed through the shop door and found it full of people. She frantically looked around the room for Olivia and saw her speaking to someone across the room. She moved to make her way over to her when Simone stepped in her path.

"Miss Dinah, what a surprise to see you here. Is there something I can help you with?" Simone asked nervously.

"I need to talk to Olivia," Dinah said, about to push past Simone.

Simone grasped Dinah's wrist with a surprisingly strong grip for such a petite woman. "Miss Olivia is busy now, and I'm sure she would appreciate not having a scene made in front of her customers. Why don't I escort you upstairs to the apartment to wait for her." Simone tightened her grip when Dinah tried to pull away.

Dinah caught Olivia's warning gaze across the room. "Thank you, Simone, I'll do that."

Simone looked visibly relieved and released Dinah's wrist. She didn't completely let her guard down until Dinah had followed her up into the apartment.

"I'm sure Miss Olivia will be with you as soon as she can. Please make yourself at home," Simone said before leaving Dinah alone.

As Dinah stood in the middle of the apartment, she found herself bombarded with memories of Celine, their first time together and all the nights that followed. Their love affair had begun as a heated flame and burned into a roaring fire within a matter of days. Maybe that had been another reason for how they ended up where they were today. Dinah knew Celine was inexperienced. She should have taken things slow, made sure Celine knew what she genuinely wanted instead of throwing herself fully into her life without giving her room to explore. Dinah could understand the temptation Philly represented to Celine, especially after learning of the role she played in Celine's past. Dinah wiped away tears and stood gazing out the window, waiting for Olivia. It was almost a half hour before she entered the apartment. When she did, she pulled Dinah into an embrace.

"I'm sorry to have kept you waiting, but if I had known you were coming, I would have made time for you," Olivia said.

Dinah felt the tears coming again and managed to hold them back as she stepped out of Olivia's arms. "I'm sorry to barge in like this, but Philly came to my home frantically looking for information on where Celine was."

"I had hoped I would be the one to break the news to you, but since we are one less person, it's been very hectic in the shop since Celine left."

"I'll understand if you don't want to tell me where she went."

"Oh, *mon ami*, I would not do that to you. Philly doesn't deserve the courtesy of knowing," Olivia said.

Dinah looked up at Olivia with relief. "Where did she go? Maybe I can go after her?"

Dinah didn't like the pity that suddenly shone in Olivia's eyes. "Olivia, please."

Olivia took Dinah's arm and guided her over to the sofa. "Sit."

Dinah did as she was told.

"She went to Paris," Olivia said.

"Paris, France?" Dinah asked in disbelief.

"Yes."

Dinah felt another emotional gut punch. "I guess she wanted to get as far away from me as possible."

Olivia grasped her hands. "You're not the only one she needed time away from. You must understand, Dinah, not only was her heart broken but she was confused about her own part in the situation. She's also never had the opportunity to go out on her own. Celine's whole life has been guided by other people's whims without consideration of what she wanted."

"But I never pushed her to do anything she didn't want to do," Dinah said.

"You didn't have to. Celine would have done anything to make you happy. That's just the person she is. But in doing that, she discovered more about herself than she anticipated. There is no doubt that she loves you, but she needs to learn to love herself as well. To understand the woman she is, and the woman she can become, if given the freedom to do so."

Dinah understood what Olivia was saying. She had never had to deal with the pressure of family and community obligations like Celine did, but understanding didn't lessen the pain.

"Is she planning to come back?"

"Yes, but not for quite some time." Olivia dashed what little hope Dinah still had left.

There was no way she would be able to go after Celine and probably wouldn't if she could. Olivia was right, Celine needed to find her own way, and Dinah didn't want to keep her from doing that.

"She left something for you." Olivia left Dinah alone for a moment as she went into Celine's room. When she returned, she handed Dinah an envelope. "She asked me to give this to you."

Dinah hesitantly took it and gazed down at her name written in Celine's neat script.

"Thank you, Olivia," Dinah said, no longer able to hold back the tears.

Olivia took her into her arms once again. "If there is anything I can do for you, please don't hesitate to call on me."

Dinah nodded then left with her heart shattering into tiny pieces with each step she took.

She didn't open the envelope from Celine until she went to bed that night.

Dearest Dinah,

I wish I didn't have to write this letter and that I was able to tell you these things in person, but I realized it would make leaving that much harder. As you have probably learned, I have left for France in the hopes that our time apart will give us both the opportunity to figure out not only what we truly want with our lives but also if our love is something that will stand the test of time.

The last thing I would ever want to do is break your heart, and my actions with Philly have done just that. I will not make excuses for what happened, but I will also not apologize for what I had to do to help you get out of your deal with Curtis and Philly. If I had to do it all over again, I would still make that same choice because you're worth any sacrifice I made. Your love was a gift that freed me and helped me to see that no matter what society has to say about our kind of love, I know that God would not give us such a gift if it was wrong. I don't know when I will be back, but I hope when I do return, it will be either to your arms or to find you happy in whatever path you choose in your life.

I have a gift for you that I hope is worthy of what you have given me. I promised to help you bring your mother and sister up from Alabama, and I will keep that promise.

Enclosed is a bank draft for what I hope is more than enough to not only bring them up but to help you and them get settled into a home of your own. Please do not worry about the amount. As I told you, my sweet Paul took incredibly good care of me and made sure I would not want for anything upon his death. I believe he would want you to have this gift as well because of my love for you.

Please take care, and if it isn't too much of an imposition, please look after my aunt for me. She may seem like she doesn't need anyone, but I think it's because she's afraid of being hurt. It seems to be a family trait.

Until we meet again,
With all my love,
Celine

When a tear splattered at the bottom of the letter, Dinah dabbed it off the paper before it could smudge the ink of Celine's signature. She looked down at the bank draft that was included and couldn't believe Celine's generosity. There was enough money to move her family up, purchase a brownstone nearby, and not have to worry about finances for some time. If Celine didn't consider this a large amount of money, then she was wealthier than Dinah could have imagined. Dinah didn't care about Celine's wealth. She would rip the draft to shreds if it meant Celine would come back to her, but she knew, after reading the letter, Celine would have to come back when she was ready, not when Dinah wanted her to. Celine knew how important Dinah's family was to her and she would not let her gift go to waste. She would bring her mother and sister up North and, like Celine, take time to figure out what she wanted not just for her heart but her life.

CHAPTER TWENTY

Montmartre, France, 1926

Celine rose from the settee she had been lounging on and wrapped herself in her silk robe lying nearby.

"You know you don't have to leave."

She gazed over and smiled at Bridgette as she cleaned paint from her fingernails with the hem of her already paint-stained blouse. Bridgette was an artist Celine had met about a month ago when Bridgette approached her in a café and asked if she would model for her. It wasn't the first time Celine had been asked that since arriving in Montmartre almost a year ago, but she was the most talented Celine had met. Bridgette's lifelike works seemed to jump off the canvas, and Celine had bought two of her paintings before she agreed to sit for her. Unlike many of the male artists who approached her, Bridgette insisted Celine would not need to take one article of clothing off. She and Bridgette would meet for dinner to talk for hours about their lives, politics, and their families. Celine learned that, like her, Bridgette was also from New Orleans's Gens de Couleur community, but unlike her, she was not forced into a life of arranged marriages and high expectations. Five years ago, when Bridgette was eighteen, her parents moved their family to Paris when they realized the extent of her talent. They'd lived in Montmartre ever since. It wasn't until she and Celine began their affair two weeks ago that Celine allowed her to sketch her nude.

"I've already stayed far too late as it is. It's almost supper time and I still have to make a few more stops before I get ready for the Chanel party this evening." Celine slipped an arm around Bridgette's waist and looked over at the partially finished painting of herself. She cocked her head to the side and studied the look on her face. "Why did you paint me with such sadness in my eyes?"

Bridgette slipped an arm around her waist and placed a soft kiss along Celine's temple. "Because, my darling Celine, I paint what I see."

Celine thought about that for a moment. "Is that what everyone sees?" she asked as she continued to study her image.

"Only if they take the time to truly look. Your beauty was not the only thing that drew me to you. There was a story in your eyes that I wanted to tell," Bridgette said.

"Sometimes I look at your paintings and think you must know voodoo to read people so well and be able to bring their secrets out in a painting." Celine stepped away from Bridgette and gathered her discarded clothes.

"My mother has said the same thing. Maybe you are both right." Bridgette gave her a mischievous grin.

"As long as you don't try any of your spells on me, then your secret is safe with me."

Celine finished dressing, and as she stood in front a large mirror in Bridgette's studio that she used when painting her self-portraits, Bridgette came up behind her.

"Is that one of your own designs?" she asked as Celine settled her feathered cloche hat on her head.

"Yes, it is. I'm almost finished with the one you requested for your mother's birthday," Celine said.

"She will be so excited. She absolutely adores you and the hats you wear, but she just can't afford them." Bridgette tucked a loose strand of hair back into the chignon Celine had hastily put her hair into.

"That's why it will be my birthday gift to her." Celine turned, stood on her toes, and placed a kiss on Bridgette's lips. "I will try to come back tonight, but I can't promise anything."

Bridgette shrugged. "I knew when I saw you that no matter what happened between us, your heart belonged to someone else and promises weren't necessary."

"You should be with someone who can make you promises," Celine said.

"My darling Celine, you know I am far too young to devote myself to anything but my art. I believe what we have is just what we both need right now." They walked arm in arm to the door.

"In that case, until we meet again," Celine said before their brief but passionate parting kiss.

❖

Later that evening, Celine stood in front of her bedroom mirror for one last look before she left for a private party thrown by French fashion designer Coco Chanel. She knew it would be obvious that she was trying to impress Mademoiselle Chanel by wearing one of her dresses, but she had bought the dress before she had been invited to the party. What better time to debut a Chanel dress than a Chanel party? It was a blue silk chiffon evening dress with blue ombré silk fringe, blue under slip, and draped collar neckline. She loved the way the fringe flowed with every movement and the way the draped collar elongated her neck. She had let her hair grow since coming to Paris and had styled it into a high bun with curls on the side and a headband with rhinestones and feathers dyed the same blue as the under slip of her dress. The outfit was completed with silk stockings and a pair of strappy silver dance heels. Satisfied with how she looked, she grabbed her silk wrap and purse and headed out to where she could pick up a taxi.

"Celine Montré, is that you?" a male voice shouted as she passed her favorite café.

Celine stopped, not used to hearing her full name being called. She had made many acquaintances in the time she had been here, but most were on a first-name basis. She rarely gave her last name. She turned and was surprised to see Lee, the drag performer who frequented her aunt's shop and stayed at Dinah's aunt's boardinghouse, hurrying toward her.

"Lee?" she said.

Montmartre had many expatriates from Harlem, but she had not encountered a familiar face since arriving. When Lee reached her, he pulled her into a tight embrace as they joyfully greeted each other.

"Your aunt told me you were in Montmartre, and I had planned to come visit you, but I've been so busy with rehearsals for our show I haven't had a chance to get away. This is the first real night off we've had in two weeks," Lee said.

"Where are you performing?" Celine asked.

"At Chez Bricktop. Our first show is next Friday night."

"Well, I will make sure I'm there."

Lee's smile faded. "You should probably know that Dinah is also here."

Celine wasn't sure she heard him correctly. "Dinah is here? In Montmartre?"

Lee nodded. "She's a featured dancer in our troupe."

Celine's legs felt weak and she grabbed onto Lee's arm for support. He guided her over to one of the outdoor tables of the café.

"Here, sit down." He waved a waiter over and asked for a glass of water.

"She's a dancer? But what about nursing?"

Lee shrugged. "She would have to answer that question. Two months before our tour started, I mentioned the troupe was looking for dancers and she asked me for details. She showed up to the auditions a few days later. With her talent she was a shoo-in. She's been on the road with us for about four months now."

"I can't believe Dinah left her nursing career behind. She worked so hard for it," Celine said in disbelief.

"After you left, Dinah just wasn't the same. She didn't seem to find joy in much of anything. From what I can see in her performances, dancing is the only thing she's given herself over to completely."

Celine thought about the joy she saw when Dinah danced and could understand what Lee saw. Celine looked frantically around her. "Is she out with you tonight?"

Lee patted Celine's hand to calm her. "No, she doesn't go out much when we're on the road. She socializes when we we're working or all out together for a meal, but she pretty much keeps to herself when we go out on the town of whatever city we're in."

Celine felt her whole body relax in relief. "Lee, you can't tell her I'm here. My aunt told me she never told her exactly where I had gone in Paris, and I think it's better that way."

"But why? It's obvious you both still care deeply for each other. There's nothing keeping you from being together again."

Celine shook her head. "There's too much hurt. I can't bear the thought of breaking her heart again."

Lee didn't look happy about not being able to reunite her and Dinah. "All right, but I think it's a mistake."

They were interrupted by someone calling Lee's name from the doorway of a nearby club. He turned and waved in their direction.

"I've gotta go, honey, but just in case you change your mind about seeing Dinah, I'll make sure to leave a ticket at the door for you for Friday's show." Lee stood and gave Celine a hug.

"Thank you, Lee."

She watched him walk away, then waved the waiter back over and ordered a bottle of her favorite wine. When the waiter returned, she paid for the wine and headed back to her cottage. She knew the designer she was apprenticing under was expecting her at the Chanel party, but she was no longer in a festive mood. A few minutes later, she arrived home, tossed her purse and wrap onto the sofa, grabbed a glass from her small bar, and poured herself a large glass of wine. She drank half the glass before she flopped down on the sofa and allowed herself to wallow in self-pity, something she hadn't done since leaving home.

Her life in Paris had been a wonderful distraction from her broken heart. She had even had brief affairs with a few women. The most recent was her current affair with Bridgette, which was more a friendship with the added benefit of staving off both their physical desires and Celine's bouts of loneliness. Bridgette knew all about Dinah and what drove Celine to run away to Paris. She never placed any pressure on Celine to make their relationship more than what it was, and Celine appreciated that.

Celine stood, grabbed the bottle of wine, her purse and wrap, and headed over to Bridgette's cottage just a short distance away. It was in the opposite direction of the main part of town, so she wasn't worried about running into Lee or Dinah. When Celine arrived, she tentatively knocked, hoping she wasn't disturbing Bridgette with her unexpected arrival.

"Come in," Bridgette called.

Celine entered Bridgette's studio cottage to find her sitting nude in front of her full-length mirror painting a self-portrait. This wasn't the first time she had walked in on Bridgette in such a provocative setup, but where it would have normally had Celine very aroused, she now only felt the slightest hint of physical attraction. All she could do was compare Bridgette's soft, minimally curved figure to memories of Dinah's curvaceous and firm dancer's body. Celine felt a sense of sadness at her suddenly dimming attraction to Bridgette. Their gazes met in the mirror and Bridgette smiled happily.

"Celine, what a pleasant surprise!" Bridgette laid her paintbrush and palette on a nearby table and greeted Celine with a soft lingering kiss on her lips, then gazed curiously down at her.

"There is something wrong," she said.

Celine found it difficult to say the words. "She's here."

Bridgette tilted her head and frowned in thought, then her eyes widened in surprise. "Your Dinah is here?"

Celine handed Bridgette the bottle of wine she had brought with her. "Yes."

Bridgette took the bottle and carried it over to the kitchen area, grabbing an oversized men's shirt along the way. After she was as dressed as she was going to get, she poured them both a full glass and led Celine over to the settee Celine had been posing on just that afternoon after a morning of lovemaking with Bridgette.

"Did you see her?" Bridgette asked.

"No, I ran into a friend who's traveling with her. It seems she left her nursing career to become a full-time dancer. She's performing at Chez Bricktop."

Bridgette considered Celine for a moment. "But isn't this good? You can finally rekindle what you lost."

Celine shook her head. "It's not that simple. There's a lot of hurt between us. It may be too much to overcome."

Bridgette waved her hand dismissively. "I don't believe that. The love you two have for one another is not something you can so easily forget. As they say, time heals all wounds. You both had plenty of time to heal."

Celine sat quietly, sipping her wine and thinking about what Bridgette said. She knew the hurt she felt over Dinah's accusations and harsh words the night of her dinner with Philly had dissipated over time, but had enough time gone by for Dinah to heal?

"You won't know if you don't talk to her," Bridgette said in that way that always made Celine believe she really could read others' thoughts.

Celine sighed heavily. "Would you come with me to the show?"

Bridgette clapped in delight. "Yes. I have not been to Chez Bricktop in some time. Are you sure you want me there? After all, we have shared more than a simple friendship for some time now."

"Yes, but I value your friendship above anything else, and I don't think I can do this alone. I can't imagine Dinah spent too many nights alone over the past year," Celine said, feeling a bit jealous at the thought of Dinah with another woman.

Bridgette took Celine's hand and gave it a gentle, supportive squeeze. "It will all work out, and I will be there to push you along if you find yourself changing your mind," Bridgette said.

Celine usually went along with Bridgette's sunny outlook, but on this occasion all she could see were rain clouds ahead.

❖

Dinah sat in front of a mirror in the dressing room the club had assigned to their troupe, applying her makeup and considering joining her fellow entertainers for a night out after the show instead of locking herself in her room like she normally did. After all, there was no telling when she would ever get the opportunity to visit Montmartre, which she found out everyone called the Harlem of the City of Lights. When they arrived a week ago, she had not expected to see so many Negroes living in this French provincial town. They were treated with respect by the French and seem to have the same lives they had back in New York but with total freedom. Dinah learned that most were artists and entertainers like her and her fellow troupe members. They had more opportunities for fame here than they did in New York or anywhere else in the United States. They experienced little, if any, prejudice living in Montmartre and Paris. At the thought of Paris, her heart skipped a beat. She knew Celine was in Paris but didn't know exactly where. It was a big city and there was no telling where she might be living.

"Girl, I'm so excited I can barely contain it," Lee said from the table beside her, grinning like a cat that just ate a mouse.

Dinah chuckled. "Well, be sure to bring that excitement out onto the stage. I peeked out and it's a packed house. One of the waitresses told me that they had to turn people away at the door, and I've never seen such a mixed crowd before. There are Coloreds and Whites sitting and dancing together. I even saw a Colored man openly holding hands with a White woman," she said in disbelief.

"I know what you mean. Me and the other queens were out having dinner and were approached by the most beautiful White man we had ever seen. He asked if he could join us. He didn't even wait for an answer, just sat right down at our table and ordered a bottle of wine. He's also a drag performer. He heard about our show from an American friend of his, so he invited us to his show in Paris so that we could watch and give him tips. Child, I was floored. A White man asking me for advice on how to be a better performer!" Lee said in wonder.

"If I didn't have my family back in New York, I would actually consider staying here for a while. Unlike Harlem, I've heard that ever since Josephine Baker came to Paris in twenty-one, dancers of darker complexion like me are popular," Dinah said.

Lee turned fully toward her. "Would you stay if an opportunity came your way that you'd be crazy to refuse?"

Dinah shrugged. "I don't know. It would depend on the offer. If it was enough to be able to send home to Mama and live here for a few months, I might consider it," she said, then looked at Lee. "Why? Is the troupe staying here longer than our four-week run?"

Lee turned back toward his mirror. "No, I was just curious."

Dinah looked at him suspiciously for a moment, then dismissed it and finished her makeup.

An hour later, she was standing backstage waiting for her entrance. Her performances as Sable had become the hit of their tour. She had been compared to Josephine Baker on many occasions and had been honored by the comments. Ms. Baker's banana dance was legendary. Dinah couldn't imagine the seductive solo that she brought with her from her days dancing with Flynn's Follies reaching such status. Thoughts of the first time she met Celine came unbidden to mind, and Dinah's heart ached as it always did when she thought about her. Dinah regretted so much. Just sitting by while Celine was with Philly and not contacting her after finding out she had gone to Paris to tell her she still loved her.

She had done as Celine asked and stayed in contact with Olivia, who had become close with her aunt and Fran. The three were like peas in a pod, so when Dinah decided to join Lee's troupe, she knew she left Olivia in good hands. Thanks to Celine, she had also left her mother and sister well cared for. Dinah had refused to use the money for some time after she found out Celine left, but Olivia had made her realize that her family's well-being was more important than her pride, so she brought her mother and sister up, bought the brownstone next to her aunt's, and made sure, with Olivia's help, both her mother and sister had a new wardrobe to replace the small amount of worn clothing they had come up with. She set the rest aside for anything else they might need and for her sister's education. Dinah had not used any of the money for herself.

After that, Dinah's work lost its appeal. She had gotten into nursing to make money to help her family. Now, because of Celine's generosity, all of that had been taken care of. She struggled with what to do when

Lee told her about his troupe looking for dancers. With her family settled and her dissatisfaction with what she was doing, she jumped at the opportunity to do something different and get out of Harlem, where memories of Celine overwhelmed her almost daily.

Despite not needing to work, Dinah's mother had taken a job as a cleaning woman at the same hospital where Dinah had recently been nursing, and her sister was attending her final year of school and excitedly looking forward to attending Spelman College the following year. When Dinah spoke to her family about what she was thinking of doing, they encouraged her to go. They all knew she was having trouble dealing with her heartbreak over Celine and thought that getting away would do her some good. Olivia had also encouraged it, telling her that she was wasting wonderful talent not sharing her dancing with as many audiences as she could. Nursing would always be there, but an opportunity like what Lee's troupe was offering would not. So here she was, across an ocean from everything she had ever known, still missing the one woman she had ever genuinely loved and nursing a heartbreak she had tried to run from.

Dinah heard the opening notes of her solo and felt the warmth of the spotlight bathing the curtain she stood behind. She went through the curtain and gazed out at the crowd, and although the spotlight kept her from seeing individual faces, she pictured a certain beautiful face as she removed her robe and began her dance. The only thing she changed from her original act was pulling strangers from the audience. Another female dancer waited in the chair onstage for her, and Dinah pictured Celine's golden eyes gazing back at her as she approached the other dancer. Dinah danced for Celine. For the love she gave to Dinah that she obviously did not deserve for her to treat her the way she did. She danced for what could have been if she had pushed pride aside and seen what was right before her.

When Dinah's performance ended, she felt drained, as if she had poured her whole being out onto that stage. She managed to gather enough energy to take the other dancer's hand to bow before the loudly cheering crowd. The spotlight clicked off and she could see the entire audience standing as they applauded. Dinah gazed around the room, and her heart skipped a beat as she spotted a woman dressed in a white pantsuit walking toward the entrance. She had briefly seen her profile before her back was to Dinah, but it was enough for her to believe it was Celine.

"No," Dinah whispered, doubting what her eyes were seeing.

She felt a slight tug on her hand and turned to find the other dancer attempting to pull her back from where she had walked to the edge of the stage. The crowd was still applauding, but people in the front row mistook her action as if she were coming out into the audience and were reaching out to touch her. She put on a smile, reached out with her free hand to grasp a few that were offered to her, then turned and went backstage.

"Are you all right, Dinah? You looked like you were in a trance and were about to step right off the edge of the stage," her dance partner said.

Dinah shook her head to clear her thoughts. "I thought I saw someone I know, but it had to have been a mistake."

The other dancer shrugged. "Oh, well, I've gotta hurry, I'm in the next number." She released Dinah's hand and rushed ahead of her.

Dinah watched her go, then stepped toward a dark corner nearby. She stood with her back to the wall, covered her face, and silently cried. The pain of losing Celine was still as fresh as it was the day it happened. She was even seeing her in crowds of strangers. Then a thought came to her. Celine was in Paris, what if it was her? Moments later, she heard the chattering and giggling of the dancers in the next performance passing by. When she peeked out and saw the last dancer pass, she made her way to the dressing room. There would still be several people in there, including Lee and the other drag performers, but it would be quieter than if the whole crew were there.

Dinah sat at her dressing table and gazed at her image in the mirror. All she could see was sadness. Since she had been on the road, she tried getting over Celine with meaningless sex with women she met along the way, but it just made her feel worse, so she stayed to herself and rarely went out with the other performers unless it was to get something to eat. Tonight, she would try and go out with Lee and the others for their planned night of dinner and dancing to celebrate their first show in Paris. She needed to forget, at least for one night, about the woman with the golden eyes and loving heart.

❖

Celine stood at the back entrance of the club with a small crowd, waiting for the performers to exit. She didn't know what to expect when she saw Dinah again, but it wasn't the intense pull she felt as soon as the curtain opened and Dinah walked into the spotlight in the very outfit she had created for her what seemed a lifetime ago. It brought her back to the night of the ball when they first laid eyes on each other. She hadn't even realized she stood until she felt Bridgette's hand tugging her back down into her seat.

"She is everything you described," Bridgette had said in awe after Dinah's performance.

To Celine, Dinah was even more beautiful than she remembered. She had to step out and get air before she found herself running backstage and grabbing Dinah up into her arms.

"Are you all right?" Bridgette asked.

"My heart is beating a mile a minute and I'm teetering between leaving and staying," Celine said.

Bridgette took her hand and squeezed it gently. "Whatever you decide, I am here for you."

Celine squeezed Bridgette's hand in return. "Thank you," she said gratefully.

Moments later, people began filtering out of the door. Celine and Bridgette stayed back from the crowd as they moved forward to excitedly speak to the performers as they exited. When Dinah made her appearance, the crowd applauded enthusiastically. Celine watched Dinah's surprised expression turn to a sweet blush as she was showered with adoration and praise for her performance. Celine was so proud of Dinah and loved seeing how humble she remained under the attention. As Celine watched, a beautiful and elegantly dressed older White woman stepped forward as the last to speak with Dinah. Celine remained in the shadows with Bridgette and watched as the woman stood just a little too close to Dinah, leaned forward, and whispered in her ear. From Dinah's shocked expression, Celine could only imagine what was being said. She began to step forward but was halted by Bridgette.

"That's Madame Voltaire, she runs a high-end gentlemen's club in Paris," Bridgette whispered.

"A gentlemen's club. Does she believe she can recruit Dinah to work for her?"

"I doubt it. She's also known to favor women of a certain type," Bridgette explained. "Dark beauties like Dinah are approached for her own personal pleasure."

"Oh," was all Celine could say.

Celine couldn't help the rise of jealousy that came over her. Did she think she would be the only woman who could want Dinah? After all, Dinah was a beautiful and sexy woman whose performances made her even more seductive and alluring. Celine was surprised she hadn't been approached by any other men and women in the crowd that greeted her after tonight's sensual performance. She watched as Dinah shook her head with a smile, took a card the woman offered, and accepted kisses on her cheeks in parting. After the woman left, Dinah chuckled in amusement and began walking arm in arm with Lee toward where she and Bridgette stood.

It's now or never, Celine thought, and stepped out into the light where Dinah could see her. Dinah was facing Lee as they chatted, so she didn't see Celine until Lee stopped and looked in her direction with a grin. Dinah turned also, and when their gazes met, Celine felt a moment of fear when Dinah looked as if she would turn and leave.

"It was you?" Dinah said in disbelief.

Celine was momentarily confused.

"I saw you leaving after my performance," Dinah explained.

Celine realized Dinah must have seen her when she stepped out to get some air. "You were wonderful as usual. Hi, Lee," Celine said.

Lee smiled. "Hi, Celine. I'll give you two some time to talk. Dinah, we'll be at the hotel freshening up."

Dinah just nodded, her gaze never leaving Celine's.

Celine saw movement out the corner of her eye. She had forgotten Bridgette was even there. "Oh, my apologies." She directed everyone's attention toward Bridgette. "Lee, Dinah, this is my friend Bridgette. Bridgette, this is Dinah and Lee."

Bridgette stepped forward and shook their hands in greeting. "I've heard so much about both of you, I feel as if I know you already."

Celine could see Dinah's gaze shifting from her to Bridgette, probably wondering about their relationship. Once again, as if she could read other's thoughts, Bridgette answered the unspoken question.

"Celine has been such a wonderful friend and fellow artist," Bridgette said, then offered her arm to Lee. "I'll walk with you. Celine, if you're not too busy, call on me tomorrow afternoon," Bridgette said in parting.

After Lee and Bridgette left, Celine turned back toward Dinah. "You're even more beautiful than I remember."

Dinah blushed. "So are you."

Celine's heart skipped a beat at the compliment. "Do you have some time to talk?" Celine asked.

"Yes. We can go to my hotel or a café nearby," Dinah said.

"Actually, I don't live too far from here, unless you prefer some-place public," Celine offered hesitantly.

Dinah smiled. "Your place is fine."

Celine offered her arm to Dinah, who took it and allowed Celine to lead the way. They strolled along in companionable silence for some time before they were stopped by people wanting to greet and chat with Celine. Not once did she release Dinah's arm clasped around hers, and she made sure to introduce her to each person she spoke with. They reached her cottage a few moments later.

"It fits you," Dinah said after they entered the small home.

"It suits my purpose. I don't spend as much time here as I would like, but it's a cozy retreat when I do get a chance to escape." Dinah gazed up at a nude portrait of Celine hanging over the fireplace.

"You seem to have acquired a lot of admirers during your time here," Dinah said. "Although whoever did this painting seems to be a bit more than an admirer."

Celine didn't miss the jealous tone in Dinah's comment. "We were intimate, but not anymore," she said, knowing it was partially true. She and Bridgette had not actually broken off their intimate relationship, but they both knew that with Dinah showing up, Celine's desire for more than a friendship had fizzled like a candle in a breeze.

Dinah turned with a sad smile. "You don't owe me any explanations."

Celine walked over to Dinah and stood close enough to touch her but too afraid to do so. "I owe you far more than explanations."

They stood just inches apart, gazes saying so much more than words could.

Celine cleared her throat and tore her gaze from Dinah's. "May I get you a glass of wine?"

"Yes, thank you."

CHAPTER TWENTY-ONE

Dinah watched Celine walk away, longing to call her back and tell her how much she loved and missed her, missed what they shared, but she didn't. She turned back toward the painting wishing she had been the one Celine had been gazing at with such desire. The artist had painted Celine so lifelike it looked as if she were about to crawl right out of the picture from the bed of pillows she was lying on. As she studied Celine's painted form, Dinah's palm itched remembering every curve and line emphasized in the painting that her hand had smoothed over when they last made love.

"Dinah," Celine said from behind her.

Dinah had to shake her head to dismiss the intimate memories flooding her mind. She turned back to Celine and accepted the glass of wine from her.

"Shall we sit?" Celine asked, waving her hand toward the sofa.

Dinah nodded and followed Celine, sitting at the other end of sofa, as far from Celine as possible. The look of disappointment on Celine's face almost tempted her to shorten the distance between them, but doubt kept her from moving.

"How have you been?" Celine asked.

"I've been doing well. The tour is keeping me busy."

"I was surprised to hear you left nursing. I thought that was your dream."

"It was but mostly because it was a way to help my family. Because of your kindness, I didn't need to do that anymore and found I no longer felt the same way about the job. Thank you, by the way, for the money," Dinah said.

Celine smiled. "It was my pleasure. I'm glad you were able to help your family."

"I guess your aunt told you."

Celine gazed down at her untouched glass of wine. "No. I don't ask my aunt about you when we communicate. It hurts too much," Celine admitted. "I had no idea what was going on until I ran into Lee a few days ago. He told me about your family and you joining the troupe."

"So, you already knew I was here when you came to the show?"

Celine lifted her gaze back to Dinah's. "It was the only reason I came to the show. Chez Bricktop is an immensely popular nightclub so I don't go often because of the crowds, but I had to see you, Dinah. I had to find out if there was anything left between us because as much as I have tried to move on with my life, I can't seem to let you go." Tears glistened in her eyes.

Dinah opened her mouth to speak, but the words wouldn't come. Fear and doubt kept her from admitting that Celine was, and would always be, the only one to deeply hold her heart, no matter what happened to bring them to this point. She watched as the tears slid from Celine's eyes, and the love that had shown there during her admission was replaced by hurt.

Celine placed her glass on the coffee table in front of the sofa and stood. "I see that you don't feel the same, and I understand." She walked over to stand in front of the large bank of windows by the door. "It was foolish of me to think that the hurt I caused you would be so easily forgotten."

Dinah's heart railed against her silence, beating frantically against her chest as if trying to push the words out since nothing was coming from her mouth. She gazed at the painting wondering if she could walk away from Celine once again. She studied the painted image of Celine's eyes and realized the artist was so good they had not only captured Celine's passion but also her loneliness. The spark of love and life she had always seen in Celine's eyes was absent from the painting. Had that spark and love only been reserved for her? Was the look in the painting the same look Philly had received? Had Celine told her the truth when she said there had been nothing more with Philly than a physical attraction? Was it the same attraction she must have felt for the person in the painting? Had she been as lonely as Dinah?

Dinah gazed back over at Celine, who was quietly looking out the window, and stood. She placed her wineglass down, went to Celine, and placed her hands on Celine's waist to gently urge her to turn around. When Celine faced her, Dinah quietly chastised herself for bringing the same hurt look in Celine's eyes that she did the night she walked out on her.

"I'm sorry, Celine. I was so overwhelmed with my own pain and jealousy that I hurtfully pushed you away. You didn't deserve to be treated that way after everything you had done to help me with Curtis and Philly. That wasn't fair. It also wasn't fair not to consider what Philly represented to you and your past. You're a passionate woman, but you were also inexperienced, and Philly took advantage of that. She's a beautiful, tempting, and confident woman who is exceptionally good at manipulating people and situations to get what she wants. I should have remembered that and fought harder for you," Dinah said.

Celine gently grasped Dinah's face in her hands. "Dinah, I'm sorry also. I won't make excuses for what I did because there is no excuse for hurting you that way. All I can do, if you allow me, is spend the rest of our lives making up for everything, including the time we lost being apart. I love you with everything I am and will go wherever you are because if I'm not with you I'm not truly living."

Dinah felt as if she could breathe deeply for the first time since learning that Celine had left Harlem. She pulled Celine into her arms, brought her lips down upon Celine's, and kissed her as if she were the very air she breathed. After several passionate kisses, Celine tore her lips from Dinah's.

"Unless you're in a hurry to meet your friends, we should move this to the bedroom before we give passersby a peep show they may not forget," Celine said breathlessly.

Dinah forgot that they stood directly in front of Celine's window with the lights behind them spotlighting them to anyone who passed by.

"I'm sure Lee will understand. Lead the way," Dinah said.

Celine led Dinah to her bedroom. The first thing that caught Dinah's attention was that the bedroom was decorated for long days in bed making love. A fireplace took up almost an entire wall. A large painting with several women lying in a bed, feeding and touching each other in very intimate ways, hung above the fireplace. To the right of the door was a large four-poster bed with white lace and pink silk draped along the posters in a canopy fashion. Large plush pillows, a fur throw, and down comforter covered the bed. The rest of the furnishings consisted of a large divan with another fur throw, a dressing table in front of a large mirror, and a few floor lamps with sheer scarves draped over them. One lamp was already turned on, bathing the room in a soft glow.

"Wow," was all she could manage to say.

Celine chuckled. "This was all my aunt's doing. It was like this when I arrived, and I never felt the need to change it. You're the first person I've ever brought here."

Dinah's eyes widened in surprise. "Not even the woman who painted you?"

Celine shook her head. "It never felt right bringing a woman back to my home. I like to keep my privacy," Celine admitted.

Just for a moment, Dinah wondered how many women's beds Celine had shared since being here but knew that it wouldn't do her any good allowing jealousy to ruin their reunion.

"I'm honored." Dinah pulled Celine into her arms and placed a soft kiss on her lips.

Their eyes locked. Celine grasped Dinah's face and brought her lips down upon her own.

Celine covered Dinah's face in feather light kisses, traveling along her neck, and whispering in her ear, "I want you so badly it hurts."

"I'm yours."

Celine shifted just enough to be able to bring her hands between their bodies to unbutton Dinah's blouse. Dinah reached in and began undressing Celine, their hands tangling and bumping into one another as they unsuccessfully made little progress. They both stopped and laughed at their fumbling attempt.

"I think we would get more accomplished if we undressed ourselves," Celine said.

"I have a lot less to take off than you." Dinah gave her a playful grin as she waved a hand indicating Celine's suit.

Celine removed her jacket, pulled her blouse over her head rather than wrestle with the remaining buttons that Dinah had not reached, and somehow wiggled out of her pants without unbuttoning them. Although Dinah only wore a blouse and slacks, Celine still managed to be undressed at the same time as Dinah. She loved the way Celine looked at her as if she were a starved woman looking at a tempting dish. Dinah knew her body had changed since they had last seen each other. She was trimmer but also firmer from dancing regularly. She noticed that Celine was also trimmer and firmer but still managed to keep her luscious curves.

"Paris seems to have agreed with you," Dinah said.

"Dancing seems to have agreed with you as well." They stepped into each other's arms and Celine ran her hands over Dinah's behind.

Even with the changes, their bodies seemed to fit together perfectly. Dinah lowered her head and Celine accepted the gift of her lips. Dinah wondered how their kisses could still be as passionate now as they were the very first time they kissed the night of the masquerade. Even after all the time apart, Celine still seemed to know just where to touch to make her moan. When Celine delved her fingers within her folds, Dinah almost orgasmed standing there. Celine gently removed her fingers and guided Dinah backward toward the bed. They separated long enough to climb into the bed before Celine overwhelmed her with kisses and caresses that had her moaning and writhing beneath her. Dinah liked this new, bold Celine. She knew experience probably made her this way, but Dinah no longer cared who shared Celine's bed before today. What mattered was the depth of the love they still had for each other. It was as if their time apart had strengthened, rather than dimmed, their feelings.

Dinah didn't have a moment to think as Celine overwhelmed her with sensation. While Celine's lips devoured Dinah's in a hungry kiss, her fingers once again did delicious things between Dinah's legs, bringing her to the brink of orgasm then slowing again, leaving Dinah begging for release.

"Not before I taste you," Celine said. "It's been so long since I've feasted from between your thighs."

"Yes, please," Dinah begged as she writhed and moaned beneath Celine.

Celine took her time moving down Dinah's body, making sure not to leave anything in between untouched by her soft lips. When Celine reached her destination and the tip of her tongue encountered Dinah's clitoris and gave it a few flicks, Dinah could no longer hold back. It was like an electrical shock started at her clitoris and surged through her entire body, leaving her hips bucking and body trembling from the intensity of her orgasm. But Celine didn't stop. She replaced her tongue with the pad of her thumb and delved her tongue into Dinah's slick opening, moaning against Dinah's lips as she lapped her up like a cat enjoying a bowl of cream. Dinah heard a keening noise and realized it came from her as another wave of pleasure crashed through her, leaving her feeling like a boneless puddle of mush as it subsided.

Dinah was almost relieved when Celine slid up along her body and lay beside her.

"You don't know how much I missed the feel, taste, and smell of you." Celine buried her nose in Dinah's neck and pulled her close.

Dinah shifted so that she could wrap her arms around Celine. "I think I have a pretty good idea." She kissed Celine tenderly. "Now it's my turn to show you how much I missed you."

Dinah laid Celine on her back and they spent all night getting reacquainted physically and emotionally. They made passionate love, talked, slept, woke up to make love again and talk some more until the early morning hours. If Dinah didn't have to get back for rehearsals for that evening's show, she would have stayed in bed with Celine the whole next day. They bathed together, which to Dinah's delight led to even more interesting and messy lovemaking, before getting dressed and going to the café for breakfast. After breakfast, Celine walked Dinah to her hotel where they said goodbye with the promise of seeing each other again that night.

❖

Celine was thrilled to have Dinah back in her life. Dinah moved into her cottage to stay during her remaining time in Montmartre. Neither discussed what would happen when the troupe's appearance in Paris came to an end. They spent their time together one day at a time, choosing to ignore the passage of it. Not having the pressure of worrying about parents' expectations and Dinah's safety gave Celine the opportunity to relax and allow herself to truly express her love for Dinah and live her life the way she wanted.

Their days were spent with Dinah in rehearsals and Celine working her apprenticeship. Their nights were spent making passionate love and Celine showing Dinah the Paris she had come to love, as well as the surprising number of nightclubs and social clubs in Montmartre and Montparnasse where homosexuals and lesbians thrived. Same-sex relationships were far from being legal in Paris, but it seemed to be fairly tolerated, particularly between women. Celine and Dinah felt a sense of freedom they could only imagine while living in Harlem.

After an evening at Le Monocle, a nightclub in Montparnasse, Dinah had become noticeably quiet when they returned to the cottage. They had retired to bed shortly after getting home and Celine pulled Dinah into her arms.

"You've been awfully quiet since we left Le Monocle," Celine said.

Dinah cuddled closer and laid her head upon Celine's chest. "You seem very happy here."

"I'm more than happy now that I have you." Celine placed a soft kiss atop Dinah's head.

"We've managed to ignore it these past couple of weeks, but the tour is coming to end. Next week the troupe heads back to America to finish out in Chicago, then back to New York."

"I've been very aware of the time passing," Celine said sadly. She knew this conversation had to happen, but it didn't make it any easier.

Dinah sat up to look at Celine. "You've made a life here, established a reputation all your own with your fashions, to the point where you could probably open your own shop and do very well."

Celine looked worriedly at Dinah. "What are you saying, Dinah?"

Tears began to shine in Dinah's eyes. "I couldn't possibly ask you to leave. Not to go back to Harlem to a place that would only dim the bright light that you've become since being in Paris."

Celine shifted so that she could grasp Dinah's face. "Dinah, I will be happy wherever you are."

"But not as happy as you are here. In Paris, you aren't looked down upon because you're a woman of color. In Paris, a love like ours doesn't have to be a complete secret. Le Monocle and the other places like it that you've taken me have shown me that. Even here in Montmartre, two women in love doesn't bring police knocking at your door ready to put you in a prison cell or an asylum like it would in America. Do you really want to go back to living like that?"

Celine could hear the fear in Dinah's voice, and she understood it. She had been seriously considering whether she wanted to go back to the pervasive intolerance of America. The other option would be to ask Dinah to stay and leave her family behind. Celine knew how important Dinah's family was to her. She couldn't ask her to move an entire ocean away from them just to make her happy.

"As long as we're together I don't care where we live. Yes, in America we'll have to be careful, but your aunt and Fran have done it for twenty years. So can we." Celine tried to reassure herself just as much as Dinah.

Dinah seemed to study her intently, as if, despite the darkness, she could see the uncertainty in Celine's eyes.

Celine leaned forward and kissed Dinah. "Remember our promise. One day at time. No looking back and no looking too far ahead. We will trek that road when we get to it," she said before pulling Dinah into her arms and making love to her until they were both too tired to do anything but sleep.

Dinah smiled out at the full house and loud applause as she and the other members of their troupe took their final bow at Chez Bricktop. In two more days, they would be boarding a ship heading back to the United States to end their tour and go back to their normal lives of auditions, domestic jobs, waiting tables, or whatever work they could find until the next tour came along. As they gathered in their dressing room, you could hear a pin drop. Their experience in Paris had been nothing like they could have imagined. Some of the performers had even considered coming back after the tour rather than live in a country that didn't respect or seem to want them.

Dinah gazed at herself in the mirror and wondered, for a moment, what that would be like. To stay here rather than go home. Unlike most of the dancers in the troupe, at twenty-eight years old, Dinah thought she would be considered too old to even think about trying to audition for shows or clubs. She could go back to nursing, but there was no guarantee she could get back in at Harlem Hospital, and she refused to take a position at a facility where she would end up doing the same menial tasks Nurse Porter had her doing before her job at Harlem Hospital. So, what did she have to go back to? Her family. That was the only thing keeping her from not boarding that ship in two days.

"Penny for your thoughts," Lee said next to her.

Dinah gave him a sad smile. "You'll need more than a penny for everything going on in my head right now."

"You and Celine still haven't decided what you're going to do?"

"Celine has decided. She's going to book passage on the next ship after ours and meet me back in New York. She's going to go into business with Olivia, and we'll move into a brownstone of our own."

"You don't sound too thrilled about that plan."

"Because I know she's only doing it for me." Dinah couldn't hide her frustration.

"Is it what you want?"

"It's not what I want for her. She has a good life here. I don't want her throwing it all away for me and then coming to regret it later."

"Have you told her that?"

Dinah shook her head. "Every time I bring it up, she just says she'll be happy wherever I am. I think she's afraid of asking me to stay because of my family."

"What if she did ask you to stay?"

Dinah looked at Lee uncertainly. "I don't know."

Lee rubbed Dinah's back. "Well, I think you better figure it out before you board that ship."

Dinah knew Lee was right, and it didn't make it easier when Celine entered the dressing room a few minutes later. It had become her habit, whether she came to a show or not, to meet Dinah backstage so they could go back to the cottage together. The troupe loudly greeted her with smiles and hugs as if she were part of their crazy little family, and Dinah realized she had become a part of it. She'd even had the entire troupe squeezed into her little home for dinner a few nights ago. When Celine turned her bright smile on her, Dinah didn't know what she had done in her life to deserve to have such a wonderful woman love her, but she knew that she would not let it slip through her fingers again, no matter what sacrifices had to be made.

Celine placed a soft kiss on her lips. "Are you almost ready to go?"

Dinah loved how open Celine was with her affection. "Yes, let me just finish packing my makeup kit."

Celine chatted with Lee until Dinah was ready, then they wished everyone a good night and left the club. When they arrived at the cottage, Celine opened the door and told Dinah to enter first. She walked in to find bouquets of white roses scattered throughout the main room of the cottage and a table set up for dinner for two in the middle of the room.

"What is all of this?" she asked in awe.

"It's for our last real night together in Paris. Since you're required to stay at the hotel with the troupe your last night, I thought I would do something special for us tonight."

Dinah didn't think her heart could be filled with any more love for Celine than it already was, but she was wrong as she looked at the love returned in Celine's eyes.

"Celine…" Dinah found she couldn't speak past the lump in her throat or stop the tears that fell down her cheeks.

Celine pulled her into an embrace. "What is it?" she asked.

It took Dinah a moment to compose herself enough to speak. "I love you so much. Too much to ask you to give up anything for me. You've spent most of your life giving up what you want for others, and I will not be one of those people who allows you to continue to do that."

"What do you mean?"

Dinah took Celine's hand and lead her to the sofa. "I'm going to ask you a question, and it's important that you really think about your answer before responding."

"All right," Celine said.

"If my family being in Harlem were not a factor in deciding whether you stayed in Paris or went back to the States, what would your decision be?" Dinah held up her hand to stop Celine from answering right away. "Take your time answering. I need to know what's truly in your heart."

Celine looked down at her lap. Dinah could tell she was seriously considering her answer.

Celine looked up at Dinah with tears shining in her eyes. "I would stay in Paris."

Dinah nodded, once again too emotional to speak.

"Why are you asking this now? My decision has been made. You're leaving in two days and I'll follow a few weeks later," Celine said.

"Because I can't bear the thought of you once again doing something you don't want to do to make me happy. That's what got us to where we are today. If you hadn't spent the night with Philly to help me get out of trouble, then you would never have been put in danger or felt you had to leave in the first place."

Celine shook her head. "I thought we were past that. I thought we had moved on."

"We have. You're here in Paris living the life you should have been living instead of spending ten years in a false marriage, being forced to leave the only home you ever knew and having your parents try to trap you into another unhappy marriage," Dinah said. "Your aunt believed that your entire life up until you left had been like living a real-life masquerade, and I agree. Since I've been here with you, I've seen the real you. I've seen the loving, lively, artistic, and joyous person you were always meant to be. Going back to Harlem with me would force you back behind that mask again, and I won't do that to you." She wiped the tears Celine cried.

"But I can't bear to lose you again, and I won't ask you to choose between me and your family who love you despite knowing who you love. That's a rare thing to have, Dinah, and it's something I will not allow you to give up by asking you to stay here."

Dinah gave Celine a soft kiss. "You don't have to ask me, Celine, because I've made my decision. I want to be here with you."

Celine looked at Dinah as if she heard her wrong. "You're coming back to Paris?"

Dinah nodded. "I love my family, but they're fine without me. My heart is here with you. I've come to love Paris as much as you do. I can't imagine taking you from it."

Celine grasped Dinah's face and poured all her love and happiness into the kiss she gave her. "Are you sure?"

"Just as sure as I am that I love you with all my heart," Dinah said.

Celine's face was split into the happiest smile Dinah had ever seen on her, and it filled her heart with joy to know that she was the one who brought it on.

"Dinah Hampton, you are my heart, my joy, and my life. The night of that masquerade was the night my world changed because you saw past my mask and accepted the real me. I can't wait to spend the rest of our lives showing you how much that means to me."

Celine and Dinah stood on the pier at the Le Havre port, holding each other's hands tightly as they waited for the boarding call for the SS *Paris* cruise liner that would be taking Dinah back to America.

"I wish I didn't have to go." Tears sparkled in Dinah's eyes.

Celine wiped away a tear that rolled down Dinah's cheek. "I wish you didn't either, but you can't break your contract with the troupe. You'll finish up the tour and be back here in no time." She attempted to put on a brave face, not sure who she was trying to convince more, herself or Dinah.

Lee joined them looking on with sympathy. "I hate to have to break this up, but Travis wants us all together when we board."

Celine almost broke when she saw the hesitation in Dinah's eyes. "You know you have to go back, at least to say a proper goodbye to your family. I have yet to meet your mother, but I have a feeling she would never forgive me if I kept you from seeing her one more time before you settle here. After all, it could be some time before you're able to visit home again."

Dinah nodded and pulled Celine into an embrace. They held tightly onto each other for a moment, then Dinah pulled away and headed toward the rest of the troupe waiting near the gangplank. Celine could no longer hold back tears as Lee gave her quick hug as well.

"I'll make sure she is on a ship back here as soon as possible," he said.

Celine smiled in appreciation. "Lee, promise me that if she changes her mind, you won't talk her out of staying in New York."

Lee looked as if he would argue. Celine grabbed his hand. "Please, Lee. I wouldn't be able to live with myself if she came all the way back here only to regret leaving her family behind for me."

"If that's what you want." Lee gave her hand a quick squeeze.

Celine nodded and pulled him into another hug. "Safe travels, and please take care of her for me."

Lee nodded, then joined their group. The ship's horn blew loudly and the call for boarding was made. Dinah looked back at her, and Celine lifted a hand tentatively. Dinah blew her a kiss and mouthed the words "I love you" in response. Celine returned the gesture and mouthed the words back to her. She was barely holding herself together and was almost relieved when the troupe headed toward the gangplank. As soon as Dinah looked away, Celine turned and hurried to the taxi waiting for her. She was barely in the car before the tears flowed freely and she covered her mouth to keep from crying out in misery.

Her heart had been broken so many times now she wasn't sure how it would ever heal. She didn't fool herself into thinking that once Dinah returned home, she wouldn't have second thoughts about her decision to come back to Paris. She could only hope that if fate had brought them together twice already, it would do it again one final time.

EPILOGUE

Celine sat in a chair in the back of the room watching Dinah dance and felt as if time had turned back to two years ago on the night they fell in love. A night that had seemed to be filled with mystery and desire had turned into more than either of them could have imagined. She felt a sense of pride as Dinah finished her performance and received a round of applause from her adult students.

"Mademoiselle Hampton, you dance so beautifully, why did you stop performing?" one of her students asked.

Dinah gazed at Celine with a warm look. "Because I found I no longer needed to perform to be happy." She looked back at the young woman who asked the question. "I also don't think I could compete with as talented a dancer as you, Antoinette." She gave a wink.

Celine almost chuckled at the blush that colored the young woman's face at Dinah's compliment.

"Now, I want everyone here at four o'clock tomorrow so that we can be at the Paris Opera Ballet House early enough for Monsieur Ferrer to give us a tour before the performances begin," she said.

As the students chattered excitedly about their trip to the Opera Ballet House on their way out, they made sure to stop and greet Celine. When the last student exited, Dinah locked the door and closed the curtains. She strolled over to Celine, slipped her arms around her waist, and gave her a sexy look.

"I thought I was meeting you at home," Dinah said.

Celine wrapped her arms around Dinah's waist. "I thought I would surprise you and walk you home."

"What a very pleasant surprise this is," Dinah said before pressing her lips to Celine's for a slow, passionate kiss.

Celine moaned against Dinah's lips when the kiss was done. "You keep that up and we're going to be late."

"Do we have to go?" Dinah whined playfully.

Celine smiled indulgently. "Yes, we do. *Tante* Olivia and Helene traveled all this way to spend time with us and to go to the Bastille Day Masquerade Ball. We can't disappoint them."

"True, your aunt would never let us hear the end of it. I still can't believe she and Helene are lovers," Dinah said.

"It seems they were in a similar situation as us once. It just took them a little longer than us to realize they were made for each other," Dinah said. "I'm happy for them and glad they came to spend time with us." Dinah gave Celine a quick kiss and stepped out of her embrace. "Let me just change and I'll be right out." She hurried toward the studio's dressing area.

Celine gazed around the small but functional storefront converted into a studio and smiled. Celine moved the curtains aside and gazed out the window.

"You would have loved it here, Paul," she said while she watched passersby chatting and as they bustled off to any number of cafés or cabarets nearby.

Tears came to Celine's eyes as she remembered his happy, outgoing personality. Paul would have fit right into the jovial spirit of Montmartre and Paris. Celine wiped the tears away, refusing to be sad at thoughts of her friend because he would not have wanted her to be. Paul would have told her to enjoy life to the fullest. Celine promised herself, in Paul's memory, that she would do just that. There was no more masquerading her life at someone else's whim. She lived openly, freely, and without regret. Celine sighed contentedly as she felt Dinah's arms wrap around her.

"It looks like it's going to be a beautiful night. Are you ready to celebrate freedom?" Dinah asked.

Celine released the curtain and turned in Dinah's arms. "I was free the moment you held me in your arms," she said before kissing Dinah with all the happiness and love she felt for her.

About the Author

Anne Shade loves writing romances about women who love women featuring strong, beautiful Characters of Color. Her dream is to retire and open a bed and breakfast so she can spend her days doing what she loves…providing wonderful hospitality, writing novels, and planning fabulous weddings.

Books Available From Bold Strokes Books

A Far Better Thing by JD Wilburn. When needs of her family and wants of her heart clash, Cass Halliburton is faced with the ultimate sacrifice. (978-1-63555-834-0)

Body Language by Renee Roman. When Mika offers to provide Jen erotic tutoring, will sex drive them into a deeper relationship or tear them apart? (978-1-63555-800-5)

Carrie and Hope by Joy Argento. For Carrie and Hope, loss brings them together but secrets and fear may tear them apart. (978-1-63555-827-2)

Detour to Love by Amanda Radley. Celia Scott and Lily Andersen are seatmates on a flight to Tokyo and by turns annoy and fascinate each other. But they're about to realize there's more than one path to love. (978-1-63555-958-3)

Ice Queen by Gun Brooke. School counselor Aislin Kennedy wants to help standoffish CEO Susanna Durr and her troubled teenage daughter become closer—even if it means risking her own heart in the process. (978-1-63555-721-3)

Masquerade by Anne Shade. In 1925 Harlem, New York, a notorious gangster sets her sights on seducing Celine, and new lovers Dinah and Celine are forced to risk their hearts, and lives, for love. (978-1-63555-831-9)

Royal Family by Jenny Frame. Loss has defined both Clay's and Katya's lives, but guarding their hearts may prove to be the biggest heartbreak of all. (978-1-63555-745-9)

Share the Moon by Toni Logan. Three best friends, an inherited vineyard, and a resident ghost come together for fun, romance, and a touch of magic. (978-1-63555-844-9)

Spirit of the Law by Carsen Taite. Attorney Owen Lassiter will do almost anything to put a murderer behind bars, but can she get past her reluctance to rely on unconventional help from the alluring Summer Byrne and keep from falling in love in the process? (978-1-63555-766-4)

The Devil Incarnate by Ali Vali. Cain Casey has so much to live for, but enemies who lurk in the shadows threaten to unravel it all. (978-1-63555-534-9)

Secret Agent by Michelle Larkin. CIA Agent Peyton North embarks on a global chase to apprehend rogue agent Zoey Blackwood, but her commitment to the mission is tested as the sparks between them ignite and their sizzling attraction approaches a point of no return. (978-1-63555-753-4)

Journey to Cash by Ashley Bartlett. Cash Braddock thought everything was great, but it looks like her history is about to become her right now. Which is a real bummer. (978-1-63555-464-9)

Liberty Bay by Karis Walsh. Wren Lindley's life is mired in tradition and untouched by trends until social media star Gina Strickland introduces an irresistible electricity into her off-the-grid world. (978-1-63555-816-6)

Scent by Kris Bryant. Nico Marshall has been burned by women in the past wanting her for her money. This time, she's determined to win Sophia Sweet over with her charm. (978-1-63555-780-0)

Shadows of Steel by Suzie Clarke. As their worlds collide and their choices come back to haunt them, Rachel and Claire must figure out how to stay together and, most of all, stay alive. (978-1-63555-810-4)

The Clinch by Nicole Disney. Eden Bauer overcame a difficult past to become a world champion mixed martial artist, but now rising star and dreamy bad girl Brooklyn Shaw is a threat both to Eden's title and her heart. (978-1-63555-820-3)

The Last First Kiss by Julie Cannon. Kelly Newsome is so ready for a tropical island vacation, but she never expects to meet the woman who could give her her last first kiss. (978-1-63555-768-8)

The Mandolin Lunch by Missouri Vaun. Despite their immediate attraction, everything about Garet Allen says short-term, and Tess Hill refuses to consider anything less than forever. (978-1-63555-566-0)

Thor: Daughter of Asgard by Genevieve McCluer. When Hannah Olsen finds out she's the reincarnation of Thor, she's thrown into a world of magic and intrigue, unexpected attraction, and a mystery she's got to unravel. (978-1-63555-814-2)

Veterinary Technician by Nancy Wheelton. When a stable of horses is threatened, Val and Ronnie must work together against the odds to save them and maybe even themselves along the way. (978-1-63555-839-5)

16 Steps to Forever by Georgia Beers. Can Brooke Sullivan and Macy Carr find themselves by finding each other? (978-1-63555-762-6)

All I Want for Christmas by Georgia Beers, Maggie Cummings & Fiona Riley. The Christmas season sparks passion and love in these stories by award-winning authors Georgia Beers, Maggie Cummings, and Fiona Riley. (978-1-63555-764-0)

From the Woods by Charlotte Greene. When Fiona goes backpacking in a protected wilderness, the last thing she expects is to be fighting for her life. (978-1-63555-793-0)

Heart of the Storm by Nicole Stiling. For Juliet Mitchell and Sienna Bennett a forbidden attraction definitely isn't worth upending the life they've worked so hard for. Is it? (978-1-63555-789-3)

If You Dare by Sandy Lowe. For Lauren West and Emma Prescott, following their passions is easy. Following their hearts, though? That's almost impossible. (978-1-63555-654-4)

Love Changes Everything by Jaime Maddox. For Samantha Brooks and Kirby Fielding, no matter how careful their plans, love will change everything. (978-1-63555-835-7)

Not This Time by MA Binfield. Flung back into each other's lives, can former bandmates Sophia and Madison have a second chance at romance? (978-1-63555-798-5)

The Found Jar by Jaycie Morrison. Fear keeps Emily Harris trapped in her emotionally vacant life; can she find the courage to let Beck Reynolds guide her toward love? (978-1-63555-825-8)

Aurora by Emma L McGeown. After a traumatic accident, Elena Ricci is stricken with amnesia, leaving her with no recollection of the last eight years, including her wife and son. (978-1-63555-824-1)

Avenging Avery by Sheri Lewis Wohl. Revenge against a vengeful vampire unites Isa Meyer and Jeni Denton, but it's love that heals them. (978-1-63555-622-3)

Bulletproof by Maggie Cummings. For Dylan Prescott and Briana Logan, the complicated NYC criminal justice system doesn't leave room for love, but where the heart is concerned, no one is bulletproof. (978-1-63555-771-8)

Her Lady to Love by Jane Walsh. A shy wallflower joins forces with the most popular woman in Regency London on a quest to catch a husband, only to discover a wild passion for each other that far eclipses their interest for the Marriage Mart. (978-1-63555-809-8)

No Regrets by Joy Argento. For Jodi and Beth, the possibility of losing their future will force them to decide what is really important. (978-1-63555-751-0)

The Holiday Treatment by Elle Spencer. Who doesn't want a gay Christmas movie? Holly Hudson asks herself that question and discovers that happy endings aren't only for the movies. (978-1-63555-660-5)

Too Good to be True by Leigh Hays. Can the promise of love survive the realities of life for Madison and Jen, or is it too good to be true? (978-1-63555-715-2)

Treacherous Seas by Radclyffe. When the choice comes down to the lives of her officers against the promise she made to her wife, Reese Conlon puts everything she cares about on the line. (978-1-63555-778-7)

Two to Tangle by Melissa Brayden. Ryan Jacks has been a player all her life, but the new chef at Tangle Valley Vineyard changes everything. If only she wasn't off the menu. (978-1-63555-747-3)

When Sparks Fly by Annie McDonald. Will the devastating incident that first brought Dr. Daniella Waveny and hockey coach Luca McCaffrey together on frozen ice now force them apart, or will their secrets and fears thaw enough for them to create sparks? (978-1-63555-782-4)